MW00588456

WHAT WONDERFUL ... found myself wondering wh... and who would be his n... ...... The story is filled with interesting and engaging characters, each with their own issues and quirks. At times I really liked most of them but at other times found myself disappointed with their poor decisions and bad behaviors. The authors kept me guessing at what would come next. Every time I thought I had something figured out; I was hit with a new surprise. I was sure one or more of the main characters would eventually fall prey to Tracy but was never quite sure who. And, what a surprise ending … I can't wait for the final book in the series.

IT IS ABSOLUTELY CAPTIVATING AND SO MUCH FUN TO READ! The plot takes unexpected twists and turns which makes the book hard to put down. The characters seem to come alive, so much so I am still thinking about them. As in the first two books of the series, I thoroughly enjoyed the authors beautifully written descriptions of the locations and settings. Book four cannot come soon enough!

NEW CHARACTERS, NEW PLOT TWISTS, I LOVED IT!! This is another fast-moving book with some new, interesting friendships for our old friends to replace those that have met their demise! We get to know Tracey better, and we get to see another side of him and his demons. I love traveling with the group of friends to some beautiful places and sharing their adventures. It's suspense to the very last page, can't wait for Book 4!!

BOOK THREE OF A SPECTRUM SERIES DOES NOT DISAPPOINT. The killer continues to kill but after getting married becomes a part of a social circle and changes his look. All the maps and drawings add a different aspect to the book. There are several characters, and each character adds their own story. The killer seems to get too comfortable and unbeknown to him someone is starting to connect the dots. Then he makes a mistake that could bring him down. If you are looking for different relationships, travel, cuisine and a good mystery this book is for you.

A Body Washes Ashore

Bradley Pay

This is a work of fiction. Names, characters, places and incidents either are the product of the authors' imaginations or are used fictitiously. Any resemblance to actual persons, living or dead, events or locales is entirely coincidental.

First paperback edition October 2022

ISBN 978-1-7345212-8-3 (paperback)
ISBN 978-1-7345212-9-0 (e-book)

https://BradleyPay.com
https://Facebook.com/BradleyPayBooks
https://Instagram.com/BradleyPayBooks

For Gavin Pay and Bis Bradley

Other books in the
SPECTRUM SERIES

Book One – *The Killings Begin*

Previously published as *Murder in Zaporozhye*

Book Two – *Death in a Dark Alley*

Previously published as *Murder in Strasbourg*

Dear Readers,

Our imaginations ran wild

When the geography of Ostia didn't quite suit our needs, we changed it. We needed the Fongs to live by the Tyrrhenian Sea with a private beach, but we also wanted them to live within easy walking distance of the downtown area where they have a piece of property where Frannie and Lee paint a mural.

We imagined, to benefit the story, how the Raleigh Police Department would be run and how they would initiate cooperation with the FBI, with the (fictitious) Trigg Pass Police Department and with Emily Bissett's company, Haypress Security, so that certain lines of inquiry could be made effectively by Haypress.

We needed to have Jane Mitchell in Raleigh, NC, so we gave the University of North Carolina School of the Arts a PhD program in filmmaking so she could begin to realize her dream of becoming a producer of documentary films.

In reality, murals take a long time to paint. But our mural painters all had other lives they had to get back to, so they had to finish the Ostia and the Slovenia murals in a week each – we aren't sure how long it took Frannie to paint the one on the side of the Pomegranate in Milan – she's been very quiet about that.

Likewise, because of the story's timeline, Lydia had little time to establish her couture business in Milan. We took great liberties with that and helped her get it up and running in about six months. (Thank goodness we are writing fiction!)

We also played a little with Italian work visa requirements. We wanted Frannie, who is self-employed as an illustrator of graphic novels and the creator of a series of comic books, to need a job in Italy so she could go to work for Lydia.

We created our own version of tactile signing because it was important for Remy and Frannie to have a way to "whisper" to one another without having to communicate openly in sign language.

These are just a few examples of how we've used poetic license throughout the novel to suit the story's needs.

We are so grateful

Our heartfelt thanks to David Mathewson for lending Jane Mitchell the layout of his San Francisco apartment for her Raleigh residence. She has found it to be a wonderful place to live.

Whoever came up with the brilliant idea to sell houses for one euro, we are forever in your debt. We took that idea as inspiration for Charlotte's house and gardens on an unknown hillside in Sicily. And like Gia's apartment in Madrid in book one, we would love to live there. Watch out, Charlotte, we're on our way! Thank you for giving us each a bedroom with a private bath and for creating a proper wine cellar.

Thanks to György and Agnes Gunst for letting us use their restaurant in Budapest, Barack & Szilva for an important assignation and for providing us with a complete menu. György and Agnes – our character, Emily, insisted that we add the physalis to their dessert because it is such a favorite of hers.

Where did that come from?

For a bit of fun, our characters created a story of their own. We wanted something for Tracey and Fong to bond over early in the book. While they each have family and work friends, neither has had a close, adult male friendship – until something clicks between the two of them when they meet at dinner. Tracey begins to tell the story of an imaginary art thief named Henri, and Fong joins in, adding details to Tracey's tale. Their friendship grows throughout the novel. But we didn't answer your question, did we? Henri was the protagonist in one of the original, crazy stories we spun back in 2016 when the Spectrum Series was conceived. While characters and bits of their stories have evolved into the current set of novels, the Henri story is the only silly one that survived more than five years of collaboration.

This isn't really a spoiler

A few characters from earlier books return throughout this novel. Some of them have small parts, and others, who made only brief cameo appearances before, have moved into more significant roles. Of course, you will encounter Sasha on Spectrum riverboat cruises, where he works as the master bartender, and again when the group visits his vineyard in Slovenia to help with the harvest. Gia finishes her stint with the cruise line and moves to Milan to take a dream job. And there, while clothes shopping, she reconnects with Lydia McKay, formerly of Paris. Gia's ex-boyfriend from Madrid, Sal, also reappears in her life. If you aren't familiar with these people, we encourage you to read *The Killings Begin* and *Death in a Dark Alley* to make their acquaintance.

And now, we'll leave it to you to read this book to find out what happens with all these folks as well as Tracey and Charlotte, Lee and Fong, and Remy and Frannie, the primary characters in this, the third Spectrum Series novel.

With love to you all,

Robin & Jody

Table of Contents

Prologue

Part One

Under Way 3

Meet Other Guests 11

Downstairs And Upstairs 20

Monet's Garden 31

See You Later 42

Part Two

Another Murder 47

Part Three

The Invitation 55

A Trip To Budapest 57

For Just One Euro 72

Part Four

The Pomegranate 93

A Dress For The Gala 103

Part Five

Never Just Settle 113

Part Six

The Harvest 123

There Is No Choice 131

The Pearls 141

Part Seven

One Lone Sock 147

Part Eight
Murder Mystery   157
The Cooking Class   173
The Mural   179

Part Nine
The Flowers   185
The Solstice Party   193
Happy Valentine's Day   203

Part Ten
Fifteen Years   207

Part Eleven
Damn You, Fong   215
Preparing For Berlin   217

Part Twelve
The Other Woman   223
They Finally Talk   239
An Unfinished Card   244

Part Thirteen
Conversation On The Hillside   251

Part Fourteen
Frannie Snoops Again   257

Part Fifteen
Tracey Visits Fong   265

Part Sixteen
Our Killer Was Here   271

Part Seventeen

Remy Confesses 281

The Christmas Cruise 295

A Body Washes Ashore 302

Epilogue

After the Killings

The Killings Begin

Death in a Dark Alley

Acknowledgements

About the Authors

Prologue

January 2012, Raleigh, North Carolina

Edgar pushed his new rimless glasses up on his nose. "You need to resolve the big question. Is this going to be about lies or about cheating?" He set the outline on her writing table and tapped it with his fingertips.

"Or both?" Jane replied. She reached up and tangled her fingers in his dark brown hair, making it even more disheveled than it ordinarily was. She pulled his head down and gave him a quick peck on the lips before taking him by the wrist and pulling him toward the door.

"And obviously, I'm going to leave you alone today to figure that out. You need to get this done." He pulled Jane into his arms and leaned against the wall by the door as he gave her a lingering kiss.

"Time for you to go then, if I'm going to get to work." She turned the knob and pulled the door open. As he walked out, she smacked him lightly on his backside.

"Owww."

She closed the door and smiled. She had thought she was an introvert until she'd met Edgar. She recalled the sweet way he had hardly been able to get the words out to ask her on a date. She smiled again and smoothed her hands down her body. *But he's certainly no introvert in bed.*

In the kitchen area of her studio, she flipped the switch on the electric kettle and ran the grinder, inhaling the aroma of freshly ground coffee, "Mmmm." She reached overhead to take her French press from the cabinet above the sink as she mumbled to herself, "What's more important? Lies or cheating? Does one exist without the other?"

The kettle clicked off, and Jane poured a small amount of boiling water into the pot, swirled it around and dumped it into her cup. She continued with her morning ritual, carefully tipping grounds into the glass carafe, slowly adding a little water, giving it a stir, filling it to the top. She picked up the cover and carefully pushed the plunger down with the flat of her hand until it just touched the water. Once she'd set the timer for four minutes, she leaned against the counter, thinking about the draft proposal she had to discuss with her advisor the following morning. She knew she needed to make it very clear, the difference between emotional and physical affairs. Was one type of cheating worse than the other? More hurtful than the other? It was going to be interesting to hear what people had to say in the interviews.

Then, remembering the towels, she dashed through the bathroom and yanked open the stackable dryer, pulling out the contents and pushing the door shut with her shoulder. As she carried them through her studio to the small sleeping area, she buried her face in the armload of clean towels, enjoying the smell of freshly washed laundry, a smell that, for her, rated up there with freshly brewed coffee. Using her foot, Jane nudged open the shoji screen that separated her sleeping alcove from the living area and dropped the towels in a pile on her bed. The sight of them reminded her that if she didn't start another load, she would run out of clean underwear. She shrugged – her outline would have to wait a few minutes more. And back she dashed to the bathroom where she pulled her clothes from a basket beneath the sink. As she pressed the start button on the washer, the coffee timer buzzed, and she hurried to turn it off.

In the kitchen, pressing the plunger down ever so slowly, she forced the grounds to the bottom of the cafetière. Jane poured herself a cup of coffee, added a luxurious dollop of cream, stirred it and took a small sip. *There's nothing like my own French press coffee.* A tendril that had escaped from her messy topknot tickled the side of her face, and she brushed it aside impatiently. She gazed across the kitchen peninsula and the living area of her junior studio. "Okay, time to stop procrastinating," she said out loud and walked determinedly to her writing table under the bay window where her laptop waited.

She set her coffee on a colorful, woven coaster and booted up her computer. With one foot tucked under her, Jane sat, idly picking at the threads of her torn jeans, staring out the window across the tops of the bare trees to the spot on the other side where the highway wound its way across Raleigh and out to the North Carolina countryside. She pushed the annoying tendril that had fallen back into her face firmly into her topknot. "Enough already, Jane," she said as she looked down at the single page she'd printed before Edgar had arrived the night before. "Getting started is always the toughest part. *Just do it.*"

"Come on," she chided herself and picked up her pen to add more detail to her outline. Her thumb clicked the top of the pen rapidly. She told herself to focus – her dissertation proposal wasn't going to write itself. She knew this was possibly the most important piece of work in her academic career so far and that she'd never become Dr. Jane Mitchell, documentary filmmaker, if she didn't get her act together.

After staring at her outline for a few more minutes, Jane began to add notes in her neat handwriting. *Does adding lies make this complicated? Aren't lies implicit in cheating?*

Jane continued to look at her outline as she thought about the scope of her project. She had already narrowed it down to examining relationships between committed or married couples but felt that lying and cheating was still too broad – one could lie about finances or cheat on taxes and not tell the other person. Would that have the same impact as something more egregious, like having an affair, where it seems to be more personal, more emotional? She thought about it further. That topic in itself had so many rich opportunities to explore, since having an affair, by its nature, involves both lying and cheating. Affairs then, she decided, would be where she would focus. She clicked her pen again with her thumb and made a note in her outline.

Since two parties are responsible for an affair, is one more culpable than the other, she wondered. *Either person could have said no. Either could have chosen not to engage with the other person.* She felt that was going to be interesting to explore – what if one party was reluctant at first?

And what about the victims, she thought. *Wow – that means there are at least three, if not more, people affected by the affair if the cheaters are in committed relationships. And victims wouldn't just include the partners but perhaps also children or extended family or even the friends of the couples.*

She wondered if she would come across relationships that survive affairs, either due to forgiving the one who strayed or because they never found out. *Are those relationships stronger? Hmmm.*

She continued clicking her pen absentmindedly as she looked at her outline, thinking about the people she would need to interview and how she was going to find her subjects. She might need to partner with someone, perhaps from the Psych Department, then she'd be able to devote more time to the actual filmmaking. She gave a little chuckle, *Wouldn't it be ironic if two of our volunteers turned out to be spouses or partners in the same relationship? That might be a little dicey.*

She leaned back and stretched her arms over her head, feeling better prepared to complete her outline before reviewing it with her advisor the next morning.

University of North Carolina School of the Arts, Film Production

Jane Mitchell

Ph.D. Dissertation Proposal
Draft 1, January 15, 2012
Advisor: Dr. Nelson Greene

Working Title   *This sentence needs work*

Collateral Damage – Damage caused by cheating or by misleading viewers with production techniques in documentaries.

Problem Statements   *Is this too much detail?*

1. When producing a documentary, how do production techniques (editing, sound recording, set design) influence the audience's emotional response?
2. What are the moral and/or ethical dilemmas caused by these production techniques when creating a non-fiction film?

High-Level Approach   *Is a lie part of cheating?*

A. Cheaters – Record three interviews:
   - Why do you lie and cheat in your relationship?
   - What caused you to cheat?
   - Who do you blame for the cheating?
   - Was it an emotional or a physical relationship? *–Or both?*
   - What happened when your partner found out?

B. Victims of Cheaters – Record three interviews:
   - Do you know if your partner cheated once or more frequently?
   - What was the impact of the cheating on your relationship?
   - Who do you blame for the cheating? *Add questions here*

C. Interview Recordings: Create one video with a bias toward victims, one video with a bias toward cheaters, and one video with no bias. Measure responses of 50 viewers to each video.

D. Psychologists: *Should this be more?*
   - Doctor watches documentaries, reviews audience responses.
   - Ask doctor what are the moral and/or ethical dilemmas caused by:
     - lying and cheating
     - manipulating the videos

Part One

Second Half of April 2012

Under Way

Onboard *The Indigo*

Tracey lay on his back with his head resting on Charlotte's shoulder. She stroked her fingers gently through his hair, and he sighed with pleasure, "That feels so good. You know just what I like." He felt her fingertips trace the faint scar along the side of his head beneath his hair.

"How's the headache, my love?"

"Better," he chuckled. "That new prescription and a bout of rousing good sex always seem to help it. I just can't get enough of you."

She sighed with pleasure, "Mmmm, I've decided there's absolutely nothing better than honeymoon sex." Her fingers slowed, and she closed her eyes. "I just need a little nap before dinner."

Lulled by the gentle movement of the riverboat as it moved away from Paris, Tracey also drifted toward sleep. He recalled the day his best friend had dared him to go higher and higher until the swing was above the top bar of the swing set and then to jump the impossible distance to the grass outside the play area. He'd pumped his legs one last time, and as the swing reached its apex, he'd given a mighty jump forward. His little six-year-old feet had hit the ground short of his goal, and he'd stumbled in the sand and fallen, half in and half out of the play area. His head had struck a jagged rock that was partially buried in the grass. And when he'd opened his eyes again, he was lying in a hospital bed with his adoptive mother holding his hand, looking anxiously at him. He reached up and gently touched the scar, and he smiled, remembering how glad she'd been that it was behind his hairline and didn't mar his looks. *Though it would have been a mark of distinction to me as a teenager to have a cool scar on my forehead. The stories I could have…*

Tracey turned on his side and slept with his head still resting on his wife's shoulder.

§

Remy came out of the bathroom in the riverboat cabin that she was sharing with her cousin. Her hair was twisted up in a towel, and she'd wrapped a second one around her torso. She looked over at Frannie in her skinny jeans and white t-shirt. Remy raised an eyebrow and waved her arms to catch her attention, "If you don't hurry up, you're not going to have time to change."

Frannie ignored her and remained seated on the twin bed next to the nightstand with her legs crossed, yoga style. Her toenails were painted fire-engine red. Her matching fingernails tapped against the letter she held in her hand. She dropped the page into her lap, next to the envelope she'd pulled it from a few minutes before. As she leaned forward, she used her hands to sign, as if for emphasis, as she slowly pronounced the words, "You slept with him?"

Remy signed back as she spoke, "What? What are you talking about?" Frannie picked up the paper again and waved it. Remy recognized the gray-colored sheet of stationery, "What are you doing, going through my stuff?"

"How else can I find out things about you?"

Remy snatched the letter out of Frannie's hand, shoved it into the envelope and stuffed it back between the pages of the old book lying on the bed.

"I just wanted to look at this ancient guidebook. I don't know why you cart these things around when you have a new one with all the right information in it." She pointed to the paper. "It fell out, and I lost your place," Frannie shrugged.

Remy's face flushed as she replied, raising her voice and signing furiously, "That was very personal – you're always digging through my stuff. Can't I have any privacy?"

Frannie stuck her chin in the air and gave a little head waggle. "It. Just. Fell. Out. And yes, it was personal. How could you do that?"

"For heaven's sake," Remy's signing became more frenetic as her exasperation increased, "it was six years ago. It was an affair. Only an affair. And there was no emotional involvement." Remy pulled the towel from her head and leaned over to fluff her thick, wavy hair with her fingers, speaking to herself, knowing that Frannie couldn't hear her, "You're too young. You wouldn't understand." She stood up and spritzed her hair and shoulders with the light, floral perfume that was her signature.

"That's gross. He's our neighbor." Frannie made an unintelligible sound of revulsion.

Remy stood up and looked at her, her hands flying as she spoke, "I'm not sure why I'm even telling you this. He was at odds with his wife at that point. We broke it off once they repaired their marriage. You saw that in the letter. So, what's the problem?"

"How could you do that? He's so old."

"He's only eight years older than me."

"Shit. That means he's fifty now. He's twice as old as me. Really?"

"Well, fortunately, it wasn't your affair. I didn't even know his wife."

Frannie sat silently for a moment, thinking about her cousin sleeping with an older man, *that* older man. Even though she thought the idea of her cousin's affair was disgusting, her curiosity finally got the better of her. "How did you meet him, anyway?" she blurted out.

"I was having lunch by myself one day down near the Embarcadero in San Francisco, and he was there. He came up to the table and asked if he could join me. We talked, and the affair just happened. He and his wife were drifting apart. Ultimately, they repaired their marriage. End of affair. End of story." She brushed her hands together. "It's all part of my rules, so no one got hurt. Maybe it even helped them. And he was a decent lover while it lasted."

"Rules?"

"We don't have enough time to talk about them. Maybe I'll tell you after dinner." Remy turned toward the closet.

Frannie shrugged as she picked up her phone and started texting.

Turning around, Remy saw her cousin's thumbs flying across the keyboard. She grabbed Frannie's wrap from the closet, wadded it up and threw it at her to get her attention.

"Hey! What was that for?"

"Who are you texting? This conversation is completely in the vault." Remy jabbed her finger toward Frannie for emphasis, "You can't tell anyone, including your mom. She would be so disappointed if she found out."

Frannie waved her phone in the air, dropped it in her lap and signed and spoke simultaneously, "Best friends have to keep in touch. Don't worry, I won't tell anyone." She shook her head, "And why would I tell Mom? That would be awk-ward!"

§

Lee stood at the window of their first-class cabin, watching the ripples across the surface of the Seine, happy to be underway with Daniel, her beloved husband. His arms snaked around her waist, and she turned toward him, her breath quickening as he bent his head and trailed kisses along her jawline to that sensitive spot below her ear. And then he began to remove her clothes, oh so slowly, teasing her skin with little nips and feather-light kisses. When there was nothing left to remove, he stepped back, and as she watched, he did a strip tease for her, swinging each garment, then letting it go to land where it might. Lee giggled. When he stood completely naked before her, she looked him up and down, admiring his sinewy arms, the slight definition of his abs, the lean muscles along his hips, and finally, her eyes lingered below his waist. "I see you are still attracted to me, Mr. Fong," she drawled in Italian, her voice low and thick with desire.

His mouth twitched as he tried not to smile, "Oh, am I just 'Mr. Fong' now?" He made a sad face. "What happened to Daniel?" he asked playfully.

"Ah, you were paying attention."

He picked her up and laid her on the bed and pinned her down, his body half covering hers, "Always, Mrs. Fong." With his hand against her bare skin, he caressed her, his touch soft and tantalizing. "But what is it that makes you think I'm still attracted to you?"

Her body began to tighten in that familiar response to his touch. "This, Daniel," she gasped, as her hand closed around him. "And this," she said as she stroked him. "This," she said as she opened her legs and brought him against her. "And that," she moaned as he entered her in one long, delicious stroke.

He held her in his arms, while their hearts pounded in the aftermath of their orgasms.

"In all the time I've known you, Daniel, you have never performed a strip tease for me."

"I'm just keeping it fresh."

"Fresh?" she giggled. "That was very fresh of you."

"Making love with you is even better now than when you first seduced me," he said. "Much better now," and he gave her luxurious auburn hair a little tug.

"Me – you?" she said. "As I recall, it was you who seduced me."

"As I recall," he laughed, his eyes crinkling at the corners, "you made the first advance."

They sat together in bed, Lee holding her champagne glass in one hand, reading aloud the card that Sasha had propped against the ice bucket, where now the ice was all but melted. "*Happy anniversary to my dear friends. I'm so pleased you were able to take this cruise. It's the most romantic of all, and it's always been one of my favorites. With love, Sasha.*' How sweet he is." Setting the card down, she reached over to her nightstand, and with a light kiss, she handed him a wrapped package.

He opened *The World Behind Art Appraisals* to the front page and read, "*My dearest Daniel, you're my world, and my heart and soul are yours forever. Happy twenty-third anniversary.*"

"How – thoughtful," he said, trying not to sound disappointed. Lee's gifts were usually so fun and innovative. He leaned over and kissed her hard on the mouth. When he pulled back, he gave her a puzzled look.

Lee laughed at his expression, "That's not the real gift, Daniel. Turn to the chapter that you wrote." She pointed to the envelope marking his chapter, "That's your anniversary gift. I had to look for a long time to find it. And while I was shopping, I ran across this book. I knew you had been waiting for it to come out."

He reached over and picked up the slim, silver penknife lying next to his wallet on the nightstand on his side of the bed. He ran his thumb over its smooth surface before carefully slitting open the envelope and pulling out a trifold brochure with colorful hot air balloons on the front. As he opened it, a ticket for a balloon ride for two fell out into his lap. He gave her the special smile he reserved only for her. "Will you be my date, my dear, dear Lee?"

She laughed, "Oh, I hope you aren't too disappointed. It was a hot air balloon trip or something made of silver. Would you have preferred a second silver penknife or another silver tray to match all the ones we've received as wedding and anniversary gifts, Daniel? I suppose I could return—"

"Never!" He pulled her to him and blew softly against her neck, "Mmmm. Air and silver? Those were the choices this year?" He nibbled her shoulder, "I think it's adorable that you look up these traditional anniversary gifts every year. And I have to say, this is one of the best." He ran his hand caressingly along her back.

"Adorable? Me? Really? Adorable?"

"Everything you do is adorable, my darling," and he pulled her to him and kissed her noisily.

"Oh, Daniel." She tapped him on the cheek and returned to their earlier discussion as he smiled in amusement. "Hallmark has such interesting choices compared to the ones on the other lists. And I like their list the best because it includes every year after the twentieth anniversary, not just the big ones. But imagine how hard it was to find air to give you!" She grinned, "Hallmark says next year is stone. Just you wait."

He paused for a moment, imagining the unusual gifts Lee might find made of stone before he threw his head back and laughed heartily. Still chuckling, he reached over to his nightstand and picked up a gift wrapped in copper-colored paper with an elaborate, charcoal chiffon bow. Before handing it to Lee, he paused, holding it away from her, "I want one last look at this masterpiece before you rip it open." He gave a dramatic sigh.

"I know I say this every single time we exchange gifts, but I'm so glad you had that holiday wrapping job in high school. Your wrappings always look so professional. I absolutely adore them." She slid her hand over very slowly and then snatched the package from him before enthusiastically tearing off the paper.

She pushed the paper and bow onto the floor and carefully unfastened the ties around a soft leather case. She stroked it gently before unrolling it to reveal a beautiful collection of brushes. With a sigh of pleasure, Lee said, "Oh, Daniel, this is beautiful," and she leaned over and rested her cheek against his. "I love you – warts and all," she murmured.

He winced at her comment, and with his forefinger, he traced the two butterflies imprinted into the leather, "I love you too. Perhaps you can say I gave you the gift of air as well? These butterflies look like they are dancing in the air—"

"—symbolizing long-lasting love." Lee's eyes glistened with tears of happiness, "Just like the origami butterflies Sasha made for us on the cruise when we met Mari and Gia."

"So, did I finally surprise you?"

I can't lie. "The butterflies were a surprise."

His face fell.

"Daniel. The credit card. You used the card. It was on the statement."

"My darling, you are far too clever. I can't ever surprise you, can I?"

After a final sip of champagne, he leaned toward her with that look in his eyes that never failed to make her catch her breath. "Daniel, we have to get a move on. I don't want to be last to the table." She slipped out of bed, went into the bathroom and started the shower.

He followed, "Are you sure you want to dine with other guests on this trip? I'm sure we could still get our usual little table by the window."

Lee stood under the spray of water, her dark hair pinned up on top of her head. "I know we've always dined on our own, but this is a new offering with Spectrum. We agreed when they sent it to us that it might be fun to try something different."

"Whatever you'd like, my darling. But – it's too bad we didn't plan this better. I know what I'd like to do." He stepped in behind her, picked up the bar of soap and as he lathered it over her body, he kissed along her neck.

"What could be better? That which came before was unparalleled lovemaking – ohhh, Daniel – ohhh—" She leaned back against him as his hands moved over her body.

Meet Other Guests

Onboard *The Indigo*

Frannie slipped her hand under Remy's palm. "Wow," she signed, "This is going to be so much fun."

Remy smiled and flipped Frannie's hand over to sign back, "I knew you'd like it."

The dining room was almost empty. Along the back wall, the staff stood waiting, dressed in black jackets and slacks with white shirts, the collars open for an elegantly casual look. The square tables were lined up beside the dark windows, one corner against the wall like diamonds, covered in crisp, white cloths, napkins laid across the plates, water and wine glasses gleaming in the light from the chandeliers above. The lights sparkled as the guests entered.

Gia recognized the two women standing at the door, one tall, with her hair loose in thick waves over her shoulders, the other about her own age, petite with sleek blond hair coiled elaborately at the nape of her neck, a black, silk shawl draped over her arm. As the newest member of the concierge staff, Gia had been assigned to be Frannie's sign language interpreter for the cruise. She had been keeping an eye out for them as she went about her other duties. She hurried over to greet them, smiling first at Remy and then Frannie, "Nice to see you both again. I was thinking about what we discussed earlier, and even though you use American Sign Language, Frannie, and I learned International Sign Language, I've been brushing up on ASL, so I think we'll be able to communicate well enough – especially since you lip-read so easily. Are you all settled in? If you need anything, feel free to call on me." She looked at their dresses appreciatively, "Frannie, I love that dress."

Remy smiled to herself at Gia's rapid-fire comments. Spectrum had obviously put great care into the selection of her as Frannie's interpreter. From their brief interaction, she was already certain that Gia would make Frannie feel comfortable if she needed to rely on her.

Smoothing her short dress over her hips, Frannie answered Gia with a happy grin, "Thank you. Little black dresses are so in style. I was texting my girlfriend earlier that all the women seem to wear them over here. I found this one in Paris yesterday."

"I adore shopping in Paris." Gia looked at her, "And your necklace. Is it new too, or vintage? I love chunky necklaces like that. You're so bold to pair such large red jewelry with a simple little dress. But it works."

Frannie giggled, "I borrowed it from my mom, so it's probably vintage. But she doesn't know I have it."

"She has a million necklaces, so I bet she won't miss just one," added Remy.

Frannie stuck her foot out, "Do you think these peep toes are too old fashioned for this dress?"

"Oh, no." Gia motioned with her hands from the top of the dress downward, "Your whole look is perfect. It's such a wonderful combination of now and retro. I wouldn't change a thing."

"I saw in the passenger information that you're from Florence," said Gia, turning toward Remy. "We'll practically be neighbors. I've just finished an architecture degree and have recently landed a killer job with a small firm in Milan doing urban revitalization, so this is my last voyage."

"You're sooo lucky. I was bummed that my cousin's job was in Florence because I would much rather spend my time in Milan," Frannie chimed in. "The fashion industry there is fabulous."

"You never know. Maybe our paths will cross. Florence is only a couple of hours by train from Milan." Gia gestured across the room, "The table we've reserved for you is over here." She walked beside Frannie as they approached the table, Remy trailing slightly behind. "You'll have the same table every night. I picked one for you, so you could sit at the end, Frannie, and be able to see everyone."

"Thank you. That's so thoughtful of you."

"Of course." She showed them the table, "The rest of your tablemates should be here shortly. They've all traveled with us before, and I know you'll like them. But I'm not going to tell you any more because, after all, this is *Meet Other Guests*."

Gia pulled out the chair at one end of the table for Frannie and with a discreet nod to one of the male crew members, indicated that he should seat Remy to Frannie's right. Remy murmured a thank-you to him, pulled her long, midnight-blue skirt to the side and slipped her feet with very high black pumps under the table.

"Would you like a drink while you wait for the other guests?" asked Gia.

Turning, so Frannie could read her lips, Remy replied, "When in France – cruising the Seine – we'll each have a glass of Bordeaux. Is that okay, cuz?"

Frannie gave a little nod, and Remy continued, "But please wait to bring it until the other guests arrive." She pointed at the ball-stemmed water glasses. "Until then we'll just have sparkling water." She put her hand lightly on Gia's arm, "Would it be appropriate to ask you to join us in the lounge after dinner so we can get to know you better?"

"The first nights of cruises are pretty hectic, but perhaps we can find a bit of time tomorrow morning to chat. I want to make sure you are comfortable and all your needs are being met, but fraternizing with passengers is not encouraged, so I need to be discreet. And you'll find plenty on this trip to keep you busy."

"Of course," said Remy.

After Gia had walked away, Frannie watched Remy bend forward to scoot her chair in another inch or two. She reached out and tapped Remy on the shoulder to get her attention. Then Frannie ran her finger down the front of her own dress, looking at the plunging neckline of Remy's midnight blue top, cut low enough to reveal her cleavage. "Oooh, la, la. That's a daring neckline, cuz," Frannie grinned impishly.

Remy smiled confidently and pushed her hair back from her face.

Frannie reached over and took Remy's fingers in hers, turning her hand from side to side. "You were right to choose the French manicure." Suddenly, she tightened her fingers around Remy's hand, turned it palm down and began to sign rapidly in the version of tactile signing that they had created to use when they were sharing secrets. "*Oh. Holy. Shit. Don't turn around.*"

Remy started to turn her head. "*Don't!*" Frannie jerked on her hand. "*The best-looking couple in the whole world just walked in.*"

Remy "whispered" back into Frannie's hand, "*What are you talking about?*"

"*Oh, he's hugging Gia. She must know them. Do you think they are going to sit at our table? Ho-ly shit!*"

Again, Remy began to turn around, Frannie yanked her hand, her fingers flying under Remy's palm, "*Don't turn around and look. It will be obvious you're staring at them.*"

"*Me staring?*" she smiled at her cousin.

"*You won't believe how they're dressed. He looks fuckin' hot. Just like 007, all in black, but he's Asian. He's wearing these European slender-cut pants and a very stylish dinner jacket. I think I might need my napkin because I'm about to seriously drool.*"

"*Don't tease me. What about his partner?*" Remy asked.

Frannie peeked at the couple from under her lashes. "*OMG,*" and she looked again. "*She's as hot as he is. Her dress is obviously vintage, draped low in the front, and the scoop in the back goes almost to — well not quite, maybe just to her tailbone. She looks like a movie star all dressed for the Academy Awards.*"

Remy giggled, "*How can you see that?*"

"*Because now she's hugging Gia.*"

"*Tell me about her dress.*"

"*You know, thirties style, fog-gray chiffon, tea-length, covered with silver beads, sheer, fitted sleeves with a stripe of fancy beadwork from the shoulder to the wrist. It's stunning.*"

"*That's a lot of beads. It must weigh a ton.*" Remy started to turn to look, and again, Frannie yanked on her wrist and signed, "*No!*" into her hand. "*Be cool. They're heading our way.*"

Remy replied, "*How can I be cool when 007 and a gorgeous movie star are walking in our direction?*"

Frannie glared at her and then started to giggle as she pulled her hand from Remy's and reached for her water glass.

The glamorous couple arrived at the table after pausing several times to chat with members of the crew. "I'm Daniel Fong, and this is my wife, Lee." A pair of waiters approached, greeted the new arrivals warmly and pulled out chairs for them.

They are breathtaking, thought Remy as she reached under the table and signed into Frannie's hand, *"You were right. They're quite the stunning couple."*

Once they were seated, he looked around the table, "Just call me Fong. Lee is the only one who calls me Daniel."

Remy smiled first at Lee and then at Fong.

Frannie looked at them, "I saw the two of you come into the dining room. Everyone knows you. You're like celebrities."

Lee said, "We've been doing cruises every year since our honeymoon twenty-three years ago. We always try to book with the same Spectrum crew, so it feels like we're traveling with family. That's why so many of them know us."

"In case you didn't notice, my speech is not very crisp. I've been deaf since childhood," said Frannie.

Remy added with a quick grin, "But be careful what you say because she does read lips quite well."

The four began to chat and discovered they were all involved in the art world in one fashion or another – Fong, an art appraiser who traveled frequently; Lee, an artist and art therapist for children; Remy, an art history professor who'd recently accepted a two-year teaching position in Florence; and Frannie, an illustrator of graphic novels who was also developing a comic book series with "Lady Scarlett" as the superhero.

Out of the blue, Frannie looked at Lee and touched her own necklace, "Wow, that diamond is gigantic."

"I'm sorry. My cousin can be a bit – forthright," murmured Remy.

"That's okay." Lee smiled and put her fingers on the enormous stone, "I think it's a little obscene myself."

"But it *was* responsibly sourced. You have no idea how hard I had to look to find it," Fong commented wryly, obviously having had this conversation before. "She wouldn't let me buy her a diamond ring. So, I had to give her that instead. I guess the joke was on me, since now she finds it 'obscene'," he said with a loving smile at his wife.

15

"He's a bit of an overachiever sometimes." Lee reached over and laid her hand over his, "He gave me this on our tenth anniversary cruise, and I've worn it on every one since then. I didn't want a diamond on my hand because I garden." She held up her left hand, revealing short, simply polished nails to show her narrow, gold band. "I don't need anything more than this. And I didn't want to put a beautiful stone into the dirt."

"But that's where the stone came from," Frannie said, and they all burst out laughing.

From behind her, Remy heard a man say in a low voice, "I just wanted more alone time with you. I don't want to eat dinner with a bunch of strangers. I'll have to make small talk with them, when the only small talk I want is with you."

"Don't be so grumpy, my love. I know you weren't so keen on the *Meet Other Guests* option for dining, but you'll have a fabulous time, I promise," she heard a woman's voice reply.

Remy turned her head to see a distinguished man with a salt-and-pepper beard and dark hair threaded with gray. He wore what was obviously a bespoke dinner jacket with a white shirt and an artistic, Hundertwasser-inspired tie with bright swirls of color.

She watched his brow relax as he leaned over to whisper something into the woman's ear. She smiled and nodded knowingly as he pulled out a chair for her at their table and dropped a kiss on the top of her head. Her hand reached up to stroke his cheek.

Fong stood up and reached over to shake the newcomer's hand. "Tracey Lauch, right? It's rare that I forget a face or a name. You were on our cruise in Ukraine. What a small world."

After a firm handshake, Tracey replied, "Fong, right? And your wife is Lee? I rarely forget names or faces either. And this is my wife, Charlotte. She and I met on that cruise."

Lee said, "Yes, I remember you both. And now you're married. How wonderful for you." Her eyes twinkled, "I suspect Gia had something to do with seating us all together."

"I suspect she did," Tracey smiled and took a seat next to Remy. She introduced herself and then Frannie, and she then signed the names of the newcomers.

"Remy Martin? Remy Martin?" Tracey turned toward her and raised one eyebrow, "Like the French cognac?"

Remy smiled at him and chuckled, "My parents were both artists, and my dad had a quirky sense of humor. They named me Rembrandt Martin, but I've always been Remy."

"Do you get teased about it?" asked Charlotte.

"All the time, especially since I was old enough to spend time with folks of drinking age."

Frannie turned toward them and said very carefully, "I'm deaf. When you speak to me, please look at me so I can read your lips."

"If you ever have trouble understanding us," Charlotte said, "please tell us. Or if we forget to look at you, don't hesitate to just bang on your glass with your fork. It will probably take some training before we get it right, so don't be shy." Charlotte laughed, and the group joined in as Frannie immediately picked up her fork and tapped on her glass.

"Like this?"

Fong threw his head back and laughed, "Exactly."

Gia set Lee and Fong's drinks in front of them and then glasses of wine in front of Remy and Frannie. "Welcome back, Tracey and Charlotte. I thought you might all like to sit together." Fong took a sip and looked up at Gia with a smile of appreciation, "Please thank Sasha for my scotch."

"What do you mean, Sasha? I'm the one who remembered it," grinned Gia.

Lee added, "And thank you for my Grievous Angel. I remember how dubious I was when Sasha first described it as a cocktail made with bourbon, elderflower liqueur and strawberry syrup. I am not a fan of sweet drinks, but somehow, Sasha created something divine. He's a magician."

"He is," replied Gia. "If there were a level above master bartender, I'm sure Sasha would hold that title. So, I think 'magician' will have to do."

Charlotte looked up at Gia, "I'll definitely have a Grievous Angel as well, please. It sounds delightful."

"Fong, what scotch are you drinking?"

"It's a twenty-five-year-old, single malt by Grangestone. Sasha tucks a bottle or two away for me when he knows we're joining him on a cruise. I often sneak down last thing as he closes up for the evening and share a dram with him."

Tracey looked at Gia, "I'll have one of those." He glanced at Fong, "If you don't mind my poaching your private stock."

"I'm happy to share."

After they all had ordered, Frannie tapped her glass and giggled. "Not to correct anyone," she smiled at Charlotte. "I just want to know more about you two." She pointed toward the end of the table where Tracey and Charlotte were seated. "The four of us all have connections to the art world. I'm a freelance illustrator of graphic novels and have a comic book series as well." She pointed to Remy, "My cousin is a photographer and an art professor who lives in Florence."

Remy added, "Amateur photographer." She looked up, and her glance met Fong's. Their eyes caught for a moment, and she flushed before she looked away.

With a twinkle in his eyes and his voice brimming with laughter, Tracey said, "I'm a serial killer and a wealthy philanthropist from Raleigh, North Carolina."

Charlotte gave a loud guffaw and shook her head at him, "Now, Tracey." She turned to the others, "As you can tell, my husband has a warped sense of humor."

"In my real life," Tracey's voice became more serious, "I was a family court judge before I retired. And I founded a unique foster home that provides housing for siblings as they await adoption. When I'm not supporting that, I travel. Life is too short not to enjoy it."

Charlotte said, "My life has been much more mundane. I am of Hungarian descent, and I taught English at the University of Washington in Seattle before I retired last month."

"But you have such a lovely British accent," said Lee.

"My grandparents emigrated from Budapest to London. I was born and grew up there. After I married for the first time," she paused, "I moved to Seattle with my husband. Tracey and I met almost two years ago on a Spectrum cruise. I overheard him having a hilarious conversation with Sasha about a toilet museum in Kyiv. I had to meet that man. Now, we're newlyweds, and we're moving to Italy because he's just bought me a house in Sicily."

"Bought you a house?" asked Remy.

"It's one of those one euro houses that need to be completely rebuilt, so I hardly bought her a house," Tracey said. "More like a pile of rocks."

"That's a huge project," Lee said thoughtfully. "But what fun! I grew up in Sicily. You'll love it there."

"We live in Ostia now," said Fong. "It's about an hour from Rome on the Tyrrhenian coast."

"We considered Sicily, but as an art appraiser, Daniel travels to Asia a lot for work. We wanted easy access to the airport in Rome, so he'd have more direct, international flights to choose from."

Charlotte asked, "So, Lee, while Fong is away, what do you do? Ohhh, gosh, sorry, that wasn't meant to sound so condescending."

"No offense taken. I'm a children's art therapist, and I also teach children's art classes. And I dabble as an artist in his absence."

"Is it coincidental that four people sitting at this table would be involved in the art world?" asked Tracey. "Actually, five. My family have been patrons of the arts for several generations. And relatively recently, I've developed an interest in iconography."

"I see Gia's hand in our seat assignments, so no coincidence there," said Fong.

"You know, everyone in the world is connected by only a few degrees of separation," said Frannie.

Charlotte chortled, "I guess I'm the one with the greatest separation. I'm merely an English professor. And like Tracey, I retired early. But I do take pictures with my phone. Does that make me an artist?" They all laughed again.

Downstairs And Upstairs

Onboard *The Indigo*

Charlotte said, as she and Remy walked away from the table, "Your fish looked delicious. If I had known you better, I would have reached over with my fork and taken a bite."

"It was fantastic. But it's a good thing you didn't do that because I would have rapped your knuckles with my knife. I'm a huge fan of fish with lemon and capers. There are some things a woman doesn't share," laughed Remy.

"I guess so." Charlotte raised her eyebrows and gave a small laugh, "My mom and I used to reach over and eat off each other's plates all the time. We had a rule that when we went out to eat, we couldn't order the same thing. Then we shared, at least a bite, with each other," Charlotte said with a little hitch in her voice. She gave Remy a tiny smile.

"What a delightful memory."

"Yeah, but sad too. She'd been ill for a while and died last month, just after Tracey and I got married."

"Oh, I'm so sorry." Remy gently touched Charlotte's hand resting on the banister of the curved staircase just outside the dining room. "The others must have gotten held up. Let's go upstairs to the lounge and find seats for us all."

At the top of the stairs, the doors to the lounge opened with a gentle swoosh. The room was spacious, dimly lit, ideal for romantic encounters and conversations among new friends still making one another's acquaintance. Between the two sets of entrance doors stood a u-shaped bar with several bartenders bustling about preparing for the night's guests. Chairs and loveseats were clustered around small tables at the edges of the room, while groupings of comfortable club chairs surrounded cocktail tables in the center. Candles in crystal tealight holders flickered on each tabletop, and toward the back of the lounge stood a baby grand piano with its lid up, waiting to be played. They paused next to the bar, and Charlotte pointed toward a corner of the room near the piano, "How about there?"

"I think it might be a bit noisy when the pianist begins to play. How about over here against the windows. It's a little farther away, so it'll probably be quieter."

"Perfect." While they walked toward the chairs, Charlotte said, "It's too bad our departure was so early. I would like to have seen the Paris skyline by night as we pulled away from the dock." She smiled to herself at the memory of how she and Tracey had spent their afternoon, definitely too preoccupied to pay attention to the skyline.

"That would have been lovely. Charlotte, I meant to tell you at dinner how much I like your dress." She leaned forward, looking at it closely, "Are those really pleats or is that decorative stitching?"

"They are actually tiny, tiny pleats that are stitched down."

"All the way around?"

Charlotte slipped her matching wrap off one arm and turned around, showing off her sleeveless, ankle-length red sheath with a low, square neckline and wide straps. Before sitting, she lifted her left arm, "I wasn't sure about the pleats at first, but I absolutely fell in love with these fabric-covered buttons." She touched the tiny fasteners that ran down the side of the dress. "But after wearing this for a couple of hours, I'm realizing they rub against my arm and are just plain annoying."

"Ahhh, the price we pay to be fashionable," said Remy. The two women laughed comfortably.

"Do you think – you have to be honest with me – do you think the red color clashes with my hair? Tracey insists that it doesn't."

"Oh, no. I was going to compliment you earlier on how flattering that dress is on you. It takes such a good eye to find reds that work well together." She touched her own auburn hair, "I have the same problem myself."

"It's nice to hear that from an artist. Thank you."

"You're welcome," Remy smiled warmly.

"Where did you buy your dress? Tracey adores plunging necklines. He's always going on about them. That one looks wonderful on you, but I'm just not sure that they're the right style for me. This," she traced her neckline with one finger, "is about as daring as I get."

"It's lovely on you. And my dress? I bought it at Nordstrom's just before I moved from San Francisco. I have a wonderful personal shopper there who is always setting things aside for me to try on. I'll miss her."

"A personal shopper? Why didn't I ever think of that?" said Charlotte.

"You could always fly up to Milan from Sicily. It's only a couple of hours at the most. A fashion capital of the world, you know. Frannie is already planning a huge shopping trip there before she heads back home. I'm sure she'll need at least one extra suitcase to carry back all her loot."

"That's an idea," said Charlotte. "I'll have to pick her brain."

"Or in a couple of weeks, when our cruise ends, you could shop in Paris. Another fashion capital," Remy smiled. "Did you and Tracey get a chance to visit many museums in Paris? I truly love museums, where I can experience life from other periods or locations, even if just vicariously, and spend as long as I like enjoying the work of one artist or school of painting. I like to analyze the work, to walk up close to the painting and see all the tiny details, how the strokes of the brush and the palette knife create a mood or a feeling, and then to step back and see how it all works together. Frannie and I arrived several days before we departed, and I dragged her all over to museums and galleries. She finally put her foot down and went off by herself to explore. She's not much of a museum person. Something about 'life is art, so why do I need to go see all those old paintings?'"

"I'm afraid I am not much of a museum person either. After a couple of hours, I want to go sit in a café and people-watch. It's highly entertaining and much easier on the feet."

"You and Frannie – I'm sure she saw a much different Paris when she was out and about on her own. She was ecstatic to find a few places that sold vintage comic books. I think those and the flea market at Les Puces de Saint-Ouen were the highlights for her. She found a couple of fun, vintage jackets at the flea market."

"We didn't do much sightseeing." Charlotte cleared her

throat delicately, "We splurged and stayed at the George V as part of our honeymoon, and I'm sure we did wonders for their revenue with all the room service we ordered. I must confess that we didn't venture out much at all," Charlotte replied, trying not to laugh.

"I wanted to stay somewhere truly French on this visit. I thought something less posh would appeal to Frannie. So, I went online and found a little hotel near all the places I wanted to visit. It was described as a quirky boutique hotel, and I found it charming, but she thought it was just pokey and inconvenient." She shook her head, affectionately thinking about the sweet building with corridors that wound around and the sunny, brick courtyard where she'd had breakfast each morning. Frannie had skipped it after the first day in order to go out and find true Parisian breakfasts like the working people ate.

"Give me good strong coffee with lots of cream and sugar and a baguette with butter and jam. And the more comfortable my surroundings, the better."

"Precisely," agreed Remy.

The women looked up, and Charlotte waved vigorously at Lee and Frannie who were just coming through the door. Frannie waved back and continued her conversation, "—and then perhaps Lady Scarlett would go off into the night to find her next good deed to do," she was saying enthusiastically. "The graphics I create for other authors' novels are my bread and butter, and I've tried writing a graphic novel or two of my own, not very successfully, but the plan for my Lady Scarlett series has my heart."

"How nice that you want to write something that appeals to children. Heroes and role models are so important. I had no idea, Frannie, how involved it is to develop storylines and illustrations for comic books. I'm so impressed."

They dropped into chairs next to the other women. Remy turned to chat with them while Charlotte reached into her oversized handbag, pulled out a Paris guidebook – its pages flagged with different colored stickies – and set it on her lap. She continued to rummage for Tracey's pipe and tobacco pouch.

Frannie pointed at the stickies throughout the book, "That's exactly what Remy does."

Charlotte nodded, "It's the only way to keep track of what we want to see and fit it all in." Finally finding the pipe and pouch that had drifted to the bottom of her bag, she set them on the small, round table next to her chair before picking up the book and flipping through it. "I scribble notes on the stickies too." She paused at one and turned the book so Frannie could see, "What we'll do on each day we're there. It's all color-coded and organized. I have one of these for almost every city we visit."

"Of course," agreed Remy, looking over at Charlotte's annotated book with interest. "I do the same, although not to that level of detail."

"She has shelves of ancient guidebooks too," Frannie chimed in with a shake of her head.

"I confess, I do have shelves and shelves full of new and older ones. But the old ones aren't just any old guidebooks. They are old Baedeker's. They give so much information about cities and countries from the period when they were published. My treasure is the 1910 version of Austria, including Hungary, Transylvania, Dalmatia and Bosnia. Imagine, some of those places don't even exist under those names anymore. And the pages are all crispy, so I rarely take it anywhere."

"That's fascinating. I've heard of the Northern Italy version because, of course, that's the guide referenced so extensively in E. M. Forster's *Room with a View*," Charlotte laughed, bonding with Remy. "I'm afraid mine are all functional and new. What made you start collecting the older ones?"

"Interestingly, one of my passions, reading espionage novels. When I was a teenager, still living in Switzerland, I read one by Helen McInnes about a British couple who traveled through Europe just before the beginning of World War Two. They had a collection of Baedeker's guides, and I was intrigued – little red guidebooks with lovely maps, designed to fit in a man's jacket pocket. I bought a new one, and I found it so useful, and then I just kind of fell into searching for older ones in second-hand bookstores."

Tracey and Fong came through the doors to the lounge, chatting away spiritedly as they walked toward the group of women.

Their animated voices caught Remy's attention, and she watched as they made their way through the lounge. Her eyes narrowed in interest as Fong's face lit up and a big grin split his face. He murmured something to Tracey and hurried over to the bartender who threw his arms around Fong, "My friend." Remy smiled at their joy as they hugged each other fiercely.

With an arm still flung over the bartender's shoulder, Fong said, "Sasha, these are our friends from dinner." Smiling at the group, he said, "I think we'll be spending a lot of time together. We're all very artsy and seem to get along wonderfully."

Fong turned to Tracey and the women, "This is my longtime friend, Sasha. Something interesting about Sasha is that he owns a hectare of vineyards in Slovenia. But more important for us at the moment is that he's the master bartender."

"Oh, then we'll get good drinks," Frannie said, and they all laughed.

Tracey leaned over and kissed Charlotte, "So this is where you ended up." He ran a finger along her thigh at the top of the slit in the side of her dress. She reached over and slid her hand under his. "Later, my love," she whispered.

Sasha smiled, "What will you be drinking this evening?"

Once their drinks had arrived, Tracey took a sip of his cognac and nodded appreciatively. He picked up his pipe and its pouch in his other hand, motioning with it, "Fong, would you like to join me on the upper deck?"

"Of course. I'll be completely outnumbered if I stay behind."

As the two of them walked away, Lee smiled fondly, "He only allows himself one cigarette a day, after dinner. But he has to have that one."

"You two are like two sides of a clam shell. You fit one another perfectly," Remy said. "How did you meet?"

Lee's eyes sparkled, "We were students in our early twenties when we met here, in Paris – I was studying painting, and he'd always wanted to be an art appraiser. So, I guess you could say, generally speaking, that art was the thing that drew us together. But, oh, my goodness, he was so good-looking and had such a vibrant personality. He caught my eye from across the room at my senior art exhibition. He made an extravagant gesture with his hand, and I noticed that he was wearing a signet ring on his little finger." She took a sip from her glass, "Mmmm, Sasha makes the best drinks."

Charlotte said, "With that look in your eyes, there has to be more to your story than that."

Lee chuckled, "He was standing across the room, discussing one of my paintings with my senior advisor, and he caught my eye when he threw his head back, put his hands out with that ring gleaming on one finger and laughed from the depths of his soul. I just had to meet that man. I made the first move when I strutted up to him." With her shoulders, she did a little imitation of an exaggerated strut as she sat. "I put my hands on my hips and – I look back and can't believe I was so bold – and I interrupted his conversation, 'What pretentious artist walks around with bling on his pink?' and I waggled my pinky finger at him, like this."

Remy said, "Oh, that silver signet ring he is wearing tonight?"

Lee nodded, "That very one. I was so brazen. As I spoke, I raised my left eyebrow, like this," she arched her eyebrow. "I continued to hold my finger up and looked at him – waiting."

"And?" said Frannie, completely caught up in the story.

"He looked at me, and for the longest time, he didn't answer. My heart was pounding. I was sure I'd ruined my opportunity. He just looked me up and down, and then finally, he smiled, '*This* pretentious artist does. I use it to seal letters and nude sketches before I send them to my lovers.' And then he asked me out for a drink."

When their howling diminished, Lee went on, "Daniel says at that moment, he fell for my spontaneity, for my sassiness. I claim I fell for his sarcasm and his romantic wit. I don't think either of us really know what it was anymore, but we've been inseparable ever since. He seduced me with his smile and that one remark."

Frannie tapped on her glass with her red fingernail and giggled, "So, Charlotte, tell us about you. Even though I'm a writer – well, sort of – I struggle with English. How do you teach it so it's not boring?"

"Well, as I said, I'm retired now, but I would try to find something that might resonate with my students. For instance, I've always been fascinated by ethical and moral dilemmas. Quite honestly, any dilemma. Most recently, in my classes, instead of having my students write about a preselected topic that they might not find interesting, I had them respond to dilemmas I posed, dilemmas from material we'd read." She looked around, realizing she was falling into her Professor French tone and then gave a quick shrug and continued, "There's almost always a good dilemma – take *Romeo and Juliet*, '*Defy thy father and refuse thy name.*' or *To Kill a Mockingbird*, when Atticus has to decide if he will properly defend Tom Robinson at trial. Think of any book, and there is some type of dilemma, a choice the characters must make – that's what makes the story interesting. I like to see how people think, and I like to understand their opinions. So, for example, I'd perhaps ask my creative writing students to write a short story based on a dilemma a character faces."

"But, Charlotte, so I get the choice thing, but what's the difference between all these kinds of dilemmas?" Frannie wrinkled her forehead.

"Oh dear, you've asked the critical question. A classic dilemma is choosing between two right things, but you have to determine what's right for you. An ethical dilemma is when a person is forced to choose between two morally sound options, for example, truth versus loyalty to a friend. And of course, moral dilemmas are between right and wrong."

"I'd like to have been a fly on the wall in one of your classes. I'm sure that led to some fascinating debates," said Remy.

§

On the upper deck, Fong glanced at Tracey with a twinkle in his eye. "I bet we are directly above our table in the lounge. Do you think we should do a tap dance, or better yet, send morse code down to them?" They both chuckled and found seats sheltered from the breeze.

Tracey watched as Fong pulled the sharp crease of his trouser leg slightly as he crossed his leg. It could be very interesting to get to know him. *Even though he's a bit formal sometimes, he's obviously quite bright, and he definitely has a wacky sense of humor.*

Fong watched Tracey's ritual – he picked up his pipe, curling his fingers around it and with his thumb and forefinger, he unzipped the pouch, dipped the pipe in to fill it with tobacco and tamped it down in the bowl of the pipe with the little device he'd pulled from a zippered pocket on one side of the pouch. He carefully closed it and took a book of matches from the other outside pocket before setting the pouch on the table. After a couple of failed attempts to keep the matches lit, he turned his back to the breeze and clamped the pipe between his teeth, striking yet another match and drawing on the stem as the tobacco caught at last.

"You even carry a pipe tamper in that little pouch? You're very precise."

"Mmmmhmmm. If you're going to do it, you have to do it right. It's an art, after all, to smoke a pipe."

Fong put his slender cigarette in his mouth and slipped the slim, silver case back into his jacket pocket before cupping one hand around the cigarette as he lit it with his silver lighter. He sat back and took a long drag. "These are much easier. Instant gratification, you know."

"True. So, what made you decide to become an art appraiser?"

"I love art, but I can't draw or paint to save my life." Fong raised his hands in an open-handed shrug.

"Yeah, I can't either."

"Lee's the artist, she's very talented. I knew from the first moment I saw her at her senior exhibition that I had to meet her. Funny thing, I've never shared this with her," he idly ran his finger along the thin, silver band that diagonally bisected his black tie, "but I'd been scheming about the perfect way to meet her that evening, so I couldn't believe it when she came over to me and made the first advance. How about you and Charlotte?"

"My meeting with Charlotte wasn't nearly as premeditated.

As she said earlier, she overheard my conversation with Sasha about, of all things, the toilet museum in Kyiv. Personally, I think she was looking for a way to meet me. And I thought she was fun from the get-go. Whatever it was, it worked. We clicked right away."

"The Toilet History Museum? I was there last year. The owners, Mykola and Maryna Bogdanenko, are lovely people. I had an appraisal in Kyiv, and Sasha said I had to stop there."

"It's certainly a small world."

"Especially among frequent Spectrum travelers," Fong added.

"It was at the end of that same cruise when I really came to appreciate iconography. I'd had a passing acquaintance because my grandparents had an icon in their house, and it was so unlike any other artwork they owned. But, like you, I can't draw or paint my way out of a box. And I hadn't focused on art, other than my duties on my family's museum board, until I traveled in Europe."

"Your family owns a museum? What kind of museum?"

"The Lauch Art Museum in Raleigh, North Carolina. My grandparents founded it, and we work hard to celebrate and support local artists."

They sat smoking and relaxing in silence. Fong put out his cigarette and turned to Tracey, "Remy is certainly charming, and her cousin is a delightful young woman."

"It's very generous that she's treated Frannie to this cruise," Tracey said. "They're both very attractive. And you know, I see a resemblance between your Lee and Remy."

"Other than the red hair, I don't see it. But they were certainly fascinating dinner companions." Fong paused, pulled another cigarette out and looked at it pensively.

Tracey heard the door to the wheelhouse open, and a beam of light shone over their shoulders. He turned slightly to watch someone exit the small room as they changed shifts, and he chuckled, "When I'm up here with my pipe in the evening on these cruises, I'm almost always alone. I have this running story in my head about a thief who uses these boats to smuggle his stolen goods."

"You have a creative mind."

"Well, you know, sitting alone in the dark, puffing on a pipe. There are endless things one can think about – art theft, bank robbery, even murder."

"So, tell me about this thief."

"Over time, the story has become quite elaborate. This guy steals priceless artwork. He takes it out of the frame and rolls it up so he can transport it in his suitcase. But even better is where he can hide it."

"Where would that be?"

"Have you ever taken a tour of one of these boats and gone inside the wheelhouse?"

"Yes, but only when we first started taking Spectrum trips."

Tracey pointed to the wheelhouse, "In addition to all the mechanics for driving the boat, there is a bin filled with rolled-up maps. They said they are only used if the computers go down—"

"As a backup?"

"Precisely. So, the thief could slip the stolen art into one of the rolled-up maps. No one would know it was there."

"Isn't the wheelhouse manned continuously?"

"Ahhh, well Henri will need an accomplice on the crew to hide his goods, won't he?"

"Henri?"

"Our thief."

Fong chuckled. He noticed that Tracey was still puffing away, and he lit his second cigarette. "I normally only allow myself one. But perhaps it's a night to break rules. After all, what are rules for, if not to be broken? Besides, I think this story could go on for a while."

Monet's Garden

Giverny, France

Fong watched Charlotte as she sat down across the room at a small table set for two. *Ah, the morning ritual. Six days into the cruise, they're still enjoying their breakfast together with no one else. How romantic, that newlyweds in their forties want to have some time with just each other.* Charlotte waved, and he nodded and gave a wave back before returning to his morning routine of coffee and the crossword puzzle.

Reaching into her oversized bag, Charlotte took out her iPad, flipped open the case and with a few clicks on the wireless keyboard, she pulled up her browser.

"Would you like some coffee, madame?" asked the waiter.

"Yes, please, with heavy cream." She looked down at the silver sugar dish, peeked under the lid to see her favorite, lumpy brown cubes, and she nodded her head in satisfaction. As the waiter began to turn away, she added, "Would you please bring a second cup. My husband will be along at some point soon." She pointed to the place setting to her left, knowing that he'd want to sit there so he could look out across the dining room.

She paused, thinking about whether to indulge in what Tracey called her "guilty obsession" or be responsible and check the news. "It is my honeymoon, and one shouldn't do anything terribly serious while honeymooning," she said very softly. "Indulge. It's like whipped cream in the morning," and she typed "*true crime*".

The waiter returned, bearing a large tray with a silver coffee pot, a small pitcher of cream and two porcelain cups and saucers with the Spectrum logo delicately painted on the side in shades of black and gray. He set a cup at Tracey's place and asked, "Shall I pour your coffee, or would you like to wait for your husband?"

"I'll have a cup now, please."

Charlotte carefully added cream and one lump of sugar and slowly stirred it around and around before taking a sip. "Mmmm

– coffee," she sighed with pleasure.

She returned to contemplating her iPad, her chin resting on her left hand, her right fingers poised over the keys, when Tracey came up behind her. "Good morning, my love," he said, resting his hands on her shoulders as he kissed the top of her head. Leaning over her shoulder, he read her query, "Really, Charlotte?"

She reached up and put her hand on his forearm gently. "We all have our guilty indulgences. You smoke your pipe, and I'm obsessed with true crime." She lifted one shoulder delicately and tapped the enter key. Responses began to scroll up on her screen.

Tracey sat down and moved his napkin to one side. Charlotte poured his coffee, rich and dark, from the silver pot and handed it to him. "Tell me about all the scandals in Raleigh."

He took a sip. "In fact, I didn't pay attention to the scandals. What I saw daily in family court was tragic – damaged families, money, separations. That was enough scandal for me. I learned pretty quickly that no family is perfect. Just like those early years with my biological mother. So, I wanted to do whatever I could to protect the kids and keep their situations from getting worse." Tracey gave Charlotte a long look as he pondered what to tell her. Then, while they ate breakfast, he told her stories about some of his cases.

When their plates had been removed, Fong came over and handed Tracey his newspaper, neatly folded to the puzzle page, "As I recall, you like to do the sudoku. In ink," he added with a shake of his head. "I thought you might like this."

Tracey grinned, "I do. Imagine you remembering that." He set the paper down and laid his hand on it, "Thank you." As Fong walked away, Tracey looked over at Charlotte and pointed to the paper, "Do you mind?"

"Not at all." She pulled her iPad back in front of her, "I have plenty to keep me busy." Tracey shook his head and gave her an indulgent smile. They sat in comfortable silence as they sipped their second cups of coffee. While he continued working methodically on his puzzle, Charlotte changed her search to "*Raleigh true crime*" and began reading through some of the links that appeared.

All of a sudden, Charlotte sat bolt upright. "Wow, that's interesting. Wow."

As he mulled over which number belonged in the next blank square, Tracey asked absently, "What's that, my love?"

"This Parking Lot Strangler in Raleigh was killing women years before we met. Do you remember him? Were people terrified? Remember the Zodiac Killer in San Francisco? Women there were petrified to go out at night."

Still focused on his puzzle, he said, "As I recall, the Raleigh murders were spread out over many years. So, I imagine it didn't have that same impact."

Charlotte looked back at her iPad, "You're right, the four killings were from 1998 to 2007. That's almost ten years. The women he strangled were all redheads. I think I would've been scared if I'd lived there then – but maybe not. That was before I had red hair."

He looked up, reached over and caressed her hair, "I like your red hair. It suits you. Coloring it was a good decision."

Charlotte took his hand in hers and held it. She continued reading silently for several minutes before she went on, "There're only a couple of articles about him. Do you know if they ever caught—"

Tracey smacked his pen down on top of the puzzle, "*Enough!*"

Startled, Charlotte looked up at him, uncertain about what had caused him to react so abruptly.

§

Later that morning, Fong leaned over and quoted Monet to Lee as they stood, looking at the pond and bridge, surrounded by weeping willows, "*Everyone discusses my art and pretends to understand, as if it were necessary to understand, when it is simply necessary to love.*"

"But who wants to ponder what someone else was thinking when you should be standing silently, absorbing the beauty? Especially in a place like this," said Lee. She sighed at the sight of the April gardens in a bloom of riotous reds and blues, yellows and purples, and with her arm tucked through his, they continued their stroll through the gardens and around the bottom of the pond. "Daniel, I'm so happy we chose this tour and were able to visit Monet's garden together again."

"Me too." Fong leaned over and gave her a kiss on her temple. "I saw Remy this morning just before you came down for breakfast. She walked in through the lounge from the bow. She had a camera around her neck and a sketchbook in her hand."

"She was probably preparing material for one of her classes." Lee smiled, "Daniel, it's been a long time since I've laughed as hard as we did the other night. I know we schedule these trips to relax but—"

"—But what a wonderfully different experience this is." Fong smiled at her. They looked back down the length of the pond and watched Remy and Frannie step off the bridge before pausing to look at their map of the garden. "Speak of the devil, there they are." He watched the sunlight reflecting off Remy's auburn hair and remarked to Lee, "Her hair is truly titian. I don't think I've ever seen that before in real life."

"I don't think I have either," Lee replied.

Fong caught Remy's eye, and they waved to each other. When they were within speaking distance, she said, "Good morning. Are you enjoying yourselves?"

"These gardens are my sanctuary whenever I have business travel to this part of France," said Fong. "Even if I can only steal an hour or so from my schedule, I like to walk along these paths and stop from time to time, imagining I'm looking over Monet's shoulder as he paints."

"I dress up as Monet," Lee winked at Fong and said with her gentle smile, "I've found Impressionism an easy style to teach children. It's not as precise as other styles of painting or drawing, but it's still based on reality. It gives children the opportunity to paint without any anxiety about their art not being perfect. I dress up as Monet and bring a bag full of berets and smocks that they put on while they giggle and become little Monets, inspired to paint clouds scudding across the sky or trees on hilltops blowing in the wind. Children love to play-act, and I like to turn that enjoyment into a lesson."

"What a fabulous way to introduce children to art," said Remy. "The younger the better! For the most part, my college students wouldn't dare put on a beret and play a role. So, I have to find other ways to inspire them. Each semester, I ask them to read the art sections of the *San Francisco Chronicle* and *New York Times*. Then at the end of the semester, they turn in a paper describing the trends they observed during the semester. It's a subtle way to teach them about research and writing in addition to art."

"Art-related research is a great skill to teach young adults. It's an ongoing part of my work in preparing appraisals," Fong said.

"Enough with the shop talk," said Frannie impatiently. "I'm hungry, so let's get lunch. We should find Charlotte and Tracey. I know they'll want to join us."

Everyone nodded in agreement.

"Look, they're over there canoodling behind those bushes." With a twinkle in his eye, Fong pulled Lee against his side, "Maybe we should have thought of that."

Remy raised her camera, focused the large lens she was using that day and took a few shots of the couple, hoping that Charlotte would like them. And then she stepped back and focused her camera on Lee and Fong's faces. As she pressed the shutter, she noticed the way he smiled at her.

"Oh, Daniel, they're newlyweds. And there's nothing wrong with a little canoodling."

"Do you have a place in mind?" he asked with a smile.

"Daniel!" Lee smacked his arm playfully.

Fong threw his head back and laughed, "No, my darling. I was merely asking Frannie about a place for lunch – of course."

Frannie teased, "You're asking me? You're the one who comes here all the time."

"Les Nympheas has an excellent lunch, and it's not far from the front entrance to the gardens."

"Sounds good." And they went off to gather up the newlyweds before heading to the restaurant.

While walking to lunch, Lee and Frannie went on ahead,

chatting, while Remy and Fong walked next to each other with Tracey and Charlotte a little way behind.

Remy turned her head slightly toward Fong and mentioned that when she'd come back in from taking some early morning photos to capture the light, she'd seen him reading a newspaper. "How do you get a real paper onboard the boat?" As she spoke, she drifted toward him, and their hands brushed. A tingle of electricity ran through her, and she quickly stepped away. "I'm sorry," she said. *Oh my, what was that?*

Fong smiled, "No need to apologize. I'm always walking into people when I'm looking toward them. About the newspaper, it's a secret," he teased in a solemn voice, and then he gave her a broad grin. "Cruising annually on Spectrum has privileges. But I'm not sure how they make it happen. A miracle occurs, and a copy of the New York Times appears when I sit down for my coffee in the morning. I'd be happy to share it with you, except for the crossword."

Tracey overheard them and added, "Thanks for the sudoku this morning. Do you only cruise with Spectrum, Fong?"

"Yes. We like to make it special since we only cruise once a year. We chose Spectrum because it is small and such an exclusive luxury line. We've traveled with them in Europe and Asia but never in the United States."

While the others were chatting, Frannie asked Lee, "Why did you decide to teach art to children?"

"Art's my passion, Frannie, and I love children." She continued quietly, "Daniel and I don't seem to be able to have any of our own. I'd hoped we would have a large family together. So, this is the next best thing. And my current job is a perfect melding of both my passions. I teach in a small school in Ostia, near where we live. Smaller classes are wonderful because I can give more attention to each child."

Charlotte took Tracey's hand in hers and slowed down, so they lagged behind the rest of the group, "Is everything okay?"

"What do you mean?"

"This morning, at breakfast, you seemed upset about something."

"I'm sorry I snapped at you. It's just that," he paused, "I knew some of the women who were killed."

For a moment she thought about asking which ones. Instead, she simply replied, "Oh, my love."

Images of the women he had killed paraded through his mind. The four in Raleigh, the prostitute in St. Petersburg, Mari in Zaporizhzhya, the unknown woman in the alley in Strasbourg, the young woman at the golf course in Washington state. He blinked and pulled Charlotte close in a quick hug.

The group exited Monet's Garden onto Rue Claude Monet, straggling down the village street as they continued to converse in pairs, and soon they arrived at the restaurant. As they waited at the entrance to be seated in the garden, Remy looked around the elegant space that looked as though it had been taken from a painting by Monet. They sat on chairs with soft, yellow cushions sheltered with large, white umbrellas, the oval, white table, topped with placemats depicting the gardens they'd just left. The weather was warm enough that they were very comfortable in their secluded corner, and soon the men were removing their light jackets while the women pulled off their sweaters and hung them over the backs of their chairs.

Tracey and Fong conferred over the wine menu, and they all agreed that a couple of bottles of crisp white wine were in order.

Frannie, who spoke fluent Italian but little French, picked up her menu and soon had them in stitches as she began to read the choices in French with a heavy Italian accent. When they'd recovered, Charlotte and Remy took control of the ordering process, and soon the table was covered with dishes they'd all agreed to share, quiches and omelets, salads and asparagus, plates of prosciutto and smoked salmon, a lovely wedge of brie and of course, crisp, fresh baguettes.

"*Bon appetit,*" said Fong, and they began to eat hungrily.

"If we eat like this every day," whispered Tracey to Charlotte, "we'll be so fat, we might need a second bed in our cabin, one for each of us."

"You aren't getting away from me that easily," Charlotte teased back. "We'll just need to walk more."

Frannie sampled bits of everything on the table as she continued her conversation with Lee, "You said you like the smaller classes. Other than giving kids more individual attention, what do you find are the other advantages?"

"Smaller groups give me much more flexibility. My classes are usually only about ten students. That means we can do things together as an entire class instead of splitting up into smaller groups, with each group having a different experience. For example, each fall, I take the class on an artistic adventure. Last year, we did a controlled graffiti evening. We painted a mural on the side of a decrepit building. Beforehand, we talked about all the steps required to get permission, that they can't just run around painting on anyone's building. It's about respect for other people's property. But once we had that permission and completed our project, they saw how our work improved the community and created a piece of art for the public to enjoy. It's wonderful that the children were able to contribute something of artistic value at such a young age. Now, when they walk past the mural, they can feel proud that it's their work."

Over coffee and dessert, Frannie's face lit up with excitement, and she returned to their earlier conversation, "Lee, you've given me a great idea."

"What do you mean?" Remy asked.

"Lee said she has super kids that do super art projects that contribute to beautifying the community."

Lee replied modestly, "I guess that's one way to look at it. The projects make them believe that they all have extraordinary powers."

"Lee, I think I'm going to steal your idea. What if Lady Scarlett doesn't work alone, but she works with kids. Each comic book in the series can be a different kind of beautification. It could be different areas, different cities, different kids. But they all work to beautify their communities – at night. In one book, she could create gardens like Monet's in overgrown lots. Because it's a story, they could plant fantastic gardens in a single night, and the residents would wake up to flowers, trees and fountains where before, it was rubble and weeds. In another one, they could paint a flat median strip that's outlined in yellow paint in the middle of the street to look like a beautiful overgrown garden with benches, and the next day, it has turned into a real garden. Of course, there has to be some kind of adversity for them to overcome, like an evil-hearted villain who wants to destroy the garden so he can buy it for himself and build a huge house on it."

"Your comic series could have subtle morals to the stories," Lee said.

"Exactly. The children learn about giving back and different ways they can change things. That they have the power to do it. That the superpower lives inside them."

As they exited the shuttle they'd taken back to the boat dock, Lee pointed out a red sports car, "Fong, is that car the same year as yours?"

"No, that's a '70, not a '66."

Tracey said to Fong, "You have a 1966 Alfa Romeo?"

"Mmmmhmmm. But mine's hunter green, it's far sexier."

"Very sexy," Tracey laughed.

"And very fast. Lee gave it to me for my birthday."

"Nice gift," said Charlotte, "but don't get any ideas, my love. We just bought a house."

"Well, there's a story behind that car." They all stopped at the bottom of the ramp to their boat to listen to Lee's story. "Daniel's birthday is on February twenty-ninth. So, on leap years, I get him big gifts because he really only has a birthday once every four years."

"Technically, it may be my car, but Lee loves it as much as I do. She likes the speed, riding with the top down. She imagines we're *that* couple, like movie stars. She wears a long scarf wrapped around her head and neck and pretends she's Isadora Duncan."

"So, you *are* like movie stars," laughed Frannie.

Charlotte chuckled, "Oh dear, the modern dancer who was strangled with her scarf when it got wrapped around the car's axle?"

Lee waved her hand and with a straight face said, "We never get to that part."

Remy said slowly, suppressing a grin, "But wait. Wait. Every four years? He only has a birthday every four years. That means, Lee, you're a cradle robber."

"That's right, my darling, I'm only twelve years old."

"Let's not go there then." Lee slipped her hand into his and stood with her head against his shoulder.

After dinner that evening, as the boat pulled away from its moorings, the group sat in the lounge of *The Indigo* talking about their day, the spectacular weather and the beautiful gardens.

Fong and Remy chatted quietly. "Florence must be a wonderful place to teach art history. I have some regular clients there, so I visit it often," he said.

"It's fabulous. I've visited frequently in the past, too. It would be amusing to figure out if we'd ever been there at the same time."

"It would. How did you manage to snag a teaching position there?"

"I was invited to come be a guest lecturer last year, and then they offered me a contract. They wanted me to make a five-year commitment, but I didn't want to be locked in for that long, so finally, we settled on two. After that, they want me to stay on as the department chair. The current chairman is retiring once they find a suitable replacement. So, I have to decide if I'm going to stay. Otherwise, they'll need to begin the search process in the middle of next year."

Frannie had been lip-reading their conversation and leaned over to add, "I have to go home in July. But I hope Remy stays because I want to come back for an extended visit – for about – for about forever. I love it in Italy."

Remy smiled at Frannie and blew her a quick kiss.

Fong asked, "Was it easy getting a visa, Remy?"

"I don't need one. My mom was a U.S. citizen, and my dad was Swiss. That makes me a dual citizen. I was born and raised in Switzerland and only moved to live with Frannie and her folks when I was eighteen, after my parents died." She looked at Frannie fondly, "She was just a little tyke, and I helped take care of her while I attended Berkeley."

Fong turned toward Frannie, "Remy can work anywhere in the EU because of her Swiss citizenship. But what about you? Are you a dual citizen as well?"

"No. I'm just an American."

"Getting a visa in Italy isn't that easy. You'll have to get a job to stay. If you'd like some help—"

"I plan to look for a job when we get back to Florence. So, yes, I probably could use your help. Thanks."

Sasha arrived with their after-dinner drinks, and once they'd all settled back in their seats, Remy asked him to take a photo of the group with her camera.

See You Later

Onboard *The Indigo*

On the last morning, they had decided to have breakfast together to say their goodbyes. Charlotte looked around the table at the group who had become such unexpectedly close friends over the previous twelve days. She chuckled to herself as Lee came to the table last with her face glowing.

"Good morning, my darling," Fong looked up at Lee with a smile.

She murmured, "Good morning, Daniel," and touched the back of his neck lightly as she passed by on her way to the buffet.

She returned with a small cheese omelet with sliced carrots, cucumbers and smoked salmon alongside. After she'd draped her napkin across her lap, she smiled at the group, who had all arrived before her. "Sorry I'm late. I overslept, and Daniel didn't wake me up until he was practically out the door." The waiter put her usual morning caffè crema in front of her. She thanked him and took a grateful sip, closing her eyes as she savored her first swallow.

Fong gave her a tender smile, "It was our last morning, and you obviously needed to sleep."

Lee turned to Tracey and Charlotte, "Are you returning to Sicily today?"

"Returning? I haven't even seen my house yet. Tracey sent me a picture of a view, and when I told him I loved it, he bought the house based on that one comment," said Charlotte.

Tracey took her hand in his, "We're flying there directly today. We have an appointment with an architect tomorrow morning to design Charlotte's house."

Lee said, "I'm puzzled. I would think, as newlyweds, you'd call it 'our house'. So, how did it become Charlotte's house?"

"That's the funny story I mentioned at dinner."

Tracey continued to hold her hand, stroking it gently, as Charlotte told the story about how they had debated about Lisbon, where Tracey wanted to live, and Sicily, where she wanted a house.

Long ago, she had fallen in love with the food, wine and people there. And the view of the sea.

"Then, for Valentine's Day this year, Tracey sent me the key to a one euro house in a long, narrow box. I thought he'd sent me a bracelet or a necklace. It was the wrong shape for an engagement ring." She winked at him and looked down to admire her sparkling diamond ring and wedding band. "But instead, it was the key to a beautiful, heavy door standing between two, almost non-existent walls."

"You two are pretty spontaneous. Daniel and I took over a year to find our house."

"And it already had lots of good sturdy walls," said Fong with a straight face.

Tracey chuckled, "On the other hand, we get to rebuild this house exactly the way Charlotte wants it."

They talked about how Lee had grown up in Sicily and discovered that Charlotte's house was in the same area where Lee still had lots of family. She smiled and took a bite of her omelet, "Last night, Daniel and I were saying that normally we don't keep in touch with anyone we cruise with."

Tracey looked at her and nodded. "Most people I've met on cruises aren't that interesting." He reached over and took Charlotte's hand, "Except for one." He lifted it and kissed the backs of her fingers.

Charlotte turned her hand over so it cupped his cheek as she looked at Fong and Lee, "With all the cruising you've done, it would be a full-time job keeping in touch with everyone you meet."

"And the purpose of our anniversary cruises is to reconnect with one another," Fong said, his smile reflecting his fondness as he looked at his wife.

Lee turned to him, "Especially since you've been traveling more and more."

"Mmmm," Fong nodded as he reached into his pocket and pulled out a few cards.

"But this cruise is different because Daniel and I feel very close to you all." She looked around at everyone, reached over to

Remy who was sitting next to her and touched her hand. "Something about this group is different. I do hope we stay in touch."

Fong handed each of them a card with his initials embossed at the center of the top and their phone numbers and email addresses written below in bold, black ink. "Here is our information. Please, call or drop us a line."

Remy turned the card between her fingers and flicked the edge with her thumb, "These cards are so elegant, Fong. I may need to steal this idea for myself."

He responded to her with a warm smile.

She felt her face grow warm in turn. *Oh my, I think I have a crush on him – as though I were just a schoolgirl. I can't let that happen if Lee and I are to be friends.*

"They have a very personal feel to them," Tracey said. "I like that."

Fong looked at him, "But that's what it's all about. The personal touch is everything."

"Daniel leaves the emailing to me for the most part. He writes personal cards for everything. He'll write one at the drop of a hat. As you can see, he even brings them on vacation."

Part Two

Early May 2012

Another Murder

Raleigh, North Carolina

Penelope Huber and Edgar Spring sat across the table in the conference room at Haypress Security. Haypress was owned by a retired Raleigh Police Department detective named Emily Bissett, an attractive, mid-forty-ish black woman, who had mentored Penelope during her early days on the force. They had remained friends since then. Emily believed firmly that all means, conventional and otherwise, should be brought to bear in solving each case she worked. Penelope was not so sure.

Emily had investigated a murder when Penelope had discovered the body. After Emily's retirement, Penelope had worked as a detective on three more similar cases. While Haypress's line of business was security with a specialty in supporting river cruise lines, Emily had kept her eye on the murder investigations informally through her friendship with Penelope.

When the cases had seemed to have stalled, Emily had made an anonymous call to Edgar causing him to author a newspaper article, in which he dubbed the killer the "Parking Lot Strangler." In that article, he reported on four, frighteningly similar murders of red-headed women.

With the reluctant permission of Penelope's boss, Emily had brought her and Edgar to Haypress to collaborate in an environment outside the police department. Penelope was hell-bent on solving the murders – even if it meant that she had to work with the press. She had frequently been heard to express her view that the murdered women deserved justice.

"I knew we would find something. I just knew it," said Edgar triumphantly.

Penelope looked at him grudgingly, "I have to give it to you, Eddie. I thought, after all these years, that you were crazier than I am to keep looking." She absentmindedly took a lock of her long, blonde hair and braided and unbraided it over and over.

"I knew we would find something. We had to. All those

newspapers – even the small-town ones, someone had to report something. Investigative reporting can be instrumental in solving crimes," he replied.

"Well, I wouldn't go that far. It takes more than reporting to solve crimes."

"I couldn't have done it without Jane. She sped up the process for me. She figured out how to make the searches more efficient—" He pressed his lips together, realizing what he had just said.

Penelope raised an eyebrow at him in annoyance, "Edddieee, what happened to not leaking our work to another soul – not even the smallest detail? Who is this Jane person anyway?"

Edgar pushed back the conference room chair and raised his hands in defense. "I promise, I didn't tell her anything. I only asked her to help me with the search and let me know if she found anything. Honestly, she doesn't know anything about the cases."

Penelope repeated, "Who's Jane? Another reporter?"

"Sh – she's, my girlfriend. She's not in the news business." He stumbled over his words as he explained, "She's working on short films for her PhD. She – she's very talented, she does a lot of research. It has nothing to do with m – murder, and I promise, she won't tell a soul. Awww, shit. I was only trying to do my searching quicker, and she offered to help. She does research all the time, and she's good at it. She – she's very fast."

Penelope took a deep breath and looked at Edgar. Her voice was deathly quiet, "Please tell this 'girlfriend' of yours to keep her big mouth shut, or—"

He shoved his glasses up on his nose as he nodded solemnly.

A couple of evenings later, Penelope and Edgar huddled around the conference room table discussing how they were going to tell Emily what they'd found and why they'd waited so long to bring her into the loop.

"Hey, I think I heard Em's TV. She must be back." Penelope knocked on the door connecting the conference room to Emily's office and then threw it open without waiting for a response.

Emily was sitting at a small table, a fork raised halfway to her lips. With her free hand, she beckoned them in. Behind her, the wall of windows set into the old brick wall gleamed, and a bonsai cedar tree stood on the credenza beneath them, silhouetted against the evening light outside. Travel posters from each company she'd signed a contract with hung on the walls. She carefully put her fork back on the plastic dish holding her microwaved chicken dinner, *I guess this will have to wait*, and glanced at her watch, "I didn't realize you guys were still here." She picked up the remote for the TV and muted it.

Bursting with excitement, Penelope stopped in front of Emily. "While you were gone, Eddie made an amazing discovery." She paused for effect.

"What did he find?" Emily looked longingly at her dinner, *such as it is.*

"This week, he was searching newspapers in Washington state—"

"And?"

"Well, it's a real long shot, but we think he's found another murder, similar to the four here in Raleigh."

Emily straightened in her chair, listening.

Reluctant to barge right in on Penelope's heels, Edgar stayed propped against the door jamb, "Oh, my God! I just *knew* we would find something that wasn't put into the national crime database. I *told* you guys, if police departments don't enter the data," he shook his head, "you'll never find it there. I told you. Oh, my God! We *had* to look in the newspapers."

"As you've said," Penelope rolled her eyes.

Emily propped her elbows on the table and leaned her chin on her hands, watching the two of them, "So, tell me."

Penelope walked over to the desk, giving Edgar time to gather his thoughts and speak. She picked up a nameplate that said "*Emily Bissett*" and perched on the front of the desk. She smacked the nameplate against her palm impatiently.

Then, as Edgar opened his mouth to answer, she jumped in, her words tumbling out over one another in her excitement to share what they'd discovered, "While you were traveling, Eddie found a newspaper article from March 2011 in this little town north of Seattle called Trigg Pass." She shook the nameplate at

Emily to emphasize her next words, "The victim was a young woman who worked for the golf course and was found in some bushes next to the parking lot."

Edgar ventured a few steps into the office to lean against the wall between two framed posters of river boats, "Red hair. Strangled. Missing earring," he ticked off on his fingers.

"I knew the bastard was still out there somewhere."

Emily made an affirmative sound and then turned her gaze to Edgar, "This was your search?" He nodded, and she looked over at Penelope, "Sooo, that search you were so skeptical of finally paid off?"

"After the newspaper article he wrote about the Parking Lot Strangler way back in 2008—"

"And the one in 2009," Edgar added defensively.

"Oh, the 'not report'? Well, they both failed to turn up any new information." She looked at him and grinned companionably. "And I still think 'Parking Lot Strangler' is a stupid name for this guy."

Emily smiled as she watched them bicker, recalling how, early on, Penelope had been so unwilling to accept him as part of the team.

"Yeah, well, I was new at crime reporting back then. But it did get the information out there. I think that was what Emily wanted," he said, looking quickly at her.

Penelope narrowed her eyes, "Anyhow, why would I think your obsession with searching the internet for murders would work?"

"You're just as obsessed with these cases. In fact, I would argue, you're more obsessed than Edgar," Emily chuckled. "So, why didn't you tell me about this yesterday when I got back from my trip?"

"I told her she should have called you. I didn't want to keep it from you," said Edgar.

"Hey, don't throw me under the bus!"

"What are you two talking about? We're a team. Just because I own Haypress Security and am about a million years older than the two of you," teased Emily, "doesn't mean I'm your boss."

"I've been dying to tell you, but I wanted to get hold of the detective for the case before bringing you the news. He's hard to reach." Penelope paused, trying not to sound like she was whining about the capabilities of the Trigg Pass PD. "It's as though he's the only cop in town, and so he does a little bit of this and a little bit of that. It's a small department. Anyway, he just called me back this afternoon."

"And?"

"He gave me the details, you know, one cop to another," she grinned at Edgar.

"He would never have talked to me," he agreed.

Penelope shook the nameplate again, "From the marks on her neck, we were able to tell that perp was left-handed, and the size of the hand looks like it's the same as the one in the Raleigh murders. I asked about the earring, and he said the victim was wearing only a left earring. There was also a hole in her right ear, but no earring. Maybe the perp took it. And the shoe print they found was also the same size as the one we have in Raleigh."

"Good research on your part, Edgar. Good on you for your chat with the detective, Penelope."

"They're faxing me a copy of their whole file. Maybe we finally have a connection, knock on wood." Penelope rapped her knuckles against the top of the desk.

"Once you get it, let me know so we can all review it together."

Penelope hopped off the desk, getting ready to leave the office, "Oh, sorry I didn't ask sooner, but how was your trip to Europe?"

"Better than expected. I got another river boat company to sign up with us."

"Did you sign Spectrum, then?" Edgar asked.

"Nope. But I haven't given up hope yet." She looked at Penelope, "My offer stands, Pens. I'm going to need more good people. Are you ready to retire yet and come to work for me?"

"We'll see. I just want to follow up on this lead."

"Okay." Emily picked up her fork and waved it in the air. "Okay you two, go on home. Let me eat my dinner. I have a few hours' worth of work to do."

Part Three

Mid-May 2012

The Invitation

Ostia, Italy

Fong set the box of new cards in the center of his desk and lifted the lid off. Fifty new, cream-colored cards, each embossed with his initials in the top center. He leaned back in his leather desk chair, thinking about the day he and Lee had designed them, understated, elegant, to celebrate going into business on his own. Before, he'd always used plain cards with a slightly raised border. But they'd decided that these would make the appropriate statement, and since then, he'd never used any others. He tipped the stack into his hand and laid one in front of him on the desk before pulling open the right-hand drawer and placing the remaining ones in the empty compartment where he always kept them. He tapped the corners gently to align the cards and then repeated the process with the matching envelopes, opening the box, tipping them into his hand, setting one aside on his desk and placing the others in their individual compartments.

Slender, gold fountain pen in hand, he ran his thumb along its worn ridges as he paused for a moment with his mind on his upcoming trip, and then he twisted off the cap. He began to write.

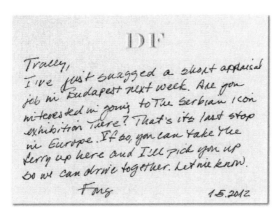

He opened his phone and copied Tracey's address onto the

envelope, slid the card inside and sealed it. Lee was in the kitchen, washing vegetables from her garden when he went to find her. "Would you like to go to lunch, my darling? I'm going to town to mail my card to Tracey, and I'd love your company."

A Trip To Budapest

Italy and Hungary

The sleek, dark green sports car, with its top stowed away, pulled up to the curb of the Civitavecchia Port ferry terminal with a screech of its tires. Fong tapped the horn to get Tracey's attention.

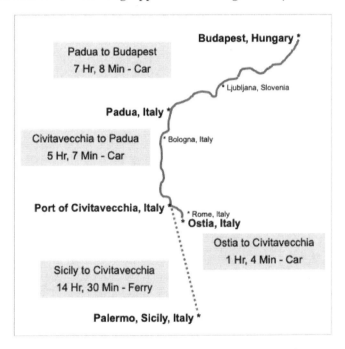

He jogged over, tossed his bag into the trunk and muttered to himself, "Small trunk. If we had this car, Charlotte and I could never travel together. She always brings too much – stuff. And there's no way my large tour bag with my golf clubs would fit in there with any luggage." As he slid into the passenger's seat, he remarked, "What a beauty. And in perfect condition. Do you refer to your car as classic, antique or vintage?"

Fong thought about it for a moment, "She's a '66 and barely

squeaks into being an antique. I'm proud of her. You said you have an old Mercedes, an antique, isn't she?"

"Technically yes, but I prefer to call her vintage. She's a '62, and vintage just suits her better. I had her repainted the original silver and replaced the leather seats. I always wonder if restoring her has diminished her value. But she's a stately old girl, and I'm fond of her."

Tracey looked over at Fong, who wore a driving hat pulled down over his forehead and dark tan driving gloves, thinking that if anyone could carry off that look, it was Fong. "Thanks for getting up so early to pick me up."

"Early morning sun with the top down, that's the best time to drive. The air is so fresh and crisp, and the trip only took an hour."

"A convertible is nice. Even when it's cold, you can roll the windows up and turn the heat on and still feel the wind in your hair."

"I knew you'd understand." Fong adjusted the heat as he pulled away from the curb. "Let me know if that's too much. It was chilly when I set out this morning, so early that Lee didn't even budge when I kissed her goodbye." He continued, remembering how soundly she'd been sleeping, "I left a note for her to find when she wakes up."

"She'll appreciate that."

"Yes, she always tucks notes somewhere in my luggage when I travel. I'm afraid I'm not usually quite so attentive."

"When Charlotte dropped me off in Palermo last night, she said she would miss me." Tracey grinned, "Hmmm, I'll need to check for a note in my luggage, though that's not her style. In fact, I'm sure she's glad to have me out of her hair. She's meeting with the interior designer. Even though we've only just finished with the architect, and the builder has barely started, she's months ahead. She wants to pick colors for the walls, window coverings, furniture, you know, all of it. She's very organized about this house of hers."

"I bet you're glad to be out of her hair, too." Fong tugged his cap down on his head, "How was the ferry trip? Was the sea calm?

Did you sleep well?"

"I had a splendid trip. The stateroom was small, but it was quite comfortable. They served a simple, Sicilian meal that was very tasty, and there was a nice single malt scotch that I took out onto the deck after dinner to do a bit of stargazing. It's so dark once you get out of port, it's ideal for looking at the stars."

Tracey pulled his sunglasses out of his pocket as Fong accelerated onto the autostrada and whipped around cars to find some open road. *And to think I imagined him as a staid and overly cautious driver.* Tracey smiled to himself.

Early that afternoon, as they arrived at the *pensione* on the outskirts of Padua's historic city center, Tracey said, "You have nice taste. This is charming."

"Life's too short to not indulge when you travel."

After checking in and unpacking, Tracey sat in the lobby, waiting for Fong. The old wooden floors creaked as guests passed back and forth through the small space, while a little old woman, hair tied up in a crisp, white kerchief, moved around, carefully polishing the dark wood trimming the windows and fireplace. *I bet this is original and probably a few hundred years old. At least.* He stepped aside for an elderly Italian man to walk by. *For Americans, this would be considered a very old building. I bet, for him, it's just middle-aged.*

"Are you okay with wandering around this afternoon and just seeing what we see?" Fong said from behind Tracey, causing him to jump. "We can walk into the old part of Padua and visit the Basilica di Sant'Antonio. It has some magnificent art and even a little surprise." Fong's eyes twinkled. "Eventually, I'm sure we can find somewhere outside to relax and have a drink."

"Sounds ideal." Tracey tapped his finger on his pocket. "It'll be a good time for an afternoon pipe."

They strolled along, taking in the sights, and then Tracey stopped in front of an imposing building and squinted up at the large turrets and domes among the rooftops. "What a beautiful church."

"This is the Basilica di Sant'Antonio. The inside is absolutely spectacular – and if you like body parts, you can see St. Anthony's relics."

They crossed the square, but before they reached the front entrance, Tracey slowed down and looked up again, admiring the architecture. A great equestrian statue by Donatello greeted them in front of three large bronze doors. Fong looked over at Tracey, and with a small nod of agreement, they entered grandly through the middle one. Their feet echoed on the inlaid checkerboard marble flooring as they turned into the Cappella delle Reliquie to join the line that was moving slowly in front of the relics.

"*Jawbone and tongue*," Tracey read from the description on the gold-framed display holding the undecayed tongue and vocal cords of St. Anthony and his lower jaw with five teeth still remaining. He pointed, "It's better than a claw-like hand."

He saw Fong's shoulders quiver as he struggled to suppress his laughter.

They continued to wander, admiring the impressive domes from the inside, more bronze statues by Donatello, the immense crucifix over the main altar and finally, the elaborate frescos. Tracey paused for a long time in the St. James Chapel in front of the immense fresco by Altichiero di Zevio, depicting the crucifixion. He murmured to Fong, "So many people there, watching that act that changed the world." He stood in silence for another moment before moving on thoughtfully. *Each act performed by anyone has the potential to change another's life, and we so rarely know the impact.*

"One last stop before we leave," Fong said as he turned into the former chapel of Maria Mater Domin with its beautiful marble reliefs.

Tracey watched him take a small piece of paper out of his pocket and tuck it under the flowers others had laid on top of the tomb. Fong stood silently with his eyes closed and his hands loosely clasped in front of him. After a few moments, he turned toward Tracey and motioned to the front door, "Shall we?"

Outside, Tracey looked at him and raised his eyebrows, "For some reason, I thought you were a Buddhist."

"Lee was raised a Roman Catholic, but we do try to practice some aspects of Buddhism, doing the right thing, keeping our lives simple, meditation, yoga. She's far better at it than I am. Anyway, we've been trying to have children since we first got married, but – it's never happened." A look of intense sadness crossed his face as he spoke about their efforts.

"That must be a strain on your marriage."

Fong nodded his head, "There have been doctors and more doctors. Tests and more tests. No one can figure out why we can't—" He shrugged one shoulder helplessly.

"So, you offer a supplication to St. Anthony?"

"Every time I come here, Lee sends me with a plea for the thing she wants most of all."

Unable to find any words that could offer comfort, Tracey reached out to rest his hand on Fong's shoulder for a second.

Fong drew a quick breath, "How about that drink?"

Seated on a patio facing the narrow street, Tracey stretched out his legs and drew on his pipe, blowing smoke off into the soft spring air. Their drinks on the table in front of them, he and Fong talked about the astoundingly beautiful frescoes they had just seen in the basilica. "But how," Tracey wondered aloud, "can a fresco, which has to be painted in fewer than a dozen hours before the plaster dries, have the same spiritual meaning to the artist as an icon, in which each stroke of the brush is executed so mindfully as a prayer. The intellectual part of me finds icons beautiful but also flat and expressionless. Nevertheless, they touch something in my soul when I consider the process as I look at them."

In turn, Fong shared how, early in his art career, he had found himself drawn to paintings containing not two or three, but multiple people. He'd tried to feel the psychology of the painting and the artist's mindset by the way people were looking at one another, the way their relationships were revealed by their posture and how they were portrayed against the background. He sat back and pointed out a group of people standing on the corner and described to Tracey what he saw in that scene – how they were listening, or not, by the tilt of their heads, their stance, the position of their arms and hands, if they were friendly or polite or even antagonistic toward one another.

"You know, as a lawyer and then as a judge," said Tracey, "I watched people in the courtroom. I could always tell a lot about what was going on without anyone saying a word. But I certainly hadn't given thought to it. It was just something that I knew, something that happened. Fascinating."

Fong took out a cigarette and contemplated it for a moment.

"What happened to having only one of those after dinner?" Tracey drew on his pipe.

"One of my weaknesses, I suppose. I know they aren't good for me, but I don't want to give them up. I like them. That's why I normally limit myself to just one – after dinner. But today—"

"Perhaps I'm a bad influence."

Fong shrugged lightly, "Just keeping you company, I suppose," he said with a smile and lit the end of the slender cigarette he still held in his fingers. After the first drag, he looked at it thoughtfully, "You know, I've been thinking about the story you were telling on the boat."

"Oh, our friend, Henri." Tracey raised an eyebrow, "Go on."

"First of all, his accomplice needs a name. What do you think of Melanie?"

"Hmmm, that works. She'll need a last name at some point."

"True. I'm sure we'll think of one when it's necessary. Meanwhile, I've given some thought as to how they move the artwork around." Fong reached into the breast pocket of his light summer jacket, took out his fountain pen and began a crude sketch.

Tracey pulled his own, well-loved fountain pen from his pocket and laid it on the table between him and Fong.

Fong looked up, his concentration broken, and threw back his head in laughter. He set his pen down next to Tracey's. "Yours looks like it's been around for a while. How long have you had it?"

"My dad gave it to me for my sixteenth birthday," said Tracey. "He believed there was an art to writing with a fountain pen. I also think it lends authority to one's handwriting."

"Sixteen? Truly? My grandfather gave me this," he held up his pen, "for *my* sixteenth birthday," and in a surprising move, he reached over to bump fists with Tracey, "Brothers. Separated at birth, no doubt."

"Brothers," responded Tracey with a chuckle. "Now, back to

Henri and Melanie—"

§

The following day, in Budapest, while Fong was off appraising the young widow's collection, Tracey spent several hours wandering through the Serbian icon exhibition, pen in hand, making notes in the catalog he'd purchased at the entrance. He left the Műcsarnok, the large Palace of Arts exhibition hall on Heroes Square, and stood at the bottom of the steps with his map in hand, contemplating what he would do next.

Charlotte had recommended that he spend the better part of his day exploring the area. Tracey focused on his map and list from her as he gazed across the impressive square in front of him. A girl zipped past on a skateboard. She passed so close that he could feel the breeze from her movements and was startled by her sudden appearance. He stepped back and hit his heel abruptly against the bottom step. The girl, her long, red hair flying out behind her, swooped on down the sidewalk, weaving in and out among the tourists, causing them to stop and glare angrily. With a rude gesture, she whizzed on and next came very close to knocking down a little old lady who shook her cane at her, yelling angrily, "*Vigyázz!*"

Tracey shook his head in astonishment. "Kids all over the world, they're all alike," he chuckled. "And old ladies too."

His stomach growled, reminding him that it was lunchtime. Jotted in his small moleskin notebook was the name of the restaurant that Charlotte had suggested because it was close to the exhibition hall. With a quick glance at the map and then around the square to orient himself, Tracey crossed to the Városligeti-to and paused to watch a family of ducks swimming in the murky green water. The early afternoon weather was far too nice to hurry, so he meandered along the path, past young families picnicking on the banks. Soon, he arrived at Robinson's restaurant, built on a little man-made island at the edge of the lake. *Clever name – I wonder who thought of that.*

Tracey finished the lunch of local fish, salad and beer that

Charlotte had recommended and wandered through the park and the surrounding area for the remainder of the afternoon. At last, tired of playing tourist, he sat at an outdoor bar, sipping a before-dinner drink, and began to write an email to Charlotte.

"Charlotte, my love,

Imagine if you had been with me today at Robinson's. It would have, no doubt, been more leisurely and culinarily, far more adventurous. The jazz was delightful, and I wanted to linger there – with you. Come along with me as I share snippets of my afternoon.

As you suggested, I went in search of your cousins' house on Stefánia út. What a lovely, stately building it is. I can picture a young you and your small cousins playing in the snow in the front yard, pelting passers-by with snowballs and then ducking behind the stone wall; celebrating the holidays there, peeking down through the stair railings at the guests all dressed in their finest party clothes, and as you grew older, descending that central staircase you described to me, ready to go to dinner with a group of friends. It's too bad your family sold that wonderful place and moved to the Balaton.

If we lived in that house now, we would have held hands as we wandered along the road through the park on our way home from dinner, and if it had been a delightful spring evening, like it is tonight, we would, no doubt, have paused outside a club that (according to my guidebook) plays Latin music. We would have smiled into each other's eyes, leaned in for a long, passionate kiss and then debated whether to stop for a while to dance before continuing on our way. After arriving home, we might have sat outside in our garden, sharing a bottle of wine, and listened to the music coming from that beautiful palace across the street.

But sadly, Charlotte, you aren't here. So, I snapped a few pictures for you and made my way back to Heroes' Square. Still following your instructions, I hopped onto that iconic yellow subway line. I was fortunate, I think, to have boarded one of the old cars with its wooden bench seats. It was a rattling, noisy ride down to Erzsébet tér. I pictured myself living there soon after it had been built, riding beneath Budapest's equivalent of the Champs-Élysées with grand houses, the Opera and fine shops along the avenue above me.

As I walked to the bank of the Danube, I was tempted to stray off to the Gerbeaud coffee house for a quick drink, but I decided to wait until we can live that part of your memories together. The porcelain and crystal in the shop windows that I passed were stunningly beautiful but so ill-suited for our house in Sicily. Fortunately, I suppose since it was certainly priced for tourists.

I rode the funicular up the hillside to the Castle District and was able to get some lovely photos of the late afternoon sunshine on the domes of the Parliament and St. Stephen's Basilica. They are, I admit, pretty good pictures for ones taken on a phone, though I'm sure Remy would put them to shame if she were here with her camera.

I had dawdled so long over lunch and my explorations on the Pest side of the city that I decided to forgo a visit to the National Art Gallery and just wandered around.

It is getting cool out here, so I'll send this on its way and save more tales for another evening.

Good night, my love. Sweet dreams.

Your Tracey"

He leaned back in his chair, wiggling his thumbs that were stiff from typing on his phone. He thought about the figurine he had bought on a whim while exploring the Castle District. He'd gone into an antique store and seen a shelf of small, old statues of children playing. After agreeing upon a good price with the owner, he came away with one of a little girl, her hair tied up in a red scarf, playing with a ball. She'd reminded him of his twin sister, Sarah, playing with the yellow ball their mother had bought for them when they were very little. They'd rolled it back and forth across their room while their mother entertained her "guests" in her room. The ball would always get stuck under the bed, and Sarah would ask him to get it because she was afraid to go underneath in the dark. His eyes moistened, wondering what had happened to her after she'd been adopted. He'd tried so hard to find her – Tracey looked at his watch and decided it was still too early for dinner, and he raised his hand to catch the waiter's attention to order another drink.

§

He overslept the next morning. So, instead of rushing to catch the end of the hotel's generous breakfast, he decided to get something light and then find somewhere to get out into nature, stretch his legs a bit and breathe some fresh air, to be less of a tourist. At a nearby café, he had a small pastry and a coffee while he read the newspaper and then returned to his hotel to ask the concierge to call him a taxi.

He made his queries at the concierge desk, staffed that morning by an elderly man who spoke with a scarcely noticeable accent. Looking at Tracey's jeans, casual button-down shirt with the sleeves rolled up and sturdy walking shoes, the old man said, "You are dressed perfectly for that. I cannot tell you how many people come down in the wrong clothing. I will send them back to their room to change. But many of them refuse." The man pulled out a map. "We are located here," he circled the location. "This is where you are going," and he put an X on Normafa. He traced the route with his pen, "It will take you an hour and a half to walk there if you feel ambitious." He looked up at Tracey, "Or you can take the tram or a bus. But if you want to spend more time there, I will call you a taxi." With his plan in place, Tracey headed out for what he felt would be a relaxing day.

After he'd hiked through the park for a couple of hours, admiring the view, he realized how hungry he was after that light breakfast. He recalled that there had been a rustic restaurant near the area where the taxi had dropped him off, and he walked back in search of it. It turned out to be a small, wooden building, with a window for takeout on one side. He perused the selections for a moment and ordered a sandwich and a beer, carrying them to the only remaining empty picnic table not far from the window. He would have preferred to have found a table farther away from the restaurant, but at least he was in the shade and surrounded by the forest.

Tracey sat with his feet tucked back under the long wooden picnic table bench, took a bite of his sandwich, savoring the unfamiliar flavors of Pick salami and local cheese. He washed it down with a long swallow of cool beer and then took another bite and chewed thoughtfully. His legs ached pleasantly from his hike along the hilly trails in the park. He was approaching his mid-forties and realized he wasn't in the best shape, but certainly not the worst either. He'd have to create an exercise regimen – perhaps lengthy hikes several days a week on the slopes of Mount Etna – if he was actually going to attempt to hike the entire length of the Appalachian Trail. Since long before he'd retired, he had imagined what it would be like out in the wilderness, relying only on himself for the two-thousand-mile trek. With a smile, he wondered how Charlotte would feel about him being gone for somewhere between five and seven months. *Perhaps she might join me for a segment here and there. It would be fun to have her companionship on the hike.*

Then, abruptly, the redhead from Heroes' Square zipped up to the restaurant and flipped her skateboard, with its bold design, into her hand. She was wearing the same jacket she'd had on the previous day and pulled it off, holding it in her other hand. She looked around at the full tables and then walked over to Tracey's table, leaned her board against the end of the opposite bench, dropped her jacket over it and turned toward the window to order her food.

He shrugged, "Oh, by all means, be my guest," not happy that his peaceful lunch was about to be interrupted by, of all people, this brash young woman.

She set down her food at the other end of the table and swung first one leg and then the other over the bench before pulling her long red hair back from her face into a ponytail with a scrunchie from her wrist. Tracey watched her, fascinated by her multiple piercings. Chewing a bite of her sandwich, she looked up and caught him staring at her, "What, man? Don't you know it's rude to stare?"

He motioned from the top to the bottom of his ear, "God, that must have hurt."

She looked at him with a grin, and he noticed the piercing in her lip, the one in her nose and another in her eyebrow. She pointed to her left ear, "These weren't too bad, but," pointing to the one above her eyebrow, "this one hurt like hell." Then she turned her head and pointed to her right ear, "But I only have one earring on this side. It's different."

He shook his head with a slight shudder and went back to his sandwich and beer.

The young woman crumpled up the paper from her

sandwich, shoved it into her beer cup, stood and said to Tracey, "You should get a piercing, man. It would be cool." She gave him a quick nod, pushed a stray strand of hair off her forehead and left.

With a fingertip, he stroked the curve of his left ear, murmuring to himself, "A piercing? Me? I wonder what Charlotte would think."

Suddenly, he stood up and dumped the remainder of his meal into the trash and followed her as she headed into the wooded area. He came up close behind her, watching her as she stopped, crouching down to tie her shoe.

She looked up at him, "Excuse me, mister. Give me some space here."

He glanced around, seeing no one, and decided. As she stood up, he stepped even closer and forced her against a tree, clasping his right hand over her mouth and the other around her neck. Her hands were trapped between her body and the tree trunk as Tracey pushed against her, squeezing tighter and tighter with his hand. As she moaned, as her athletic body writhed against him, his heart pounded, and he began to breathe heavily. Groaning, he pressed harder against her.

She struggled, finally freeing one hand, reaching up, grabbing Tracey's right arm, scratching it with a ragged fingernail, trying to pull his hand from her mouth so she could scream for help. When he felt the stinging on his arm, he intensified his grip on her neck. Her arm flailed as she tried to reach back and hit him on the head.

And then – she went limp.

He held her, pinned against the tree, pushing his body against her one final time before he pulled away and laid her gently on the ground. With his left hand, he stroked her hair away from her forehead as though he were her lover and gently removed the hoop from her right ear.

Still gasping, Tracey stood up, putting the earring in his pocket. He leaned against the tree, taking calming breaths in through his nose and out through his mouth, trying to control his arousal. His arm still stung, and he looked down at the beads of blood in a stripe parallel to the two red lines of the birthmark that marred his lower arm. With his left hand, he pulled out a handkerchief from his trouser pocket and pressed it firmly against the scratch as he walked back toward the restaurant to catch a tram to the other side of the river.

Back in his room, his head was pounding. *I'm glad tonight Fong has more business. This gives me a quiet evening to myself.* A bottle of water in one hand, he went into the bathroom where the small container of tablets lay amidst his toiletries. He shook the prescribed two pills into his hand and swallowed them with a long gulp, leaned against the counter, staring off at nothing and slowly pressed his fingers against his temples.

Carefully placing the earring on the bathroom counter, he removed his clothes as the events of the afternoon looped slowly through his thoughts.

His hands moved deliberately, working the soap over his body, the bright gold of her earring catching in the corner of his eye as the glass walls of the shower enclosure steamed up. With one shoulder braced against the shower wall, the earring gradually blurring in the steam, he began to move his hands quickly, his breath coming faster and faster until, at last, he gave a long groan of release.

Wrapped in the thick hotel robe, he looked at himself in the bathroom mirror and rubbed his beard. "It's time for you to go, my friend. Just in case someone saw us." He opened his bag, carefully trimmed his beard very close and shaved the remainder off. After splashing water onto his face and drying it carefully, he wiped a few stray whiskers from the counter and from his razor with the damp towel. He polished the blades to his scissors, slipped them into their tan leather cover and laid them in the bag as well. He reached back amongst his grooming paraphernalia for the small jar of liquid bandage, and his breath hissed as he stroked the clear liquid over the scratch on his arm. He blew on it gently to ease the burning.

Tracey decided to stop for a pre-dinner drink in a bar along the Danube embankment. It was cooler than the night before, but with his jacket, it was still comfortable sitting outside. People strolled past between the bar tables and the riverbank. Reflections of the Chain Bridge's lights and those from the palace on the hill wavered in the quickly moving current. He leaned back, stretched out his legs and relaxed, puffing away on his pipe.

Tracey stretched his arms over his head and felt the tenderness on his arm where the girl had scratched it. *That's the first time I've left DNA that could be linked to me. I wonder if it will become a problem. But the chances of them connecting it to me are virtually non-existent. A single murder in a city with no other similar murders, where I'm merely a visitor?*

He thought about the woman he'd killed in St. Petersburg. *She was a prostitute. She had to have DNA from lots of men on her. So, I'm sure they didn't even bother to investigate.*

Is giving into my urge to kill worth the risk of getting caught? But, my God, I really like the way killing makes me feel.

He slid his hand into his pocket and removed the skateboarder's earring and toyed with it, putting it on the tip of his little finger and twisting it around and around, watching the light gleam against it. And all the while, the killing played on in an unending loop.

§

The following morning, Fong set down his coffee cup and wiped his lips as he focused on his crossword puzzle.

Tracey approached the table, and the waiter pulled out a chair for him. After he'd sat down, the waiter shook open a napkin onto his lap. "How did the appraisals go?" Tracey asked. "Were your clients easy to work with?"

With a shocked glance at Tracey's clean-shaven face, Fong replied, "All normal stuff on this trip, thank goodness." He cocked his head and ran his hand along his jawline, "But you – you obviously didn't have enough to keep you busy over the past couple of days. What made you decide the beard had to go?"

Tracey reached up to touch his bare chin, "It was too itchy. Charlotte loves the beard, but I have to live with it, and I decided I couldn't any longer."

Fong reached up and touched his left ear, "And the earring?"

Tracey reached up and touched the tiny, black, carbon fiber stud. "It seemed like a fun thing to do, and it will amuse Charlotte."

Fong shook his head, "You look so different. I wouldn't have recognized you."

For Just One Euro

Sicily, Italy

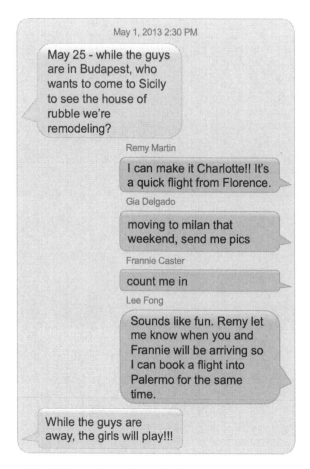

May 1, 2013 2:30 PM

May 25 - while the guys are in Budapest, who wants to come to Sicily to see the house of rubble we're remodeling?

Remy Martin

I can make it Charlotte!! It's a quick flight from Florence.

Gia Delgado

moving to milan that weekend, send me pics

Frannie Caster

count me in

Lee Fong

Sounds like fun. Remy let me know when you and Frannie will be arriving so I can book a flight into Palermo for the same time.

While the guys are away, the girls will play!!!

Remy grabbed her suitcase from the luggage carousel. "How is it that yours came off the plane first and mine was at the very end?" she asked Frannie.

"Because I am lucky? I don't know. My bags always come out quickly."

The cousins wheeled their suitcases out the door from baggage claim to the curb. Sure enough, just as she'd promised, there stood Charlotte next to her dusty, turquoise Mini, her arms waving excitedly. Lee stood beside her, a broad smile on her face.

"Small car, three suitcases, and four women. This could be interesting," said Remy as they reached the car.

"And picnic paraphernalia," Charlotte grinned. "Obviously you've never owned a Mini. The space inside just keeps going."

"I see," Remy commented, as she and Lee squeezed in behind Charlotte and Frannie. "And how far is the drive to your house?"

"Oh, just up there in the hills," said Charlotte with a nonchalant wave of her hand.

Lee giggled, "Yeah, just up there. Up is the operative word here." She leaned toward Charlotte, "You know, your house isn't far from the village where my mom lives."

Crowded in the back seat, Remy and Lee's shoulders bumped together as Charlotte drove her Mini at a breakneck pace up the rough driveway with clouds of dust billowing out behind them. Lee leaned forward between Charlotte and Frannie and said loudly, "You and Fong are the fastest drivers I know. You must be kindred spirits."

Charlotte laughed, "Is there any other way to drive?" They reached the level area at the top of the driveway and passed a dilapidated old stone building; it was difficult to tell what it had been in its prior incarnation. She slammed on the brakes, and the car skidded to an abrupt stop, flinging all four women forward against their seat belts.

Frannie and Charlotte unfolded themselves from the front seats, reached for the levers and pulled the seats forward. Frannie grabbed Lee's hands and tugged her out of the back. When she popped out, she accidentally fell against Frannie, who caught her. After steadying her, Frannie finally turned around, "Where's the house?"

"This is what you get for a euro. An old outbuilding and a house that has tumbled down into piles of stones," Charlotte laughed. "But it has potential. A lot of work, but a lot of potential. Let me show you around, and you'll see what I'm thinking." She went to the back of the car and pulled out a rolled-up set of plans.

Lee rubbed her hands together in excitement, "Yes, let's check this out."

Charlotte reached into the console between the front seats and held up a heavy old key. "This is the key Tracey sent me for Valentine's Day."

"But you don't need a key to open the door. You can just walk in through a gap in the wall," Frannie said, walking through the wide space to the left of the door, "like this."

With great ceremony, Charlotte unlocked the tall wooden door and pushed it inward. "It was so romantic. After the cruise, Tracey brought me up here. He made me keep my eyes closed as we drove up the last bumpy bits and while we walked up to the house. He finally let me open them and look around for a moment, and then he told me to unlock the door. He pushed it open, turned around and swept me up into his arms and carried me over this threshold. And then he gave me a long steamy kiss." She fanned her hand in front of her face, "What more does a woman need? A hot, sexy man who gives you a house and incredible kisses—"

Then, remembering her friends, she stepped aside and held her hand toward the open door, "Welcome to my home."

Entering first, Remy slowed down and ran her fingers over the carvings on the door, "I hope you're keeping this door, it's wonderful."

As she followed Remy inside, Charlotte assured her, "Oh yes, we're keeping it. That, the fireplaces and as many stones as we can reuse will be almost the only part of this old house that will remain by the time we're through." With a grand gesture to the left, she said, "The room will be divided into two parts. Over here is the living room where that massive fireplace will be rebuilt." Then she showed them how the other half would be laid out, the kitchen against the opposite end where remnants of another huge fireplace were centered on the wall. It would be an open space with cabinets that would wrap around each corner, run along the wall and butt up against either side of the fireplace. A long farm table, rough enough to act as additional workspace, would separate it from the living room. "We want everybody to be together when we entertain. We don't want someone stuck in the kitchen or isolated in the living room, and we want a dining area that is big enough for everyone."

Remy sighed happily, "A second fireplace – in your kitchen? I am so envious."

"But this is our favorite part of the house." Charlotte led them over to a hole in the floor near the foundation with stone steps leading down into a cellar. "Eventually, we'll put a wine cave down there. A real wine cave. I've always wanted one."

Then she pointed toward the partial staircase that went nowhere, tucked against the front wall. "Those will eventually lead up to two guest bedrooms with good-sized, built-in closets. None of this wardrobe stuff for my dream house. And, of course, each bedroom will have its own bathroom."

She walked through the living room, tapping the roll of plans against her leg, "There'll be an addition for the master suite beyond the living room. It'll be almost as large as this original house. We'll add a fireplace on the other side of this one." Charlotte pointed at the living room fireplace. "The two will share a chimney, but you won't be able to see through. Oh, no, no, no, that wouldn't do," she snickered. "There will be a spa-like bathroom over there with two walk-in closets. The front end of the addition will be a bright, good-sized room with a desk, a comfortable daybed and a good chair for reading."

Lee hesitated a moment, "Will you share a bedroom? Or is the room with the desk to be Tracey's?"

"Oh, we'll have separate beds," said Charlotte, widening her eyes in mock innocence, "just like in the old TV shows."

It was Frannie's turn to snicker.

"No, actually," Charlotte went on, "I've already found an antique bed for my non-existent bedroom in my non-existent house," she laughed. "It's kind of rustic-looking and enormous, perfect for lazy Sunday mornings – and good romps with my man."

Lee laughed with her, "I see. You're building the house to fit the bed then?"

"I guess I am. And it will fit in with the decor I've decided on. Simple, traditional, not a lot of ornate carvings or tchotchkes. Pillows, cushions and throws, comfortable seating, lots of candles," she paused, "and fresh flowers all the time, all over the place."

Confused, Remy turned to Lee, "Separate bedrooms?"

"Daniel and I each have our own bedroom. That's how we keep our marriage fresh and exciting." She thought about the many times she'd sent him to sleep in the other bedroom, those times when he had misbehaved.

"Hmmm, I never thought about that," said Charlotte. "So, that's all I have to show you at this point. I know it's just a bunch of crumbling stone walls and chimneys, a hole in the ground and a partial roof, but someday, it's going to be beautiful."

Lee added, "And I can imagine the garden out back." She swung around to gaze toward the overgrown area at the back of the house.

"Sure," replied Charlotte with a little less certainty in her voice. "I'm completely lost as far as the garden goes, and our architect hasn't designed anything for the outside. We'll have to hire a landscape guy for that."

"If you don't mind, I could come up with some ideas for

you."

"Lee, that would be great, thank you," said Charlotte. "You grew up around here and know what will grow best."

"May I tag along with you?" Remy asked. "I want to see how you create magic like in the pictures you showed me of your gardens in Ostia."

Suddenly, they'd all scattered. Remy and Lee hopped over the remains of the back wall and began to explore the outdoor space. Frannie found a comfortable spot in the sun, perched on top of a wall facing the house, and opened the small portfolio slung over her shoulder. She contemplated her pencils for a moment and selecting one, she glanced up at the crumbling stones and began to sketch.

"I just got these drawings from our architect," Charlotte held up the roll of plans and then, looking around, she realized she was alone in the space and chuckled, "so I'm going to take another look at them," she said to herself. She wandered around the house, talking out loud, referring to the drawings and imagining what it would look like when it was finally completed.

Remy and Lee leaned against one of the partial exterior walls, debating what size to make the kitchen garden, what vegetables should be included and what herbs to plant. Glancing up at the sun from time to time, they talked about full-sun and partial-sun exposures.

Lee looked around. "Charlotte – where will the kitchen door be?" she shouted.

Charlotte picked up a couple of stones and placed them along the back wall, "About here. What difference does it make?"

"Herbs," Lee said. "The herbs have to be right outside the kitchen door. If you need something, you don't want to run across the garden to get it."

Charlotte chortled, "Especially if you are cooking in the buff?" She returned to her drawings without waiting for a response.

"Cooking in the buff?" Remy began to laugh, and soon she and Lee were doubled over with tears running down their faces. When she'd finally caught her breath, Remy asked, "So, where should the flower garden be?"

After a final hiccup of laughter, Lee took a deep breath and looked around. "I think it should be off the living room," she said, pointing toward the other end of the house. "From the entrance, you'll have a magnificent view to the sea. And behind the house, you'll see herbs and vegetables from the kitchen windows and riotous flowers from the living room and master bedroom. And behind all of that, this hillside that goes up and up will serve as a spectacular background. I think I'll suggest a flagstone patio separating the two sets of plants, with little paved pathways trailing off through the gardens." Lee continued, "My mom lives about an hour's drive from here." She went on to describe the flowers her mother had grown over the years. "Now, she has mostly native ones that do well here and a few hardy plants that she brought in to try that have actually managed to survive in Sicily's hot summers. Of course, there were the ones that didn't make it. It's been a lot of trial and error, but her goal was to have something always in bloom."

"I bet it looks beautiful."

"Charlotte, please come here for a second," called out Lee. "Do you want a formal garden or a natural garden?"

"I'm more of a natural-garden type of gal," she smiled as she joined them.

"What about edible flowers?" Remy asked. She turned to Lee, "Would those go in the herb garden?"

"Of course," Lee answered.

"Edible flowers? Sure. Sounds like fun. I imagine Tracey will find something to do with them." Charlotte grinned, "He's constantly telling me I need a cooking class. He teases me and says I cook like a stereotypical Brit – overcooking everything."

"Tracey cooks?" Remy asked. "I'm liking this man of yours more and more."

"He's become quite accomplished during the time I've known him. Someday—" she gestured at the kitchen area, "he'll be able to do it here. But now, it's time to take a selfie out in front of the house and then lunch." She led the way back through the house and out the front door.

"Give me a couple of minutes to get my tripod set up, and we can do a proper picture as well." Remy reached into her backpack and pulled it out. As she began to set it up, she said to Lee, "Would you please get Frannie? She won't have heard Charlotte. And she's so lost in her drawing that I'm sure she hasn't noticed anything is going on over here." She paused her work with the tripod to snap a quick picture of Frannie, perched cross-legged on top of the wall, her head bent in concentration over her sketchbook.

"Or you could just take a picture with your phone like Charlotte does," said Lee over her shoulder as she went off to fetch Frannie.

"This is a photograph, not a selfie or a spontaneous snapshot. This is for posterity. And I want to make a large copy of the photo for my watercolor class. But most importantly, I need a number of very clear pictures to get the feel of the light here."

While they waited for the delayed shutter to click, Charlotte and Remy stood in the back, smiling at Frannie and Lee horsing around in the front, striking silly poses with their arms around each other's shoulders.

After the photos had all been taken, Lee spun Frannie around and said, "I'm so glad you were able to join us on this trip." She felt like she and Frannie were kindred spirits, and she wanted to spend more time getting to know her.

"Me too," smiled Frannie, giving Lee a quick hug.

While Remy took a few more pictures of the landscape, trying to catch colors and shadows and light, Charlotte handed bags and baskets and blankets from the back of the car to the others.

"Charlotte, what is in this tote, some of those rocks from your house?" asked Frannie as she puffed her way up the hillside.

"Just a few bottles of wine and some ice packs. Don't worry, it'll be lighter coming down."

They finally paused at a flat area under a tree higher up on the hillside with a view of the top of Mount Etna to one side and the sea to the other. Lee dropped the blankets she'd been carrying and stood, looking around, breathing deeply. She turned her head toward Frannie, "The perfect place to meditate."

"You meditate? So do I," Frannie replied happily. "Outdoors is the best place to practice it." She turned toward Charlotte, "Where do you want this killer bag of wine?"

Charlotte laid out a blanket and set down the picnic basket. "That was heavy. Put it right here beside mine." While Charlotte stood, flexing and stretching her hands, Frannie set down the insulated tote, plunked herself down beside it and peeked into the picnic basket. "Wow, there's lots of good stuff in here!" Remy shook her head at Frannie's unabashed curiosity.

Frannie reached into the insulated tote bag and pulled out a bottle. "Charlotte, do you want me to pour?"

Charlotte grinned, "Sure." She dropped down next to Frannie. "Somewhere in the basket you'll find four glasses and a corkscrew," she said as the other women joined them on the blankets.

Frannie pulled a bottle of cold, crisp Grillo from the tote and held it up. "Oh, yes!" she said, eyeing the wine in anticipation. "Good call, using those stinkin' heavy ice packs." She expertly pulled the cork and divided the wine among four large glasses.

"Frannie has been like this her whole life. She's curious about what's inside everything, how it works, and she's not afraid to figure it out." Remy glanced over at her cousin. "I've lived with her family since she was a toddler. We've always been close, but we got even closer after she got sick and lost her hearing. She was always poking around in my room." Frannie looked up at Remy, and Remy signed, "I'm telling them about how curious you've always been."

Frannie waved her hand at Remy, "I call it having an enquiring mind. When I was little, I idolized Remy and wanted to be just like her. I loved looking at her stuff. I would go through her drawers and closets and try on her clothes, put on her makeup, and I followed her everywhere. I wanted to figure out how to be just like her."

Lee said, "It's so much better to be yourself." She reached over to take Frannie's hand.

Charlotte laid out plates and napkins and began taking items for lunch out of her picnic basket and laying them on a platter she had produced from somewhere. Remy arranged them skillfully as Charlotte told her what each thing was. "We like this local bread. The crust is crisp, but the inside is wonderfully chewy. There, that's a local sheep's cheese with green olives. It's called *Belicino*. I can't get enough of it. These odd-looking fruits," she said, holding one up, "are *Ficodindia dell'Etna*. They are prickly pears, and they taste like a cross between watermelon and lemon. They'll be a nice combination with the cheese. And, finally, this jar has Leonforte peaches in it. They don't ripen until much later in the summer, but I thought you should try them. There's this little old woman I bought them from – she puts them up in a very light syrup so you can taste how sweet they are."

Lee sat watching Charlotte in astonishment. "Wow, your pronunciation is excellent, almost like a native. And I'm so impressed with your knowledge of Sicilian food. You're quite brave to make a picnic of only local foods and wines."

Charlotte blushed, "I studied Italian for years and years, so I'm glad to hear you think I speak so well. And then, you know, Tracey is such a foodie. I have to confess, he helped me sort this out. Come on and dig in. I'm starving. I imagine you all must be too."

With just crumbs left on their plates and the wine low in their glasses, Remy yawned and complimented Charlotte on the picnic. "Just perfect for a May day on a hillside in Sicily with a group of good friends." She yawned again and closed her eyes, leaning back on her elbows. "Mmmmmm, a nap would be nice." Remy slid down onto her back and bent an arm over her forehead.

Lee picked up the sketchbook from beside Frannie, "May I see what you drew?"

"Sure." Frannie flipped the book to the page she'd been working on. "This is how I envision Charlotte's house when it's finished."

"This is fantastic, Frannie."

Charlotte looked at the drawing upside down, "That's exactly how I want it to look." She reached over to indicate that she wanted to look at it more closely, "May I?"

"Sure," Frannie grinned at the compliment as she handed the

book to Charlotte.

Charlotte studied it before taking out her phone and snapping a picture of the sketch.

Lee said, "You're so talented. Maybe when you come to visit Daniel and me in Ostia, we can find a way to do something together."

"Thanks," she blushed. "I would like that." She smiled at Lee and then said, "Charlotte, flip to the next page."

Charlotte turned the page and immediately began to laugh. "This is wonderful. Tracey, my superhero."

Remy opened her eyes and sat up, "Hey, I need to see that." She leaned over the page, "What's his superpower?"

"Best not to go there," Charlotte said with a cheeky grin.

They continued to chat, enjoying the shade of the tree and the spring breeze. Frannie opened a second bottle of wine. "Shall I cool off your drinks?"

"Cool them off?" Charlotte said sarcastically. "They're all empty. I think we need them filled up again before we go on." Once their glasses were full again, she continued, "So here's the first dilemma. How much do you share about your love life with your new friends?"

No one said a word.

"With this group, I think anything goes," Charlotte went on. "Don't you?"

Frannie watched Remy sign what Charlotte had just said and raised her eyebrows in a silent, "*Oh, really?*"

Finally, Remy looked at Charlotte, "Then you start."

"Are you satisfied with your sex lives?" Charlotte asked.

Slightly uncomfortable, everyone stayed silent, and Charlotte chuckled, "I always love it when my questions stun people into silence – into thinking. I'm not prying, I'm just curious."

Remy's fingers flew, translating for Frannie.

"Well, Remy can answer that," said Frannie, breaking the silence at last. "When she's not satisfied, she just moves on. She loves 'em and leaves 'em like men do to women all the time."

Remy winced at her cousin's comment, "Well – it's not as simple as that." *I don't like this at all, being put on the spot. For all of*

Frannie's curiosity about me, she's never respected where I draw the line in my life between what I don't mind being public and what I want to be kept private. Even though I told her a little bit about the background to the rules, she just doesn't get why I have them or how they protect me and my emotions. She recalled how loving her parents had been, but they'd been a close pair, her mother and father, and she'd always felt like she had been on the outside looking in at them. She'd kept her emotions close. Over time, it had become a habit, watching how people felt but not engaging with them on an emotional level. And then after the disastrous affair in college, she'd become even more emotionally remote.

"Relationships can be very complicated – if you let them," said Remy.

Relieved that she didn't have to talk about Daniel's and her sex life, something that she wasn't comfortable sharing, Lee looked around the group quickly and then said, "Oh, come on, tell us about it, Remy."

Frannie persisted, "She only sleeps with married men. She has rules, you know."

"Rules?" Charlotte asked.

Damn it, Frannie, can't you keep a secret? "Now that you've let that cat out of the bag," she took a gulp of wine, a deep breath, and then she gave a little shrug. "This isn't the kind of thing I would normally share, but here goes." She took another gulp of wine, "My first and most important rule is that I don't sleep with my friends' husbands." Remy gave a quick grin. "So, you two are safe."

Charlotte said, "Well, you couldn't get my husband. He notices other women, and I let him talk to me about them – and I notice other men and tell him about them."

"But you're newlyweds," said Lee. "Why would you talk about other people?"

"We're middle-aged and secure with ourselves. And I was divorced and don't want to do that again." Charlotte smirked, "So I spice things to keep him happy. Sometimes, I point out women and ask him to tell me a fantasy about them. Sometimes, it has nothing to do with sex. Sometimes, it does. He does the same with me."

Remy turned to Charlotte, "You're so fortunate. I find Tracey an absolutely fascinating man – so comfortable in his own skin that he can have those discussions with his wife. A guy who likes religious art, who cooks. A romantic who looked for exactly the place you wanted and bought it, who carried you over the doorstep—"

"Pshaw, thanks. It took me forty-six years to find him, and I love him so much it's scary. I don't know what I would do if something happened to us. And I'll share a little secret. He wasn't always so comfortable having those conversations. We had to work on it, along with a few other things." The corners of Charlotte's mouth turned upward mysteriously before she turned back to Remy, "But enough about me. What are your other rules?"

"I think we need another glass of wine before I dive into them." Remy picked up the bottle and tipped it, "Oh, no. I guess we have to open another bottle." She handed it to Frannie and then signed, "Sommelier, another, please."

Frannie zipped open the tote, pulled out a bottle and poured each one another generous glass.

After a deep swallow, Remy said, "There are six more rules." She ticked them off on her fingers.

"I'm serially monogamous, so I'm only involved with one man at a time.

"I only sleep with married men who have no intention of leaving their wives.

"I break it off if I feel as though either of us may become emotionally involved.

"I don't introduce the men to my friends – or my friends to them.

"The men never know where I live.

"We don't engage in any public displays of affection, no kissing, no hugging, no touching except to shake hands."

Remy finished reciting her list and held up her hands, "Okay, now it's your turn, Charlotte."

"Oh, no, no, no," Charlotte shook her head. "We need to hear the rest of this first. Why do you need these rules?"

Lee chimed in, trying not to sound judgmental, "Well, that's an interesting way to date – for a single woman."

"For me, it's normal. I've been doing it since college – over twenty years now, I guess."

Frannie said, "Hey, you never told me it was that long."

"It was because you were just a young child when it started. For me, it's just – simpler that way. I abide by my rules. My life stays uncomplicated." She paused before adding, "And satisfying."

"How do you meet these guys? In a bar?" asked Lee.

Remy's hands flashed, translating for Frannie as she spoke, "I never pick up a stranger. It isn't like that at all. I'm almost always introduced by someone I know, or it's someone I know professionally. It just happens. I never think, 'Oh I'm feeling a little horny, I guess I'll go find a guy.' No, it's not like that at all."

"No strings attached," said Lee. "Men do it all the time. But doesn't it get lonely?"

Remy looked around at the group of women, "I'm content. It works for me." Remy was relieved that none of them seemed at all shocked. Curious certainly, but not shocked.

"But you haven't told us why you do it," said Charlotte. "You can't leave us hanging."

This is the hard part. "My childhood friend and I both went to Berkeley at the same time. She came from Switzerland to study. We were roommates, but she betrayed me." Remy paused at the painful memory. "She tried to steal the man I was in love with. She blackmailed him, and he gave in and dumped me. And I don't want to talk about it anymore."

Lee reached out and took her hand.

Surprised that it still hurt so much after all those years, she decided it was time to change the direction of the discussion. "Charlotte, here's one for you. How do you address conflict in your relationship?"

Charlotte smiled, "I have strong feelings about things, and I like to express them. So, sometimes they turn into, uhmmm, arguments. Not fights. Just a sort of spirited discussion. On the other hand, Tracey stays very calm and measured and presents all the pros and cons. It always irritates me that he's so calm. The important thing is that we keep at it until we reach some consensus. I don't always give in. Neither does he." She looked around at them with a wicked gleam in her eyes, "And of course, the sex afterward is always wonderful."

Lee finished the last of her wine and stared into her empty glass. She took a deep breath and shared that she and Fong had very few things they disagreed on. "I want to be centered. I've studied Buddhism because I find the principles grounding. I don't want to follow all of it, but I've distilled it and taken the things that are important like kindness, compassion, generosity, contentment, dependability. However, when you get to avoiding excesses – every now and then, I think a little excess is okay. Speaking of excess," she lifted her glass and turned toward Frannie, "do we have another bottle?"

Frannie smiled, "Another? We have three more. Charlotte's spoiling us."

"Or spoiling our livers," Remy said wryly.

While Frannie poured more wine into their glasses, Lee continued, "When I started studying Buddhism, I also started meditating. It helps me let go of my stress and keeps me centered. Fong doesn't follow these principles as closely as I do, but we've found some common ground to base our lifestyle on. We don't have any marital strife – I'm a peacemaker – but at the same time, we have a passionate love life. It's great because we are so much alike – two peas in a pod."

Charlotte frowned, "How do you have passion without strife? How can you agree on everything? Isn't that boring?" She reached over and touched Lee's arm. "That wasn't meant to be a judgment, I just can't imagine it."

"We have stimulating discussions about many things, so our relationship isn't boring. In my marriage, I want things to be peaceful. I lived with my parents' stressful, drama-filled relationship, and I swore my marriage would never be like that."

Lee suddenly realized how much she had shared about her life after four large glasses of wine.

Remy watched, noticing Lee's discomfort. "It must be soothing to have no conflict, Lee." Remy thought about her own relationships, "Or you can just stay emotionally detached like I do, and then there's no conflict either."

"If you can call them relationships," Frannie observed.

Charlotte asked, "You're able to keep up a barrier and not get hurt?"

"Yes. I have good sex and good company. And I can walk away at any point."

Frannie listened, "Why do marriages and relationships have to be so complicated? I wonder how my parents do it? They're very comfortable together."

"Comfortable? Do you think they have good sex?"

"Remy, do you think anyone wants to think about their parents having sex?" Frannie asked, thinking about precisely that. About the times she'd come into the room and caught her parents in a passionate embrace. About the way one would spontaneously get up from a chair and walk over and kiss the other. And about the way they would wander into the house at the end of an evening out, hand in hand, and go directly to the bedroom with only the most distracted of good nights to her. *But no one wants to actually think about their parents' sex life.*

"That's how we all got here." The women all laughed, and then Charlotte asked her next question, "So, have either of you cheated on someone?" She pointed to Lee and Frannie.

Frannie replied quickly, "I haven't been in a significant enough relationship to cheat on anyone."

Lee flushed a deep red, "This is where I need another glass of wine!" She put her hands up to her cheeks for a second. "Well, a long time ago, in a weird way, I did cheat." She told them about when she'd been in college, before meeting Fong, how she and her friends used to dare one another to do outrageous things. How the dares had escalated over time. Her last dare had been to forge a painting and try to sell it to a gallery. But the owner had noticed something that wasn't right – and he'd called her out.

"Oh, my," Remy exclaimed. "Were you arrested?"

"Nooo, not arrested."

"Did he ask for a sexual favor?" Charlotte narrowed her eyes as she watched Lee.

Lee turned toward her abruptly, "Yes. How did you know? The agreement was he wouldn't tell anyone about the painting if I slept with him."

"Was he married?" asked Remy.

"Yes. And he was attractive and an excellent lover. I liked it. It made me feel quite sophisticated, sleeping with an older man. Then I met Daniel, but I continued to sneak away to have sex slept with the gallery owner for a while. So technically, yes, I was cheating on him while the gallery owner was cheating on his wife. Whew, that sounds complicated. It only went on for a few weeks after I met Daniel. But the worst part is that I've never told him about the forgery – or the man."

"Lee, there are things that spouses don't need to know. And you were just young and dumb." Charlotte smiled at Frannie, "No offense."

Frannie lifted her glass to Charlotte, "None taken."

Charlotte looked at Remy and Lee, "But more importantly, how does it feel to be the other woman?"

Lee replied, "I was so young and flattered, I never thought about that. And not to make excuses, but I think, in the case of the gallery owner, there were a lot of other women. In hindsight, that makes me feel sad for his wife."

Remy shook her head, "I don't let myself think about it that way."

Lee turned toward Remy, "How can that be?"

"Because there's no emotional attachment. No love. Just good sex. So, I don't feel like I'm taking anything away from their wives." Remy shrugged. Though she'd always kept this part of her life a secret, she found it was a relief to talk about it, as if it were the most normal thing in the world to bare her soul to these women.

"That's what I like about all of you. You're so comfortable talking about this." Lee lifted her glass and giggled, the wine sloshing precariously, "Although I do have to rely on this liquid courage."

Suddenly, there was the sound of a car speeding up the hill. They all looked over as a green convertible with its top down slid to a halt next to Charlotte's Mini. Tracey and Fong were singing loudly to the radio.

Remy's heart began to beat faster. *Where did that come from? Damn it, Remy, he's Lee's husband. Enough.* She cleared her throat. "And your fascinating husband sings as well," Remy said to Charlotte.

"He has a wonderful voice. He likes to sing, and not just in the shower," she chortled.

"But wait, what happened to his beard?" asked Remy.

Charlotte looked more closely, "Oh, dear. We'll have to discuss that this evening."

Remy murmured, "He's certainly handsome either way."

Charlotte glanced at her and grinned.

"It looks like they've both had a good time. Daniel enjoyed Tracey's company so much on the cruise. I do hope they'll become close friends. Daniel has lots of professional friendships, but except for Sasha, he doesn't have any real friends outside of work," said Lee.

"I hope so too. I sometimes think Tracey and I spend too much time with each other. He needs a male friend here in Italy."

Remy said, "They certainly must have developed some kind of bond, to come back in such good spirits after spending more than a week together, mostly in the car."

"It would be awkward if we were all friends, but they disliked each other," Frannie said.

Charlotte smiled, happy to see how much her husband appeared to be enjoying himself. "Ever since the cruise, Tracey has been talking about how much he's enjoyed elaborating on that Henri story with Fong. In fact, I'm sure Henri accompanied them on much of their trip."

Lee raised her glass in an exuberant toast, "To Henri," and wine splashed on Remy. The two of them giggled when Remy jumped at the cold liquid. Lee wrapped her arms around her, and more wine spilled down Remy's back.

Fong pointed at Lee and Remy, wine glasses in hand, laughing and hugging, and he smiled, "Look at how much fun they're having. I would guess they've already become close friends.

I wonder what they're talking about?"

Tracey looked up at the group and grinned, "Wine – and secrets, no doubt."

Part Four

Summer 2012

The Pomegranate

Milan, Italy

After several weeks that Frannie had spent alternating between staying with her cousin in Florence, job hunting and touring around Italy, she made a trip to Milan to visit Gia, who had moved there in early May.

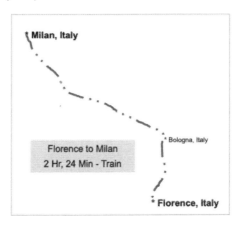

Gia had found a large apartment she loved in an old building on the outskirts of the Quadrilater d'Oro, Milan's fashion district. Her close friend, Sal, had made good on his offer to help her furnish it. They'd spent several pleasant weekends together, going around to flea markets and secondhand stores to find just the right pieces of furniture that she was in the process of refurbishing. She had settled into her new job comfortably but was tired of trying to disguise the fact that she was making do with the few office-appropriate clothes she possessed.

Frannie stopped in front of the display window of a smart boutique in Milan's Navigli district, "Gia, look here. I think this shop might have exactly what you're looking for." They stood looking at the display of stylish women's clothing in the shop window.

Gia tapped Frannie on the shoulder, signing, "Good find. You know, I think you might be right."

Frannie giggled, "I just love being in Italy and speaking Italian. All those years in school learning it. It was unbelievably difficult for me. And now, look at me." She grabbed Gia's hand and pulled her toward the door. "Come on. Let's go in. Shopping in a fashion capital of the world is so much fun."

A bell chimed when they opened the door. As they looked around, Gia heard soft music playing and began to laugh.

"What's so funny? This is a beautiful place."

"It reminds me of the very first high-end shop I went into after moving to Madrid. It was a lingerie shop."

Frannie looked around, "There's no lingerie here."

"I know. It's the music, the deep carpet, the vases of roses. I was barely eighteen, and it intimidated me so much that I was almost ready to leave." She looked around, "The clothes here are arranged by color, just like they were in that shop in Madrid. It was so lovely."

"And that's funny because—?"

"I don't know, it just made me laugh, remembering how naïve I was, and the ratty underwear I was replacing with nice lingerie. I was too embarrassed to have Sal see me in it."

"Sal?"

"A former boyfriend in Madrid."

"Ah, boyfriends and ratty underwear," Frannie laughed.

They walked around, touching the fabrics, holding up pieces and looking at the seams and finishes, draping a few over their arms, when a woman approached them from behind, speaking Italian in a soft voice with just the lightest Irish accent.

"May I help you find something today, madame?"

She froze at the familiar voice. Turning around, Gia saw a stranger with short, spiky black hair, freckles, round, horn-rimmed glasses. Then, looking more closely, she noticed her green eyes. "Lydia?" she exclaimed. "Is that you? You look so different!"

"You mean, compared to her?" With an impish grin, she pointed to the row of fashion shots hanging along one wall, shots of her in the beautiful dresses she had designed, her long, curly red hair falling over her shoulders or pulled up in a sophisticated knot on top of her head, flawless makeup covering her freckles. Lydia smiled broadly, "Hello, Gia." She threw her arms wide and pulled Gia into a warm hug.

They embraced for a few moments before Gia pulled away, "How long have you been in Milan? Whatever happened to Lydia McKay of Paris?"

Lydia reached into her pocket, "It became this." She pulled out a card and handed it to Gia.

"*The Pomegranate. Women's Couture*." She flipped it over to the back where Lydia's name, followed by "*Proprietor*" and all the contact details for her boutique were inscribed in fancy black script.

"So, this is your business? You finally made it?"

Lydia nodded and gave a huge grin of excitement.

"Oh, my goodness, I'm so happy for you," Gia said. "Oh, let me introduce you. Frannie, this is Lydia. Lydia, this is Frannie." Gia signed to Frannie as she spoke, "Lydia and I met in Paris."

Frannie nodded and smiled, "It's very nice to meet you." She stuck out her hand to shake Lydia's.

"And it's nice to meet you. Would you like a coffee or a glass of wine?" Lydia offered.

"Wine," they said in unison.

With glasses in their hands, Lydia's eyes danced in excitement as she shared her news with Gia, "Finally, I made it." She pointed around the salon filled with fashionable women's dresses, slacks, tops and jackets, perfect for work, all made of fine summer-weight wool, soft cotton and crisp linen. "But this isn't all *my* stuff. Not yet. It takes time to create enough inventory to fill a display area. Especially since people keep buying it," she laughed. "Eventually, I'll have to hire some help."

"But I see your hand in these dresses," said Gia, pointing to one corner where dresses for cocktail parties and special occasions were carefully displayed.

While they were talking, Frannie had walked over to look closely at the fashion photos on the wall. When she rejoined the women, she pointed at the pictures and said, "You don't look anything like those."

Lydia turned her head to look at the photos, "Oh, well, I've reinvented myself."

Gia appraised her. *She looks so chic and edgy and so very now.*

Frannie tapped Lydia on the shoulder, "Just to let you know, I'm deaf so I need to see your face to read your lips."

Lydia turned toward her, "Oh. I'm sorry. I said I reinvented myself." She asked Gia, "So, what are you doing here in Milan?"

"I quit Spectrum because I finished my degree, and I landed a fabulous job working in urban revitalization at a small architecture firm here. So, finally, we're both living our dreams."

"Yes, we are."

"Frannie and I've been out shopping for work clothes. I lived in Spectrum uniforms for so many years that I have almost nothing suitable for my new job. When we saw your display window—"

"This place is amazing," said Frannie, looking around. "I've never known someone who designs clothes."

"Would you like a tour of my establishment?" And Lydia grinned with pride that she finally had a business that she could call an establishment – *her* establishment.

"Of course."

She showed them around the small salon, the two little dressing rooms and the back workroom. In the back, Frannie walked over to a rack and began looking through the colorful garments, "These are interesting. Are you making costumes for something?"

"Yes, I am." They heard a soft chime. "Oops, that means I have another customer. Look around and try on anything you want. But don't go away. We need to catch up."

"Okay. But be prepared. I may have to buy a lot of your merchandise," Gia said.

Several hours later, their arms weighed down by bags bearing the name of Lydia's boutique, the women stood at the door to the shop. "I think this constitutes a successful shopping trip. But you've been so busy with customers that we didn't have much time to talk. How about we plan a dinner at my place?"

"I would love that."

"I have your card," said Gia. "I'll call you."

§

As Frannie bounced through Gia's apartment door a few weeks later, she exclaimed, "I can't believe the changes you've made to this place since the first time I visited."

"I still have a way to go. But I've had a lot of help from my friend, Sal."

"Sal, the former boyfriend? Does that mean he's *not* former anymore?"

"We're only friends. Let me show you to your room. When you've finished unpacking, come join us in the kitchen."

Gia and Lydia carried plates of tapas to the table. Frannie followed with an open bottle of wine and poured some for each woman. Gia lifted her glass and said, "To old friends and new ones, to Lydia McKay of Paris and The Pomegranate." They clinked their glasses.

Lydia added, "And to your new job." They raised their glasses in another toast.

Gia signed along as they talked.

"This food is delicious," Lydia said after the first bite. "You missed your calling, Gia. Why would you want to design buildings when you can create food like this? You could open a Spanish restaurant here in Milan."

"Thanks for the compliment, but I wouldn't want to cook full time. Then it would be a chore."

Lydia nodded.

"What was Lydia McKay of Paris?" Frannie asked. "You know, if you face me so I can read your lips and you don't talk with your mouth full," she giggled, "then Gia won't have to sign, and she'll be able to eat."

Lydia turned to Frannie and grinned, "I guess I could air my dirty laundry."

"Only if you want to." Gia looked at her closely.

"I haven't told anyone all the details of what happened before

I moved here, except for Shane, my boss at the pawnshop in Paris."

"I didn't mean to put you on the spot."

"Frannie, it's okay."

Lydia leaned forward, her elbows propped on the table. "Once upon a time, Lydia McKay of Paris was just me and a sewing machine in a tiny room in a boarding house. No meals, no amenities. And a shared toilet and tub down the hall." She took a mouthful of food, chewed it, thinking about what she should share, and swallowed before she continued. "And then I fell in love with this man named Frank. But it was all so complicated. It turned out that he was in love with Isabelle, a riverboat captain who was his best friend. She was practically married to Frank's uncle, Victor. They were madly in love with one another and had four adorable little girls. And then she was murdered this past February in Strasbourg. Frank and I were on that cruise." Lydia paused, "I saw the murder."

"What? Murdered? Oh, shit." Frannie's eyes grew round in astonishment.

"Your Frank was in love with *her*? Isabelle? Captain Ronaldo?" Gia said.

"Mmmmhmmm," Lydia said, nodding with her mouth full.

"I was on that cruise too, Frannie." Gia continued sadly. "Isabelle was a fantastic boss and a lovely woman, and it was her last cruise before she was going to retire." She took a deep breath, "You were there, Lydia? You saw the murder?"

Lydia nodded and looked away. "I saw the whole thing, but it was dark and rainy. I'm afraid the murderer might know that I saw him. That's why I left France."

"Didn't you go to the police?" Frannie asked.

"Yeah, I finally did. But I was a mess that night. Frank had just told me that he loved Isabelle and not me. And then I saw Isabelle lying there, dead. The murderer came back and stood beside me and spoke to me. He was watching Frank leaning over Isabelle's body. He said, "Do you think he did it?" I looked at him, but I was in shock and didn't *really* see him. The police took my statement, but I couldn't tell them much about the man. I thought

I recognized him from the bar I'd been in earlier that night, but when I tried to describe him, a few days had passed, and I realized, with all the emotional chaos that night, I could only tell them that he was tall, had a beard and he was wearing a hat and raincoat. It was the worst night of my life." Lydia shivered.

"Could you repeat that? I'm not sure I followed it all," said Frannie.

Lydia repeated it more slowly.

"Did they catch him?" Frannie asked.

"As far as I know, they never found him."

"Oh, you poor thing." Gia reached over and put her hand on Lydia's wrist. "So that's why you cut off all your hair and dyed it?"

Lydia nodded solemnly. "I felt like I'd had such a close brush with death that maybe it was a sign that I should turn my life around and not steal anymore."

"Steal?" Frannie's voice squeaked.

"I had a stash of expensive jewelry that Frank and I—" she paused and cleared her throat, "had acquired over the years. Shane let me stay with him for a while, and he helped me sell the jewelry to start my business here. He got good prices for me. We're both Irish, and I think he thought of me as a daughter of sorts." She paused to take a sip of wine, "I always tried to justify that the jewelry Frank and I stole had come from rich people who would have it insured and could afford to replace it. But we didn't give away the money we made from stealing. We kept it. Those costumes you saw in the workroom? I felt like I needed to give back something, somehow. So, I volunteered to design and make costumes for the community theater. I donate my time and the material. It's something they need and something I can give – sort of an atonement for my sins."

Frannie shook her head in disbelief. "Wow. You've had an exciting life."

"In hindsight, I'm not sure I'd call it exciting. I'm almost thirty. It was time for me to own up to things. I was good at stealing, but it was wrong."

"I'm not much younger than you. I feel like my life has been boring in comparison."

"I've simplified things – I have my shop and a small apartment above it – and I'm doing what I love full-time, designing and making beautiful clothing." Lydia went on sadly, "I loved Paris, and I miss traveling all over Europe. I miss the glitzy, glamorous events we attended, I miss seeing women wearing the dresses I designed, but this was a good place for a fresh start." She looked at Gia, "Why didn't you go back to Madrid?"

"I considered taking a job there doing urban renewal, the pay would have been great, but after my best friend, Mari was murdered and with my bad history with Sal, I needed a fresh start too."

"Sal? The not so former, former boyfriend?"

Gia looked at Frannie, "Yes."

"That sounds like another story. The two of you are fascinating."

"Hang on, Gia. I thought you and Sal went your separate ways when you started working for Spectrum," said Lydia.

Frannie tapped on her glass again to remind them to look at her.

"We did." Gia turned to Frannie to fill her in on her background with Sal. "Frannie, I know we're talking about a bunch of strangers to you. Sal and I had a special relationship. There was a spark right from the beginning. We were together for about five years. Then, we had a huge fight, and he dropped off the face of the earth, and then he showed up about ten months ago at the wedding of some friends."

"That must have been hard for you. Did he tell you where he'd gone?" Frannie asked.

"When I saw him at the wedding, he told me he'd been in a year-long rehab program for drugs and alcohol."

"So, what's happened since then?" Lydia asked. "Do you have a photo of him?"

Gia showed the two women a picture of them together. "This is us at my Madrid condo at Christmas several years ago."

"He's a hottie. I could fall into those black eyes of his," gushed Frannie. "Wow, that place you're standing in looks fabulous," she added as she eagerly examined the background in the picture.

"The building is called The Peacock. It *is* fabulous."

"Ah, when you were a kept woman," Lydia teased.

Gia laughed.

Frannie gave a romantic sigh, "He's so handsome. He could keep me anytime."

Gia laughed at Frannie, "I told him we would only be friends, but he still wants to move here to Milan. He wants to get back together. But we're taking it slowly, very slowly. He broke my heart when he called me a whore—"

"Whore? What? Is that another story?"

Gia held her hand up, "It is, but that one, I'm not sharing. I still can't commit yet, emotionally, to sleep with him again. He's very patient, letting me set the pace. He wants to be around me, and we have a lot of fun. He's a good friend."

"Good friends are hard to come by," Lydia said.

"Yeah," replied Gia.

"So, what's your story, Frannie?" asked Lydia. "We've shared our sordid pasts, what about yours?"

"Nothing sordid. My parents have been protective of me because of my disability." She paused for a moment before continuing, "Maybe too protective. I have a walkout basement apartment in their house in the Berkeley hills."

"So, you grew up right across the bay from San Francisco? How cool is that?" Lydia said.

"It was. I used to go over the City, walk around and people-watch. A lot of ideas for my comic book series came from those trips. When I dropped out of college to write and illustrate graphic novels, I found the writing part wasn't something I liked as much as I thought I would, but I do well illustrating other writers' work. And now, I'm planning a comic book series. But the most exciting thing I've done is to take a cruise with my cousin, Remy, and spend these past two months here in Italy."

"You live in California? You're a writer?" Lydia responded.

"Yes, I do, and I am. But I've met so many interesting people in Italy, and I've fallen completely in love with Milan. The different districts, the fashion – I've decided I want to move here, and modern technology means I can work anywhere. And my superhero, Lady Scarlett, comes with me wherever I go."

"Well, you should do it then," Gia smiled.

"I wish. But I've looked into it, and I have to have a real job to stay in Italy long term."

Lydia looked at her, "A real job?"

"Yeah, being self-employed when you're trying to stay in the country is too difficult. I need to work for someone in Italy and earn a paycheck to prove I can support myself and, I suppose, more importantly, pay taxes."

"You could work for me. I could hire you. I would enjoy the company and the help."

"You don't know me, Lydia, and I've never worked retail."

"But you already speak Italian fluently." Lydia looked at Frannie's skinny jeans, asymmetrically cut black top and high-heeled sandals, "Your sense of fashion is so current. Women will look at you and want your help selecting clothes. You'll see, selling clothes is easy."

"She's right. Lydia has all that beautiful clothing at The Pomegranate. With you to help clients put it together, it will practically sell itself. And Lydia will train you," said Gia, trying to convince Frannie to do this thing that obviously would make her happy.

"Of course, I would. I can't pay much, but at least you'd have employment."

"That's all I need, because I have my freelance work, and soon, I hope to have royalties from the comic book series coming in too. It's not about the money for me."

"When there are no customers, you could also work on your books."

"That would work. But I'll still need to find a place to live."

"What if you moved in here?" offered Gia. "I have a spare bedroom and plenty of space. I'd love to have you."

"Are you kidding? Thank you both." Frannie smiled broadly. "This is happening so fast. My head is spinning. I know Remy will say it's too sudden. But sometimes, things happen that way for a reason."

A Dress For The Gala

Milan, Italy

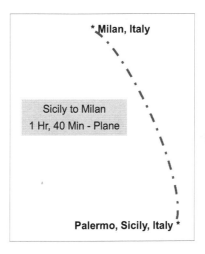

Following the brief flight from Sicily, Charlotte had immediately taken a taxi to the Navigli district in Milan. She walked through the narrow streets, looking into the windows of the fascinating little shops that were everywhere, even tucked away down the side alleys. There were art galleries, cafés, little bars and shops selling vintage clothing and accessories. She realized how easily she could become distracted and end up buying endless furnishings for their new house. She needed to focus on her dress. She stopped to look at the hand-drawn map that Frannie had texted to her, realizing she needed to cross over the canal to get to the boutique. Then, standing at the top of a bridge, she saw the mural – exactly as Frannie had described in her message.

A stylized, Art Deco mural of The Pomegranate, with its front door open welcomingly and beautiful 1920s and thirties-inspired dresses on mannequins in the windows, covered the side of the building. It was far more professional than Charlotte had expected and so real that it felt as though she could walk through the door and be back there in that era. She smiled and went around the corner, where she saw how similar the mural was to the actual front of the building, except that in the real window, the dresses were all unique, modern pieces. "Oh, this will be fun," she whispered to herself.

When she opened the door, soft chimes sounded, and she noticed a small light flash discreetly three times in the back corner, the light Lydia had installed to alert Frannie when customers entered and exited the shop. She looked around curiously, noticing that all the dresses were arranged by color, but before she had time to explore further, a young woman came out of the back room, taking off her black smock and tossing it over the chair behind the cash register. Her hair was short, spiky, black, and light freckles covered her face and neck. She pushed her round, owlish, horn-rimmed glasses up on her nose as she came around the counter. Charlotte tried to be discreet as she admired her high-heeled sandals with a small platform and her flowing, wide-legged, black pants topped by a fitted, sleeveless shirt made from pale cream fabric. A necklace made from chunky pieces of honey-colored Baltic amber lay intertwined with a tape measure around the young woman's neck, and matching earrings hung from her earlobes. She felt a thrill of excitement to finally meet Frannie's good friend, Lydia.

Charlotte extended her hand, "I'm Charlotte French. Some friends of mine referred this shop to me. They said I might be able to have a dress made for a special occasion."

Returning her firm handshake, Lydia smiled broadly, "I'm Lydia McKay, proprietor and designer. Frannie told me that she and Gia had recommended my shop when you said you needed something formal. I'm so glad you found it."

"They can't stop talking about you. It's nice to finally meet you, Ms. McKay."

"Please, call me Lydia. They are wonderful friends. I know Gia from Paris, and Frannie works for me now."

"I'm glad that you're open. So many places are closed for the entire month of August."

"My business is new enough that I don't have the luxury yet

to close for an entire month. Two weeks this year will have to suffice."

Charlotte looked around at the elegant clothing on display. "This is marvelous, but I don't know how to begin designing a formal gown. I've just always bought them off the rack. I'd like to spend some time getting to know you and hearing about your work. Would that be okay?"

"That would be perfect because it will allow me to get to know you and get a feel for your style and what you're looking for."

Charlotte outlined her body with her hands, "I've never thought about style. I'm not sure I have one. I could certainly use some help with that."

"You have a good sense of what goes together and what suits you. Those slim yellow slacks and orange tunic? You wear those colors remarkably well, even with your red hair. Your height, swimmer's shoulders and long legs mean you can get away with wearing things that short women, like me, can't. You have a definite presence. So, yes, I would say you certainly have style. Maybe, it's a matter of you not recognizing it."

Looking down at her clothes, Charlotte smiled at the compliment.

Lydia walked over to a display case and removed pieces of jewelry identical to the ones she was wearing. She fastened the necklace around Charlotte's neck and held an earring to her ear. "These would complete your outfit perfectly."

Charlotte looked in the mirror, ran her fingers along the strand of smooth amber chunks and grinned at Lydia, "I'll definitely take the necklace – *and* the earrings." She slipped them on and turned her head from side to side, "I love the way they dangle against my neck."

Lydia grinned and pointed to the two upholstered chairs placed in front of a coffee table with thick albums laid out on top of it. "Would you like a glass of wine? I only serve white." She smiled, gesturing at the luxurious pale carpet, and shrugged.

"White would be lovely."

As the women settled into their seats, glasses in hand, Lydia asked, "To get started, why don't you tell me about your event."

"Oh my!" Charlotte lightly clapped her hands together in front of her, "It's a huge, fundraising gala, a ball and a dinner that my husband's family hosts every year. It's held in their art museum in Raleigh, North Carolina and is attended by the crème de la crème of society there. I want to make Tracey proud. I want to make sure I'm dressed just right."

"That sounds like fun. I used to attend a lot of those when I was building my business in Paris. I think I have some ideas for you already, but, please, tell me more."

"Paris is my all-time favorite European city. Why didn't you keep your business there?"

"I had a falling out with my business partner, and I wanted a change. It was just the push I needed, and why not come to Milan?" She gestured with her glass toward the window, "It is, after all, a center of fashion."

They chatted a while longer about Charlotte's life and what she liked to do, what kind of clothing she found most comfortable, and how she would like to look in an ideal world. Finally, Lydia pointed to the album on the left, "This has photos of costumes I've designed for a local community theater here in Milan." She laid her hand on the album on the right, "And these are photos and sketches of clothes I've designed for my clients."

Charlotte picked up the album of costumes and began leafing through it, "Oh, I love theater. Especially small, local ones. These are wonderful costumes, Lydia. How did you get involved doing this?"

"A client of mine took me to one of their plays. Afterward, she introduced me to the owner of the theater. To make a long story short, I volunteered to assist with costume design for them. Even when I worked in Paris, I wanted to give back. I've done some things earlier in my life that I'm not happy about. When I met the theater owner, it seemed like working with them would be a good way to make amends. But enough about me." Lydia picked up the other album, "Let me show you my designs, and we'll see if we get some ideas about what will work for you."

Charlotte set the book of costumes on the table and leaned

forward to look at the photos and drawings.

Lydia flipped to a page in the album, "I start off with sketches of my ideas. I like to keep the drawings I make and then take a photo of the final product. Here's a design I did for Anne. She used to sing with the New York City Opera Company. I had the opportunity to design an entire wardrobe for her just as my career was taking off. She and her husband travel constantly, so she's always needing something new. And she provides wonderful, word-of-mouth advertising."

They turned a few more pages to one with a flamenco dancer.

"Oh, look how you've captured the movement of her body here. You're such a talented artist, Lydia." Charlotte ran her finger over the drawing. "It's obviously not what I need for my gala, but it's incredibly beautiful."

"That was the first dress I made in Paris," Lydia said nostalgically. "She had a perfect body to design for. She died unexpectedly, and that drawing always reminds me of her love for life." Lydia quickly moved to another page. "I think something along these lines might suit you. It's a design I did for the wife of an Australian diplomat. She needed something for an evening reception that was being attended by the president of France on Bastille Day."

"She looks lovely." Charlotte took a sip of her wine, "My husband says that a friend of his who will attend the gala this year is planning to run for president in the U.S. in a few years." She rolled her eyes and gave a wry grin.

"Then we need to make sure your dress is perfect. Why don't you stand up and let me take a look at you?" She stood as well and began to look carefully at Charlotte.

"What about getting something off the rack." Charlotte looked around the showroom, uncomfortable with Lydia's scrutiny.

"Oh no." Lydia set her wine down and lifted the tape measure from her neck, "You need something special. Something unique, something made just for you. Something that complements your body and makes heads turn."

"Like Cinderella?" Charlotte set down her drink and smiled

as she lifted the skirt to her imaginary dress in her hand and curtsied deeply.

Lydia laughed, "Well, not as elaborate as her dress." She pointed toward the back of the salon, "Come, let me take your measurements in the workroom where it's more private."

While Lydia measured her up and down and sideways and jotted numbers in her sketchbook, she asked, "So, Charlotte, tell me, when do you need this gown?"

"Not for a while. Tracey said he wants to leave for the States shortly before Christmas."

"Then we'll want to do a final fitting in November and get you the dress, packed and ready for travel, by early December. Nobody wants to fret over whether or not their dress will be finished on time. I'm glad you came in early because I'm always extraordinarily busy at the end of the year with everyone going to holiday parties and waiting to order their dresses until the last minute."

Notebook in hand, Lydia suggested they return to the comfortable chairs out front where she could make some initial sketches, and then they could talk about which one would best suit Charlotte.

Charlotte watched Lydia work, noticing how completely focused she was as she drew, her pencil moving confidently across the page with bold strokes and intricate little marks outlining the designs.

Finally, Lydia showed her two sketches. Charlotte just stared, speechless.

"Are they okay, Charlotte? If you don't like them, we can try another design. We have unlimited options. The only absolute is that you need to like the dress and feel beautiful in it."

"I – I – I don't know what to say, which doesn't happen very often," Charlotte chortled. "Both of them are perfect. You've captured exactly what I like."

"This design," Lydia pointed to the sketch in the upper left corner of the page, "is slim fitting to accentuate your figure, and because it's shorter, it will show off your long legs. I wasn't sure if you wanted to be bold and go against convention by wearing something that short. Now, this design," she moved her pencil to point at the sketch in the lower right corner, "what do you think of it?"

"Not having been to one of these galas, I want to keep with something a little more conservative. But, you know, as I think about it, I should have you make both dresses. Who knows, I may need a cocktail dress while I'm there. And that design is beautiful. What colors are you thinking about?"

"I made a wonderful, emerald green, silk gown for myself. That's it right there," Lydia pointed to one of the photos on the wall. "That color looks fabulous with red hair. So, I think that's the color for the short dress. Perhaps I'll even use the same fabric. We'll make a matching little jacket to go over it, since the first time you'll wear it will be in the winter."

"I love that color."

Lydia continued, "As for the dress for the gala – you know the mural on the building?" Lydia gestured toward the wall with the mural on the other side. "I was thinking of making the formal gown with a nod to the Art Deco era. Pale, seafoam blue and straight. Since you're tall, we don't want the dress to be flared at all. I can design a simple silk shift as the underdress, and the outer layer could be chiffon, sleeveless, covered with tiny, silver beads. The weight of the beads will cause it to hang beautifully. We want it to be simple but very elegant. And of course, I'll pack them so that they'll travel safely."

"That would be wonderful. When I met my friend, Lee, she was wearing a dress similar to that in feel, but in gray, and it was shorter, cocktail length, with long sleeves."

At last, with the designs agreed upon, the women stood up, and Lydia put out her hand to say goodbye. Surprised, Charlotte leaned over slightly and gave her a hug, "Thank you, Lydia. This has been so much fun. Now, I understand why women like to have clothes designed especially for them. You know, I'm becoming quite excited about the gala."

Part Five

Late August 2012

Never Just Settle

Ostia, Italy

Oh, that's Remy's ringtone. Lee jumped up and stuck her trowel into the dirt where she'd been digging. As she ran up the curving stairs to the terrace above, she pulled off her gardening gloves, dropping them on the table next to her phone. Breathing heavily, she said, "Remy, I'm here. How are you?"

"I'm fine. I interrupted you, didn't I?"

"I was just puttering around down in my garden. You know, the usual when Daniel's gone. And, of course, I left my phone up here on the terrace."

"Oh, that's right. Singapore and Hong Kong again?"

"Actually, he went to Hong Kong first for business and then on to Singapore to see his parents. He has several more trips back there before he finishes up this appraisal. It's pretty complicated."

"If it's not being too nosey – why don't you join him when he visits his family? That is, when you're not teaching."

"His parents aren't happy that he married a European woman. They had a nice girl from Singapore picked out for him."

"After two decades, they still feel that way?"

"Yes. But I don't mind having time to do things that fulfill me, things that I don't spend as much time on when Daniel's here. Like spending hours in my garden. And I'm more creative when he's gone, I paint and sketch. Then, when he comes back, we have time together."

"We do very well on our own, the two of us, don't we?" said Remy. "But Lee, the reason I called is to pick your brain. Lydia's closing her shop for the last couple of weeks in August. She'll work on some new designs and sew like a fiend. But that leaves Frannie at loose ends in Milan. We thought it would be nice to get away this coming week, away from all the city heat and tourists. I'm hoping you can recommend some out-of-the-way, non-touristy places we can go."

"What do you and Frannie want to do during this getaway?"

"Relax, walk on a beach, eat good food, drink good wine, read, sketch, take photographs."

"You know you can do all of that here. Why don't the two of you come spend this next week with me? Daniel will be gone for a few weeks, so we can have some quality girl-time together."

"Well, if it wouldn't be an imposition, we'd love to come to your place. I was *hoping* you would invite us." Remy gave a quiet laugh. "Frannie and I can meet up here in Florence and drive on down."

"Remy, you know you're welcome here anytime you want," said Lee softly. "Shall we invite Charlotte as well?"

"Charlotte and Tracey are making a quick trip back to Seattle to check on her house there. She said that Tracey wants her to consider selling it. So, she's not available."

§

Spoosh! exploded the handful of little weeds with bits of dirt attached as it landed on the brim of Remy's straw hat. At lightning speed, Frannie pulled another handful from her bucket. *Spoosh!* That one landed on Lee's hat. Frannie grinned and ducked down behind the row of tomato plants, separating her from the others, and watched.

Startled, the two women looked up. Then Lee leaned toward Remy and said something that Frannie couldn't see. They laughed. Lee gave a shrug and reached out to pick some arugula. She handed a leaf to Remy and bit off a piece of the one she held in her own hand. They sat for a moment, chatting and then, very slowly, they stood and walked off toward opposite ends of their row of vegetables. Frannie jumped up and took off running, only to find her way blocked by Remy coming around the end of the row. Frannie had begun to back up slowly, her eyes on Remy, when Lee grabbed her around the waist from behind and marched her out to the lawn.

With her eyes locked on Frannie's and a sly smile playing across her lips, Remy said, "You got very dirty while you were weeding. I think you need a shower." She picked up a watering can and poured it over Frannie.

"Hey, you're getting me wet too," screeched Lee.

Lee let Frannie go, spun around quickly and picked up the garden hose, spraying first Remy and then Frannie. The three women horsed around, tussling and pushing each other and laughing until they collapsed on the grass. Remy threw up her arms and gloated, "We've won! The old ladies are victorious." She dropped an arm over Lee's shoulder and gave her a quick squeeze. "You can never win, cuz," she said to Frannie, her hands moving quickly as she signed.

Lee leaned against Remy. "You two are very competitive, aren't you?" she asked.

"We've been that way all my life. She's always challenged me to see who can win. It could be a race, cards, dancing—" replied Frannie.

"Anything really, even who can peel and eat a banana faster." Remy laughed at the memory of them doing that.

They all flopped back on the grass, enjoying the afternoon sunshine.

Suddenly, Frannie sat up and turned toward Lee. "I had this great idea."

Lee sat up and looked at Frannie, "Yes?"

"You know that vacant lot you showed us yesterday, the one where you're going to plant a garden with your students? There's an empty wall next to it where I could paint a mural."

"Like the Art Deco one you painted on the side of Lydia's building in Milan?" asked Remy.

"Sort of. Lydia, Gia and I designed and painted that one to be very stylized to attract people to the shop. Lydia says that mural lures so many customers in, and it's been the talk of the town. She thinks we may be asked to do some other murals in Milan. But for yours, I was thinking about having superheroes that can resemble your students. It could depict them planting the garden."

"Ah, the superheroes transforming the lot," said Lee.

"That's right. One side of the mural can be the original lot with the kids in their normal clothes. The mural can transition, ombre-like, into the garden after it's fully planted. There can be birds and butterflies and bees, too. And the superheroes are there, putting the finishing touches on their work."

"I'll give my friend at the city planning department a call this afternoon. But Fong and I bought that building and the lot for a song when we moved here, so I can't imagine there will be any problem. And I'm sure he'll love the idea too."

Lee stood and reached out to pull Remy up from the ground. "Let's go clean up and have a glass of wine on the terrace while we plan it out, and then we can walk to town for dinner. Could you start this tomorrow, Frannie? Or do you need more time?"

As the women walked into the house, Frannie said, "After we talk a bit, I'll do a final sketch, and tomorrow, we can go buy the brushes and paint." With a wicked little grin, she continued, "If it's okay with you, I may have to stay an extra week to get it finished."

§

On Remy's last day, while Frannie was getting ready to continue her work on the mural, Remy and Lee took a sunrise walk, arm in arm, along the beach. "It's magical here, Lee."

"I can't imagine living anywhere else. When Daniel and I came to Ostia to see the house and the property, I knew immediately that this was the only place I could see myself living. The huge gardens, the beach, and it's so close to the school where I teach."

"I can see why. The house is charming. From here its size is deceptive because of the way the stone makes it blend into the coastline. I think that the way it was built against the hillside gives it the same feel of being part of the landscape as Frank Lloyd Wright's buildings do – but very Italian."

"It does, doesn't it? Daniel's only requirement was that we had to live near an international airport. Other than that, he let me pick the location since I'd be home alone so much while he travels. If I hadn't fallen in love with Ostia, I probably would have picked Sicily to be near my family."

"I can see that Fong loves you very much."

"I think I must be the luckiest woman in the world, Remy."

They walked along in comfortable silence toward the water and let the waves wash over their feet and ankles. Remy leaned down and picked up a seashell, using the tips of her fingers to brush away the sand. She put it in her pocket and smiled at Lee. "I'll set it on my writing table and think of you when I'm back in Florence."

"That's sweet."

"I'm looking forward to seeing you again next month at Sasha's vineyard for the harvest. I've never picked grapes before, but I'm sure I'll catch on."

"It will be about a week of hard work, but it'll be nice to have us all together. Sasha always needs all the hands he can get. He's bought several adjoining plots of land over the past couple of years, and now, he has a lot more vines to harvest. Gia, Daniel and I have been going there for the harvest since he and Kisho bought the house and original vineyard in 2009."

"Who's Kisho?"

"Kisho was Sasha's partner. They bought the place to retire to, and just a few months after they moved there, Kisho died suddenly of a massive stroke. They were so in love. They always described themselves as soulmates."

"The unexpected death of someone you love is just the worst thing."

"It is. Anyway, Gia always brings friends along to help with the harvest. Sasha says the more hands the better. With Gia and Sal, and you and Frannie, and Tracey and Charlotte, that will make things go faster. Oh, and I forgot, this year, Gia has invited her friend Lydia from Milan."

Remy said, "I've heard so much about Lydia. Frannie likes working for her, and Charlotte says she's charming. It will be nice to meet her. With all of us together, I suspect we'll eat well, drink lots of wine and laugh a lot."

"There always is a lot of laughter, especially at the end of the evening when we all gather out back by the firepit. Sasha has a way of making everyone feel so welcome."

"That sounds like a wonderful break from my city life in Florence."

"Sometimes, I wonder if you're lonely up there."

"I'm not lonely. I don't have time to be lonely. I'm very busy."

Lee put her arm around Remy and hugged her waist. "We've spent so much time together this summer that I've grown to feel like you could be the sister I've always wanted. I only want the best for you."

"I feel the same way. And I tell you things I've never told anyone."

"Like your affair this summer?"

"Exactly. I've never told anyone about any of them."

"It's good to have someone to talk to."

"It is. Anyway, I broke it off last week because I felt he was becoming too attached."

"Oh, Remy, I'm worried about you with your 'only married

men' thing and all your rules. What if he's still attached and stalks you?"

Remy pulled away from Lee's hug, her voice becoming defensive at what she perceived as judgment by Lee. "That can happen with any relationship. Don't worry, I've been doing this for twenty years, and it's been fine."

"Remy, Remy, I'm not judging you."

"It sounds like it." Her jaw tightened.

"It's just that I've come to care about you very much." Lee paused, reaching out to rest her hand on Remy's arm.

"It's worked for this long, and I'm content." Remy put her hands up in defense.

"Are you really willing to settle for just contentment for the rest of your life?"

"I don't know what's going to happen with the rest of my life, Lee. But I have a fulfilling career. I get offers from around the world to lecture, and I meet so many fascinating people. If that's contentment, I'm happy to settle for it."

Lee took Remy's hands in hers and looked her in the eyes for a long time before she spoke sadly, "Oh Remy, you deserve so much more. No matter how hard it is, don't ever just settle."

Part Six

September 2012

The Harvest

Slovenia

They worked hard in the vineyard that day, filling the baskets they carried with lush, ripe grapes. Remy paused to wipe her face on her sleeve and take a long drink of tepid water from her bottle. She smiled, watching Fong lift Lee's hair lovingly and fan the back of her hot, sweaty neck before giving her a quick kiss. Fong looked up, and Remy waved. He continued to watch as she went back to work.

As the sun dropped lower in the sky, Sasha walked through the vineyard, pausing to say something to each individual as he passed them. After they'd filled their baskets one last time, they took them to the end of the aisle to empty them into the cart before heading back toward the house and the guest quarters. Sasha stopped next to Remy and rested his hand on her shoulder, "I think we've done a good day's work out here. Everyone is exhausted. Let's go shower and give Gia and Tracey a hand in the kitchen."

At dinner, Sasha stood at the end of the long refectory table on the terrace, cutting the pork roast and laying slices on bright blue plates before handing them to Gia. With a large serving spoon, she piled roasted vegetables and tiny potatoes alongside the meat and then passed them down the table.

Frannie jumped up, "I'll pour." From the nearby sideboard, she took a bottle of rich cabernet franc from Sasha's vineyard in each hand and began to fill everyone's glasses. They raised them in a silent toast and began to eat hungrily.

"Mmmmmmm, wow," Tracey closed his eyes as he took his first bite. "Gia, would you come live with me and Charlotte and cook for us? This is absolutely wonderful."

Gia grinned at him, "Nope, I saw how well you cooked tonight, but I'm happy to come stay when that wonderful house is finished. I'll even give Charlotte cooking lessons."

Sal reached over and took Gia's hand in his, "She is a

spectacular cook, isn't she? Did you see that cake she baked? Yummm." With full mouths, everyone murmured their agreement.

"Sasha, you're at least as good a cook as I am, if not better," said Gia, turning to her friend. "I can't believe that you were able to roast that pork to such perfection and work in the vineyard too. Perfectly cooked meat is a real art. Tracey prepared the vegetables, that's hard too, getting them just right. I just baked the bread and the cake."

"Ahhh, but no one can bake a chocolate cake like you." Sasha looked down the table toward Tracey, "It's nice to see," his eyes twinkled, "that you are so proficient in the kitchen too. The more of us the better. By the way, I've been meaning to ask you, is there a story behind your earring?"

Self-consciously, Tracey reached up and touched it.

Charlotte chortled, "Something happened in Budapest. He came back a changed man, without his beard but with that earring. I like this new look."

"There's probably room in all of our lives for change," Sasha smiled.

Frannie changed the subject, "Sasha, I've been thinking about that barn of yours."

Sasha looked down the table toward her, "You know, we renovated it together, Kisho and I, before we moved in – to store things."

"I understand that," Charlotte laughed. "Everyone needs more storage."

Tracey looked at her and shook his head with a smile, "You and your stuff."

Frannie banged on her glass, "About the barn. I'm itching to paint a mural on the side of it. Your barn could become a landmark, Sasha, because you can see it from the main road."

Gia chimed in, "Sasha, you have to let us do it. It would be so unusual."

Lydia added, "Great idea, Frannie. I get so many compliments on the one we did on my building. It is definitely eye-catching."

"And the one she painted on the side of our old building in Ostia is wonderful, the perfect backdrop for my students' garden," said Lee.

"Hmmm. I'm not sure I want to do that. This is an old vineyard, out in the countryside. Why would I want a mural painted on the side of my barn?"

Charlotte said, "Sasha, I wasn't so sure about this whole mural thing. That was until I saw Lydia's. It's so professional."

"Well—"

"Frannie can sketch what she has in mind, and you'll see what we're talking about," Gia said. "I think you'll like it."

Frannie jumped up and ran inside to get a piece of paper and pencil. She came back and with short, confident strokes, she began to sketch. When she finished, she passed the paper down to Sasha. "Here, this is what I was thinking. Imagine it in color."

Before handing him the paper, Gia examined it carefully. "Look, Sasha. This way, we'll always be here with you."

He held the sketch in his hand, scrutinizing it. Everyone sat in silence, waiting for his reaction. Then, slowly his mouth turned up in a smile, and he nodded his head. "I suppose. And if I don't like it, I can always paint over it." He winked at Frannie.

Fong shook his head, "Sasha, Sasha, Sasha, you never cover a masterpiece." He turned to Frannie, "But how in the world will you find the time to get this done?"

"Today's Saturday," Frannie said, thinking out loud. "Is there a store that's open tomorrow where we can buy paint, Sasha?"

"The closest and only store open on Sundays is a general store with a little bit of everything, from groceries to nails and tools. They have basic house paint colors. Will that do until Monday when we can go get more at the paint store?"

"Sasha, the three of us can start picking grapes early," Gia gestured at Frannie, Lydia and herself. "We can work hard all morning every day."

"I always get up early anyway," said Lydia.

Frannie said excitedly, "That would give me and Lydia and Gia all afternoon and until dusk to work on the mural. If we work long hours every day for the entire week, we could be ready for its big reveal next Sunday before we leave."

The three younger women grinned at one another in excitement.

Charlotte sighed, "Ahhh, how energetic the young are," and the older members of the group all nodded their agreement.

On the final Sunday morning, they all crowded together in front of the mural to get into the selfie Charlotte was trying to compose. "Sasha, I can't see you. You need to move closer to Sal."

Under his breath, Sasha said, "Remy has a camera with a tripod, why do we need a selfie?"

"Sasha, I heard you." Charlotte lowered her phone and looked back at him. "Come on. Selfies are spontaneous and fun to share. We can do this." As she snapped the picture, Sal put his arm around Gia and gave her a smacking kiss on the cheek. Charlotte looked at her phone, "This is perfect."

"Okay, everyone, now it's time for the real picture." Remy rearranged the group before she walked over to her camera, set the timer and dashed back to her spot. *Click, click, click* went the shutter.

With the group photos out of the way, Lydia, Gia and Frannie stood off to one side, watching everyone's reactions to the mural. Sasha looked at it for a long time, his face solemn. Frannie jiggled up and down in excitement, gripping Lydia and Gia's hands. Finally, he said, "I'm pleasantly surprised. No, truly, I'm thoroughly impressed. This mural is a work of art. Look how you've painted yourselves and all of us into it. There you are, Gia, up on a ladder painting those storm clouds, with your hair held up in a bun by a pair of chopsticks. You always do that when you cook."

"We tried to capture the essence of each person," Lydia said, "but they all still had to work together." With a cheeky glance at Tracey and Charlotte, she pointed, "They're always canoodling. That's why we had them kissing in the vineyard."

"Sal is always near Gia, not enough to cramp her style but always doing something helpful for her," said Frannie. "See, there he is in his white shirt and light tan linen pants, cleaning her paint brushes while she glances down, happy at having him nearby."

"It has a very impressionist feel, not quite the angular clarity of that Art Deco mural on your shop, Lydia," said Remy.

Fong moved nearer to examine the details. "This is a splendid idea," he breathed, gesturing at the depiction of his friends, all dressed as though they were going to a garden party in the eighteen hundreds but with bare feet. "And this," his hand moved toward the images of the painters, who in contrast, wore modern shorts, t-shirts and tennis shoes, "is genius. My word, look at all those tiny brush strokes they've used to create the movement of our clothing and the light reflecting off the women's hair. How interesting to see that technique used in a mural, in a painting this size." He glanced at Sasha and continued his appraisal, "See how they used that same technique in the trees to give the feeling that the breeze is blowing. Look at the way Frannie's blond hair is moving, the way the light shifts along the length of it. It's true artistry."

Sasha nodded and quietly continued to examine the massive work of art.

Charlotte stepped close to Tracey and murmured, "Look, my love, they've shown each of us with something that is unique to our personalities – Tracey, she captured you perfectly with that straw hat you wear everywhere in the summer, and Fong with his driving cap, Lydia's spiky hair and glasses as she leans in with her paintbrush, concentrating so hard. And look, there are Lee and Remy sitting over there on the stone wall, taking one of their long breaks." Tracey draped his arm across her shoulders and nodded his head, nuzzling her with his face. She squirmed as his rough face scratched her neck, "You didn't shave. Are you growing your beard back?"

Tracey shook his head decisively, "No way. It was too itchy."

Tugging on his chin, Fong walked close to the mural and scrutinized the pair of women, how Remy and Lee leaned into one another, their heads bent together as though they were sharing a secret.

He turned to share his thoughts with them and saw them standing at the edge of the vineyard. Remy, her hair loose and occasionally blowing into her face in the gentle breeze, was down on one knee, her camera in hand, giving directions to Lee, who stood very still, posing with her hair twisted over one shoulder. In her hands she held a bunch of grapes from the last few rows that remained to be picked. His eyes crinkled in pleasure as he watched Remy's confident movements, the way her hands cradled the camera, the way she reached up with one hand to absently brush her hair aside, the way she leaned forward just before she pressed the shutter.

Sal walked into the middle of the road for a better look. Suddenly, he gave a shout, "Anyone driving past would think that they're just now painting the mural. Look at how they've painted themselves on the ladders with their brushes and cans, and the tarp covering the ground under the ladder. This is brilliant."

Fong smiled at him. "Sal, what they've done is called the Droste effect, the use of a picture within a picture, putting themselves on the ladders painting the mural. Now, look at the barn in the mural. There the three of them are again, perched on ladders, painting another mural. And see how Lydia is balanced on the top rung, holding Frannie's sketch with the same picture in her hand? Very clever," he murmured almost to himself.

Gia went over to stand next to Sasha, who grinned suddenly and gave her a little nudge with his elbow. "You've made me a superhero," he said, peering up at the figure flying above the vineyards, his hands held before him, holding off a storm. "What fun!"

She hugged him, "That was Frannie's idea." Then she pointed at his hair that over the years had turned more silver than black, "I hope you don't mind that we made your hair a little longer. It needed to move as you flew over us."

"Perhaps I should grow it that way. I think it suits me," he said, self-consciously touching his head. "But what's that little thing on my shoulder?" he asked as he squinted upward.

"Look again," said Gia quietly.

"Kisho?" he whispered.

"I thought it was appropriate that he'd just ride along with you since he never seems to be far away from here."

Sasha wiped his eyes with the backs of his hands and turned to give her a hug. "Thank you, Gia," he said gruffly. "Thank you for thinking of us."

Fong had been standing nearby and overheard their conversation. "I guess you won't be painting over this masterpiece, my friend."

"No, never."

"I like your signature, cuz." Remy turned to Frannie, "*Scarlett.*"

"Of course, as in Lady Scarlett."

"We have to celebrate. Champagne, Sasha?" Gia asked.

Fong was about to take Tracey, Charlotte and Lee to the airport, but the prospect of champagne was too enticing for Tracey. Glancing at his watch, he said, "Oh, yes, let's do that before we have to go, it'll be a perfect toast for the mural and a perfect send-off for us."

"I'll take a pass since I'm driving," Fong shrugged, "but when I get back—"

Sasha laughed, "You'll come back and help us pick those last rows of grapes, my friend," and led the way back to the farmhouse.

Remy leaned against Lee, "Awww, I'm going to miss you so

much."

Lee reached down and took Remy's hand in hers. "I wish I didn't have to go back so soon. I just couldn't take more time off. I'm so envious that Daniel gets an extra day with you and Sasha and everyone."

There Is No Choice

Slovenia

Remy lay in the big bed in the old bedroom at the top of the house, her window wide open and the cool evening breeze rustling the pages of the spy novel by John Le Carré that she'd left lying open on the table next to her. Sleep wouldn't come. *I've never felt that kind of attraction, that – closeness – to anyone. Why Fong?* Her unexpected reactions that afternoon played over and over in her head. *What happened today?*

She'd looked up to see him back from the airport already, working his way closer and closer down her row of vines. Her heart had pounded as she felt him moving toward her. Her breath shortening. Fingers reaching for that same last bunch of grapes hanging amidst the dusty leaves, the electricity when their hands touched. Startled, dropping her pruning shears, both of them crouching to pick them up. Fong, faster than she was, taking them and pressing them into her palm, closing her fingers around them, never looking down but only at her face, her mouth and into her eyes. His slender hand coming up to brush a bit of dirt from her face, leaving her scarcely able to breathe, his touch sending another frisson of electricity coursing through her. Steadying herself before they'd both stood. Hearing the snick of his shears cutting through the stem holding the bunch of grapes. The heat of his body as they stood side by side. Fong, looking at the grapes for a long moment, wondering about something before placing them carefully into her full basket. Running his finger across her mouth, stroking her lips open. Her touching his finger with her tongue. Him gently pulling his hand from her face, turning and walking away. Her eyes lingering on him as he'd begun working his way up the opposite row, away from her. Looking at his back as he'd moved away, slowly cutting grapes with his long, graceful fingers. Longing for the feel of those fingers against her skin.

All through dinner, he hadn't looked at her, instead, talking with Sasha and Sal, with Gia and Frannie and Lydia but never with her. She'd sat and listened, lost in the sound of his voice, the cadence of his words, sad that none of them were meant for her. She'd sat straight, turning her glass by its stem, peering in at the wine and then taking small sips, but inside, she'd been leaning, pulled toward him. When dinner had ended, Gia had cleared the plates and scraped them while Remy washed and handed them to Lydia to dry. Sasha, Sal and Fong had stood on the terrace, and she'd heard their low voices as they talked about grapes and agriculture and buildings and art. She'd wanted to be part of that conversation, but instead, she spoke with the women indoors. Then, she'd pleaded a headache from too much sun and wine and went upstairs.

She'd turned the shower from hot to cold and back to hot again, and it had beaten against her skin, oversensitive with longing for him. She'd pulled on her pajamas, opened the windows and gone to bed, lying there, waiting for sleep that wouldn't come.

Remy groaned in frustration and swung her legs out of bed, felt around for her worn leather sandals and slipped her feet into them.

In the room next door, Fong heard her movements. He lay there, recalling how that afternoon as he'd driven back from the airport, his thoughts had gravitated over and over to this friend of his wife. How his eyes had met hers over dinner that first night of the cruise and how his stomach had tightened. The electricity he'd felt when their hands brushed accidentally as they'd walked side by side in Giverny. The unexpected pleasure he'd felt when he saw her sitting on the hillside in Sicily, drinking wine with her friends. His anticipation as he'd pulled into the driveway next to the house and walked to the vineyard and worked his way down the row toward Remy, cutting heavy bunches of grapes and laying them gently in his basket. Finally, he was there beside her. He'd reached out to cut the bunch of grapes she was reaching for, and his hand grazed first the back of her hand and then her fingers. He'd felt her startled response at the sharp jolt of electricity between them before her shears fell into the dirt. They'd both crouched down, his forearm brushing hers, the feel of her arm warmed by the sun against his. He'd been faster than she was and picked up and pressed the shears into her hand, his eyes caressing her face, watching her mouth, catching her in his gaze. He'd noticed how her throat convulsed as she swallowed. When he'd reached out and run his fingers lightly across the drift of dirt on her cheek, his stomach had tightened at its softness. He'd heard her gasp at his touch and had seen her eyes close briefly, her lashes dark against her sun-reddened skin. And then they'd stood at the same moment. He'd reached out, his shears making a crisp, slicing sound as they severed the stem from the vine. He'd held the ripe fruit in his hand, looking at it, thinking about feeding the grapes to her one by one, wondering how her lips would feel against his fingers. Instead, he'd placed the bunch tenderly into her full basket, and then, he'd stretched out his hand and caressed one finger across her mouth, gently parting her lips. His heart had pounded as she'd touched his finger tentatively with her tongue. He'd pulled his hand away, even though he'd wanted to stay, to replace his finger with his lips, to touch the tip of his tongue to hers, cover her mouth with his. Instead, he'd turned and begun to work his way back along the other side of the aisle, refusing the temptation to look back at her.

He lay there, thinking about how he'd felt her eyes on him from time to time through dinner, how she'd carefully sipped her wine without a word to him, how after dinner, he'd wanted to go to the kitchen and take the wet plates from her hands and let his fingers touch hers. Instead, he'd stood on the veranda, talking with Sasha and Sal, and he'd felt the cool evening air on his skin and imagined it was her hands on him.

He heard her door open, and her quiet footsteps move down the hall and then onto the stairs, the kitchen door creaking lightly as she opened it. Fong stood up and went to the window and watched her walk out into the vineyard to the aisle they'd cut together. He saw her pause and touch her mouth and then tip her head back and breathe. He slid his feet into his sandals and crept down the stairs and out to the vineyard.

Remy heard his footsteps in the soft dirt and turned around. Fong stretched out his hand, "Come."

A shudder of anticipation like she'd never felt before ran

through her, and with no thought for her rules, she put her hand in his and walked beside him into the barn where they'd taken the photos of the mural that morning. He pulled an old blanket from the side of a stall and flicked on the light before leading her up the ladder to the loft. He spread the blanket on the hay and turned and pulled her to him. His mouth moved against hers, he probed her lips gently with his tongue, and her mouth opened eagerly beneath his kiss. Finally, his breath coming quickly, Fong took a step back, his fingers nimble on the buttons to her top. He slid it from her shoulders and dropped it into the hay. With gentle hands, he removed the bottoms and laid them beside her top. Then his fingers, so quick and confident just a moment before, were suddenly clumsy on his own buttons.

"Here, let me do that," she whispered and removed his clothing, piece by piece.

They stood, looking at each other in the dim light from the bulb below. Fong reached out and lightly ran his fingers along her cheek, down her neck and the length of her collarbone. He flattened his hand and stroked downward to her breasts and lowered his mouth to them. Her body clenched with excitement, and she pulled him to her and down onto the blanket. And then nothing mattered but their bodies against each other.

Fong stroked his fingers down her thighs and then replaced his fingers with his lips, whispering kisses along each leg. "I want you so—"

"Yes, oh, yes," she called out as he knelt between her legs and entered her slowly. She raised her hips to meet each stroke, moaning, tightening around him a little more with each movement. And then she came with a long cry of pleasure in a shattering explosion of sensation.

With one final deep thrust, he cried out, "Noooooo. Noooooo," and he came too.

They lay together, Fong heavy on top of her, his mouth pressed against her neck, his breath coming in long, harsh gasps, his heart pounding. Remy's heart pounded in counter rhythm, her head was thrown back, her chest heaving as she tried to catch her breath. He felt the small aftershocks of her orgasm, as her muscles clenched gently again and again. He slipped his hands under her smooth buttocks and pressed her against him, and he moaned each time she tightened around him.

"Fong?"

"Mmmm?"

"Why did you call out, 'No,' just before you came?"

"Because I didn't want it to end. Because right before the end is the most exquisite moment in all of life." He lay quietly, thinking. "I'd like to stay like this forever, beside you, inside you, making love over and over. I didn't want it to end."

"I didn't want it to end either. How can it feel so right when what we've done is so wrong? Oh, Fong, what happened?"

"I don't know, my sweet." He stroked her hair, winding a piece around his finger, "But I don't ever want it to end."

He felt her shoulders shake as she began to laugh. "We would starve – if we stayed here forever and just made love," she said, laughing harder. "They would write on our headstones, '*They died making love.*' But more realistically, at some point, it will be light again. And Sasha will come looking for us. It wouldn't be wise to be found together," she answered, and suddenly solemn again, she tugged his ear gently with her teeth.

He cupped his hand around her breast, loving it with his fingertips, and he hardened, groaning with desire as he pushed against her, surprised that he was ready again so soon. With a sudden twist, Remy rolled on top of him and straddled his hips, sinking down onto him. He moaned and began to move inside her. With her hands on his shoulders for balance, she said, "I want to watch you when you cry out at that exquisite moment, I want to go there with you." So, with his hands on her hips guiding her, their eyes on each other's faces, they made slow love again in the coolness of the barn, and then Remy stood and pulled on her pajamas and sandals and disappeared down the ladder.

I've been married to Lee for nearly twenty-five years. What is it about Remy that makes me want her so? What am I going to do? What will we do? He put his arm over his eyes, overcome by his longing and by his betrayal.

Fong returned to the house quietly. As he stepped up onto

the terrace, he heard Sasha's voice, "Be careful, Fong. Someone will get hurt if you continue like this."

He turned in surprise, "What? What are you doing out here in the dark, Sasha? Why aren't you sleeping?"

"I know you, my friend. I watched you and Remy at dinner. The way you constantly glanced at her from the corners of your eyes. You wanted her. The way she twisted her glass in her fingers, never looking at you, just wanting."

"But nothing happened."

"No, nothing then. I watched you both. You avoiding looking directly at her. Her longing for you. Then I heard Remy go out, and your door opened, and you followed her. I saw you from my window, in the vineyard and when you went into the barn. When you didn't come back out, I came down here to wait for you."

"Why?"

"Fong, you're my oldest friends, you and Lee. I don't want to see her hurt. Not by you. Not like this. Please, don't do it."

Fong sat down heavily in the chair facing Sasha, "I don't know what happened. Neither of us did anything or said anything before today. I've been noticing her since we all met. But – driving back from the airport – suddenly, Lee was gone, and Remy was all I could think of. And when we were in the vineyard this afternoon, I touched her hand and her face. And I wanted her. Dear God, I wanted her. I've never felt this kind of attraction before, Sasha. Not even to Lee."

"I thought you had stopped cheating on Lee."

"I keep trying. But this time, I think it's different. The other times, there were no emotions."

"Cheating. Emotions. No emotions. You're still betraying your vows to her." Fong winced as Sasha continued. "But this time – Lee knows Remy. They're friends. And you and Remy are part of a circle of friends. You'll continue to see each other regularly. Just like you have since you met."

"We're mature enough to keep what happened tonight separate from our friendship."

Sasha sighed and scrubbed his hands over his tired face, "Oh, my friend, be careful. What you and Lee have…" His voice trailed off. "If you don't stop, someone's going to get hurt."

"I would never hurt my wife." Fong stood up and touched Sasha lightly on the shoulder, "Thanks, my friend." He went inside to bed.

Early the next morning, Fong chased after Remy as she walked down the road away from the house and cut through an opening into the meadow. "Wait. We have to talk about last night."

Remy pretended she hadn't heard him and continued walking through the meadow grass, her ankles and shoes wet with the early morning dew.

Breathing heavily as he caught up with her, he reached out and touched her shoulder, "Later today, I leave for Hong Kong and Singapore for two weeks. We have to talk. We can't leave things like this."

She pulled away from him and looked bleakly across the fields, "I can't break the heart of another woman – a friend – the way my heart was broken by my friend." The pain from the betrayal twenty years earlier showed on her face.

"What are you talking about?" he said, still breathing heavily from his sprint.

Remy turned her back toward him, and haltingly, she shared the painful memory. "When I was at the university, I fell madly in love with my history professor, and we had a long affair – across a couple of years. My best friend was jealous because she had a crush on him too. She came on to him, and he refused her. She told him she knew about us and that if he didn't break it off with me, she would tell the university about our affair. If she'd told, he would have been fired. Ultimately, he chose his job *and her* over me. I was heartbroken – I'd lost my lover. Although I know better now, I thought I was the love of his life and he of mine. I never talked to my best friend after that. I lost both of them. And I dropped out of school for two years."

She turned to look directly at him, "Once I went back, I focused completely on my education, my art, my goals. Fong, women can be so cruel. I didn't want to be the subject of that kind of cruelty again, so I never allowed myself to have another close woman friend – until I met Charlotte and Lee. After that breakup, I put a wall around my heart. My God, it sounds so melodramatic. I did it by creating rules that I've lived by since – to protect myself – until now, until you, until yesterday and last night." She folded her arms, looking down at the grass, refusing to look at him.

"Let's sit here so we can talk this through." He pointed to a large oak tree with a bench beneath it that Sasha had put there to admire the view.

"What's there to talk through? We should never have made love."

"Remy—" Fong pleaded.

Remy sat as far as possible to one end of the bench, intentionally keeping her distance from Fong. She stared into space.

"You know Sasha saw us go into the barn last night," he said finally.

"Oh, no! Now, I've lost another friend."

"He never judges." He reached out to touch her face, and she pulled away. "Talk to me, Remy."

"This," she pointed to him and then to herself, "this is why I have my rules. When you break rules, bad things happen, and people get hurt."

"Tell me about your rules," he said in a gentle voice.

Resigned, she ticked off on her fingers, one at a time, her rules about relationships with married men. "My rules protect me and the man I am with and make us look like we're just friends doing things friends do together." She chuckled wryly, "Except in the privacy of a hotel room."

"I don't understand why you don't date single men, so you don't run the risk of breaking up any relationships. Wouldn't that make you that 'other woman'?"

"Someone else asked me about that recently. Fong, I don't want the complications and expectations of relationships. The married men I choose don't want to leave their wives. They just want something different for a little while, and so we have sex without any emotional attachment. I don't break up marriages, so

I'm not the 'other woman'."

"I don't have mistresses, but sometimes when I travel, I get incredibly lonely. Sometimes, I just need sex and a warm body in my bed."

"A warm body?"

Fong said, "Sometimes, I have – mmm, indiscretions – when I'm away from home on business for several weeks. They are women I don't know, who don't know me, who mean nothing to me. There is no emotion involved. I don't hurt these women. I don't take these women out. We don't go to dinner or to a play or a movie. It's only ever one night. And I never sleep with the same woman again."

"So, you have rules too," Remy said bitterly, still staring away at nothing. "How long has this been going on?"

"For the first five years, Lee and I had a fairytale marriage. No cracks and no flaws. Once I started traveling, especially on longer trips – three or four weeks at a time, several times a year – I needed to be with a woman. I'm a very sexual man. But somehow, Lee always knows about my indiscretions. Whenever she senses it has happened, she makes me sleep in my bedroom until she's ready to take me back. She takes me back – eventually. It's the way we've come to terms with it."

Remy was shocked, "How can you do that to her?" She'd never thought about the wife just instinctively knowing about an affair. "Do you believe Lee ever really comes to terms with it? Don't you think it hurts the same amount every time?"

"Why does she take me back then?"

"Because she loves you more. She gets through it. But my guess is that she doesn't get over it. I think a small piece of her heart must break off every time you cheat on her. Someday, Fong, there won't be anything left."

"I hadn't thought about that. My father told me – he was the same way. He and my mother were very happy together. When he traveled for business, he needed a woman too, but when he returned, he was there for our family and my mother. They are still happily married, and so am I." He paused a moment, "But this time – with you – was different." He turned toward her, "Remy, this time, I felt something different, more than the need for a warm body."

"I did too. I didn't expect it. Suddenly, there you were at the end of the row of grapes, and my whole world tilted, shifted. Even before you touched my hand and my face, I wanted you – sexually and emotionally – I wanted you, all of you. The sex was wonderful, but more importantly, it was as though you were a part of me. But we can't continue this, Fong. I'm afraid. Our time together has set off something inside me, and I'm so afraid."

"What are you afraid of?"

"I'm afraid of feeling deeply for someone, of becoming involved. I don't want to get hurt. Even more, I don't want to hurt Lee. She and Charlotte are the only close friends I've had since college. I can't have you as a lover and Lee as a friend. It just won't work for me. And I'm afraid because I don't want to lose you and whatever this thing is between us."

"You can't lose me, Remy. You're my friend, and I'm your friend. What we did was wrong."

"Yes, it was very wrong." A look of intense sadness crossed Remy's face, "I let my guard down with you, but I can't continue this. You need to go back to Lee as though this never happened. She deserves you, all of you." Her eyes pleaded with him to understand.

His voice shook, "If I could choose, without hurting anyone, Remy, I would choose to be with you."

"It's breaking my heart. I wish I could choose you too—" On the verge of tears, she said, "But I can't. Lee is my friend. There is no choice, Fong."

The Pearls

Ostia, Italy

"Daniel, what's this?" Lee took the beautifully wrapped box from him, turning it around and over in her hands with a troubled look on her face. He never brought her gifts from his travels anymore. He never called while he was away. And suddenly, he'd called before he left Slovenia and while he was in Hong Kong and again from Singapore. Normally, it would be brief arrival and departure text messages. "What's going on?" she accused him.

"Can't I bring my wife something after a long business trip, something I know she'll like?"

"I suppose," she said uncertainly.

"I thought a lot on this trip – about you – about us – and wanted you to know how much I love you."

Fong watched her remove the paper carefully instead of ripping it apart in her usual exuberant fashion. She paused, looking up at him with her fingers curved around the flat, velvet box, holding it, weighing it, afraid to open it, afraid of what she might find inside. Finally, her fingers shaking, she lifted the lid. Inside lay a beautiful, long strand of creamy white pearls.

"What did you do, Daniel?"

Knifelike, her words cut through him, and he pulled her close and held her tightly against his chest. Forcing himself to speak calmly as tears ran down his cheeks, he said, "I've finally realized how much I hurt you each time I was unfaithful."

She noticed that he finally hadn't used "indiscretions", that word he always chose to hide behind and convince himself they meant nothing. She pushed him away and looked at him silently, watching the tears that continued to pour down his face. "I know I've strayed in the past, but I can't do that to you anymore."

"I hope not," she said, "but this isn't the first time you've promised it would never happen again. Why is this time different?"

Lifting the pearls from their box, Fong clasped them gently around her neck. "I can't continue to break your heart, Lee."

She reached up and touched the cool strand, the strand that had so many symbols, but the one she'd heard most often was "*pearls are for tears*". On the verge of tears herself, she said, "I'm tired. I'm going up to bed, Daniel."

He touched her cheek, "I missed you. I truly missed you, my darling. Will you leave your door open for me, please?"

Fong stretched, thinking about how wonderful the previous night had been. He'd wished, as they'd made love, that it could go on forever – her body writhing under his touch, her hands moving over him, caressing him, arousing him, the pearls, the last thing she'd removed, lying puddled on her nightstand.

He looked over to the other side of the bed, rumpled and empty, and then at his watch. He realized it was just dawn and that Lee would be at the beach, in the position she used for her sunrise meditation.

He rolled out of bed when he heard the sound of an incoming text message from Sasha confirming their 7:30 call.

After his shower, he pulled on his comfortable jogging suit and wandered barefoot down to the kitchen to make coffee. Cup in hand, he walked through his office and stood at the window, smiling as he watched Lee in the distance, sitting motionless on her usual flat rock facing the sea. He recalled her delight when she'd meditated that first morning after they'd bought the house, when she'd come back and told him how she loved having the sunrise on her back while watching it reflect off the sea, that it was like having two sunrises every day.

He sat down at his desk and turned on his laptop. While it was booting, he said to himself, "I need to get this note taken care of before life overtakes me." He pulled one of his personal notecards out of his desk drawer, picked up his fountain pen, running his thumb over its smooth surface as he mentally composed the card. As he was addressing the envelope, his phone rang, "Hello, Sasha."

"Welcome home. How did it go?"

"Very well. This widow has an enormous, unusual collection of art. It was so large that I didn't finish the appraisal, and so I'll have to go back at least once more. I did manage to get it all photographed, but I have a tremendous amount of research to do before my next trip."

"How are your parents?"

"They're still doing well. They said to tell you hello."

"Tell them hello back from me. Will you take Lee with you next time when you go to Hong Kong?"

"To make me behave?" Fong asked with a tinge of bitterness. "Probably not. I'll go on to Singapore from there, and frankly, there's always the issue with my parents. Besides, she isn't particularly fond of Asia."

"But she married an Asian."

"You know I'm a European at heart."

Fong heard Lee come into the kitchen and clatter around before coming to the door and pointing to the phone. "Sasha?" she mouthed and chuckled at their habit of talking to one another the morning after Fong returned from his trips.

Fong nodded.

"Give him my love," she said.

"Lee says hello and to give you her love."

"Breakfast in twenty minutes."

Fong gave her a thumbs-up as she pulled the door closed quietly.

"Did she leave the door open for you last night?"

His jaw clenched, "She did."

"Even after what happened in Slovenia?"

"Lee doesn't know about Slovenia. I won't ever tell her. I finally realized that I've hurt her too much. So, I've stopped."

"Stopped?"

"It was because of Remy. She was very clear that because Lee is her friend, I can't be her lover. She also said that every time I cheat, it breaks off a bit of Lee's heart. I'd never thought about that before."

"Ahhh, Fong, you haven't been successful at ending your infidelities yet."

"But this time it's different."

"It's apparent how much Lee loves you, that she's tolerated this for all these years."

"I know how much she loves me. I guess I've finally come to my senses."

"A warm body in your bed is an indulgence. I hope you can be stronger than before."

"I hope so too."

Part Seven

Early October 2012

One Lone Sock

Raleigh, North Carolina

The sun was just below her visor as Penelope zipped her new, red Miata sports car into an open spot against the curb in the gentrified Raleigh warehouse district, only a block away from Emily's building. She sang along to the radio before switching it off. As she continued to hum the song, she pulled off her driving gloves and unzipped the front of the lightweight jacket that she always wore to drive in cooler weather like that evening. Her jacket and the heater made it possible to keep the top down and enjoy the changing leaves and the crisp, cool air. She hopped out of the car to lift and lock the top in place before raising the windows and turning off the engine.

Penelope patted the dashboard lovingly, "I'll take good care of you, baby." She'd wanted a convertible since she'd been a teenager, and with her recent promotion, she'd decided to splurge and go for it. She smiled, thinking about how protective her late, adoptive parents had been, how opposed they'd been to her having anything that wasn't built like a tank, despite the fact that she was a skilled driver.

Penelope pulled the elastic band out of the end of her loose braid and ran her fingers through her long hair, feeling the plait unravel. With short, evenly filed fingernails, she massaged her scalp. Reaching back into the footwell, she grabbed her purse from where it sat on top of a sports bag that held her running clothes. And then, after locking the door, she started off toward Haypress at a brisk walk, being careful to step over the cracks in the sidewalk.

Down the block, Edgar stood in front of the Haypress building, hugging a petite woman with very dark hair pulled up into a messy topknot and a camera with a large lens slung over her shoulder. Penelope watched Edgar lower his head and give Jane a long kiss. Edgar had her face in his hands, and she was moving her hands up and down his back. Penelope had been surprised that

Edgar had a girlfriend, especially one as sweet and talented as Jane. Despite the fun it would have been to see Edgar's embarrassed face if she interrupted their kiss, she slowed down to give them some privacy.

Pulling her phone out of her jacket pocket, she checked her messages, peeking every now and again at the two lovers. After several peeks, she saw Jane at the corner looking for a break in the traffic before she crossed to the other side of the street. Edgar stood watching her with a goofy smile on his face. They waved to each other, and she turned and headed off down the sidewalk.

By the time Penelope reached the entrance to the old, red brick warehouse with large windows and the doorway encased in white stone, Edgar had vanished inside. The heavy front door hadn't quite closed behind him, and she put out her hand to push it back open.

Edgar stood in front of the empty reception desk. The late afternoon sun shone through the door's original isinglass sidelights and lit his face, still bearing that goofy smile. "Hello Eddie," she said.

"You know I hate that name," he complained, though he was actually flattered that she'd finally given him a nickname.

"Yep, why do you think I call you that?"

"Ever since Eric moved away from Raleigh last year, you've been picking on me more and more. What, you miss him, so I'm your new target? Why don't you pick on your new partner instead?"

"You're way more fun to tease," Penelope grinned at him. She glanced down the length of the huge space with several doors along one side. Halfway down, Emily came out of her office and walked toward them, the wood floor creaking under her feet. "Hi Em. I would have been here a few minutes sooner, but I had to wait for Casanova here," she swung her thumb toward Edgar, "to finish smooching with Jane. Don't want to mess with true love."

Emily smiled at her teasing and handed each of them a small bottle of water before leading the way to the conference room next to her office. As they entered, Penelope took a final swig from her bottle, crushed it in one hand and made a basketball shot toward the recycling can. It bounced off the edge and landed on the floor. "Denied," she said before scooping it up and dropping it into the container.

"Don't give up your day job, Pens," teased Edgar.

"That was your last opportunity to practice with plastic. Tomorrow, the water cooler will be here, and you'll be tossing paper cups instead," Emily said.

"They don't work as well."

"Then you'll have to practice harder," Edgar snickered.

Penelope remained standing, staring at the information on the whiteboard in front of her. In her typical style, she recapped the status of the cases as she thought out loud, "So, we know this guy killed four red-headed women in Raleigh between 1998 and 2007."

She stepped over to the board that had the newer murder written in and pointed at it, "Then we think he killed that young red-headed woman in Trigg Pass, Washington, in March 2011. We just don't have any solid evidence yet."

Emily added, "That was a good piece of work. Who knows what we'll find if we keep digging?"

Penelope paused, pursing her lips as she continued to think out loud, "I regularly go through the FBI's Crime Data Explorer. So far, I've found nothing. And if a department, like the one in Trigg Pass, doesn't input their homicides into the FBI's database, the only choice we have to find them is in newspapers. Eddie's still searching for those."

Penelope's phone rang, and she grinned as she looked down at the number. "Hang on a sec." Holding up a finger to indicate they should wait, she said, "This could be important. I'll be right back – Hello? This is Detective Huber. Yes. Yes." She stepped out into the hall to talk. Several minutes later, she burst back into the room, waving her phone in excitement. "You're not going to believe it. I have something that's solid. It was a long shot that paid off."

"What are you talking about, Pens?"

"Okay." Scarcely able to contain herself, she shook her phone at them again, "You already know it took a long time for me to finally get the Trigg Pass PD to fax me a copy of the crime file. The detective there is so slow. It would have been easier if I'd been able to get the time off and go out there last spring."

Edgar motioned with his hand for her to move along, "Pens, get to the point."

"I made a copy of the file on my computer and spent almost all my free time combing through it – I studied the evidence every night for hours and hours. Then one night, I noticed a single sock in one of the photos of the items from the scene. Allegedly, it was in the victim's jacket pocket. I then realized she was wearing golf shoes with both socks. I asked myself why the young woman would have a single sock in her pocket when she was wearing two socks." She paused and took a deep breath, "I asked my golfer friends, and it's very common after a round for them to take off their golf shoes and socks and slip into shoes that are more comfortable. My theory of what happened is that the young woman found a stray sock, saw the murderer and went over to see if it was his. I reached out to the detective again and asked him for the size of the sock and the victim's shoe size."

"Why didn't you tell us about this, Pens?"

"Em, it was a long shot, and the detective in Trigg Pass kept taking forever to get back to me because he thought it was a stupid question, so he kept letting it go to the bottom of his to-do list. Anyway, let me tell you the best part."

"Finally." Edgar looked at Emily and grinned.

"He told me in an email that the lone sock was larger than the victim's shoe size. So, I called the detective to ask him to send the sock to our lab so we could see if there was any DNA on it – the Trigg Pass PD is so small, I was afraid it would take as long to get those results as it did to get the fax in the first place. Good thing I called him because it took some sweet talking to convince him, and then he had to check with his boss to see what the policy was with turning over evidence. It took a lot of back-and-forth."

"Pens, you're killing us, what did you find out?"

Her voice rose, "Well that was our lab on the phone. I've kept my fingers crossed, and guess what? We have a match!" She did a little dance before continuing, "The DNA in the hair we found on Zoe Abrams here in Raleigh matches DNA in the skin we found inside the sock from Trigg Pass! And – the killer probably doesn't know we have his DNA at all," she said in a cocky tone.

Emily added, "But the young woman never got a chance to hand the guy the sock because he killed her first."

Penelope nodded, "Precisely."

Edgar stood up, shaking his hands vigorously, "Oh. My. God. We have a DNA match. Oh. My. God!"

Emily stood as well, and with a broad smile, she went over and gave Penelope a hug. "Well done, Pens!" Then she turned to Edgar to shake his hand firmly, "Good work, Edgar."

"Thanks, Em."

Emily continued, "Our Raleigh Parking Lot Strangler has been in Washington State. So, have you reached out to the golf course to interview them? Who had tee times that day?"

"While the sock was at the lab, I called and spoke to the manager at the course. I asked about everything."

"What did they say?" Emily and Edgar asked simultaneously.

"Nothing came of it. It's a small town. The course keeps tee times in a paper calendar on the counter and only writes down first names, no phone numbers. They toss the whole year's calendar at the end of each year. And after a certain time in the day, after all the regular morning golfers have finished their rounds, they take walk-ons, and no names are tracked for them. The victim was strangled near sunset according to the police report. So, the murderer is most likely one of those walk-ons."

Edgar asked, "Any video cameras around the place?"

"Yeah, I grilled the manager on that, Eddie. They converted a farm into the golf course. It's an inexpensive course, and so it has no cameras on or in their building, and it's surrounded by cherry orchards. Just trees and trees around the course, as far as the eye can see."

"And credit cards?" asked Emily.

"Inexpensive course," she repeated, "so it's cash-only. Other than the DNA, it's a dead end."

Edgar jumped back into the conversation, "But what about

fingerprints on the golf carts?"

"Nope. The Trigg Pass detective didn't check for those."

Emily turned to Penelope, "Now that we know for sure that he's killed in more than one state, we have to turn this over to your lieutenant to pass to the FBI. It's gone beyond Raleigh's jurisdiction and our informal inquiries."

"Yeah." Penelope turned slowly and stared at the evidence, "But I sure would like to have been the one to solve it."

"It's hard to believe – this is all happening so fast," Edgar said.

Emily answered, "There's a point in every case when all of a sudden, things move quickly."

Penelope tilted her head, still looking at the evidence boards, before turning back to the others, "These cases were the only things keeping me at the PD."

"Then you'd better get your retirement paperwork submitted so you can come work for me."

"I guess it's time to take your 'cushy security job'," chuckled Penelope, making air quotes as she spoke. "But passing this all to the Bureau isn't going to bring *me* closure," she muttered. "Here, Em, let me take all this down." She raised her phone, snapped a few photos of the wall and shrugged at the other two, "A souvenir." Penelope began to remove everything from the wall, stacking it neatly on the table. "I'll put this in a box in the storeroom."

"Thanks to you both. This case would have gone nowhere without your diligent work. Well done." Emily stood, and this time, she hugged both of them.

"Well, this is just too sad," Edgar said. "I can't stay and watch. Bye, Pens. Bye, Emily. Stay in touch."

"I have to get back to my office. I'll leave you to finish up here, Pens. I'll walk you out, Edgar." On the way to the door, Emily said, "Come by in the next week or so, Edgar, and we can discuss other articles. But before you go, tell me how Jane's dissertation is coming along."

"She's taking a break. She's finished her research and all the interviews. She wants to step away from it before she takes all the information she's collected and makes that chaos, as she calls it, into a cohesive documentary."

"What is she going to do for her break?"

"She takes an annual trip to an ashram for some time away from the hustle and bustle of life. She meditates a lot and does yoga. I'm not sure what she does there, but she always comes home relaxed and refreshed. Sometimes she goes with her mom and sometimes she goes alone. She's always really excited about it."

"Why don't you go with her?"

"This is her thing. Hers and her mom's or hers alone. She doesn't need company. I don't think she wants it either."

"I've been thinking a lot about her dissertation. Cheating and lying – a fascinating subject. Everyone lies from time to time. But whether it's in a romantic relationship, like Jane is looking at, or just between friends, personally, I think it's intolerable."

"That's a tough one, because sometimes, people lie with the best of intentions." He looked at his watch, "You're right, it's so interesting and complex. I wish we could talk more, but I have to run to do an interview. When Jane gets back, why don't you come over to my place for a drink, and we can all discuss it?"

"It's a date."

Edgar gave her a quick hug before he pushed the front door open.

As she left the building with the evidence in a box in her arms, Penelope yelled out, "I'm out of here. See you later, Em," She glanced around guiltily to make sure Emily was in her office before she ducked out the door.

Back in the spare bedroom of her townhouse, referring to the pictures on her phone, Penelope stuck all the evidence up on the wall in the same order it had hung in the evidence room at Haypress. She sat on the sofa bed, staring at the photos and notes. Her eyes paused on the information from Trigg Pass as she talked to herself.

She was certain that no one cared about the victims as much as she did. She had been working on the case right from the first murder and wasn't ready to give it up yet. "I'll just wait a little longer before I hand it over to my boss. Once he passes it off to the Bureau, I'll lose all visibility into their progress."

Penelope's phone dinged as a text message came in from Emily, "*Come by tomorrow. We need to talk about your job.*"

Part Eight

Fall 2012

Murder Mystery

Milan, Italy

* Ljubljana, Slovenia

Milan, Italy *

Padua, Italy

| Ljubljana to Milan |
| 5 Hr, 26 Min - Car |

** Bologna, Italy

Pisa, Italy *

* Florence, Italy

| Florence to Milan |
| 2 Hr, 24 Min - Train |

* Rome, Italy

Ostia, Italy *

| Ostia to Milan |
| 7 Hr, 6 Min - Car |

| Sicily to Milan |
| 1 Hr, 40 Min - Plane |

Palermo, Sicily, Italy *

"Everyone has been warned that this will be a most unusual party," Gia said to Lydia and Fong with a broad grin as she looked around her living room to make sure everything was ready. "The scripts are over there on the table. The place cards and character lists are ready. There are a few guests who might be difficult to keep under control, but I think we'll all have a wonderful—" A tap at the door in the small entry hall interrupted her.

"Welcome, ladies and gentlemen." Fong opened the door with a flourish, greeting the guests with an exaggerated bow. Lee, Charlotte, Sal and Frannie filed into the apartment.

"So, this is why you had to come separately from us," Lee giggled as she passed Fong, "Wow, what a get-up." She waved her hand at his white gloves, white shirt with a Windsor collar and panel front, black coat with tails over gray, striped trousers and a red bow tie and giggled again, "I'm glad to see you're still getting mileage out of all those bits of old evening wear."

"Yes, and I'm donating it all to Lydia's theater group after tonight," Fong whispered to her.

When Charlotte realized that Fong was not only in costume but already playing his role as butler, she put her nose in the air, gave a little nod and winked at him, "Why, thank you, Fong."

Fong closed the door, and with one hand resting at the small of his back, he said in his most ceremonious, butler-like tone, "Please set your phones on mute, and place them here." He held out a small basket and continued, "Her ladyship is in the reception room." He gestured toward the living room, "Please go on through."

Soft string music played in the background, and Lydia and Gia stood in the middle of the room. In her role as lady of the manor, Lydia greeted her guests in a gracious tone. She wore the deep-emerald, raw-silk gown trimmed in mink that she had made for her first visit to the opera with Frank several years earlier. She'd made no effort to cover the freckles scattered across her nose and cheeks, but she had tamed her spiky black hair to lie in flat curls in front of her ears. A turban, adorned with her beloved pomegranate brooch attached above her left eye, was fashioned from the same fabric as her dress.

Loudly enough for Gia to hear, Sal leaned over and whispered to Lydia, "If I weren't spoken for, you would have to watch out."

Lydia held up her lorgnette in front of her glasses and peered through it at him, "Sir, please behave. We have standards in this household."

Frannie laughed, "So now you need glasses to see through your glasses?"

"Wait 'til you see your props, Frannie," Gia laughed back at her.

Lydia instructed Sal, "Go stand over there with your cousins and mind your manners." She gestured imperiously toward Gia and Lee.

Sal flashed a smile toward his "cousins" and asked, "Are they kissing cousins?"

Lydia gave him a stern look, "You will understand your role once we hand out the scripts, and you must remain in character for the entire evening." She turned toward Fong, "Fong, please bring champagne for our guests."

Sal chuckled and walked over to Gia and gave her a kiss on her bare neck. She snapped her fan at him. "Cousin," she said arrogantly. Then she broke character. "Hands off the goods, buddy," she giggled.

Fong walked to each guest, and with a little bow from the waist, he held out a silver tray with glasses of champagne, his other hand still flat against the small of his back.

There came a quick tap at the door, and Sasha poked his head into the foyer with Tracey close behind him. Charlotte saw them enter and said, "Sasha, Tracey, come on in. You're missing the champagne."

Fong turned to Charlotte, "I beg your pardon, madam. Please do not usurp my role." And they all laughed at his comment.

Sasha handed Fong a bag, "Three bottles of my best cabernet franc. You requested it for dinner tonight."

"Oh, yummy," said Gia.

Fong bowed to Tracey, "Welcome home, my lord." He turned to Sasha, "Welcome, Colonel." Leaning toward them, Fong whispered, "This is going to be quite a night." They chuckled, and each of them picked up a champagne glass from the tray Fong extended toward them.

Lee asked anxiously, "Does anyone know where Remy is? She *is* coming, isn't she?"

Fong set the tray down on a side table and went to answer another knock at the door. Remy's stomach did a little flip of surprise when he answered. She hadn't seen him or Lee since Slovenia and had wondered if it would be awkward spending time with them that evening.

"I'm glad you made it," Fong bowed slightly. "Or should I say, 'Welcome, madam.'" He smiled tenderly at her.

"I wasn't sure if I would come or not."

He put out his hand and opened his mouth to respond when she gently pushed past him into the room. Nervous that her betrayal of Lee was apparent to everyone, Remy's fingers shook slightly as she turned on the camera hanging around her neck. Fong picked up the tray with a final glass standing on it. She looked up, and he smiled at her. *Don't look at me like that. You're Lee's husband.* She turned her shoulder slightly as she took the glass and joined the others.

Gia gave her a little wave, and Lydia sent a smile her way before drawling, "So glad you've finally arrived, daaahling. Now we can begin." Lydia rested her hand on Tracey's arm as she turned to the group and raised her glass, "Welcome to our home, my friends. I'm looking forward to our evening of entertainment. My daughter, Gia, will describe what you can expect."

"Thank you, Mother." Gia stepped into the center of the room wearing a modest, white empire gown tied with turquoise ribbons, her hair partially pulled up into a knot at the right side of her head with a single peacock feather tucked into it. She rested her hand on a stack of small pamphlets on the table next to her with a guest list tucked inside each cover. "Dear friends," Gia began in a soft voice, "I tried to mix things up and get people out of their comfort zones as I assigned your roles, and—"

Charlotte interrupted, "So, who's the murderer?"

"We won't know until the end of the evening. That's the mystery of it."

"Who's the victim?" Tracey asked.

"Shortly, I will give each of you a small booklet that describes the role you will play in our murder-mystery evening and a guest list so you will know who the other players are."

MURDER AT THE MANOR

Guest List

Lord of the Manor _Tracey_

Lady of the Manor _Lydia_

Daughters _Gia, Lee_

Distant Cousin _Sal_

Colonel _Sasha_

Colonel's Wife _Frannie_

Neighbor _Charlotte_

Butler _Fong_

Maid _Remy_

"Please don't read ahead and spoil the surprise. Even the murderer and the victim will only know who they are when we get to that point in the evening."

"That's clever," Sasha commented in a low voice.

"And so much fun," Gia smiled at him. "Throughout the evening, we'll all be looking at and speaking to each other, not knowing who will die, how they will die, or who will commit the murder."

She went to Tracey, "Father, here is your script," and then teased, "And please, try to stay in character."

She handed a booklet to Lee, "You'll be my sister."

Lee raised her eyebrows with a demure smile, "Your older sister, of course. What will my name be?"

"Everyone will keep their own name." Gia turned to Remy next, "You will be our housemaid." She handed her a small pamphlet. "That will leave you free to take photos as well. And as the housemaid, you'll take your instructions from Fong, of course."

Oh, shit. This could be awkward. Remy took a deep breath and forced a smile. "Maid? Do I get to wear a very short black dress with a white apron and a frilly little cap?" she quipped, bobbing a little curtsy.

"Naturally. What else would you wear?" Gia shrugged her shoulders. "By the way, there is a rumor that my sister, Lee, is having an affair with the butler, so please keep an eye on them." Gia shook her finger at Fong, "Don't let any hanky-panky go on." The room erupted in a roar of laughter.

Gia went to Charlotte, "You're a neighbor and a good friend of the family. You will entertain us this evening after dinner with your beautiful singing," she said, handing her a booklet.

Charlotte took her script and caught everyone by surprise when she sang out in a lovely voice, "La, la, la, la, la, laaa. I had to warm up," and gave the group a saucy grin.

Gia moved back into the middle of the room, "Now, for our other guests." She looked at Sal, "You are our distant cousin, visiting from far away."

"You're very lovely." Then he whispered loudly, "I do hope we turn out to be kissing cousins."

She reached out with her fan again and rapped him on the knuckles. "Here is your script, cousin. We will just have to wait and see how our relationship turns out." He bowed slightly and blew her a kiss from the tips of his fingers.

"As a very wise man, Sasha," she said with a warm smile, "I'm sure you have figured out from Fong's greeting that you are the colonel – but what you don't know is that Frannie is your much younger wife." After she had handed each of them a booklet, she said to the group, "Welcome to our manor."

"Now that you all know your roles, please go and change. The men's changing room is down the hall on the right while the women's is on the left." Pointing to the hall, she added, "The rooms have signs on the doors, and each outfit is laid out on the bed, labeled with your name. Once you have changed into your costumes, which our lovely Lydia has created specially for each of you, we will assemble here to await dinner. Leave your clothing and your true selves in the changing rooms. Please emerge in character."

In the women's changing room, Frannie grabbed Remy's hand and signed into her palm, *"Is something wrong? You don't look well."*

"I'm okay. It was just a rough week."

"We'll talk later," Frannie signed back and gave her a quick hug.

As Fong cleared away the champagne glasses, Gia explained to him that dinner was in the kitchen. "We'll be using a caterer so we can all concentrate on our roles. The caterers will prepare the plates and food offstage and out of sight." She took him into the kitchen and introduced the caterers. As they walked back through the dining room, she said, "There'll be seven courses with accompanying wines." She handed him a copy of the menu.

MENÙ DELLA CENA

Appetizer	Frico (cheese crisp) Cups with Creamy Polenta & Nutty Brown Butter	Prosecco, Italy
Soup Course & Bread	Clear Chicken Broth with Green Peas & Fresh Tarragon, Crusty Rolls	Sancerre, France
Fish Course	Risotto with Shrimp, Lemon, & Rosemary	Vermentino di Gallura, Sardinia
Palate Cleanser	Lemon Sorbet	Prosecco, Italy
Meat Course	Osso Buco with Autumn Vegetables	Cabernet Franc, Sasha's Vineyard
Salad Course	Insalata di Carciofi e Bottarga (artichoke salad)	Sauvignon Blanc, Northern Italy
Dessert	Flan with Warm Carmel Sauce	Espresso, 6 p. Tokaj, Hungary

"You'll be responsible for ensuring our glasses remain full as well as instructing Remy with what help you need with serving. Oh, and Sal's sparkling water is in the ice bucket along with the champagne."

The guests began to drift back into the main room. Frannie was the last one to emerge, and everyone howled as she made her grand entrance.

"Remy, you've got to take a picture of this," said Gia.

As Remy framed the shot and pressed the shutter, Frannie reached up and cupped the enormous breasts that Lydia had built into her dress. "Whose idea was this? There's enough bosom here for five women." Frannie tossed her head saucily as Remy snapped another photo.

"My dear," Lydia said. "I bet the colonel fell in love with those breasts before he even noticed your good looks."

Sasha went over to his wife and picked up her hand. He bent over to kiss it, keeping his eyes on her breasts the whole time. "Easy now, cowboy, as we say in America," laughed Frannie. "We'll save those for later."

With a smile, Remy snapped several photos of them. Then, after a quick word with Gia, she went into the dining room and rang the bell on the sideboard, and Fong announced dinner.

They paired off to enter the dining room. Lydia led the way with Tracey, Sasha and Frannie came next followed by Charlotte on Sal's arm, with Gia and Lee coming last, arms intertwined, heads bent, whispering to each other. Fong stood at the sideboard, a long, narrow table that Gia had refurbished with gold and silver paint, his hands clasped loosely behind him while Remy moved quickly around the room, capturing the scene in picture after picture.

The large, round, oak table that Gia had found at an estate sale was covered with a heavy white tablecloth and surrounded by mismatched chairs. Gleaming silver candlesticks, none the same, were arranged in the center with beeswax candles that had been lit moments earlier by Remy. The candlesticks were entwined with vines and bright autumn leaves, and multi-colored gourds and tiny orange pumpkins were scattered about their bases.

Remy paused to take a photo of the table, and through her viewfinder saw Fong standing motionless in the background, watching – she wondered what he was looking at.

Gia said, "There are place cards marking where each of you should sit. Please take your assigned seats."

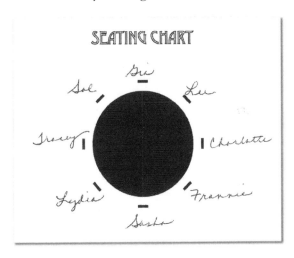

Fong added, smiling at Frannie, "The beautiful cards were all designed and handwritten by the lovely, young wife of the colonel. She is an accomplished artist and has to find ways to amuse herself when the colonel is traveling."

Frannie nodded her head, simpering in acknowledgement.

As Lee sat down next to Gia, she commented, "Sister, as always, you've outdone yourself with the table decorations this evening."

Gia leaned over and kissed her on the cheek, "Why, thank you. You are so kind. Lydia borrowed a lot of these props from the community theater that she makes costumes for. It does look very festive, doesn't it?" They giggled together.

Once everyone was seated, they all looked around with suspicion, wondering who the murderer was and who would be the victim.

Gia rapped the back of her spoon against her water glass and announced, "Please open your scripts to page two where you will see "*Before Appetizers*". Everyone's script is different. Some will be instructed to only listen while others will have more involvement at the table during this scene." Remy stood behind Sal, signing for Frannie.

Sal picked up the menu card from the plate in front of him. "Gia, you must have been slaving in the kitchen for days to prepare all of this."

"Cousin, whatever made you think that I cook? We have wonderful staff in our kitchens who prepare our food."

"Oh, of course, I guess I'm thinking of someone else I knew in Madrid." She blushed as he winked at her.

Seated beside Lydia, Tracey glanced at the instructions in his script, *Welcome your guests*. He cleared his throat and lifted the fresh glass of champagne that Fong had placed in front of him, "Welcome to our home."

Frannie chimed in, "Lydia already welcomed us."

Gia looked at Frannie, "Frannie—" The group laughed as she said, "I don't think that's in your script."

Frannie looked down and then back up with wide, innocent eyes, "Oh, but it is." She nodded emphatically.

"Frannie?" Sasha tapped Frannie on the arm and pointed to Gia. Once she'd looked up, Gia motioned as though she was turning a key in front of her mouth.

Frannie sassed back, "What are you, the script police or something?" and smiled sweetly, causing everyone to break out in laughter yet again.

Remy silently set a plate bearing a crispy cheese cup filled with polenta in front of each guest, and Fong moved behind her, refilling the champagne glasses. They quickly ducked into the kitchen to eat their appetizers before returning to stand in silence at the sideboard.

As instructed in their scripts, the guests chatted amongst themselves as they ate. They grew quiet as Fong cleared away the appetizer plates and the champagne glasses, setting them on the tray Remy carried as she walked behind him.

Gia announced, "You may turn to the section in your books,

'*With Soup*'."

Remy returned with a large tray of soup dishes and muttered, "Well, this maid is certainly going to get her steps in going back and forth."

Lee heard her and snickered, "Don't let that butler overwork you."

Fong moved around the table, setting a warm, crusty roll on each person's bread plate. Then, followed by Remy, holding the heavy tray of soup, he returned to place bowls of aromatic broth flecked with fresh herbs in front of them. He took a bottle from the sideboard and poured cold, crisp Sancerre into each glass. As Fong poured Lee's wine, he placed his free hand on her back and caressed it lightly.

Sasha looked across the table at Lee and saw Fong's gentle touch. He was relieved that things seemed to be all right between them. He glanced up to see Remy, standing behind Lee, looking at them with a peculiar expression on her face.

Remy watched attentively, and when the bottle was empty, she was there at Fong's side, handing him another. Finally, he poured bubbling water into Sal's glass from a bottle carefully wrapped in a napkin to catch any drips from the ice bucket.

Sal glanced at his script, turned slightly toward Fong and said in a hushed voice, "So the rumors of you two are true. Don't worry, I won't tell the master of the house that the hired help is flirting with his daughter. I'm all about equality for all." He winked at Fong.

"Thank you, sir. It wouldn't be good to confirm those rumors," he responded solemnly.

Wait for His Lordship and his wife to begin eating their soup, read the instructions in each script.

During the soup course, Tracey fiddled with his fake mustache. Charlotte smiled at him from where she sat at the other side of the table and discreetly tapped her upper lip.

"These walrus mustaches are a food magnet." He brushed away another crumb from his roll. "I don't know if I can stand to leave this on all night," he grumbled. Charlotte mimed pulling it off.

"Tracey, you have to keep it on." Gia gave Charlotte a stern look, "Charlotte, you're such a troublemaker."

"Of course. It's in my script," she lied, giving her the same innocent look that Frannie had earlier.

"Stop encouraging his bad behavior. One troublemaker is enough. We all have to stay in character," Gia teased Charlotte.

"But bad behavior is so much fun! Isn't it Tracey?"

He leered at her and nodded in agreement.

After finishing the sixth course, Charlotte sat back and sighed in satisfaction. She closed her script and fanned herself, "The food and drink have been splendid." She glanced over at Gia and saw her signing across the table at Frannie. She lowered her script into her lap, trying to peek at the end.

Gia looked up and caught her. She wagged her finger, and in a mock-serious tone, said, "Charlotte, don't you dare look ahead. Everyone has been following the script. Don't ruin the end."

"I can't stand it. I don't want to die!"

Everyone looked at Charlotte, wondering if she was, in fact, the victim and if she knew something they didn't.

Gia said, "No one knows who dies until they die. This is serious stuff." One corner of her mouth turned up in amusement.

"Besides, I know Sal did it," Charlotte said. "I just know it."

Tracey stopped pressing his mustache back onto his upper lip and looked at Charlotte playfully, "So, a distant cousin pops out of the woodwork for no apparent reason, and that's why you think he did it?" Tracey looked around the table at the others, "Do *you* think he did it?"

Lydia stopped at the sound of his voice saying those words. She played them over and over in her mind, *"Do you think he did it?"* She pushed her script off the table and leaned over to hide her face as she composed herself. *It can't be him. What are the odds? That the murderer from the alley in Strasbourg is sitting at this table with these people at this party?* She picked up the booklet up from the floor, taking a few deep breaths to calm herself before sitting up. She glanced at him sideways, *Is it actually him?*

Charlotte pointed across the table at Sal and said, "He's the quiet type. Always watching us. He's barely said a word, but he's been looking. Tracey, maybe he's jealous of your fortune and wants to kill you!" She swiveled in her chair to look at Remy, "Or maybe the maid? It could be the maid." She wagged her finger at Remy, "She's been very quiet too, standing there, waving her hands. I'm sure she's sending signals to someone."

Frannie laughed as Remy signed Charlotte's remarks to her.

"Maybe she's in it with him," Charlotte finished triumphantly, staring first at Remy and then at Sal.

While Tracey watched Charlotte with an amused look on his face, Lydia looked down, pretending to examine her script, unable to believe that she might be seated next to the killer from Strasbourg.

Trying hard not to laugh at her unruly friend, Gia said, "Okay, I have to be the script police again. Charlotte, you have got to stick to your lines."

"How do you know that's not part of my script? You didn't write it, did you?"

"I'm guessing?" Gia smirked.

"Well, you'll never know, will you," Charlotte said with a sassy toss of her head. Laughing, she took another sip of wine.

After the dishes from the sixth course had been cleared away and dessert placed in front of them, at a nod from Fong, Remy handed him a wine bottle from the sideboard. He bowed slightly, presenting it to Tracey, "My lord, six *puttonyos* Tokaj, the king of wines and the wine of kings," he said reverently.

Tracey nodded and in his best British accent said, "Splendid."

While Tracey's head was turned toward Fong, Lydia sneaked another glance at him. A shiver ran between her shoulder blades.

Fong walked around the table, pouring the deep golden dessert wine from northern Hungary with great care into the small wine glasses that remained at each place.

"Please turn to the '*During Dessert*' section of your scripts," announced Gia solemnly.

There is a loud commotion outside, said their scripts.

Gia read from her booklet, "Oh, my, what a loud noise. Let's go to the window in the reception room. It has the best view of the street."

The instructions continued, *Everyone leaves the table to look out the window.*

They all stood up immediately and began to move to the living room. Lee lingered for a moment to read her additional instructions, that she should empty the container of poison in her pocket onto the victim's dessert. Lee pretended to follow the instructions and then joined the group at the front window.

Tracey disappeared down the hall into the bathroom.

As Lee came in to join the group, Lydia heard the special ringtone she used for Shane. "Oops. I forgot to turn off my ringer." She immediately walked away from the group to answer her phone.

"I'm glad you called, there's something I need to tell you." She dropped her voice to a whisper, "The strangest thing has just happened."

Shane heard the strain in her voice and said, "I'm calling with some news about Frank, but that can wait."

"Hang on a minute. I need to find someplace quieter." She looked around for somewhere more private, her eyes darting between the dining room and the living room where everyone was gathered. Lydia briefly considered the kitchen, but Fong, Remy and the caterers were all in and out. She ducked quickly into Gia's bedroom which was scattered with the women's clothes from when they'd changed earlier that evening.

With her back to the doorway, she put the phone to her ear. Her voice was low and panicked, "I think he's here. I can't believe it. I can't believe he's right here. He's part of the group of friends at this party."

"Hold on, slow down, kid. Where are you? Who are you talking about?"

"I'm at a party. And he's here. I think—"

Tracey had just turned out the light and opened the bathroom door when he heard Lydia's voice coming from across the hall.

"—it's him, Shane, the one who murdered her!"

"What? Who are you talking about, Lydia?"

"The woman. On Valentine's Day. The one in the alleyway

in Strasbourg. Isabelle."

Tracey stepped back into the dark bathroom to listen. *Shit.*

Shane exclaimed, "What's he doing there?"

"He's here, at this party. Now I know his name."

"How do you know it's him?"

"It was familiar – his voice – and the words. They were the exact same words. 'Do you think he killed her?'"

She must be the woman who was standing next to me in the rain that night. I should never have gone back to watch. But what are the odds that I would run into her here in Italy as part of this group of friends? Tracey stood still, waiting to hear what else she would say.

"Has he recognized you?" Shane asked.

"Oh, no. My hair is still the same as when you cut it all off and dyed it. And I don't ever cover my freckles anymore. And my glasses make me look completely different. Even Gia didn't recognize me when we ran into each other."

"Are you going to the police?"

"Police? I don't know if I'm *that* sure. I have to think about it."

Shit. Tracey quietly slid out of the bathroom and walked down the hall and through the door to the living room.

"I'll be careful. Yes, yes. I promise. I have to go back to the party, Shane."

"Then I'll tell you about Frank later."

"Okay. Bye." Lydia turned off her phone and stood thinking for a moment before slipping it into her pocket and returning to the dining room. Everyone was already back at the table when she took her seat next to Tracey.

Gia tapped her dessert spoon on her water glass, "Now that you're all back, let's continue. We haven't even had the murder yet. Please turn to the final page."

Tracey glanced at his script, and after setting it down, he took another bite of his flan, and then, in an exaggerated fashion, he grabbed his chest, gasping. He struggled for a moment or two before sliding out of his chair and onto the floor next to Sal. He thumped his feet on the floor a couple of times before flinging his arms out, playing dead.

Remy tried to stop laughing long enough to snap a photo of Tracey laid out on the floor and then a few quick shots of the group around the table as they half stood for a better view of Tracey.

Lydia watched. She looked down at her script and realized she had a speaking role. She took a deep breath and willed herself back into character. With her script gripped in both hands, she delivered her lines in a flat monotone, "Oh. My. Goodness. My husband. He's dead. He's been murdered."

Everyone broke out laughing at her unexpected delivery.

Charlotte pointed her finger at Sal, "And he did it. I know he did it."

Fong came from the kitchen, looked at his script, tossed it over his shoulder and high-fived Sal, "You're the next male heir, Sal, so you inherit everything."

Sal flashed his big smile and stood up, nudging Tracey with his toe. Tracey opened one eye and glared at him. Then Sal winked before stepping over the body, still lying on the floor, and sat down in Tracey's chair. Sal looked at Lydia, "I'm now in charge of the manor. And I'm giving Fong permission to marry Lee. Fong, please come join your new family."

Before taking Sal's seat, Fong went to Lee, dropped on one knee and taking her hand in his, he followed his script, "I've loved you for so long. We now have the blessing of the master of the house. Will you marry me?" He gazed romantically into her eyes.

"Yes," she said. "Yes," and pulled him into a long embrace. Lee murmured near his ear, loudly enough for the others to hear, "I murdered him. I did it. While my father was alive, I couldn't be with you."

Remy watched them – and him – through the viewfinder before she took a photo, and then she went to Frannie and "whispered" into her palm, "*I have a splitting headache. I'm going back to my hotel. I'll get my clothes later.*"

Frannie signed back, "*You look a little pale.*"

"*Please thank Gia for hosting a wonderful party. You two did a great job.*" She gave her a little smile.

The Cooking Class

Milan, Italy

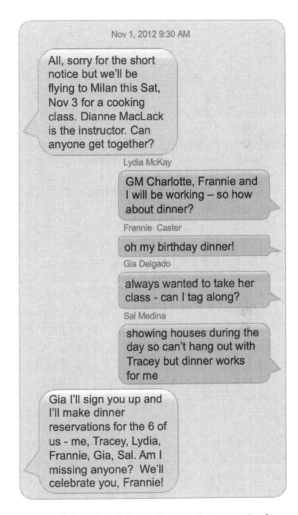

Nov 1, 2012 9:30 AM

All, sorry for the short notice but we'll be flying to Milan this Sat, Nov 3 for a cooking class. Dianne MacLack is the instructor. Can anyone get together?

Lydia McKay

GM Charlotte, Frannie and I will be working – so how about dinner?

Frannie Caster

oh my birthday dinner!

Gia Delgado

always wanted to take her class - can I tag along?

Sal Medina

showing houses during the day so can't hang out with Tracey but dinner works for me

Gia I'll sign you up and I'll make dinner reservations for the 6 of us - me, Tracey, Lydia, Frannie, Gia, Sal. Am I missing anyone? We'll celebrate you, Frannie!

Frannie popped her head into the workshop, "Lydia, can you cover while I use the toilet?"

Lydia looked up from her sewing machine, "Of course."

"I'll close up when I get back."

Absently nodding her thanks, Lydia went back to work. The evening jacket in front of her was the last in a large collection of cruise outfits for her long-time customer, Anne Gold, whom Lydia had met at the opera with Frank in Zurich. She and her husband were finally taking the around-the-world cruise she'd always longed for. Every piece of clothing in the collection had to be perfect because Anne showed off Lydia's creations whenever she wore them, constantly recommending her work to friends and acquaintances. The piece she was finishing, although called an evening jacket in the description, was one that Anne insisted had to be able to be worn with not only its matching long black gown but also with little dresses to make them cocktail-hour suitable or even with a pair of slim-cut jeans and heels for a fun evening of clubbing. "With leggings, Anne?" she murmured. "I'm not so sure about that, but we'll give it a try when you come in next week for the final fitting for your 'Seaborne Collection'."

A soft chime sounded, and the light flashed, indicating the front door had opened. "It figures. No one comes in for hours, and just when Frannie steps away, a last-minute customer appears," she muttered to herself. "I'll be right there, take a look around," Lydia called out as she tied off the final seam and laid the jacket on her sewing table, scrutinizing it carefully for any loose threads or flaws. She held it up, pleased with the way it had turned out.

She heard nothing, and then the door to the workshop clicked shut. Thinking it must be Gia and Charlotte there to meet them for dinner, Lydia looked up with a welcoming smile. Her smile faded when she saw it was Tracey, standing just inside the closed door, leaning against the jamb, watching her. *I don't like being alone with him back here.*

"Oh, Tracey," she said, trying to sound casual, hoping the others would arrive soon. "You startled me. Customers usually only come back here for fittings. But that's right, you've never been here before, so you wouldn't know that. What a nice surprise to see you. Did you come early to pick up Charlotte's gala dresses and surprise her? They aren't ready yet. Why don't you wait out front with Frannie while I finish up here? She can get you a nice glass of wine. I'll just be a few more minutes, and then I'll join you."

Tracey hadn't moved or said anything since he'd entered the room and closed the door. He'd just stood there watching her, his face somber. Her heart began to pound. *Did he see the fashion pictures of me out front? With my red hair? Did he recognize me?*

Willing her hands not to shake and betray her fear, Lydia slipped her bare feet back into her fashionable stilettos, stood and picked up the jacket, "Just let me hang this up." She turned toward the back of the room and hung the jacket carefully with the rest of Anne's collection. *Why doesn't he say something?*

"Are you trying to find something for Charlotte before she gets here with Gia?" Lydia straightened another garment, glancing around nervously. *He's scaring me.*

Inching along the rack of clothing toward the back door, adjusting hangers and dresses that needed no adjustment, trying to buy time, she continued her one-sided conversation, "Oh, tonight's your last night in Milan, right? I have some things that would look wonderful on Charlotte. Do you want something in her favorite color? Is this a gift? Is it—"

"I liked you, Lydia, I really liked you," he said in a quiet voice. "You shouldn't have done that. You shouldn't have told Shane." He shook his head sadly.

Lydia stared at him in panic, as she realized he'd overheard her conversation.

Frannie came back from the restroom and sat down on the stool behind the counter. She glanced at the closed door to the workshop, assuming that Lydia was on the call she had been waiting for. She picked up her sketchbook, admiring the drawing of Lady Scarlett she'd created for the next comic book in her series.

Lydia continued to edge toward the back door. Tracey moved quickly so he was between it and her. She turned to her left, toward him, and pretending she had no idea what he'd been talking about, she said, "Tracey, this is my private workroom. I don't like to have people wandering back here. Please go back out front to wait for the others."

Tracey stood, blocking the door. "I'm sorry. But you shouldn't have told him. You really shouldn't have."

She looked desperately toward the door to the salon. He shook his head slowly. And then she let out an ear-piercing scream.

"There's no one here except Frannie, and you know she can't hear you."

She yelled at the top of her lungs, "You're going to get caught. The police in Strasbourg have a sketch of you." If he believes that, maybe he'll leave. "You can't get away with this." She ducked to the right and knocked over several bolts of fabric she'd left leaning against the wall earlier that day. "Charlotte and Gia will be here any minute. Murderer! Do you want your wife to find out that you are a murderer?" she screeched. He paused for a second.

Glancing at her watch, Frannie set down her sketchbook and walked to the front of the boutique. She flipped over the sign to the side that said, *Chiuso.* Out of habit, she started to lock the door and then paused and left it open for Gia and Charlotte. She dimmed the lights, and as she walked through the store, she straightened a few items on the racks and shelves.

When Tracey grabbed her wrist, Lydia's eyes widened, and she screamed again. He spun her around and pulled her against him, his hand over her mouth, "Be quiet." She kicked and struggled, pulling at his hand, and then she bit down hard.

"Bitch!" He gave her a massive shove, and she lost her balance, twisting and turning in her high heels, trying to grab something, anything, to break the momentum. With her arm outstretched, reaching and missing, she fell backwards, striking her head with a crack against the sharp corner of her sewing table, and landed on the floor, her head twisted at an odd angle.

Bending over, he caressed her forehead like a lover before quickly removing the earring that dangled against her neck and running out the back door into the alley.

Gia came into the shop with Charlotte, the two of them

chattering away about their class, and walked over to Frannie. Charlotte gave her a kiss on each cheek, "Happy birthday!"

"Thanks. How was your class?"

"It was fabulous. We had so much fun," Gia said. "Tracey and Sal are meeting us here. They're coming separately. I just talked to Sal. He should be here any minute."

After they'd chatted for a few minutes about the cooking class, Frannie poked her head into the workshop, "Lydia, are you done with that call? Gia and Charlotte are here. As soon as Tracey and Sal arrive, we can leave for dinner."

Not seeing her at her sewing table, Frannie took a couple of steps into the room and glanced around. She saw the lower part of Lydia's body on the floor behind the table, "Lydia?" She walked over cautiously and saw how she lay, one arm flung out, her body twisted, not moving. She noticed that she still had her mother's pincushion fastened around her wrist with a wide piece of elastic, filled with sharp sewing pins, a few safety pins and a couple of threaded needles. "Are you okay?" When she didn't answer, Frannie screamed, "You guys, help! Something's wrong with Lydia." She frantically looked around the room and realized that the back door was partway open. "Help! Someone was here. Help!" she yelled as she ran out into the alley.

Gia came running into the workshop with Charlotte close behind her. Bolts of fabric were spilled across the floor on one side of the room and on the other side – Lydia. Gia dropped to her knees. "She's bleeding." She carefully slid her hands under Lydia's head. "Oh, my God. It feels like her skull has a big dent in it. She must have hit her head when she fell." She slowly pulled her hands away, looking down at the warm blood covering her palms, "And her head is crooked." She touched Lydia's neck, feeling for a pulse.

"I'll call the police." Charlotte ran into the salon and, picking up the phone receiver, dialed 1-1-3.

Frannie came back into the workshop, gasping for breath, "I couldn't find them. They're gone." And then she saw Gia, sitting on the floor next to Lydia, crying, her hands covered in blood.

Gia looked up at her, "I think she's dead, Frannie. I think

she's dead."

"Noooooo," Frannie howled as she burst into tears and threw herself down into Gia's arms.

Charlotte stood in shock against the counter by the phone, her face ashen and her lips pale. She stared straight in front of herself, not seeing anything. When the bell over the front door chimed, Charlotte looked and saw Tracey and Sal enter. "Look who I ran into on the doorstep," said Sal cheerfully.

"It's awful, Tracey." Charlotte ran over to her husband and buried her face in his shoulder, "It's terrible. Lydia's *dead*. With all that blood under her head." She pointed to the back room.

Tracey put his arms around her to comfort her, "Shhh, shhh, my love. Tell me what happened. I'm here now."

Sal dashed past them into the workroom, calling out, "Have you called the police?"

Charlotte replied, her face still buried in Tracey's shoulder and her body shaking violently, "They're on their way."

With his arms still wrapped tightly around her, Tracey winced as he rubbed the bruise that was beginning to form on his right palm. *I wish I hadn't had to do that.*

The Mural

Slovenia

Gia thought back to how she and Lydia had laughed about having identical phone cases and how she'd picked Lydia's phone up off the worktable that night without thinking and dropped it into her pocket. She'd only realized later that she had both phones.

"Good thing she never locked her screen," Gia said to Frannie as she scrolled through Lydia's contacts. "She was so organized. I've already called everyone she identified as clients."

"What about that guy, Frank? The one who she was in love with. Should we notify him?"

Gia looked at the phone, "There's no Frank in her contact list."

"Oh. What about her friend in Paris – you know that guy who helped her sell the jewelry?"

"Shane? Oh, yeah, I should call him. I wonder if it'll be as easy as looking for 'Shane' in her contacts?" She scrolled down and found his name. "Yep, here he is." She looked over at Frannie, "Here goes," and pressed his number.

Gia heard him say, "I haven't heard anything more from Frank. You know, I would've called you if I had."

"Shane? Is this Shane?" Gia said softly.

"Yeah, who's this? What do you want?"

"It's Gia Delgado. I'm a friend of Lydia's in Milan. I'm afraid I'm calling with some very bad news. You might want to prepare yourself."

"Bad news? Has something happened to Lydia, what's going on?"

Gia hated doing this, and although she'd broken the news many times by now, it didn't get any easier. "I'm so sorry to be telling you like this, Shane, but a couple of weeks ago, Lydia was murdered."

"Murdered? She's dead? What happened? Do they know who did it?"

"She was killed in her shop, and as far as I know, the police think it was a random burglary gone bad."

"This is terrible. I can't believe it. She was such a sweet kid. Worked her tail off. She was just starting to make a success of her life. Is there anything I can do to help?"

"There's nothing to do. I can call you if the police tell us anything more."

"Sure. Yes, please do that." His voice choked, "Thanks for the call," and he hung up abruptly.

§

Frannie, Gia and Sasha stood in front of the mural they'd painted on the barn during the harvest earlier that fall. Frannie explained to Sasha, "We want to move Lydia from earth to heaven. We want her to be an angel."

"We'll paint her out from here," Gia pointed to Lydia in the mural, "and move her up there," and she pointed to the sky.

Sasha stood with his hands clasped behind his back, contemplating the mural. Then a big grin filled his face. "Why doesn't Lydia, the angel, hitch a ride on my superhero shoulders? With Kisho."

"What a marvelous idea!" Gia said. "That would make her laugh!" Suddenly, she began to cry. "First Mari died, and now Lydia's gone. I told myself I was going to hold it together."

Frannie went to pick up the urn from the low stone wall where they had set it earlier. She took the urn holding Lydia's ashes in her arms and sat down and sobbed.

"We'd like to sprinkle some of her ashes at your vineyard," Gia said, gulping as she tried to stop her tears. "Under the mural

– here." She pointed along the side of the barn.

"Some? Of course. But what about the rest of them?" he asked.

"We took some to Paris and sprinkled them in front of the apartment building where she and Mari lived," Gia sniffled.

"Some of them we buried at the base of the tree out in front of her boutique," Frannie added. "We did it at night because we're pretty sure it's not allowed." Her tears ran over and dripped down her cheeks, "And if we spread some here, she can be in the places that were most important to her."

Sasha pulled Gia into a hard hug and reached up and touched the pomegranate brooch she had pinned to her hat, "And she'll always be with you too." He extended his arm to pull Frannie close, and the three of them embraced.

"You know, I'm going to add the brooch to your hat in the mural, Gia," Frannie said with a loud sob. "I miss her. I miss her so much. She was the best friend I've ever had."

Gia replied almost inaudibly into Sasha's shoulder, "She had no one. Her mother is dead, her father beat her, her sisters want nothing to do with her. She might have just been our friend, but we were the only family she had."

Part Nine

Winter 2012–2013

The Flowers

Florence, Italy

Florence, Italy *

Ostia to Florence
3 Hr, 27 Min - Car

Rome, Italy *
Ostia, Italy *

Remy opened the door to Fong standing there with a bouquet of flowers in his hand. She hadn't seen him since the murder mystery party, and her heart pounded – in happiness? Confusion? She gave him a look of dismay. "No, Fong," she said and started to close the door.

He put his hand out to keep it from shutting, "Remy, these flowers are from Lee. She asked me to bring them to you."

She was silent.

"May I please come in?" She shrugged and opened the door. Without a word, she took the flowers and walked away into the small kitchen where she pulled a vase out of the cabinet, slowly filled it with water and carefully arranged the flowers.

Fong followed her, stopping in the doorway so she wouldn't feel he was invading her space. "I'm sorry to barge in and surprise you. Lee's tried calling several times but hasn't been able to reach you. She's worried about you." He looked at her pale, strained face. "I'm worried too, Remy."

"Worried? What does she know?"

"Nothing. You can't honestly believe I would tell my wife?"

"Why not, you told Sasha?"

"No. He saw us. We need to talk, Remy."

Her shoulders were as stiff as the tone of her voice, "Would you like an apéritif?"

"That would be lovely."

"I only have a very small liquor collection. Campari and soda?"

"Sure."

As she made their drinks, Fong continued, "Lee was worried. She has a sixth sense that somehow tells her when something isn't quite right. She thinks she did something to offend you. You're not returning her calls, and you barely spoke to her or anyone at the party."

"Soda?" she asked. "Ice?"

"Yes, both please."

Silent, she dropped cubed ice into two glasses and poured a generous quantity of Campari into each. He watched her capable fingers cut a lime into wedges and squeeze one over the red liqueur. She let the wedge fall into the first glass. She repeated this with the second glass, squeezing a wedge of lime and letting the fruit fall into the liquid as she continued making their drinks. He watched the water fizz and bubble into his glass. She didn't pour anything over hers. He raised an eyebrow.

"I like the bitter taste." She arranged the drinks on a tiled tray with a small dish of almonds and another of fat Castelvetrano olives and then added two small napkins. "The afternoon sun warms my balcony, so let's sit out there." Fong shivered at her cold voice. She gestured with her chin toward the door, "Would you open it, please?"

Walking out ahead of him, she set the tray on the bistro table, and they sat down, crowded together on the narrow balcony. He raised his glass toward her. Slowly, she responded. After he took a sip, he asked, "Are you okay?"

Remy slowly turned her glass on the table in front of her, watching the wet rings it made as the ice dissolved. In a tight voice, she said, "Okay? No, I'm not okay. And this is very awkward. I don't think we should be seeing each other."

"I'm here because Lee asked me to check in on you. For her,

we need to be friends going forward."

"It can never be the same going forward. I slept with you. No, I made love with you. I wanted you, Fong – with my body and my heart and my soul."

"I did – I wanted – I'm trying to—" He sat back and closed his eyes.

She watched his face.

"You're Lee's friend. I can't avoid you. I can't walk out every time you appear. I don't know how to do this," he said in despair. "But we have to – for Lee."

In a tight, small voice she said, "I've tried very hard not to think about what we did." With a clenched fist pressed against her heart, she went on, "So my solution has been to back away. That's why, except for that one evening, I haven't spent any time with any of you." Her voice ratcheted tighter, "I need to shut out the thoughts of Slovenia. To separate myself from that. I can't do that when I see you, Fong. How can you pretend nothing happened?"

"How do you know what I'm thinking and feeling?" he said, his voice more heated than he'd intended. "Anyway, isn't 'pretending nothing happened' what you do with your lovers?"

Her voice shook, "How dare you? They are not my lovers, they are the men I sleep with. And we don't make love. We just have very satisfying sex. Nothing more."

He looked off down the street. "I apologize. But isn't that what you said we should do? To put it behind us? You chose Lee over me, but now, you're pushing us both out of your life. Is that how you deal with your emotions? You just shut them out. You put that wall around any feelings you could possibly have for people. You're doing it again, now."

She nodded her head, unable to respond to his accusations. She could feel her eyes brimming with tears and quickly blinked them back, "I'm a mess. I've been seeing a therapist since Slovenia. I have a lot of issues, but I told her I want to work on this first."

Fong reached over and touched her wrist, his fingers cool from his glass, "Lee has missed you terribly over the past few months, your chats and company, your laughter. And I feel at least partially responsible."

She pulled her hand away. Confused, she replied in a strained voice, "Why didn't you worry about Lee in the vineyard?"

"Remy, look at me. Look – at – me." She looked up, and against her will, her heart began to pound. "The attraction is – was on both sides. But I wouldn't have reached out to you if I hadn't felt it so strongly. Yes, what I did was wrong. What *we* did was wrong."

Remy held her breath and took another sip. She stared away and said softly, "I want to go back, you know, and I'm trying hard – so hard to do that. I miss Lee too. And you. I miss you. I miss all of our friends. The way we were on the cruise when we all first met. The fun we all had in Sicily and Ostia, the lightheartedness among us. That week we all spent together in Slovenia before—" She bit down hard on her lip.

She shivered. The sun had shifted, and she rubbed her arms as the terrace gradually fell into the shadows of the other buildings. "You're cold." He looked at his watch, "And it's late. I have to go. I'm meeting a colleague for dinner." Fong looked at her, "Can we try again – as friends?"

She sighed, "I don't know, Fong."

§

Later that week, Lee lay stretched out on the wicker chaise on the bedroom balcony and listened to the waves breaking on the beach below as the early afternoon tide came in. She tightened the belt on her pale blue wool robe and leaned back, closing her eyes with a sigh of contentment.

That morning, after she'd meditated on the beach and pampered herself with a long, hot bath, she'd been standing in the kitchen, washing and cutting vegetables from the garden. She'd hummed to herself, thinking about the rich soup she would make for herself and Daniel for dinner that evening. A hearty soup, bursting with flavors that would stand up to the loaf of bread she'd just taken from the oven. A soup that would come together quickly that evening.

She'd heard the rapid approach of his car and the crunch of

gravel under his tires as he'd braked to a quick, hard stop in front of the house instead of pulling into the garage below. The car door had slammed – her heart had pounded in anticipation as she'd heard him take the steps two at a time – he'd burst through the kitchen door, slipped his arms around her and buried his cold face in her hair.

Then he'd turned her in his arms, smelling of wind and fresh air from his drive from Florence because, of course, he'd had the top down the entire way. While she'd leaned back against the counter with her arms holding him to her, he'd kissed her greedily for a long time, so long that she could hardly breathe by the time he had raised his face from hers.

"Come upstairs with me, my darling," he'd demanded, "I want to make love to you – now." She'd scarcely had time to wipe her hands on a kitchen towel before he was pulling her toward the stairs.

When they'd reached the top step, Daniel had put one hand on either side of her face and his mouth on hers in another hungry kiss, pressing his body against hers, and then he'd guided her into her bedroom.

She'd put fresh linens on the bed that morning in anticipation of his arrival home and had turned one side back in a crisp, welcoming triangle. He'd lifted her in his arms and laid her gently on the sheets—

Lee gave a long sigh of pleasure, relaxed from that earlier lovemaking. She heard soft footsteps crossing her bedroom and opened her eyes to see Fong coming out onto the balcony, trying not to drop the glasses, bottle, kitchen knife and something wrapped up in pale, jade-green paper.

Lee laughed and helped him carefully set down some of it on the small table next to her.

He leaned over and kissed her neck. "I love it when you smell of me, Daniel." She reached up and pulled his head toward her, and she put her lips on his. "It just gets better and better between us, doesn't it?"

"Mmmmhmmm."

With his foot, Fong pulled the small armchair closer to her

and handed her the package, "I saw Remy again before I left Florence. She sent this with me."

Lee ripped it open, and Fong smiled at how she always loved to be given presents. She touched the glass of the framed photo and ran a fingertip across the figures behind the glass. "What a charming picture. Look – we were so happy on that cruise."

"That was taken by the waiter on our first night, if I'm not mistaken. No, in fact, I think Gia may have taken it."

"I'm sure it was the first night. That's the only time I wore that dress."

"Look, that was before Tracey shaved off his beard."

"He was handsome with it. But he is equally attractive without it."

"The four of you women are glowing. Who would have known that night that the six of us would become so close?"

"Remember how you fought against signing up to share a table?"

"Tracey fought against it too. We're just a couple of curmudgeons."

Lee smiled into his eyes, "You're my curmudgeon. And I know the perfect place for this – your desk."

"Yes, you're right. That would be good." He stood and took the bottle of prosecco, pointing it out over the edge of the balcony, and sabered it with the kitchen knife. "A crescendo of metal on glass, and the anticipated gush of bubbling ecstasy," he turned, cocking his head at Lee and raising his eyebrows as the cork and the bottle top flew off into the flower bed next to the slate patio two stories below.

"Show off," Lee snickered, and he threw back his head and laughed with joy.

He poured crisp, bubbling, straw-colored wine into the glasses. They picked them up, held them up to the bright sky and admired the bubbles.

"How was your trip?"

"Very interesting. The entire time I was there, the couple who hired me quibbled over the value of their collection of abstract paintings by an up-and-coming Hungarian artist."

"A divorce?"

"Yep. It's shaping up to be quite ugly. The husband kept taking me aside and asking me to lower the value so he could have more pieces."

"I can't ever imagine us having to divide up our property under those kinds of circumstances, Daniel."

He looked at her with his crooked smile and reached over to stroke her cheek with the backs of his fingers, "Never, my darling. Never."

They sat in the sun, drinking another glass of wine, quietly chatting about this and that.

"Remy called me while you were gone. We talked for a couple of hours. Things seem to be back to where we were in Slovenia. Thanks for talking to her."

"Your friendship is important to her." A memory of him and Remy in the barn flashed through his mind. He closed his eyes for a moment.

Lee took a sip of her prosecco, "Whatever she was going through seems to have passed."

Fong opened his eyes and looked at Lee, "She told me that she started seeing a therapist this fall to work through some issues. Apparently, he suggested that one option is for her to go back home."

"Oh, no. She didn't say anything about that to me, Daniel. Did she say what was wrong? Do you think she's planning to go? What about that department chair position? I would miss her dreadfully."

"She didn't say – just that she was seeing a therapist, and it seemed to be helping."

"She must feel so lonely, all by herself up there in Florence."

"You're a good friend to look out for her, my darling. She told me that she only has Frannie and work colleagues, but no close female friends other than you and Charlotte."

"It's tough moving to a new country. At our age, we don't make close friends easily. I'm looking forward to seeing her again at our solstice party. I just wish I could see her sooner."

The wicker chaise creaked as Lee stretched and stood up,

languorously untying the belt to her robe. Fong's eyes narrowed ever so slightly, knowing what would come next as she walked over to him. Her robe fell open when she leaned over, her mouth meeting his in an enticing kiss. With one hand resting on her waist, the other molding the curve of her breast, his thumb circling, teasing, his lips and tongue responded to her invitation.

The Solstice Party

Ostia, Italy

A horn honked two quick times. "They're here," said Lee, grabbing Frannie's hand and pulling her over to the window. They watched a driver getting out of what looked like Sal's car. "Daniel, did any of them say anything to you about hiring a chauffeur?" asked Lee as she opened the door.

Fong came up behind her, slipping his arms around her waist, resting his cheek against hers, "A chauffeur?"

They watched the man open the back doors of the car for Remy and Gia. As the women crossed the patio to the front door, Lee said cheerily, "Oh, my, you're traveling in style. A hired driver?"

Just inside the door, Remy paused and hugged Lee, whispering against her cheek, "It's so good to see you."

Lee leaned back a little so she could look at Remy before saying, "I know. It's been too long. This is going to be such fun. It will be nice to have us all together again." Remy smiled and nodded her head, her eyes tearing up. Lee reached up and brushed away a stray tear that had spilled over onto Remy's cheek. "I love you. Welcome back." She gave Remy another tight hug, and then she turned to wrap her arms welcomingly around Gia.

Remy sniffled and then stopped in front of Fong, who reached out and took her hands, pulling her toward him. "I'm glad you came." He wrapped her in a warm hug, and she surprised herself, embracing him back equally warmly. A waft of her light perfume took him back for the briefest moment to that night in the barn. He closed his eyes, swallowed hard and held her tightly for a moment before letting go. He cleared his throat. "You look well, Remy," he said with his kind smile before passing her on to Frannie.

The man in a black suit with a little black brimmed cap, pulled down rakishly over one eye, crossed the wide patio to the house with bags under both arms and in each hand. He set them by the door.

Fong looked around Lee, "That's Sal." He stuck out his hand, "Hello, Sal. When did you change careers?"

"Mr. Fong, it's so good to see you again. Mrs. Fong, where would you like me to put the bags?"

With a smile, Lee played along, "The ladies will be staying in the room that's at the top of the stairs to the right. It's the one with the door open and three beds."

Fong said, "And whatever you do, don't go into the room where the door is closed. Mr. Lauch and Ms. French may be — ahem — occupied, and you wouldn't want to embarrass our guests."

"I don't think you can embarrass Charlotte. Tracey, on the other hand—" They all laughed at Remy's comment.

"Yes, sir," said Sal with a cheeky grin.

Lee watched Sal pick up the bags again and head up. She looked at Gia, "What's that about?"

"He's been playing these crazy roles ever since our murder

mystery party. He's very good. Lydia wanted him to audition for some parts in that little theater where she volunteered. I'm just happy he's not taking himself so seriously these days." She grinned, "But I never know who will turn up to take me to dinner. One time, I came to his apartment, and he was out on a bench in front being a bum. He wore ragged clothes, and he hadn't shaved for days. Another time, he knocked on my door dressed in a tuxedo and top hat. It's nice to see him in good humor and enjoying life after the rough times we went through in Madrid."

Lee said, "How delightful."

"Every man needs a hobby," Fong added, trying not to laugh.

"You know," Frannie said, "he used to come into The Pomegranate, and Lydia would help him with his costumes."

"Aha, I thought he must have had some help," Gia said.

When Sal came back down to the main floor, Fong handed him a twenty euro note, "Thank you, kind sir." Sal tucked it into his pants pocket.

"Where will the hired help be staying, Mrs. Fong?" Sal asked.

Lee chuckled, "There's a sofa bed made up for you in my studio downstairs. It's not as elegant as our guest rooms, but I think you'll find it very comfortable. And you'll have a private bath." She couldn't stand it any longer and threw her arms around him, "I'm so glad you made it, Sal."

While Sal was off taking his bag to his room, Tracey and Charlotte came downstairs, holding hands, shoulders touching and looking extremely pleased with themselves.

By the time everyone in the group had given one another several hugs, Sal had returned. Lee asked, "Would you help me serve drinks? In memory of Lydia, I've made pomegranate blackberry gin fizzes." She whispered, "And for you, we have a super special one with all the fizz, but no alcohol."

Gia smiled as she watched Sal follow Lee, taking off his hat and hanging it on a chair. In the kitchen, he reached into his pocket and handed the twenty euro note to Lee. "It's only a game," he said. He took a napkin, placed it over his arm and picked up a silver tray, and she watched as he transformed himself into a waiter, carefully placing the glasses on the tray after Lee had poured the drinks.

With their glasses in hand, Lee wrapped her arm through Remy's, and the women walked around, looking at the elaborate decorations. Lee said, "Normally, I decorate in a more traditional fashion. But this year, I decided to use only white and silver and just a touch of natural greenery, in honor of our first winter solstice party."

"It's beautiful," Remy said as she looked up at the nine-foot fir tree, dripping with white, crystal and silver ornaments and small, white lights. All the magnificent packages piled on the white tree skirt were wrapped in silver paper with white grosgrain bows, the diligent work of Fong a few days earlier.

Gia walked over to the greenery-covered mantle with Frannie and touched a crystal candlestick with a white beeswax taper. "This is exactly what we're doing on our mantle next year. It's so elegant."

"This place is a winter wonderland," said Charlotte to Lee. Then she whispered to Tracey, "I just know I'm going to spill something and mar this perfection."

"When did you get here?" Remy asked Charlotte.

"Just a couple of hours ago." Charlotte whispered loudly to Remy and Lee, "We've, err, been in our room, you know, attending to an urgent matter." She winked, "I dared Tracey to have sex immediately upon arrival." Charlotte glanced at Lee, "Sorry if that was a bit rude, but you know how it is—"

Remy's hands flashed as she translated for Frannie, who glanced at them and giggled.

"No apologies necessary," Lee grinned. "We did tell you to make yourselves at home."

Fong looked at his watch, "I need to run to the airport and pick up Sasha. I'll be a couple of hours." Looking over at Sal and Tracey, he asked, "Would the two of you like to ride along so you're not left with this household of crazy women? We can take Lee's car."

Tracey immediately replied, "Definitely. I need to escape."

"I think your hubby is a little embarrassed," Remy said, nudging Charlotte.

"I know, isn't it charming?"

"And you're not leaving me here alone. They'll start on me next." Sal grabbed his cap, "I can drive."

Fong raised his hands in a slight shrug and nodded his head, "Sure."

Lee turned to the men, "While you're gone, we'll put the finishing touches on dinner. It should be ready shortly after you get back."

"And we'll have another drink, of course," Charlotte added.

Gia turned to Lee, "We'll all help."

As Lee walked into the kitchen, she tucked her arm through Frannie's and turned toward her, "Thanks for coming early to help."

"I'm glad I was able to get away. It was such fun decorating with you. I'm glad everyone loves it."

The next evening as dinner was ending, Fong stood, looked around the table at all his friends, dressed in mandatory white for the solstice, and raised his glass, "I'd like to make a toast to all of you, our splendid friends. And Tracey, it's rare to develop such close friendships at our age. Here's to you."

Tracey responded, "And to you, my friend." They all drank. He raised his glass again and smiled, "And here's to Henri."

After they took a sip, Sal asked, "Who's Henri?"

"Tracey and Fong's imaginary friend," chortled Charlotte. She caught Lee's eye, and Lee began to laugh. One by one, the others joined in, and soon the entire table was laughing heartily.

Tracey relished the moment, *What a wonderfully crazy group of friends. I can't remember a time when my family ever let go like this. We were a pretty somber lot. What a pity that is.*

After dessert, Lee stood up and handed each person several slips of paper and a pen.

Sasha said, "I bet I know what these are for."

"You may, but the others won't." Lee touched Sasha on the shoulder as she moved back to her seat. "To celebrate the winter solstice, tonight, you will discard anything you don't want in your life. Anything bad. Anything that's not necessary. Anything that is holding you back. Write one thing on each slip."

"Give me a few hundred of those, then," laughed Charlotte.

Gia, Frannie, Sasha, and Lee went to work right away. They pushed aside their forks and empty white china plates, littered with crumbs from the cake that Gia had prepared especially for Sasha – a delicious chocolate cake, covered with white chocolate icing and silver sprinkles.

Lee put her pen on the paper and then paused before she wrote, "*The pain from Fong's indiscretions.*" She carefully folded it in half and took a sip of her wine.

Sasha watched Lee and saw a look of sadness drift across her face as she wrote. He looked over at his best friend before writing, "*My friends' burdens.*"

Gia looked across at Sal. "*Lack of trust,*" she wrote.

Sal stretched over the table, trying to read what Gia was writing, but she covered her paper with her hand. "Just like kids who cheat in school."

Sal winked at her. "*My addictions,*" he scrawled.

Frannie stared at the blank slip of paper. She scribbled, "*My parents' overprotectiveness.*"

Charlotte quickly wrote on separate slips, "*Gray hair*", "*Wrinkles*", "*Aging*", and then she paused for a minute before writing, "*My vanity*". She chuckled and looked over at Tracey, sitting motionless across from her with an odd look on his face.

He looked down at the empty papers in front of him and very slowly and carefully, he printed, "*Maggie*", "*Zoe*", "*Sheila*"… As he noted each name, he folded the paper in half and went on to the next. Charlotte raised an eyebrow at the growing stack.

Remy gazed out the window, holding her paper in one hand, flicking the edge as she thought. Then she scribbled something quickly and covered it with her palm. Fong watched her as he moved the dishes in front of him and accidentally knocked against his wine glass, splashing a little onto the table.

Lee looked up and saw the splash of wine on the white tablecloth. She caught his eye, smiled at him, and as he gave a little shrug, she shook her head indulgently. *He always does that when we drink red wine, and then he says, with that charming little shrug of his hands, "It's like the Chinese who put a small flaw in their porcelain because only*

God can create perfection. No one's perfect."

Fong picked up his fountain pen, turning it between his fingers, watching the light play off it before he began filling out his slips of paper. *"Remy,"* he wrote. He looked at it for a moment and then crumpled it up and slipped it into the pocket of his dinner jacket. On another slip of paper, he wrote, *"My indiscretions"*, folded it and put it into his pocket as well.

As they headed out to the beach, Fong handed each of them a flashlight and said, "I suggest that you take off your shoes and wear these instead." He pointed to the flip flops that they'd bought for everyone and lined up under the table by size.

After changing their shoes, the group followed Lee and Fong, holding hands, down the path to the bonfire that the men had prepared on the beach that afternoon. They broke into groups of two or three. Sasha walked with Frannie on one side and Remy on the other, their arms linked.

Charlotte and Tracey watched the beams from the flashlights bounce up and down as the group wound down the side of the hill along a sandy path. "Look at how pretty it is with everyone dressed in white," she said.

He squeezed her hand and whispered, "White is both purity and a symbol of death. In eastern culture, white is linked to sadness."

"Yes, and tonight we're getting rid of sadness and bad things in our lives." They carefully continued down the path. "Don't you think Remy looks fabulous tonight, my love?"

"She does. If I weren't so in love with you—"

"Yes, I could see you chasing after her. But she doesn't sleep with her friends' husbands. So, you're stuck with me," and she bumped her shoulder against his.

"And if sex with you weren't so damn good—"

She chuckled and squeezed his hand, "That's the plan, my love."

Gia leaned against Sal and whispered, "Oh, look at the moonlight reflecting off the sea. It's so calm tonight. What a perfect time for a bonfire."

Lee handed the women shawls that had been placed in a

basket at the foot of the path.

Fong pulled his silver lighter from his pocket and lit a small stick of kindling. He touched it to the edge of the bonfire, and with a whoosh, the dry driftwood caught.

As the flames climbed, Lee explained to the group, "One by one, you'll step up to the fire, think about the things you want to discard in your life and throw the slips of paper into the fire. They will disappear, and you'll be rid of them." Lee held her slip up to her forehead and closed her eyes. She reached out her arms, and she dropped her paper onto the flames. She watched the smoke rise, carrying away the bad things in her life.

One by one, the rest of them followed Lee's example.

The final one to approach the roaring fire was Tracey. He closed his eyes, holding the papers in his palms, and raised them to his face, thinking about how badly he wanted to leave the killing behind as he made a life with Charlotte. He tossed his slips with the names of all the women he'd killed into the fire, one by one.

Remy watched Tracey turn back to Charlotte and press his lips against hers in a long kiss.

Next to them, she saw Gia step between Sal and the fire, turning her back to the flames, facing him.

"May I come to you tonight?" she asked.

"You don't need to ask. I'm yours when you're ready." Sal touched her sapphire necklace, the gift he had given her in Madrid. "This is the first time I've seen you wear this since—"

"Since too long," said Gia as she wrapped her hand around his. "I'm ready. I love you, Sal Medina."

He took her face in his hands and kissed her gently, "That means the world to me."

Remy's gaze wandered on around the circle of friends. She saw Frannie teaching Sasha sign language – fire, moon, sea, sand. Frannie looked up and caught her eye. Remy smiled and signed, "I love you." She watched Frannie sign the word "*love*" to Sasha.

She continued looking at her friends and smiled. Her eyes rested on Lee, whose head was nestled against Fong's shoulder. His arm was around her as they gazed into the fire.

Lee asked Fong, "What did you put into the fire?"

He looked at her, "You know." He was caught by surprise when Lee stood on her tippy toes and kissed him. He put his hands around her waist, dipping her deeply. She giggled and kissed him again.

This is what I need. Friends. I'm glad I let them back into my life. Contently, Remy listened to the waves gently lapping against the beach and the crackle of the wood as it burned. Those rules should have gone up in flames a long time ago. She watched the smoke swirl upward.

Spontaneously, Remy kicked off her flip flops, threw her wrap onto a rock and began to dance around the fire with her head thrown back and her arms in the air. One by one, the rest of the women joined in. Their white dresses billowing, their hair cascading down their backs, they danced and twirled and laughed while the men looked on.

Fong reached into his pocket and touched the crumpled paper.

§

The next week, with choral music from *The Messiah* pouring into his office, Fong had finished writing the addresses on their traditional New Year's cards. He listened to Lee's voice as she sang along with the recording while she packed away the Christmas decorations in the living room.

He opened the right-hand drawer for postage stamps and spotted the wrinkled piece of paper lying next to the stack of his personalized cards. Pulling it out, he smoothed it with his fingers, seeing Remy's name written in his bold hand. He looked at it for a long time and then closed his eyes – he pictured her, dancing in her white dress in the firelight, her slender body bending and twirling, her long hair streaming behind her. His thoughts drifted to the electricity between them that hot September afternoon in— Guiltily, he forced his thoughts to Lee, her spontaneous kiss at the bonfire, how he'd held her in his arms, how familiar her body had felt as he dipped her low before she kissed him again.

He picked the paper up and looked at it once more. *Remy.* He caressed it with his fingers and carefully placed it back in the drawer. Laying one of his personal cards on his desk, he picked up his pen and turned it in his fingers. Lee still sang with the music, and he looked out the window toward the sea. *Someone's going to get hurt if you don't stop.* His heart felt raw as Sasha's warning echoed in his mind. *Am I willing to take that risk?* Fong pressed the heels of his hands against his eyes and drew a deep breath, letting it out very, very slowly. *Is this what I want? The first step—?* He sat, staring at the blank notecard, and after a long time, he began to write.

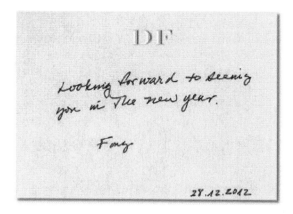

He slid the card inside the envelope, scrawled Remy's address across the front and sat looking at it, lying on his desk, before sealing it and adding a stamp. He slowly pushed it into the middle of the stack of New Year's cards.

With the cards in his hands, he walked to the door between his office and the living room. "Lee, I'm off. I need to mail these."

"Give me a second, and I'll come with you. We can have lunch in town."

Happy Valentine's Day

Florence, Italy

Remy came in from her mailbox in the entryway, a few letters and a card in her hand. She pulled the cream-colored envelope from the stack with a tingle of anticipation at the familiar, bold handwriting. "Oh, Fong. First, that personal New Year's card," she turned the card over, "and then the next – '*I wanted to hear your voice when you called Lee last night.*' And now—?"

She slid her old palette knife – that she had repurposed as a letter opener – under the flap, making a crisp sound as she cut through the paper and eased the card out.

She dropped it onto her writing table as though it had burned her fingers, the emotions she thought she had worked through with her therapist flooding back. "*Yours?* No, Fong. You're not mine, and I'm not yours. I've been working so hard to move on, but every card you send pulls me back."

She put her hand on the card, and over and over, she caressed the words with her thumb before she picked it up, sat down in the small wooden chair and held it to her heart. Then, with the card still clutched in her hand, she put her head down on her arms and sobbed.

Part Ten

Late February 2013

Fifteen Years

Raleigh, North Carolina

"Good. I look forward to seeing you. Unless it's raining, I'll meet you in the garden outside the restaurant. I'm average height, wear glasses and have dark brown hair. It's not too short, but not too long. I'll be wearing my navy-blue windbreaker and a fedora."

"Okay. How are you going to know me?"

"Don't worry. I'll know you." Edgar disconnected the call and flipped to the following weekend in the calendar he'd set on the desk in front of himself. He wrote, "*Michael Wilson interview, Raleigh Brew Pub, 3pm.*"

On the day of their meeting, Edgar waited on the bench under a heater in the garden with his hat shoved back on his head, a half-drunk beer in front of him on the picnic table. For the most part, the weather was crisp and bright, but each time a gray cloud drifted in front of the sun, the temperature dropped.

Whenever a young man walked through the entrance, Edgar nervously flipped the top corner of his notebook down and peeked at the high school graduation photo he'd tucked into the back. When he finally saw a lean, muscular, young man with red hair and green eyes come through the gate to the patio, he stood, pushed his glasses back up on his nose and waved his arm vigorously.

As they shook hands, Edgar leaned back to look up at the tall young man. He introduced himself and asked, "So what should I call you? Michael? Or Mike? I know your dad used to call you Mikey, but what do you go by these days?"

"Mikey. Everyone calls me Mikey – like my mom did."

"You *do* resemble her."

"Yes, I do, don't I?"

Before Mikey sat down, Edgar asked, "Is it too cold out here?"

"No. I'm fine. I'm up at Penn State, so I'm used to much colder winter weather than this."

"Can I get you a beer?"

"I wish. Unfortunately, they don't serve nineteen-year-olds. I'll take a soft drink. Make it a coke, please."

Edgar flagged down a waiter and ordered Mikey's drink and another beer for himself.

"You're lucky to have caught me in Raleigh for this long weekend. So, what exactly is this article you mentioned?" asked Mikey.

"I'm doing an in-depth, follow-up series about the victims of the Parking Lot Strangler here in Raleigh." The waiter set down a soda in front of Mikey and a beer in front of Edgar. He picked up Edgar's empty glass and carried it away.

"My dad saved your article on the murders. He showed it to me when I told him I was coming for this interview."

"This article I'm working on will be the first of a four-part series. We'll publish one story each month, starting on the fifteenth anniversary of that first murder back in April 1998."

"That would be Maggie, my mom."

"How were things for you after her murder? It must have been hard on someone so young. You were only four years old, right?"

"Yeah. I didn't understand exactly why she wasn't coming back. My dad told me she'd gone to live with the angels and wouldn't be home, but that he'd take care of me. The concept of death didn't mean anything. I just knew that she'd abandoned me and never came back."

Edgar flipped open his notebook, pulled a well-chewed pencil from behind his ear and began taking quick notes.

"My dad was very kind and gentle with me. But even with that, I was rebellious and angry."

"What did you do? You were so young."

"It started out as little things – not helping out with chores like putting my plate by the sink after dinner, and then as I got older, I started refusing to do my homework, I played hooky regularly, and I smarted off to my dad when he called me on it. Then I started flagrantly breaking his rules, right and left. It escalated over time, I picked fights with other kids; I even tried to punch my dad."

Edgar looked up from his notepad, "So it got bad."

"Bad enough that by the time I was twelve, my dad couldn't handle me anymore and sent me off to military school."

"That must have been tough."

"It was, but it was the best thing he ever did."

"What do you mean?"

"The teachers and administrators kicked my ass. Every time I whined about something or misbehaved, they would ask me, 'What are you going to do about it? How are you going to fix it?' Sometimes, I didn't even know what 'it' was, but ultimately, I got the message that I had to take responsibility for my life."

Edgar stopped scribbling in his notebook, "I think they call that tough love."

"Tough something, I guess. Anyway, it was what I needed."

"Did you graduate from there?"

"Oh, no, my dad brought me home when I was sixteen, after he remarried."

"How was that?"

"She'll never be a replacement for my mom, and she told me right away that wasn't what she wanted. She has a very different personality and even looks different from my mom. She is short and blond and plump, not tall, redheaded and big-boned. It wasn't all smooth sailing, but we've made it work. I think, by then, I was ready to have someone take care of me."

"Did she bring kids to the marriage?"

"I have a stepbrother who is also nineteen. He's a cabinet designer and maker. He's an artist, like *my* mom."

"What are you studying at Penn State?"

"Forensic science."

"Wow. Tough subject."

"My mom's murder has really influenced me. It's why I chose forensics. I used to watch all those reality shows where they use forensic evidence to solve murders. I never want a murder to go cold like my mom's has. It's a hard thing for survivors and loved ones to live with, the lack of closure. I want to dedicate myself to solving cases, to giving them that."

"What ever happened to your mom's gallery, Mikey?"

"MJM Expressions? The owner sold the building, and then my dad donated all her work to the Lauch Art Museum."

"Who owned the building?"

"Just some guy. My dad rented the space so my mom could have her own studio. Eventually, she got more space, and for a short time before she was murdered, it had become her gallery too. After the murder, Dad terminated the lease and cleared the place out. He didn't want the association with her murder bringing all the creeps in to look at what the murdered artist had painted or where she had worked."

"Why did he donate her art?"

"My dad said that the museum supports local artists, and it seemed like the right place for it, since my mother also supported new artists."

"So, her legacy lives on."

"It does. Who else are you interviewing?"

"I'm going to interview your dad and get his perspective."

"You should also talk to my dad's sister, my Aunt Elizabeth. She helped my dad a lot right after my mom was killed."

Edgar made a note before continuing, "After I finish Maggie's article, I'll talk with the families and friends of Ruth Sampson, Zoe Abrams and Sheila Kovacs to complete the series."

"They're the other victims?"

"That's right. One article for each woman. What else can you tell me about your mom?"

"Um, well, I know that she gave back to the community. She taught art to underprivileged women."

"You remember that?"

"No, no. But when I came back from military school, my art teacher here told me that my mom was her first instructor. She spoke very highly of her."

"That's so cool. You took art classes. Do you draw or paint or do any kind of art?"

"No, I couldn't paint my way out of a box," said Mikey.

The two of them chatted for a while, Mikey talking about what he remembered from those first four years and sharing stories his dad had told him.

"Could you give me a list of people who knew your mom? Like your art teacher, neighbors or friends. People from before she and your dad were married. I want people to know Maggie. Not just that she was the first victim of the Parking Lot Strangler."

"My dad hasn't told me anything about her life before they met. You'll have to ask him. I'll talk to him, and we'll put together a list for you."

As their conversation wound down, Mikey asked, "Do you need anything else from me?"

"No – thank you – I think that covers it for now."

Part Eleven

April 2013

Damn You, Fong

Florence, Italy

Remy dropped a stack of books onto her writing table. The card that had arrived the day before was still propped against a small vase holding a single, yellow tulip. She stared at the envelope and sighed – no, it hadn't magically vanished while she was teaching classes. She walked over to stare out the window. Walked back to the table. Looked at the card again. Stretched out her hand. Touched a corner. "Don't do it, Remy." She shook her head, "Don't do it."

In the kitchen, she poured herself a glass of water. As she leaned against the counter, drinking from the glass, she looked into the living room where the unopened card leaned against the vase, waiting. She slammed her glass onto the counter and walked over to the table, grabbed the card and tore it in half. With the two pieces in her hand, she looked at them, wondering what he'd written this time. Her thumbnail flicked against the torn edges as she stood, undecided. Then, slowly, she dropped first one half and then the other into the small trash can on top of the other bits of unwanted paper. *I'll feel better, I'll feel better about myself if I don't give in.* "My therapist told me that."

She moved around the room, straightening items, adjusting books on their shelves, pulling the curtains open to catch the late afternoon sun, her eyes drifting back again and again to the trash can where, in her mind's eye, she saw the torn halves of his card lying rejected. She walked back to her writing table and touched the tulip petals while she looked down at the pieces of the card on top of the trash.

"But I don't feel better," she whispered to herself. She reached into the can and pulled out the two pieces. Holding them, she tapped one half against the other, "It might be something important. More important than all his other cards." She sat down on the small chair in front of the table.

Remy laid the halves in the middle of her writing table and

slowly pushed them toward each other, trying to match the tear perfectly. She sat very still, scarcely breathing, looking down at it for a long time before she carefully pulled each half of the card out of the envelope and placed it face down, first one piece and then the other.

She took out the roll of tape that had migrated to the back of the small drawer, behind the stack of cards from Fong. After carefully repairing the back of the card, she closed her eyes and let her fingers rest on it, as though, if she concentrated hard enough, she might feel its message.

"Read it. It's just words on a piece of paper. Nothing more." She took a deep breath and turned the card over.

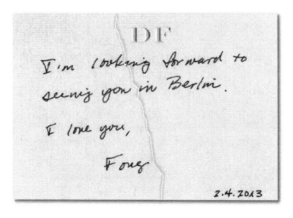

She pressed her fingertips against her eyelids to keep from crying. "*Love?* Goddammit, Fong. Why did you write that? It isn't fair. Damn you, Fong. Damn you!"

Preparing For Berlin

Onboard *The Aquamarine*

It was their annual anniversary cruise. Lee lay sleepily on the lounge chair on the upper deck of *The Aquamarine,* her book face-down on her stomach, "This is the perfect way to relax before you leave for your trip to Berlin. Are you ready for your course, Daniel?"

Distracted, he looked at her, his face blank, "Mmmm, what did you say?"

She stretched an arm out from under the warm throw and stroked his hair, "A senior moment so early in your life?" she teased.

"Obviously. I'm sorry, what did you ask me?"

"Your course, are you prepared?"

He looked at her with a grin, "Am I prepared, you ask? When am I not prepared?" They both chuckled.

Lee smiled at the small arrangement of flowers mixed with aromatic herbs on the table between them. "This crew always makes us feel special. Year after year." She examined the bouquet, "All my favorites."

When she looked up, Sasha was coming toward them, a bottle of champagne and two glasses in his hands.

"You two look so relaxed up here," he said. "But are you sure it isn't too chilly for you?"

"Lee loves the fresh air."

"It's a tradition. You know, we always sit up here. And there are these wonderful warm throws the crew gave us."

"Well, according to my calendar," he held up the bottle with a wink, "today's your anniversary. I brought you a little gift." Sasha popped the cork with a big smile and poured. "I wanted to wish my two dear friends a very happy anniversary." He gave Lee a kiss on both cheeks.

"Dear Sasha, you're so sweet."

Sasha squeezed Fong's shoulder before heading back to the

bar.

Fong lifted his glass to Lee, "Happy twenty-fourth, my darling." She touched the rim of her glass to his. He reached over and took Lee's hand, holding it tightly. They looked at each other happily, took a first appreciative sip and sat, comfortably silent, holding hands, watching the scenery go by.

Lee turned her head toward Fong and looked into his eyes, "What a life we have."

He smiled at her, "Mmmm, that we do. That we do."

One evening, later that week, they sat on their usual stools at the bar. Sasha set their drinks in front of them, and after looking around to check on his customers, he paused to chat.

"Thank you, Sasha," said Lee, following the first sip of her Grievous Angel with a sigh of pleasure. "Daniel mentioned that you put in Pinela vines this year. How are they doing? I'm looking forward to trying some white wine from your vineyard."

He nodded, "I spoke to the viticulturist this morning, and he said they are flourishing." He glanced over at Fong, who was staring off into space, "Fong, are you okay?"

He shook his head, "What – oh, yes. Thanks, Sasha." He took a sip of scotch. "Mmmm. My favorite."

"You seem a bit preoccupied."

Lee leaned against Fong, and he reached up and stroked her hair, absently twisting a lock around his finger and giving it a little tug. "He's been thinking all week about the course he's teaching in Berlin in a couple of weeks. Daniel's always looking for ways to tailor his material for his audience."

Fong cleared his throat, "Lee knows me too well." He ran his hand along the length of her hair again.

§

Ostia, Italy

Lee slid her arm through his as they walked out of their house to his car, which stood ready with the top down. He laid his suit bag neatly in the trunk, and she handed him his tote which he slung into the passenger seat.

"I'm glad Remy is attending your course. While you're there, please make some time to have dinner and find out what's going on with her. We haven't seen her since the solstice party. Whenever I talk to her on the phone, I feel like there's something wrong, but I can't put my finger on it. Get her to tell you about it. Oh, you know, Daniel, I wonder if it has something to do with renewing her contract in Florence. She's coming up on that deadline. I hope she decides to stay."

"I'll talk to her. Your spidey sense usually isn't wrong."

"Right. Just please get her to talk to you."

Fong hugged her.

"I'll miss you, Daniel."

He gave her a kiss, quick and hard.

"Are you sure you want to make this long, two-day drive? Why not fly from Rome? You'll be on the road almost as long as you'll be in Berlin."

Fong laughed at her gently, at the conversation they had every time he drove off for an extended trip. "Lee, you like being at the destination, and I like the process of getting there. I like to drive. By the time I get to Berlin, I'll have taught my course three times over in my mind and will have solved all the world's problems." He checked to make sure the top was securely fastened down under its leather cover. "You know, world peace, global warming, or more likely, whether or not the window frames need to be resealed this year," he chuckled.

"Drive safely, my darling."

He brushed his lips against hers before he climbed into the car.

As he drove out of Ostia, his thoughts turned to Remy.

What's going on with Remy — it's me — that's what. But she's our friend, and Lee worries about her. Lee keeps pushing me toward her, and I can't tell her why she shouldn't. Whatever it was that drew us together in Slovenia, I've tried so hard, and I haven't been able to put it behind me. I thought it was working last fall, but it isn't.

Remy, when I brought you those flowers from Lee, I thought, finally, I can do this, we can do this, we can move on as friends. Then, when you came to the solstice party – being in the same house with you – I desperately wanted you.

"Fuck," he yelled against the wind, "*fuck!*" He slammed his hand down against the steering wheel. "Fuck!" He looked ahead and put his foot on the accelerator, and then he pushed down harder and carelessly passed four cars, one after another.

§

Florence, Italy

Remy walked over to her writing table to get her passport, just in case she needed it in Berlin, but instead, she opened the drawer with Fong's cards in it and picked them up and held them, flipping through the stack with her thumb like a dealer with a deck of cards.

She paused, pulled the card he'd written after the solstice from its envelope. "I thought this one was so kind," Remy murmured as she recalled how touched she had been to get that first note on the same day she received the New Year's card signed by both him and Lee. She slid it back into the envelope.

She pulled them out, one at a time – his cards that had begun to come every week – reading them and carefully slipping them back into their envelopes. She looked at the latest, and not for the first time, noticed that the date was the day after his and Lee's anniversary, "Oh, Fong."

I love you, too, and I can't even tell you that. My therapist said that I needed to stop reading your cards. That I should throw all these away. That I shouldn't open any new ones. But I can't do that. I get the same butterflies in my stomach every time a new one arrives. Each one makes me miss you. You're not mine, Fong. But I still want you.

Part Twelve

Summer 2013

The Other Woman

Rome, Italy

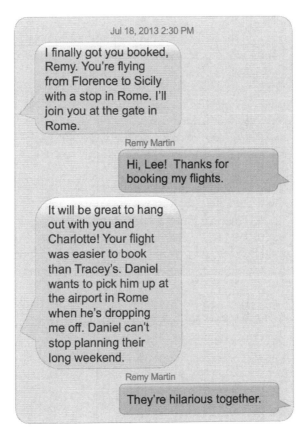

Jul 18, 2013 2:30 PM

I finally got you booked, Remy. You're flying from Florence to Sicily with a stop in Rome. I'll join you at the gate in Rome.

Remy Martin

Hi, Lee! Thanks for booking my flights.

It will be great to hang out with you and Charlotte! Your flight was easier to book than Tracey's. Daniel wants to pick him up at the airport in Rome when he's dropping me off. Daniel can't stop planning their long weekend.

Remy Martin

They're hilarious together.

Remy's stomach churned as she looked around for the nearest trash can, feeling as though she might throw up at any minute. She dreaded seeing Lee after all those months since Berlin, months filled with loneliness and longing for Fong, even as she tried to move on. She sat, holding a coffee, its warmth comforting her despite her churning stomach.

She saw Lee approach. "Yoo-hoo," Lee waved.

Remy set down her cup and stood, and Lee threw her arms around her in an affectionate hug. Remy returned it hesitantly.

"I've missed you, Remy. It's been too long."

"I've missed you too."

Remy took Lee's bag and set it next to her own. They dropped down onto the ugly plastic airport chairs, Lee talking a mile a minute. Ashamed of having fallen in love with her friend's husband and wanting him so badly, Remy struggled to keep up her end of the conversation.

Lee handed her one of the bottles of water she'd bought after going through security. She laughed as Remy reached into her bag, took out a bottle and handed it to Lee, "I got you one too."

Lee took a sip of her water and heaved a long sigh, "Whew. The logistics for this trip were so complicated – and all to finally get a long weekend together."

"That was a big sigh. Sounds like you need something stronger than water."

"Oh, no, I'm saving myself for the good Sicilian wine that Charlotte promised us," Lee said. "I've been looking forward to finally spending time with you and Charlotte. It's been too long since the solstice party." Lee reached over and rubbed Remy's shoulder.

"Wherever does the time go?" Remy felt the tension in her shoulders lessen slightly as they continued to make small talk. "Did you have a good drive from Ostia to the airport?"

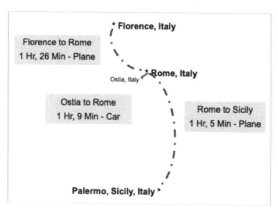

"We did. Much better than Tracey's trip. Apparently, he got tied up going through security in Sicily and thought he was going to miss his flight. Can you believe they flagged him and made him go through an extra search? He claims they interrogated him," said Lee, her eyes twinkling. "I'm sure whatever happened will make its way into an Henri tale."

"I'm sure it will," Remy laughed.

Lee continued, "Tracey has no idea why he was searched. It was probably just a random choice. But he was hopping mad. I would have been even madder if he'd missed that flight after all the work it took me to orchestrate this trip."

"What did he and Fong finally decide to do?"

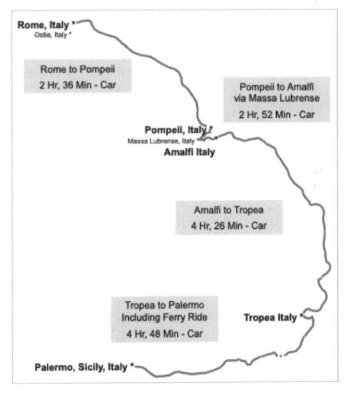

Rome, Italy *
Ostia, Italy *

Rome to Pompeii
2 Hr, 36 Min - Car

Pompeii to Amalfi
via Massa Lubrense
2 Hr, 52 Min - Car

Pompeii, Italy *
Massa Lubrense, Italy *
Amalfi Italy

Amalfi to Tropea
4 Hr, 26 Min - Car

Tropea to Palermo
Including Ferry Ride
4 Hr, 48 Min - Car

Tropea Italy *

Palermo, Sicily, Italy *

"They decided to take a leisurely drive from Rome to the tip of the boot. From there, they'll pick up a ferry to Sicily. Fong wants to take Tracey down the Amalfi coast in the Alfa – with the top down, of course." Lee reached into her purse and pulled out a piece of paper, "Here's the itinerary Daniel gave me. They'll spend the first night in Pompeii and then on to Amalfi." She glanced down at the itinerary. "They'll stay overnight in Tropea before driving on to Palermo. This trip," she shook her head with a giggle, "it's all part of their bromance."

Remy laughed, finally beginning to relax, "Yeah, Charlotte said Tracey is unbelievably excited about it."

"He and Fong drove off, singing at the top of their lungs. Ever since their trip to Budapest, whenever they're together, they put the top down on that car and sing their hearts out."

"What a pair they are," Remy said.

"How was your flight from Florence?"

"Uneventful. I'm looking forward to seeing how Charlotte's house has turned out. She says it's almost done, that it just needs final decorating touches before they can throw their housewarming party."

"And we get to be her assistants. How fun! I'm sure we'll have a lot of stories and good times."

"Lots of Sicilian food. Lots of wine." Remy told herself to relax and be in the moment.

§

Sicily, Italy

Remy hugged her friend, "Charlotte, this is beautiful – I can't figure out what still remains to be done."

"I would never have recognized it," said Lee as Charlotte turned to give her a hug as well.

Remy laughed, "Thanks for arranging the car service from the airport. But I have to tell you, when that car pulled up, we laughed so hard, remembering when Sal played chauffeur for the solstice party – do you know, Sal stayed in character and pretended he was a chauffeur during the entire drive from Milan to Florence and from there on to Ostia? Well, most of the time. Perhaps he's missed his calling and should become an actor."

"Or a chauffeur," said Charlotte. "Speaking of the solstice," she continued, "can you believe it's been that long since the three of us have seen one another? Just leave those bags right here for now. Let me show you around."

"This place is stunning. It's like something from a magazine," Lee said. "It's even better than I imagined from your descriptions and all those photos you took with your phone."

"And look at all the unique pieces you've collected – is that a Turkish rug in the living room? It looks great on these wonderful floors," Remy said.

"You know, we considered terracotta tiles, and we looked at marble. We felt the local-colored tiles were too busy for this space, and the marble was definitely too formal. We finally looked at terrazzo and fell in love with it."

"It's beautiful."

Charlotte continued, "It is. I'd never heard of it until our builder offered it as an alternative. He said we could buy it in large tiles or have it poured so it's practically seamless. At first, I was dubious about concrete floors, but all the little bits of marble give it such an interesting look. And the idea of no grout lines really attracted me."

"Cleaning grout is expensive," Lee added.

"And Remy – that rug – you were right it is Turkish – but we bought it in France."

"A French Turkish rug?" Remy laughed.

"We bought it on a driving trip through the south of France, in this quaint little town. We'd had lunch in a small café and then wandered down the street and discovered this Turkish rug shop. I tell you what, the guy who owned it was hot – and he's a widow – he'd be perfect for you, Remy.

Remy smiled, "What a lovely story and—"

"You're so his type. If you're ever in the south of France, you should stop there."

"Charlotte, the matchmaker," Lee teased.

"We'd only gone in out of curiosity, but not only were we charmed by him," Charlotte fanned her face with both hands and batted her eyes, "but his daughter was just so sweet. He was American, but he spoke very good French, and she spoke perfect English but with an interesting accent that I couldn't quite place. Anyway, she was adorable. She told us stories about the rugs that her father had told her, it was just so cute."

They inspected every detail of the house, from the master suite to the wine cellar, before finally ending up back in the kitchen. Charlotte poured glasses of cold, white Sicilian wine for Remy and Lee and a glass of sparkling water for herself, and they went out from the kitchen into the gardens.

Lee looked around, set her glass on the table and wandered a few steps away from the other women. "Oh, my gosh, Charlotte! This is exactly the space I designed for you. It looks spectacular now that it's had time to mature. That was a good call to plant as soon as the outside work on the house was finished and to use larger plants to start with." She allowed her fingers to stroke the leaves of the plants as she moved through the space. She plucked off a sprig of mint and crushed it gently with her fingers before taking a deep whiff. "Oh, my, this is even better than my garden." Then she went off again, a look of contentment on her face.

Charlotte sat down at the small, round table placed on pea gravel, surrounded by four wicker chairs. "She's in her element. Sunshine, herbs, flowers."

"And wine," called out Lee. "I can hear you. Yummy Sicilian wine."

"She certainly is." Remy sat next to Charlotte. "Lee knows exactly what makes her happy in life. I admire her for it."

"So, have you come to a decision about what you're going to do next? What will make you happy, Remy?"

"The department is pushing me for a decision. I love Italy, but I also love San Francisco – it's always been home. It's all so complicated." Remy paused. "I hate the thought of leaving the life I've built here – I've become so close to all you expats. But California, that's my place, with my aunt and uncle just across the bay. I'm leaning that way."

"Well, I'm selfish and wish you would stay here so I can spend time with you. I'll miss you." Charlotte leaned down and picked up the small tabby cat rubbing against her calf. "Little Phebe Cat, meet Remy."

"She's a cutie." Remy leaned over and rubbed her between the ears. "I didn't know you liked cats."

"I've adjusted. It's Tracey who's the cat lover. His Mrs. Whiskers died just before we got married, and he's been pining for another one. Little Phebe Cat just showed up one day and never left. Now, she's part of the family." The cat jumped off Charlotte's lap. "She would sleep with us if Tracey had his way, but I had to put my foot down." Charlotte slapped her hand on the table with a laugh, "Enough is enough. I'm the only woman allowed in his bed."

Charlotte and Remy watched as Lee walked to the table, a zucchini, cucumber, tomatoes, garlic, shallots and some herbs cradled in the front of her shirt that she'd twisted up to use as a basket. She stacked them on the table and reached up into the tree that was shading them to pick a few lemons. She laid them on the table beside the vegetables and went back into the garden.

"I wonder what she has in mind for dinner tonight?" Charlotte chuckled, looking at the pile.

Lee yelled over her shoulder from the arugula patch, "A salad. It's important to eat lots of greens and other vegetables. And locally made pasta. Lovely, fresh pasta with a homemade sauce." She continued picking arugula.

Remy picked up a large plant saucer and set it next to the vegetables. She began to arrange them artistically. "This semester, I'm focusing on painting arrangements of food. You know, *natura morta* – still life."

§

As they cleaned up after dinner on the next-to-last night of their visit, Lee said, "Charlotte, why don't you go and get your shower while Remy and I finish up here? Then we'll get our jammies on too. We can have a final girls' night before Remy leaves and Daniel and Tracey arrive tomorrow."

When they had all gathered back downstairs, Remy said, "I don't think I'm ever going to leave. I think I'll just move in. My room is so comfortable, and the ensuite is heavenly. I feel as if I'm at a spa."

"As much as I love being here with all the luxury you've built in," said Lee, "I miss my own home. My own bed. The sound of the sea. And my husband. I miss him most of all."

Charlotte watched as Remy picked up her empty wine glass and fiddled with it, tilting it one way and then the other, watching the dregs as they slipped around the bottom, pondering something before she set it on the coffee table and immediately picked it up again. Her eyes followed Remy as she stood and walked to the other end of the room to the dining table to refill her glass.

Remy raised the bottle, saw that it was empty and went to get another from the large kitchen area that ran across the entire end of the house. She stared out the window, feeling guilty for missing Lee's husband too. Then she stabbed the corkscrew into the bottle and pulled the cork with an angry twist of her arm.

Remy returned with the bottle and refilled Lee's glass before sitting down in one of the big, overstuffed chairs directly across from Lee who'd curled up in the middle of the sofa. She tipped the bottle toward Charlotte, who was sitting on another long sofa with her knees pulled up and her chin resting on them, "Shall I get you a glass?"

"No, I'm okay. My stomach has just been a little off this weekend."

"This room is so homey," said Lee, admiring the floor-to-ceiling fireplace, its opening filled with a huge arrangement of purple thistles and yellow wildflowers with two large candles positioned on each side.

"It's very peaceful, Charlotte," Remy said quietly.

They sat, sipping their drinks, relaxing, watching the flicker of the candle flames on the ceiling.

Lee gnawed on the side of her thumb, and in a low voice, she asked, "So, Charlotte, what made you decide to get divorced after

– how many years of marriage?"

"Twenty-one. Can you believe it? It wasn't an easy decision. I knew for a long time that my husband had been seeing someone. It didn't start until long after we'd been married – oh, probably sixteen or seventeen years. But then I wondered if there had been other affairs. He said there hadn't, and I believed him. Funny how those times are imprinted so firmly in my memory. I thought it would end. I thought it was a mid-life crisis, and he would get over it. I thought I could handle it, and it wouldn't hurt so much."

"How did you get through it?"

"Therapy. Lots of therapy."

Remy thought about the immensity of her feelings for Fong and the years of therapy she'd need. Years and years of therapy. She smiled bleakly to herself.

Charlotte continued, "We'd had a bumpy time the previous few years – before the affair. But we wanted it to work, and so we went together. The irony is that then he met *that woman*. I found out and confronted him. He said he would stop. And I think he did – for a while. But I sensed when they got back together. Then I continued the therapy on my own, trying to decide what to do. Should I try to salvage our marriage, or should I give up? I loved him – I still do. Just differently. Our marriage eventually just wore out, but we've remained friends. I've come to accept the other woman. They're still together." She grinned, "But I've never been able to call her his wife. She'll always be 'the other woman' to me, even though now I'm remarried too."

Lee took a few deep breaths, preparing herself for her next question. "Charlotte, how did you know for sure that your husband was having an affair? How did you know?"

"He became distant. He was there but not really there. It felt like he was off somewhere else. He wasn't interested in sex. And he wasn't interested in me either."

Charlotte looked over and saw Lee crying quietly, "Oh Lee, Lee – what's wrong?"

Remy took a sip from her glass, set it on the table beside her and leaned back in the chair, pulling her legs up underneath her with her hands gripped tightly together, afraid of what Lee might be about to say.

Lee gave a long, miserable sigh and dried her cheeks with her palms. She looked over at Charlotte, "I've lived through variations of everything you've just said, on and off, for a long time."

Confused, Charlotte asked, "What? I thought—"

"We did. We had a fairytale romance during the first part of our marriage."

"What about your relationship with the art dealer?" Charlotte asked.

"That was while we were dating, and it was very short-lived. He pressured me to keep it up, but I had fallen for Daniel. And once we said our vows, I never let anyone else into our marriage. We were inseparable. Daniel worked in Paris. I painted and taught. Even though our parents offered to help us out, we were proud. We wanted to do everything on our own. So, we didn't have a lot of money or anything, you know, a young couple just starting out in an expensive city. We had a tiny, one-bedroom apartment. We were lucky to have that and not a studio like many of our friends. But it was so good – until he started traveling."

Charlotte muttered, "Uh-oh."

"When he came back after his first long trip, I knew something was wrong. I asked him, and he told me. He called it an 'indiscretion'," she said bitterly. "He said he'd been lonely, that it had just been sex and a warm body and just one night. But he cried and was so sad that he'd broken our wedding vows. He promised it would never happen again. I couldn't share a bed with him, so I made him sleep on the couch. The next time didn't happen until months later. I confronted him again, and he cried again and promised he would stop. Then, once or twice a year, whenever he'd take a long trip, when he came back, I knew it had happened again. He never lied, but eventually, I stopped asking because I dreaded hearing the answer, and so we would sleep apart until I was ready to take him back. That's why I insisted on two bedrooms for us when we moved to Ostia. Every time he does it, it chips away a piece of my heart, and every time, it takes me longer and longer to get over it. I'm scared that someday, there won't be anything left."

Remy remembered sitting on the hillside in Slovenia, having the same conversation with Fong. She picked up her wine glass by the stem, turning it around and around, watching the wine swirl, burying her nose in it for a long sniff, hiding her face, before she took a sip.

"Then last fall, after Slovenia and his trip to Hong Kong and Singapore, he brought me pearls. I knew something was different, and out of the blue, without me asking, he promised that he had stopped. For a few months, our marriage returned to the way it had been before he started traveling. It was wonderful. The attention, the affection, the love, the passion, the sex," tears spilled over again, "the sex was better than ever. We were back, living our fairytale marriage."

Charlotte moved over to sit next to Lee, brushing her thick, auburn hair away from her face, "Are you crying tears of sadness then? Or happiness?"

Lee looked up at Charlotte in despair, "In January, it changed again, and something completely new started to happen."

Remy set her glass down on the table as she thought about the New Year's card from Fong and then all the others that had followed. She clenched her hands tightly, digging her nails into her palms.

"We're sitting together or lying in bed, and he's there, laughing, completely engaged in our conversation, and then he's gone – somewhere else in his head. Emptiness. Eventually, he returns. But all the time, he is still carrying on a conversation with me. He's there, but he's not there. It's happening more and more frequently."

Remy bit down on the inside of her cheek, almost hard enough to draw blood. She reached down and picked up her wine glass, cradling it against her chest.

"Do you think he's sleeping with someone else?" asked Charlotte.

"I don't know. Before, when he came home, I always knew when he had committed one of his indiscretions. But this is different. It just feels different. Before, *my* Daniel was always there. But now, he's there sometimes, and sometimes he's gone. And this year, on our anniversary cruise, even then, he was there sometimes and not others. Even Sasha noticed it."

Charlotte leaned forward, "Maybe he's sick? Are there financial problems?"

"No. If it's anything big, we always go to the doctor together. We've talked about health and money endlessly. We've always talked about those things. We're comfortable having those conversations."

Charlotte set her glass of water on the coffee table and took Lee's hands in hers, "I'm going to ask the hard question, Lee." She paused, "Do you think he's having an affair?"

Remy held her breath, not wanting to hear Lee's answer.

"I'm terrified to go there, to even think about it. I don't want to say it out loud. I'm afraid that will make it real. And that would be the end of my marriage. I couldn't stay with him if I knew he wanted someone else. I keep telling myself not to jump to conclusions. But this is so completely different from how it's been before. It *feels* different than all the other times. This time, I think he's fallen in love." Lee's face turned red, and she hesitated, and finally, she blurted out, "When we make love, there's this word he cries out. He doesn't do that anymore, as though that part of the passion is gone."

Remy sat, unable to move. *Fong, you should just tell her. You should tell her that the woman sent you away, that she said that she loves you too much to break up your marriage.* In her head, she yelled it so loudly that she felt everyone in the room must have heard her. Remy looked around in shock to make sure it was only a thought.

"This affair," asked Charlotte, "do you think it's physical or emotional?" She saw the confusion on Lee's face. "Sometimes it can be both, but you can have one without the other."

"Really? Does it matter? Isn't an affair just an affair? When people sleep with the same person over and over outside their marriage? His indiscretions were with someone different every time. That's why I could get beyond them." Lee took a deep breath in through her nose and blew out through her mouth before shaking her head.

"One-night stands are one thing, but even in emotional

affairs, a person spends more time thinking about someone other than their partner. They may not be sleeping together, but frequently they share things with the other person that they won't share with their partner."

"Yeah, he might be having an emotional affair, but this isn't academia, Charlotte," she said bitterly. "I think he's sleeping with someone. I think he's fallen in love. He's only physically present with me sometimes. The last few months, since he returned from Berlin, he wanders around completely lost. He does come back, and he's warm and kind, putting his arms around me. We even have sex sometimes. But he doesn't want me as a lover, as his wife. I'm just the warm body now. It's as though he needs to be comforted for something, like he's lost his best friend. Then he walks out and sits on the beach, just staring at the sea."

"Do you think he broke it off and that's why he's so sad?" Charlotte asked.

Lee burst into tears. "Remy, was there anything out of the ordinary with him while you were in Berlin?"

Remy's stomach churned as she told Lee a partial truth. "No. We visited museums. We had dinner, and we talked a lot, like we always do. We talked about what a wonderful woman you are and how fortunate he is to have you." Remy went over and sat on the other side of Lee. She put her arms around her and held her, stroking her back gently. With her cheek against Lee's, she said hoarsely, "He loves you very much. It would make him sad to see you hurting like this." *And it makes me sad too. I've become the 'other woman'. I never ever wanted to be that. I've never wanted to be the one to cause a wife so much pain. What a mess we've made. I wish we'd never started this.*

"I miss Daniel. I miss who he was."

"I'm so sorry. It must hurt so much, Lee. I can't even imagine what you're going through." Remy held Lee tighter.

"Charlotte, you've been through this. What am I going to do?"

"I can only tell you what I would do if I were in your place. I would follow him out to the beach, sit down in front of him, take his hands and ask him what the *hell* is going on. I would tell him to talk, to tell you what is going on, to tell you the truth. Tell him that you can't solve anything if you don't talk to each other."

Late that evening, sitting on her bed in the dark, Remy pressed his number on her phone. She cupped her hand over her mouth as she rocked back and forth, waiting for him to answer. Finally, she heard, "Remy, why are you calling?"

"Fong," she said, her voice barely above a whisper, "Fong, Lee knows."

"About us?"

"Not about me, but she knows you're having an affair."

"What do you mean? We only slept together that one time – last year. What are you talking about?"

"Come on, Fong. She knows there's something wrong. She knows you've fallen in love with someone else."

"I love you, Remy. What about us?"

"There is no 'us'. There can never be an 'us'," she said with an edge of irritation in her voice. "We're both guilty, but Lee's your wife. Go back to the woman you married twenty-four years ago, Fong. She loves you."

"I love you, Remy."

"No, you can't. I won't allow it." Remy pressed the button, ending their conversation. *Goodbye, Fong. I love you, too.*

After a sleepless night, tossing and turning, thinking about Fong, thinking about Lee, Remy sat at the kitchen table with her hands curved around her coffee cup. She watched Charlotte take a sip of herbal tea. "I noticed you didn't drink caffeine or alcohol this weekend. And your tummy was upset last night. Are you—"

"I'm pregnant," Charlotte grinned.

Remy squealed and pulled Charlotte into a hug. "How far along?"

"Barely three months. I didn't want to say anything in front of Lee." She and Remy glanced out the window at Lee, sitting on the flat area up the hill with her legs crossed in a traditional yoga pose, her hands lying loosely, palms up, on her knees. "She and Fong want children so badly, and she's about the same age as me, so she still could have them. I didn't want to upset her on this visit and make her have to put on a brave face. I was going to announce it over the phone or something, when she'd have Fong around to support her. And after what she told us last night, I'm even more certain it was the right thing to do – best not to mention it to her yet."

Remy sat back down, "Yeah, that would be tough for her to hear right now. But Charlotte, I'm so excited for you!"

"I've had to stop drinking completely, and you know how I like wine when I'm with friends."

"Yes, you do enjoy it. And you're so funny when you've had a few," Remy chuckled. "Do you have any names picked out, yet?"

"We do. If it's a girl, we'll call her Sarah, after Tracey's twin sister. And if it's a boy, we'll call him Albert or Al, after my father." Charlotte laughed, "Because the other choices were Adelbert, my father's given name before he anglicized it. My cousin's also named after him. Or Oden, after my uncle. We didn't want to burden our child with either of those."

"It's always nice to carry on family names. But I didn't realize he had a twin sister. Where does she live?"

"He has no idea. They were abandoned at the age of four, and he and his sister were separated in the fostering process. All the records were lost in a fire, and he hasn't been able to locate her."

"How sad for him."

"Oh, Remy, he's even more excited about this child than I am. He loves kids. The way he talks about the children at Sarah's House, you can tell how much it matters to him."

"Sarah's House?"

"That's the foster home he established in Raleigh. They won't allow siblings to be adopted separately, no matter what."

"Oh, so the house is named after his sister, Sarah."

"Exactly. The way he cares about the wellbeing of the children there stems from being adopted himself. He knows every name and each one's background – it's as though they are family to him – he oversees every case and ensures they move on to the most suitable families for their needs and backgrounds. Even from here, he's constantly on the phone with the staff there. I can't wait to visit again when we go back there for the New Year's gala at the family's museum."

Remy grinned at Charlotte and looked her up and down, "But how did this happen?"

"The usual way," Charlotte chortled. "I thought I had gone through early menopause. So, we've never taken any precautions. Who gets pregnant at forty-nine years old, for heaven's sake? If it hadn't been for the morning sickness, I wouldn't have even gone to the doctor."

"Well, this will certainly change your lives."

Charlotte nodded seriously, "Diapers, midnight feedings, car seats—" Her face lit up with excitement, "Remy, I just had a brilliant idea. Let's see who wants to get together for a Christmas cruise to celebrate – it will be my last big trip for a while."

They Finally Talk

Ostia, Italy

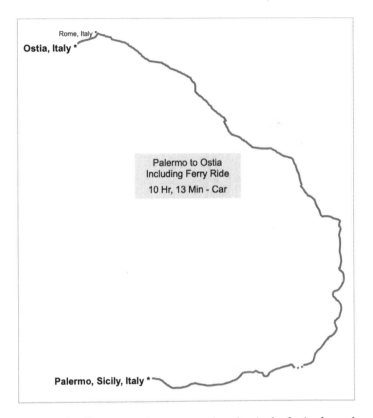

Rome, Italy *

Ostia, Italy *

Palermo to Ostia
Including Ferry Ride

10 Hr, 13 Min - Car

Palermo, Sicily, Italy *

After a light dinner on the terrace, they lay in bed, tired out by their long drive back from Sicily. Fong reached out and took Lee in his arms, pressing his lips to her neck, and began to caress her breasts. Lee lifted his hand, and turning it, she kissed his palm, "Not tonight, Daniel, I'm exhausted." She moved his hand to rest on her stomach, "I just need you to hold me. I want to be close to you."

Turning her, pulling her close, spooning against her back, he buried his face in her hair and wrapped his arms around her waist. She laid her hands over his. *Tomorrow, we'll talk. We'll really talk. I need the truth.*

After having lain awake for hours, Lee overslept the next morning. Bright sunshine woke her, and she turned to find that the other side of her bed was already empty. She stood up and pulled on a light summer robe before walking over to the double glass doors. On the beach below, she saw Fong seated in the sand, his knees bent up and his arms loosely clasped around them, leaning against the side of her meditation rock, staring at the waves, not moving.

Slowly, deliberately, reciting each step in her head, she went through her morning routine, not allowing herself to think about the conversation that they had to have.

Shower. Dry off. Hang up towel.

Put on robe.

Brush teeth for two minutes. Put brush back on charging stand.

Take moisturizer from drawer. Dot on face. Massage in with upward strokes for thirty seconds.

Brush hair, one hundred strokes; pull it up into a knot on head.

She walked into the closet.

Take yoga clothes from drawer and lay them on bed.

Pull on bottoms and then top.

Finally dressed, before she went downstairs, she walked over and looked out the doors again. Fong was still sitting there, staring, in the exact position he'd been in when she'd first looked for him.

Moving like an automaton, Lee went down into the kitchen and filled the kettle with fresh water, and while the water heated, she scooped loose herb leaves into two infusers and latched them before placing one in each mug. She poured boiling water into the cups. As she waited for the tea to steep, she stared out the kitchen window at her husband. *I wonder what he's thinking about.*

Barefoot, with a mug in each hand, she walked down to the beach, her emotions finally waking up, fear, anger, sadness roiling in her stomach, her heart aching, tears pricking the backs of her eyes. And in her head, Charlotte's voice saying over and over, "*Talk to him. Ask him. Explain to him that you can't solve anything if you don't talk to each other.*"

She stopped in front of him and held out a mug, "Careful, it's hot."

Fong, so lost in his thoughts that he hadn't seen her coming along the beach toward him, jumped at the sound of her voice. Lee looked at him as he took the cup with a strained smile, his eyes not quite meeting hers. She sat down in front of him in the sand and set her mug by her knee.

He looked down into the mug, blew across it and took a sip.

"Daniel, we need to talk."

"Talk? About what, my darling?"

"I would like you to tell me what's going on. What are you thinking about when you spend hours down here, looking at the sea? Where do you go?" She tapped two fingers in the center of her forehead, "In here."

He hesitated for a long time before answering, "I've been carrying this heavy burden around on my own, Lee. I've had no one I can talk to about it, not you, not Sasha, no one."

She leaned forward and put her hand under his chin, tipping his head up so he was forced to look at her. *What is he so afraid to tell me that he has that terrified look in his eyes?* His eyes slid away, and he stared out over her shoulder.

"Please. Please talk to me, Daniel. I want our marriage to work. I've loved you and stood by you for a quarter of a century. I want it to work, but it's not working right now."

He continued to look over her shoulder out into the distance before replying, "You asked where I go? I'm all over the place."

"What do you mean?"

"I think about you—"

"So, what do you think about me? Because it feels like you're not here." She picked up her tea, brushed the sand off the bottom of the mug and took a sip.

"I think about how much I've hurt you."

"How much you've hurt me? Shutting me out hurts too, Daniel." She imagined Charlotte whispering in her ear, *Get to the point, Lee.* She took a deep breath, "Something happened in January, and as your wife, Daniel, I have a right to know what it was."

She watched his stricken face as he stammered, trying to answer and not finding the words, "I – I – I—"

"When we're together, sitting and talking or lying in bed, you're there and then you aren't. It's like you just go away. It even happened on our anniversary cruise."

Fong took her tea, set it down next to his and took both her hands in his and looked at her with frightened eyes. Nausea pushed against the back of her throat, and she held her breath.

"Last fall I slept with someone."

She watched relief sweep over his face as he finally said the words. "But you said you were going to stop your *indiscretions.*" She spat the last word at him. "You promised, Daniel." Sadly, she repeated, "You brought me pearls, and you promised me."

"I've kept that promise. This was before. It's only been you since then."

She shook her head and snatched her hands back. "Then what's wrong? Things were wonderful last fall, better than they've been in a long time, but after the Christmas holidays, you changed. Are you thinking about her when you come out here for hours on end?"

"Yes," he whispered.

The single word that confirmed what she'd been afraid of for so long – *Now I know what it means in those silly books when women talk about their hearts breaking.* She took a deep breath, "Do you think about her a lot, more than about me? Do you think about her when we're together?"

"Yes," he whispered, "Yes, I do."

Lee looked up at the sky and watched a seagull swooping and diving as she took long, shaky breaths, thinking about what Charlotte had said. "You may not be sleeping with her, but your preoccupation with her is every bit as much a violation of our marriage vows, Daniel, as if you were sneaking off behind my back to sleep with her."

He heard the pain in her voice, and tears shimmered in his

eyes. "I'm sorry, Lee. I didn't want to hurt you."

"I thought the warm bodies in your bed were behind us – and now this?"

"I never meant to fall in love with someone else."

"Love?" she whispered. Then she stood up, throwing her mug into the sand, her palms pushing toward him, never touching, but pushing him away, nonetheless, before she finally yelled, "*Love?* Get the hell out of my house, Daniel." She pointed away, "Just get *out!*"

An Unfinished Card

Ostia, Italy

Seated at Fong's desk, Lee shoved the large pile of mail to one side to make room to write and opened the right-hand drawer for one of Daniel's cards to let him know her decision. She would have to send it to him through Sasha, she decided, since he was the only one who knew where Daniel was. A much-handled, wrinkled slip of paper, like those they'd used at the winter solstice party, lay on top of the cards. Picking it up, she saw Remy's name written in Daniel's bold script. "What is this?" She reached back into the drawer and picked up a partially finished card that lay on top of the stack.

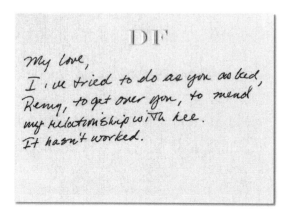

Shocked, Lee dropped the unfinished note on the desk in front of her. "It's Remy? You're in love with Remy?" She pressed her hands flat on the desk in front of her, trying to control their shaking. "Noooooo, not Remy!" she howled. "Not her!" She sat staring at the card in disbelief. "Remy?" she repeated over and over, "Remy? Remy? Why did I have to go into your desk and find this? Why did you leave this here, Daniel? Why didn't you just tell me it was her?" Teardrops streamed down her face and splashed down onto the card. Her nose ran, and her breath came in harsh

244

gasps as she stood up and shoved the desk chair away, hearing it crash into something behind her but not caring enough to look.

Scarcely able to see through her tears, she stumbled out onto the terrace and down the stairs into her garden. And she strode from one end of the patio to the other and back again, and again and again as tears continued to pour from her eyes. "You destroyed our marriage – for *her*? After she told us about all her rules, after she assured us that she *never* sleeps with her friends' husbands. What did she give you, Daniel, that I didn't?" Lee stretched her hands toward the sea, begging it for an answer. "Does she call you Daniel too?"

She cried hard, harder than she'd ever cried in her life. "When were you going to tell me it was Remy? Did you go to her in Florence? Is that where you've gone? Are you with her now, Daniel? Are you?"

Lee sat down in the dirt in the middle of her garden, in the bed she'd been preparing so lovingly just that morning. She rocked back and forth and then picked up a rock and threw it as hard as she could. "All the times I sent you to be with her because she was sad, because I felt like there was something wrong." Lee hit her forehead over and over with her palm. "How could I have been – so – stupid?"

The tears came faster still, and she pulled up the front of her shirt to wipe her nose. "Why did it have to be her, Daniel? Why?" she screamed. "Why did it have to be Remy? I loved her. Why did you have to fall in love with my friend? *Bastardo!*"

She wiped her running nose on her shirt again and buried her face in her palms. "Remy, how could you do that to me? How could you betray me?" she moaned. "He was *my* husband—" She beat her fist against her chest, "—my husband!" Looking around, frantic for something to destroy, to hurt the way she was hurting, she reached down and pulled up a flower from next to her and threw it onto the ground as hard as she could. "You betrayed our friendship!" She stood and pulled another and another, throwing each one as hard as she could against the ground, stomping on them and crushing them beneath her feet.

Needing to destroy more, to do more damage, to ruin the

peaceful refuge they had created together, she marched over to the garage and grabbed a shovel and pruning shears and rushed back to her garden. She hacked and slashed at the shrubs and flowers until there was nothing left but heaps of dirt and broken plants, and then she began to throw great shovels full of the debris into her beloved Monet pond.

"Why did you have to betray us? Why did you have to ruin us, Remy?" she screamed. "I could live with your pathetic indiscretions, Daniel, and your *warm bodies*. But now you've fallen in love – with my *friend*. You've destroyed everything we built together."

She looked around her garden with damp eyes, out of tears for the time being. She kicked a pile of dirt next to the pond, "Ruined. Like my marriage."

§

Gravel crunched under the tires, a week later, as Fong slowly braked in front of the house. He crossed the front patio, dreading the conversation he was about to have, when he'd tell Lee his decision. As he tried the handle and then unlocked the door and pushed it open, he felt a resistance. He looked down at the mail spread across the floor at his feet. Confused, he pushed the door closed with his foot and picked up the envelopes, and with them in his hands, he walked through the kitchen into his office. He pushed the desk drawer shut with his thigh and set down the mail.

A window stood open, and a light film of dust covered the desk and bookshelves. When he glanced out his office door into the living room, he saw dust motes dancing in the late afternoon sunlight and a trail of leaves, dirt and garden debris leading across the room to the open terrace door. Running out, he looked down onto the ruined garden below. It looked as though a terrible storm had blown through, uprooting and destroying everything. "My God! Lee, what's happened here?" he yelled as he turned to go back into the house. "Lee? Are you hurt? Where are you?"

The trail of debris led up the stairs. "Lee, where are you?" he called out. Dresser drawers stood ajar with clothing pulled half out, the closet door also hung open, clothes and hangers and jewelry were strewn about. "Lee, are you okay?"

There was just quiet – death-like quiet.

The bathroom sink was piled with Lee's beautiful auburn hair. He reached out and picked up a soft lock and stroked its length and wound the end around his finger. Pearls lay scattered across the counter and floor, the long strand hacked and broken. He recognized them immediately – the symbol of his promise that there would be no more indiscretions and no more betrayals. He bent and picked one up and held it cupped in his hand.

Back in the bedroom, Fong stood, looking at the havoc surrounding him before walking over to her bedside table where her simple gold band lay abandoned next to a card torn into four pieces. He picked them up, and in his handwriting, he saw Remy's name. "Oh, no, Lee, not like this – it wasn't supposed to end like this." He placed the pearl in the center of her ring and sat down on the floor, leaning against the side of her bed.

§

Out on the terrace in the dark, Fong sat listening to the sea with his face buried in his hands and the last of a glass of Scotch at his elbow. When his phone rang, he reached for it quickly, hoping it was Lee.

"Oh – Sasha. Have you heard from Lee? She's not answering my calls. I'm worried sick about her. Has she come to you?"

"No, but she's been in touch. She's safe, but she doesn't want you to know where she is. She just wants you to leave her alone."

"I hurt her, and I need to explain."

"She doesn't want to talk to you. She doesn't want excuses from you. She doesn't want anything from you, Fong – except to be left alone."

"Sasha, you said someone would get hurt. You were right. Everyone got hurt." Fong sat up straight and took a sip of his drink. "I need to talk to her."

"Remy was the last straw, Fong. You betrayed Lee, not with a stranger, but with her friend. What could you possibly say to her anyway?"

"That I'm sorry and I'm a shit?"

"And what good would it do to tell her that – except to make you feel better? I'm so disappointed in you, my friend. And yes, you are a shit."

Fong's voice cracked, "I have been for years. I just don't know what to do. I'm so lost, Sasha."

"Why don't you take some time off and come here? Come here to the vineyard. Come and spend some time away from it all."

Part Thirteen

September 2013

Conversation On The Hillside

Sicily, Italy

Seated on the shady flagstone patio they'd built on the hillside above their house, Charlotte and Tracey reminisced about the housewarming party they'd hosted the night before. The weather was hot and sultry, but at least, up there, they had the benefit of a light, intermittent breeze. He poured them each a glass of cold, sparkling water from the cooler he'd brought up the hill and took a long drink. Then he stretched out his legs and closed his eyes as though he were napping.

"I think our party was a great success," said Charlotte.

"I guess we can just be glad that most of the gifts were food and wine. We won't have to find a place to store more stuff," he teased.

Reaching out, she gave him a playful smack on the arm and then groaned, "Oh dear, that was a mistake. It's too warm to move even just one arm."

Tracey leaned over and lifted the lid to the bin Charlotte had stocked with "essentials" such as throws and extra pillows. He took out her much loved, pleated paper fan and began waving it lazily in front of her face.

"Oh, you're such a love."

"That I am," he replied with a grin. "I must admit," he continued, "it was a great idea to build this patio to match the one in the garden below. Not that you can see this from down there, mind you, but looking down, it's a pretty sight. It's like you've extended our garden all the way up the hillside." He looked admiringly at the gravel and flagstone path, bordered with lantana, caper bushes and other native shrubs, that wound its leisurely way up the hillside to the patio's low walls.

Charlotte recalled how she and Lee had come up with the idea while they were sitting there one afternoon on a blanket. They'd decided it wasn't the most comfortable spot if you were sitting on the ground, even though it was shady and the view was spectacular. So, they planned the transformation, which included the comfortable seating and little table. "Mmmm," she said, "Lee was right, it does take advantage of the location."

"Listen," he said, abruptly changing topics as he handed her the fan. I'm sorry for being so irritable this morning." He was feeling bad for snapping at her when she'd shown him a series of articles about the victims of the Parking Lot Strangler. He picked up the black horse-shaped knight from the outdoor chess set on the low table in front of them and twisted it between his fingers.

"After your reaction last year, I never should have brought up those Raleigh cases again."

"You should be able to talk to me about anything, my love. It's just—"

Her fan held to one side, Charlotte looked over at him, raising her eyebrows.

"It's just, I think one of those women was – may have been my mother."

"What?" She closed the fan and laid it on the table beside her, aligning it very precisely with the edge of the table. "Your birth mother? You knew who she was?"

He leaned his head back, his thumb pressing against the sharp ears on the head of the horse, and closed his eyes, not wanting to look at her while he spoke. "It's hard to talk about it. I keep going back over my memories, and I've been piecing it together. She had a lot of visitors. Male visitors. She told us they were 'friends'. They always came at night."

"Was she a sex worker?"

"I'm sure she was." He sighed, opened his eyes and turned toward his wife, "My mother was a prostitute. There, I can't believe I've finally said it out loud." He repeated slowly, "My mother was a prostitute." Shame and relief chased across his face.

"The older woman? Maggie?" Charlotte's eyes widened with interest.

Tracey nodded, "Maggie Jackson Wilson."

"Are you sure Maggie is your mother?"

"The pictures in the newspaper article look just like I remember my mother looking." He chose his words carefully as he decided what to tell Charlotte about his relationship with her.

"No wonder you lost your temper. You know, you could do a DNA test to find out if she's your mother. I've sent mine in, it's easy."

"I don't know what I want to do."

"If Maggie is your mother, according to the article Edgar wrote, her son, Mikey, could be your half-brother. You know you would share DNA. That would be the easy way to find out if she's your mother. Wouldn't it be exciting to know you have a family? Who knows, maybe you could even find your sister by sending off your DNA for analysis."

"Charlotte, I don't know what I want. I'm so angry with her for abandoning me and Sarah." He sat up and looked at her, his face turning red in embarrassment. "She had one friend, I think he was one of her regulars. He always wanted to read me a story. I would bring my book out, climb up onto his lap, and my mother would say, 'I'll go slip into something more comfortable while you read to him.' While she was gone, he would start to read. I would turn the pages for him, and he would slip his hand down my pajama bottoms and fondle me."

"You were molested? Oh, my love," and she reached over to take his hand.

"I suppressed those memories for a long time. Once I realized it, I was angry, very, very angry at her."

Charlotte went to Tracey and knelt on the cool flagstones beside him, and she kissed him before sitting back on her heels. "And I brought it all back up. I'm so sorry, Tracey."

"I'm still so *angry*, Charlotte."

"I think it would be good if you could try to forgive her – for the sake of our baby," she said, taking his hand and placing it on her belly. "I'll do whatever I can to help."

"I don't know, Charlotte. I just don't know if I want to go there."

Sensing he didn't want to talk anymore, Charlotte decided to let him take the lead as to when to bring it up again. She gave a little yawn, "I think I just need to close my eyes and take a little nap, my love." She pulled her feet up onto the sofa and lay down with her head in Tracey's lap. He put his hand on her hair and stroked it gently. "Mmmm, that feels good. You can do that forever."

Tracey looked at Mount Etna in the distance and then back down at his wife, her breathing slow and soft. He continued to run his hand over her hair, *Red hair. What is it about red-haired women?* He recalled the night in Rotterdam when he'd thought, ever so briefly, about covering her mouth with his hand and putting the other hand around her neck, about hearing her moan like the other women he'd strangled, their soft breathing turning to harsh panting, about feeling the life drain from her. But then, they'd kissed passionately, and the moment had passed. *Why do I do it? Why do I like it so much?*

Part Fourteen

September 2013

Frannie Snoops Again

Florence, Italy

Milan, Italy

Bologna, Italy

Milan to Florence
2 Hr, 24 Min - Train

Florence, Italy

Slightly breathless from her climb to the fourth floor, Frannie turned the key in the door to Remy's apartment, wondering how her cousin made that climb every day.

As she tossed her bag and sketchbook onto the sofa, her stomach gave a loud growl. She glanced at her watch. It was still an hour before Remy would get home from her class and they would begin to prepare dinner. Wandering into the kitchen, she rifled through the cabinets and then the refrigerator, looking for something to munch on, but there was nothing that caught her fancy. She saw the bowl of small, red apples on the counter, grabbed one, and after polishing it on a towel that hung by the sink, she took a satisfying bite.

She wandered around the living room, absently munching away, pausing to look out the window. The monthly get-togethers with her cousin – when they caught up on what was happening in each other's lives – reminded Frannie of home in the best way possible. She knew she would miss her terribly once Remy moved back to San Francisco in December, but it was only September, and she refused to think about it yet. Frannie looked down at the street and admired a fit, male student with a backpack cycling past, and at a group of three young women walking by, chattering among themselves.

After she'd finished her apple, she threw the core away in the kitchen and went into Remy's bedroom. She opened the wardrobe and slid the hangers along the rod slowly, looking at the neat row of slacks and skirts and dresses, thinking how stylish her cousin was – for a woman of her age, of course. She took out a dress and held it against her, turning this way and that before the mirror. "No, not me. So not me." She threw it on the bed and took out another dress, and then another, shaking her head each time. Finally, she posed in front of the mirror, admiring her cute little top and skinny black jeans with her favorite, very comfortable black heels. *Oh, I am quite fashionable these days. I learned so much about style from Lydia.* "I miss her," she murmured sadly, tears filling her eyes. She sat down on the bed amidst Remy's dresses and cried for her friend and for her loss.

Frannie remembered sadly all the fun she and Lydia had had, working together at the Pomegranate, the cool and the cranky customers, and how much Lydia had taught her. She thought about all the things they had planned but would now never do together. How dull her assistant job at Gia's architectural firm seemed in comparison, but at least that job had allowed her to stay on in Milan. And she cried a little more before wiping her eyes and standing up.

With a final sniffle, she glanced at the things she'd tossed onto the bed, hung them back in the wardrobe haphazardly and went back into the living room to the corner formed by two windows, where Remy had set up her office space. She took a few books off the shelf and flipped through them and then stuck them back.

Frannie picked up her sketchbook and bag, and deciding to get a little more work done on her latest Lady Scarlett comic, she sat down at Remy's writing table. She opened the sketchbook and then dug in her bag. "Shit. Where's my pencil?" She pulled out the center drawer to the small table and scrabbled through it, looking for a suitable drawing pencil. A rock, a seashell, lots of random stuff but no pencils. Frannie picked up the seashell and looked at it curiously before dropping it back where she'd found it. She moved on to the right-hand drawer. There she discovered a compartment with a trove of drawing pencils. She ran her fingers through them, searching for one with the right hardness. Finally, with the one she needed in hand, she started to close the drawer when a pile of cream-colored envelopes, shoved to the back, caught her eye. "Love letters, cuz?" She pulled the drawer back open and removed the stack.

As she sat back in the chair with the envelopes in her hand, she saw that they were all addressed to her cousin, all in the same bold handwriting and judging by the postmarks, all in date order with the most recent one on top. "Hmmm. Remy, what are you up to? Why do you hang onto envelopes—" she flipped through them. "Same handwriting, same person." Turning the top one over, she recognized the address as the Fongs'. *Strange. That's not Lee's writing. Hers is much more delicate. And she usually calls or emails or texts.* She set the cards on the writing table and looked at them for a second, tapping her bright red fingernail on the stack, staring out the window at the building across the street.

Frannie looked at them a moment longer, and then with a glance at her watch, she decided. "Heck, why not." She picked up the most recent one, looking curiously at the torn envelope that had been so carefully mended with tape, and pulled out the card.

I'm looking forward to seeing you in Berlin.

I love you,

Fong

"What the hell?" Shocked, her hand jerked, knocking the stack of cards off the table. Looking down at the envelopes scattered across the floor, she muttered, "Oh, crap." She picked them up, using the postmarks to put them back in their original order. Then she opened them one by one, and with each card she read, she grew angrier. *How could you do this, Remy? To Lee? She's your friend. Is this why she left?*

Remy walked in and saw Frannie sitting at her writing table. She tapped her on the shoulder and signed, "You're here early. I'll only take a few minutes to freshen up before I start dinner." Then she noticed the cards and envelopes scattered across the table. "Are those mine? What are you doing with them?"

Frannie looked at her stonily, "How could you sleep with him?" She pointed to the cards in front of her. She picked up one and shook it at Remy, "Lee was our friend. She was my friend. Did she leave because of *you*?"

"What were you doing, going through my things?"

"Well, if you didn't keep secret cards in the drawer with your pencils, it wouldn't be a problem."

"How dare you snoop through my things! You had no right—" Remy snatched the cards and envelopes off the writing table and the card from her cousin's hand and stormed into the bedroom. Yanking open the drawer in her nightstand, she threw them inside, slammed it shut and returned to the living room.

Appalled, Frannie framed each word slowly and carefully, "How could you sleep with him?" She shook her head, "What happened to your I-don't-sleep-with-friends'-husbands rule? I'm so humiliated. How can I face any of our friends again? Just knowing what you've done is too embarrassing. How could you?" Her eyes and lips scrunched into a peevish scowl.

Remy spoke, her hands moving emphatically, "You're assuming I slept with him. This isn't what you think it is anyway."

"I can't believe he wrote that – '*I love you, Fong*' – that's more than just a friend," Frannie spat at her. "How could you?" She raised her hands to dramatize her question.

Furious, Remy signed, "I don't need to justify what I do to you."

"Do you love him?"

"It's none of your business," she said angrily, and turned away, walking over to the balcony doors, breathing hard, her heart pounding in shame and anger.

Frannie stood up, stomped over and poked her in the shoulder to get her attention, "Do you love him?" she snapped loudly, her hands flying in accompaniment. With a cocky waggle of her head, she said, "I *knew* at some point you'd break your rules."

Remy slapped her across the face. "I've had enough of you. And I've had enough of your eternal snooping." She jabbed her finger toward Frannie, "Don't judge what you don't understand."

Frannie grabbed her sketchbook and bag and reached for the door handle. Then she turned back to Remy, "What I don't understand? There's nothing to explain about sleeping with your friend's husband. I'm so embarrassed by you. I never want to see you again. I'm glad you're moving back to the States." She wrenched the door open and walked out, slamming it hard behind her.

"Dammit, Fong, why do I still love you?" Remy yelled, "I wish we'd never done it." Picking up a glossy magazine, she heaved it across the room.

Part Fifteen

Early December 2013

Tracey Visits Fong

Slovenia

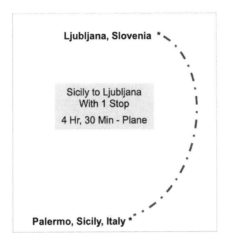

Ljubljana, Slovenia *

Sicily to Ljubljana
With 1 Stop

4 Hr, 30 Min - Plane

Palermo, Sicily, Italy *

As they walked through the vineyard with their hands in their pockets for warmth, the sun had just begun to peek over the horizon, and its light sparkled on the bare, frost-covered vines stretching out into the distance.

Tracey inhaled the crisp, cold air and shivered. He looked over at Fong. "It's too bad that Charlotte and Remy and I are the only ones who were able to take the Christmas cruise. Charlotte was so excited about getting everyone together for one last trip before the baby arrives."

"So, Frannie and Remy still aren't speaking?"

"No, not even Charlotte knows what happened between them. You know, Fong, our boat is fully booked, but what do you think about joining us in Budapest for a few days to say goodbye to Remy before she leaves for San Francisco? We've done the pre-cruise add-on, so Charlotte can visit with her relatives, and Remy said she wants to use the time to wander around and take some photos."

Fong pulled his driving cap down more firmly on his head as

he said, "There's so much to do here. I don't think I can get away on such short notice." *And Remy's made it clear that she doesn't want anything to do with me. I don't think I would be comfortable barging in to say goodbye after all this time.*

"That's a shame. Think about it." From the other side of the row, Tracey glanced at Fong, "You've really settled in here."

"I have. I didn't think I would ever be happy again. But now, every morning, I walk through the vineyard to make sure everything's in order. The solitude and the routine have helped me finally find peace with myself and my life."

"What about Ostia? Will you go back there?"

"No. Lee loved living there, it was her house. I liked being near the sea, but that place had too many memories for me. When she sent instructions, I put it on the market immediately. I received the final divorce papers about the same time. When it rains, it pours."

"Where is Lee? Charlotte said her number has changed, and her emails all come back undeliverable."

"All our communications are through her lawyer. I don't know where she is. Only Sasha does. He'll only tell me that she's safe and content. That's all I need to know."

"Has it been long enough that I can ask what happened?"

Fong stopped and looked at Tracey, sadness lurking behind his eyes, as he tried to decide what to tell. "In short, I met another woman. I slept with her, and then I fell in love. Lee found out. She was devastated. I didn't handle that situation well."

"We all make mistakes."

Fong looked at him gratefully.

"You know, Charlotte had that happen to her. It's never a good thing. When she told me the story, I promised her that I would never stray. It wouldn't be fair to put her through that again."

"I thought the same thing about Lee. I never imagined getting old without her."

"And now?"

"Working here, I'm gradually putting the pieces of my life back together. It's been nice not to travel, to spend time with Sasha when he's home. He's been such a good friend over the years. I was there for him in Tokyo when his partner died a few years ago, and now he's here for me."

"What about the woman you fell in love with?"

"I haven't let myself think about her yet."

Part Sixteen

Mid-December 2013

Our Killer Was Here

Budapest, Hungary

After exploring the Christmas market, Tibor and Emily wandered through the tiny, winding streets leading away from the square. Suddenly, he stopped and took her hand, "Would you have dinner with me, Emily?"

She smiled and leaned toward him to give him a kiss on the cheek, but he turned his head, and it landed on his lips instead. "Oooh, that was nice," he said and kissed her again.

"I'd like to go to dinner with you, but it's too early, isn't it?"

"We can have a drink first and talk."

Emily nodded, "Let's go somewhere fun."

Tibor led her down the street to Erzsébet tér. He took Emily's hand in his as they approached the stairs leading down to the yellow line of the Budapest Metro. "This is the oldest subway line on the European continent," he said. "Everybody should ride it for at least a stop or two. The stations are beautiful. Each one has the feel of old Budapest."

Standing in the crowded car that swayed with the movement of the train, they held onto the upright metal poles with one hand, and Emily held tightly to her cross-body purse with the other. Tibor kept a hand on her shoulder to help her balance.

"How do you say the name of that square we were just at?" she asked.

Tibor said, pronouncing it very slowly the first time, "*AIR-zhe-bait tare.*" And then he said it again more quickly, "*Erzsébet tér.* In Hungarian, the stress is always on the first syllable."

Emily sighed, "I'll never get used to this language."

The train lurched, and Tibor's hand tightened on Emily's shoulder to steady her. "Well, it is one of the most difficult ones in the world. This is our stop."

They left the train and were carried along toward the exit by the crowd. They walked, holding hands so they wouldn't get separated. She looked around, trying to take it all in. The bright, white subway tiles, trimmed with maroon, an ornate sign with the station name. "Look, I can pronounce that one – Opera."

At the top of the stairs, Tibor pulled Emily to the side, out of the stream of exiting and entering passengers. He pointed across the street at the impressive neo-Renaissance building, "This is the Hungarian State Opera House."

"Wow. I saw some pictures of it in my guidebook. It is absolutely breathtaking, Tibor."

"It's too bad that you won't be here longer, or we could get tickets to a performance. As a proud, music-loving Hungarian, I will tell you that it's one of the best in the world for its acoustics. At least we can enjoy the outside. We'll walk by it on the way back to your hotel this evening, and you can enjoy seeing it all lit up after dark."

They strolled along Andrássy street toward Liszt Ferenc tér, Emily constantly slowing down to admire the nineteenth-century buildings. "This reminds me of Les Champs-Élysées in Paris or the Kurfürstendamm in Berlin," she said.

"It does," replied Tibor.

"Whoa, this place is hopping," said Emily as they turned into the square named for Franz Liszt, the famous Hungarian composer. It was surrounded by trees wrapped in tiny white lights with green hedges delineating the outdoor eating areas for each café. "It's a popular place with young people." As they walked by the Franz Liszt statue, Tibor reached out and rubbed his knee.

"For good luck?" asked Emily.

"No, I have a certain fondness for him." She raised her eyebrows in a question, and he continued, "He was a jack of all trades in the music world. But most definitely not a 'master of none'. He was a virtuoso pianist and possibly the first musician celebrity. Apparently, he was a real heartthrob. I wish I had his breadth of experience in my field. I suppose that's the attraction."

"So, this," she gestured, "is not like that horse?" She laughed as she recalled all the people she'd seen earlier in the castle district, climbing up the statue to rub its balls for good luck. "I can't believe they did that."

"I confess, I did that any number of times when I was young, and I never got my wish or any particular good luck that I could associate with the act." Tibor put his hand on her shoulder to guide her to their left. "Let's get a glass of wine here, and we can decide where we want to have dinner." He left his hand resting on her shoulder until he reached over to pull out a chair for her. "I like this café because it's close to the music academy, so if we're lucky, we'll be able to hear the students practicing."

Seated at a table under a large, bare tree, they sipped their wine, a lovely red from Villány in southern Hungary, a Blauer Portugieser. "You want to know a bit of the history of Hungarian wine?" he asked. When Emily nodded, he went on to tell her that it had formerly been called a Kékoportó, because it was from the blue *portugieser* grape. "Then, a few years ago, when Hungary became a member of the European Union, they had to remove the oporto part of the name, because the name of the country takes precedence over the name of the grape. In this instance, the sticking point was the implied connection to Portugal's fortified wines known as 'port'. So, no more *oporto* here in Hungary," he sighed melodramatically.

"Ah, like sparkling wine can only be called champagne if it comes from the Champagne region of France," she said.

"Precisely."

"It's very nice, regardless of what you call it."

Suddenly, pouring from the academy windows was the sound of students practicing Liszt's *Mephisto Waltz*. They sat, relaxed, listening to the music and talking about the international security conference that had just concluded. He asked, "How long have you been coming to these conferences?"

"Six years."

He closed his fingers around hers, "I have to admit that you caught my eye that year in Paris. I was so impressed by you that it took me a long time to get up the courage to even talk to you outside of the business sessions."

"I can remember looking at you too. I thought you were really attractive, but I was so busy building *my* company that I didn't have time to think about anything that wasn't exclusively business-related. After years of lusting after each other," she said with a grin, "what finally made you decide to ask me out?"

"I'm on my home turf, here in Budapest, and I figured you wouldn't be able to resist a personal tour," he grinned at her, "by a devastatingly handsome Hungarian." He tightened his fingers around hers.

She squeezed his fingers back, and then, her eyes sparkling, Emily said, "Tibor, they've asked me to present at next year's conference."

"How exciting for you. You should do it. You have an excellent reputation. What security issues would you talk about?"

"I think I'd discuss real examples of security problems we've uncovered and how the solutions have saved these riverboat companies from lawsuits or bad press."

"That sounds fascinating."

They continued chatting about ideas for her presentation and the conference and their experiences in law enforcement and security until the lights on the lamp posts flickered on.

Tibor noticed that her attention had drifted. "What are you thinking about, Emily?"

She looked at him and gave a big grin, "I got a call this afternoon just before the conference ended. I finally landed a contract with a riverboat company that I've been pursuing for years."

"Wow. Wow. Wow!"

"Spectrum River Cruise Line has told me, 'No thank you,' so many times I've lost count. I was about ready to give up." She reached out and put her hand on his. "Tibor, they are a premier line and only offer small, exclusive cruises. This is such a big deal for Haypress."

He turned his hand palm up and put his other hand over hers, giving it a gentle squeeze. "Now, that's cause for celebration. Let me take you to a very special restaurant, Barack & Szilva Étterem." She nodded, and he pulled out his phone, and after a rapid-fire conversation in Hungarian, he turned and smiled at her, "We're all set. The owners are my good friends. They'll have a table ready for us in thirty minutes. It's just a few minutes' walk from here," he lifted his glass to her, "so we can take our time."

The owners, György and Agnes, greeted them warmly and seated them at an outdoor table, its umbrella wound through with small lights. A heater set next to them made the space comfortable, and over the backs of their chairs were warm blankets for later in the evening if they became a little chilly. After a quick consultation with György, Tibor asked if she'd mind if they let the owner choose for them. "The food here is so good. Since we are celebrating, he recommends a full meal, starting with appetizers all the way through to dessert. They will pair wines with each course to give you the best possible Hungarian dining experience."

Agnes came out a little while later and handed a handwritten paper to Emily. "Here is what we'll be serving you tonight. We thought you might like this as a memento of your evening."

> Sautéed Foie Gras on lamb lettuce with grapes, toasted hazelnuts and Tokaj wine vinaigrette
>
> Sauska Sárgamuskotály Tokaj
>
> Goulash soup
>
> Paprika veal medallions with gnocchi, wild mushrooms and a dill-paprika sauce
>
> St· Andrea Pinot Noir Eger
>
> Apple Crêpe and Fried Apple Ring with vanilla ice-cream and Calvados sauce
>
> Babits Furmint Tokaj
>
> Mineral water and coffee

What felt to Emily like moments later but was actually several hours, they had worked their way through everything but dessert, and Tibor said, "So let me tell you about this interesting, unsolved case I heard about recently."

The waiter set the dessert between them and placed a fork in front of each of them. Even though Emily had said she was too full, the waiter knew she might well change her mind when she saw it. Emily looked at the apple crêpe and fried apple ring with vanilla ice cream and calvados sauce. She whispered to Tibor, "Oh my, I don't want to hurt their feelings, but I was so hoping to have something with a goldenberry on top."

Tibor immediately called the waiter over, and after a brief discussion, he disappeared and came back with a small dish. With a smile, the waiter took a round, golden-yellow berry, its husk turned back artistically from the dish and placed it precisely on top of their dessert. Once he'd disappeared, she reached over, snatched the golden fruit and popped it into her mouth. "Mmmm." She closed her eyes, a look of pure pleasure crossing her face, "That's one of my favorite fruits."

Tibor smiled at Emily, amused by her enjoyment, "When I was in Vienna on business, one of my colleagues ordered a dessert, and when the waiter-in-training brought it out, it was topped by one of those berries with those papery husks, looking very artistic, like yours did. He asked the name of the fruit. The young man said he wasn't sure, but it was something that sounded like see-fah-liss. He offered to go and confirm it for us, and the minute he vanished into the back, we all burst out laughing. When he returned, he told us it is called physalis."

"Oh, my, the poor young man. I hope he didn't hear you laughing at him." She took a tiny bite of the crêpe with some ice cream. "Mmmm, delicious. Oh, my golden berry – I mean *physalis* – interrupted you," she said with a chuckle. "You didn't get a chance to tell me about that case you heard about."

"I hadn't thought much about it until this evening when you told me about the serial killer case you worked on for years. I've been doing some consulting for the Hungarian *rendőrség*," he glanced at her, and his lips curved up in a smile, "the Hungarian police. Earlier this week, I had lunch with a friend who works there. He told me that in May last year, they found a young woman dead in the forest up on Normafa. She had red hair and had been strangled. The murderer was left-handed and had a shoe size of forty-three."

"What's that in American sizes?"

"I think that's about a twelve. That's the same as your killer."

Emily's hand holding her fork froze, suspended in the air, "Whoa," she breathed. "The similarities are uncanny, Tibor."

"And the woman was missing an earring – from her right ear."

Her breath hissed in through her teeth. *I need to call the Raleigh police department about this so they can notify the Bureau.* She turned to look at him, a mixture of excitement and concern in her eyes, "Oh, shit, Tibor, it sounds like our killer was here."

Part Seventeen

Mid to Late December 2013

Remy Confesses

Budapest, Hungary

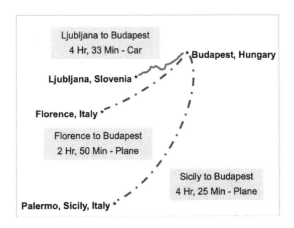

Ljubljana to Budapest
4 Hr, 33 Min - Car

Ljubljana, Slovenia *

* Budapest, Hungary

Florence, Italy *

Florence to Budapest
2 Hr, 50 Min - Plane

Sicily to Budapest
4 Hr, 25 Min - Plane

Palermo, Sicily, Italy *

Standing on the sidewalk next to their car, Charlotte kissed her elderly aunt Erzsébet and her two cousins Adelbert and Miklós goodbye. "*Viszlát!* I'm so glad we were able to see each other again today. It was great to have all of us here together in Budapest like when we were kids. Have a safe drive home."

Her aunt said, "Next time, you must come out to Lake Balaton and stay with us there."

Tracey shook hands with her cousins, "Thanks for a great afternoon." He patted his stomach, "At least I won't need to eat dinner before the concert tonight."

As Adelbert shook his hand, he said, "Too bad you're not staying longer. We could have gone hunting."

"I've never hunted, but I'm game to try," he said with a small chuckle.

As her relatives pulled away, Charlotte waved and shouted out, "*Viszontlátásra!*"

She turned to Tracey, "Game to try? *Really*? Game hunting? Anyhow, I'm so glad I got to go shopping with my aunt." Charlotte had enjoyed spending those few precious hours with her aging aunt. Shopping was something they'd always done together, whether for food or more frivolous things like Christmas gifts.

Tracey took her hand and turned toward the Vörösmarty tér Christmas market, "Your cousins certainly can eat and drink."

"But did you enjoy yourself, my love?"

"Absolutely. I look forward to visiting them someday at Lake Balaton."

They walked into the square, filled with stalls with their Christmas lights shining and holiday music playing. As they strolled around, hand-in-hand, Tracey was astounded at how similar this market felt to the Christmas markets his mom and dad had taken him to in Germany and Austria when he was young.

"So, tell me again how to say the name of this square, Charlotte."

"*Vörösmarty tér, Vörösmarty tér, Vörösmarty tér, Vörösmarty tér, Vörösmarty tér,*" she said very quickly and then began to laugh uncontrollably.

Tracey tried to say it one more time and failed. Charlotte laughed some more.

"Good lord, Hungarian is impossible to pronounce."

She continued to laugh, "So, how come I and millions of Hungarians can do it?"

Tracey shrugged and shook his head affectionately.

Suddenly, Charlotte pulled her hand away from Tracey's and entered a little stall to look at the Christmas ornaments. While she browsed, he wandered over to a booth selling hot mulled wine. He bought a glass of the spiced wine in a souvenir cup with a picture of the market printed in gold on the side. A deep sniff of the hot liquid brought back memories of the cups of similar wine his parents had bought at the Weihnachts markets when he was a teenager and how they'd always allowed him to have just one small taste. He sipped the hot wine, its steam rising into the freezing cold air, and lost himself for a moment in memories of those trips with his parents.

When Charlotte met back up with him, he offered her a drink, "No thanks. I hate the taste of it, and it's not good for Baby." She patted her very round belly and shook her head. "But the *kürtőskalács*," she pointed to another stall with a laugh, "is what she wants. Every kid, born and unborn, loves those wonderful-smelling chimney cakes."

"What're they made of?"

"They are a long strip of sweet bread dough that's wrapped around a cone-shaped spit and rolled in cinnamon and sugar. Then they're baked in that oven over there." She pointed toward the back of the stall where a row of the sweets was cooking. "But they smell a thousand times better than they taste."

"Anything that smells that good can't be all bad," said Tracey with an appreciative sniff.

She grimaced at him and then laughed at the hard kick to her stomach, "Ooof! Baby Sarah wants one very badly."

"Then Baby shall have one," he said and pulled some coins from his pocket to pay for a fresh, hot pastry wrapped in paper. Holding the *kalács* in one hand, he offered it to Charlotte. She pulled off a piece, took a small bite and fed the rest to him. "I see what you mean." He made a face, "I don't think I care for it either." They looked at each other, and he tossed the rest of the sweet bread into a trash can. They wandered around, hand-in-hand, while Tracey finished his wine.

Then Charlotte spotted a stall selling men's and women's hats. "Look, hats! We have to try some on." She picked up a big, leather cowboy hat, looked at Tracey and quickly discarded it. After examining several others, a smart, dark green Tyrolean hat caught her eye. It had a feather tucked into the ribbon that was wrapped around its brim. She picked it up, "Tracey, you should try this one on. I think you would look quite smart in it." Placing it on his head, she stood back to admire him and then stepped back in to give him a little kiss, "You should get that one. You look so debonair."

He peered into the mirror and adjusted the angle, pulling it down a little over one eyebrow. "You know, I think you're right."

"Now help me find one." They looked around, first finding a big, round fur hat. She tried it on and struck a pose.

"You look like a Russian model, but I don't think it's quite you. And it's even bigger than your belly."

She laughed, "Yeah, if I wanted a Russian hat, I should have gotten one when we were in St. Petersburg." She took it off and tried on one made of fox fur. "Uhhh, no. It clashes with my hair." She wandered around, picking up and trying on a few more. Finally, she placed a mink pillbox hat on her head, just so.

Tracey smiled, "That one's perfect. A slight nod to Jackie Kennedy, especially with your new, shorter hair."

"It is, isn't it, my love?" She admired herself in a mirror, turning her head left and right.

After paying for the hats and asking the stall owner to remove the tags, they put them back on and continued to stroll around the market, stopping occasionally at stalls to look at crafts that vendors had brought in from all over the country.

Charlotte said, "I'm so hungry. The food stalls are tempting, but I'm saving myself for dinner with Remy."

§

They entered a café not far from their hotel in the Castle District on the Buda side of the city. Piano music drifted from the back as a waiter quickly seated them at a table with a pure white tablecloth and tiny candles flickering in crystal holders. Remy looked around, "Oh, how lovely."

"Mmmm," Charlotte murmured in agreement. She rubbed her belly and looked down, "I can't see my feet anymore, but they're certainly letting me know they are there - goodness, they're killing me."

"We haven't walked that much. Are you okay?" Remy asked.

"After we left you at breakfast, my aunt and I traipsed all over Pest shopping, and then Tracey and I wandered through the *Vörösmarty* Christmas market for a couple of hours. That's where I got this." She put her hands up around her hat, showing off its shape.

"It's beautiful. When I went through the market this afternoon, taking photos, I didn't see it. Lucky for you because I might have bought it first."

"If you're into fur, I can recommend a wonderful store. My

aunt took me to a little hole in a wall with lightly used fur coats that were just killer deals. I tried on several, but with this bulge, I wasn't sure how they would fit after Sarah's born. I'll have to get one next time we're here. Do you want to go there tomorrow before we board the boat?"

"No, back in the States, they'll just throw blood and stuff all over it."

"That's true." Looking at the menu, Charlotte continued, "Tracey is going to have to start pushing me around in a wheelchair soon." She looked at her belly again, "Not that I'm vain or anything, but thank goodness I'm carrying Baby Sarah straight out front, so my hips and my bum haven't gotten too wide." The two women laughed.

"Wine. I need wine. Probably several glasses," said Remy.

After a quick glance at the wine list that the waiter had discreetly laid in front of her, Charlotte said, "I recommend the Egri Bikavér. It's perfect for a cold winter's night." She asked the waiter to bring a bottle, along with one of mineral water. "With gas," she added.

Remy chuckled at the description, "That always makes me laugh."

"That's a translation of the Hungarian for sparkling water. They also say that in England."

"Very – errr – descriptive."

Charlotte laughed with her, "A lot of Hungarian words are more descriptive than English ones."

When he returned, bottles in hand, the waiter said, "*Egri* means the wine is from Eger in northern Hungary, near the Mátra and Bükk mountains. *Bikavér* means 'bull's blood'. As the name implies, it is a splendid red blend, rich in tannin and spice." He poured a small quantity into Remy's large wine glass.

She swirled it around, held the glass up to examine the legs and dipped her nose in and inhaled deeply before taking a small amount and holding it on her tongue. Then she swallowed, breathed in slowly through her mouth and sighed with enjoyment, "Mmmm – that's lovely."

He poured her a glass and then turned to Charlotte. She

quickly covered her glass with her hand. "None for me," and she pointed to her stomach. "Just the mineral water with lemon. And we'll start with lots of warm bread and some of your house goose-liver pâté, please."

As their waiter whisked away Charlotte's wineglass and went off to place their order, she said, "There's a great story about that wine. Supposedly, it gets its name from a famous incident during the Ottoman siege of Eger in 1552. One night, the Hungarian troops drank copious amounts of that spicy, local, red wine," she pointed at the bottle, "and the following morning, when the battle commenced, the Turks saw the Hungarians' bloodshot eyes and their beards stained with red. And when they saw how fiercely they fought, the Turkish soldiers rushed back to their leader, insisting that they should leave the Hungarians alone, because they'd obviously been drinking the blood of a bull, and it had turned them into ferocious warriors!"

"What a wonderful story! Perhaps this wine will make me as brave as they were." Remy held up her glass, "Would you like a sip?"

"I suppose one small one won't hurt." Charlotte took a tiny mouthful, savoring it before she finally swallowed. While they waited for their appetizer, Charlotte said, "It's too bad all of us expats couldn't make it for this trip."

"So much has changed in these past two years."

"I'm excited about seeing Sasha tomorrow. We can grill him about where Lee is," said Charlotte.

"You know he won't share much about her. He'll just say that he's heard from her and she's okay or she's fine. I'm sorry we've lost such a dear friend," Remy shook her head sadly.

The waiter brought their first course, and immediately, Charlotte reached for a slice of bread and smeared pâté thickly on top. "Sasha's the one person who hasn't lost either friend, Lee or Fong." She took a bite, "Mmmm, I'm starving."

"You always are nowadays."

Charlotte laughed, "I'm not only eating for two, but Tracey claims I'm sleeping for two as well. It seems like I'm always hungry or tired."

"I hope Lee's happy, wherever she is. She deserves it." Remy reached for a slice of bread and absently crumbled it between her fingers.

Charlotte watched before asking, "Where do you think she is? Do you suppose she went off to an ashram like she always talked about?"

"When I asked him early on, Sasha hinted that she'd left Italy to find herself. Which makes sense. She was so young when she got married, and she had been with Fong for a while before that."

"I was in my early twenties, too, when I got married. After my divorce, I had to spend time figuring out who I was as an individual. I'm sure Lee is going through the same thing."

The waiter arrived with their soups, for Remy, an aromatic venison goulash soup, redolent with fresh tarragon, and for Charlotte, a sour cream kohlrabi soup with dumplings.

"I would be so fat if I lived here," groaned Remy, as she finished the last spoonful of her soup.

"No, because you would walk everywhere, or ride public transportation. There's no need to have a car here, though you'd never know it to look at evening traffic. There are taxis to take you home in the evening after dinner or a concert. And you can take a train or rent a car when you do want to go somewhere. It's much more economical."

"That's true," replied Remy. She leaned back and looked around at the restaurant. Her lips curved in pleasure as the pianist began to play jazz noir music from old movies. "How delightful."

The waiter arrived back at the table, accompanied by a young man carrying a large tray. The older man placed their main courses carefully in front of them and set a small dish of thinly sliced cucumber, dressed with a sweetened vinaigrette beside each plate. "Will there be anything else for the ladies?" he asked.

They shook their heads and said in unison, "No, thank you." He bowed slightly, and he and his helper walked away.

"Ahhh, this *Paprikás Csirke* is decadent," said Charlotte. "Chicken with paprika has always been one of my favorites, ever since I was a small child and would come to Hungary with my parents. They used to tease me and say I would turn into a chicken one day if I didn't eat other things."

"My favorite food as a child in Switzerland was always – drum roll here – cheese," said Remy. "I could never get enough of it. I'm still that way, especially with fresh, young cheeses that are almost juicy because they haven't aged and hardened yet."

"Try your *Töltött Káposzta*. Stuffed cabbage is so Hungarian, and it's something we eat frequently at holiday time."

Remy put a bite in her mouth and gave an appreciative groan. "Our waiter had me when he described the pork mince, rice and sour cream. And look, I have some of your paprika here in my dish too."

Remy pushed away her empty plate and poured the last of the wine into her glass.

Charlotte raised an eyebrow.

"It's not like we're driving." Remy picked her glass up and twisted the stem between her fingers, tilting it first one way and then the other, watching the movement of the wine, mesmerized as she tipped the glass and then straightened it, and the wine ran downward in straight, viscous lines.

"You sound like Tracey. That's what he always says." Charlotte looked at Remy closely, "Is there something that's bothering you? Something you want to talk about?"

Remy looked at her, "What do you mean?"

"Well, you totally destroyed your bread, and now you've finished that entire bottle and are fiddling with your wine glass like you do when you're upset."

Remy took a sip, set her glass down and folded her hands together, resting her chin on them. "I need to talk, to share with someone, Charlotte. I need a voice of reason."

"I can be that. I'm your friend. I won't judge you, whatever it is."

The young helper cleared the dinner plates while their waiter asked them about dessert. "Of course," said Charlotte without hesitating. She looked at Remy, "Sarah had her dessert at the market. She only needed a couple of bites. This one's for me," and she burst out laughing, immediately joined by Remy.

"Count me out. I'm stuffed. I don't have room for another

bite," Remy said to the waiter. "But I will have an espresso, please." She looked at Charlotte and broke out laughing again, "While you continue eating."

Charlotte tried very hard to glare at Remy. "You're implying that I'm a glutton?" she said, her eyes twinkling.

"No, no, no, never. I'm envious. It seems like you can eat whatever you want and not put on weight. But what are you going to have?"

Charlotte turned to the waiter, "I'll have a palacsinta Gundel módra, please."

"A wonderful choice, madame."

Charlotte turned to Remy, and in response to her puzzled look, said, "It's called a pancake, but actually, it's a crêpe. The Gundel pancake is filled with the most scrumptious, rum-soaked, ground walnut and raisin filling, then fried in butter and served with warm, chocolate sauce on top. It's to die for," she said, her face brightening in anticipation. "You can have a bite."

And then, Charlotte reached over and laid her hand on Remy's forearm, "Talk to me. Tell me."

Ducking her head to avoid Charlotte's eyes, Remy blurted out, "I slept with Fong."

"What? How? Where? When?"

"It was in Slovenia. During the harvest. The night after you, Tracey and Lee left."

"You slept with Fong? In Slovenia? When we were all there for the harvest?" Charlotte repeated slowly.

"It was magical. Heaven. But it was only ever that one night."

"What's happened since then?"

"We talked about it and decided it could never happen again."

"Okaaay."

"But that affair Lee was talking about when we came to stay at yours – do you remember – that evening, when she told us about Fong's indiscretions and the emotional affair she suspected he was having?" She took a breath, "Well, that was me. I was the emotional affair."

"Yes, yes – I remember how upset she was."

Remy sighed deeply and took another swallow of her wine.

"So, let's put this into perspective, Remy. You were just one of Fong's many women over the span of his marriage."

"But it wasn't just the sex. We were emotionally involved – right up until Lee left."

"So, you're feeling guilty?"

"Well, I could have told him no. I could have said no in Slovenia. But I didn't want to."

"Don't beat yourself up. You're only partially responsible for this. You're not responsible for his marriage or his behavior. Who started it? At Sasha's vineyard, who—"

"He made the first move, but I responded."

"And after that?"

"We tried to go back to being just friends, and for a little while, it seemed to work."

"And then what happened?"

"I don't know – but it changed after the solstice party. He started sending me cards, letting me know he was thinking about me. That he cared about me. Not just as a friend. After they'd been coming for a while, he started signing them with '*Love*' and '*I love you*'. It all just escalated."

"What did you do?"

"Nothing. I did nothing. I should have told him to stop, but I didn't."

"How did you feel?"

"I knew it was wrong, but I wanted to hear from him."

"Oh, that sucks. But you tried to do the right thing by not responding. Right?"

"Not responding was good, but I should have told him to stop." She paused, "And then there was Berlin."

"You were there together, right? Did something happen there?"

"We talked and talked and talked. We talked about everything under the sun. We talked about his marriage. We talked about Lee. And we talked about us."

"Did you sleep with him?"

"Almost," she whispered.

"But you didn't. What happened?"

"We'd gone to the Pergamon Museum and wandered there for hours. I'd always wanted to visit the Altar of Zeus. You know, it was shipped to Berlin from Greece in the early twentieth century. You are right there – in Greece – at this temple that sits in a museum in the heart of Berlin. We visited the Market Gate of Miletus, the Ishtar Gate, the Processional Way of Babylon. They are actual architectural pieces. All rebuilt inside the museum. It's spectacular, Charlotte. And of course, it's very controversial, because—"

"Remy, just tell me."

"We held hands, and we walked around – as though we were lovers. We pretended we were visiting those ancient cities – together. It was magical. There was that same kind of electricity that we'd felt in Slovenia. Then, finally, we left and went out and wandered along the Spree Kanal. We talked and talked and talked. Finally, we found a bench and sat and watched the boats go past. And talked some more."

"Go on."

"He told me that when he's with Lee, he often thinks of me. I asked him if he'd thought about Lee while we were in Berlin. He said no. Then we stopped talking, and we turned toward each other – and we just looked at each other's faces – eyes and mouths – and then we leaned so close, I could feel his breath on my lips. I was frightened, Charlotte, frightened that if we kissed, we would make love – and if that happened, we would be lost. I couldn't let that happen, I couldn't do that to Lee."

Another one of life's difficult dilemmas. Charlotte shook her head gently, "And—?"

"I pulled away, and I told him there could never be an 'us' again. That he was Lee's husband, not mine. That he needed to go away. That *I* was going away, back to San Francisco, and I didn't want to see him again. Ever. Ever. Charlotte, he was devastated. I think it broke his heart."

"Ahhh, Remy."

"And then to sit there in your living room and listen to Lee describe how hurt and lost he was when he returned from Berlin.

My heart broke that night too." Remy closed her eyes, and her lips trembled. "That night, after I'd gone to bed, I called him. I told him no. I told him it had to stop. *He* had to stop. To stop thinking about me. He had to pay attention – as a husband – to Lee. And shortly after our Sicily trip, Lee left."

"I honestly don't think Lee had been happy for a long time, no matter how many times she insisted they had a fairytale marriage."

"I don't know, and I don't think we'll ever know." Remy paused and looked across the room, thinking about what she was going to say next. "It probably sounds horrible, but a part of me really wanted him – even though he was Lee's husband. A part of me was just a tiny bit happy that maybe we could have another chance."

Charlotte saw how bleak her face had become and how her eyes were drowning in misery before Remy tipped her head down. As Charlotte reached across to her again, Remy looked up, "I broke up their marriage."

"Oh, no, no, no," Charlotte shook her head. "What happened between Fong and Lee had been brewing for years before they met you."

"I'd walled myself off emotionally after my friend in college betrayed me. What happened with Fong opened my heart and made me feel again. God, how sappy that sounds. But if I hadn't been with him or wanted him, they would probably still be married."

"You don't know that for sure. But that's why you're leaving and going back home, isn't it?"

"Yes. I still want him desperately, but I need to get away. In Slovenia, he's only a few hours away from Florence, and the temptation is always there." She paused for a brief moment. "You and Tracey have visited him at the vineyard. How is he? What's he like?"

"I went along a few times, but it's mostly Tracey who goes to him. At first, when we visited, he was sad. He said he was the reason Lee had left. Tracey saw him a couple of weeks ago, and he said he seemed almost like his old self, like he's finally accepted that it's over. And working in the vineyard these last months, it seems as though he's found a peace of sorts."

"Oh, good, I'm glad to hear that."

Charlotte gave Remy a shrewd look, "What brought all this up? Have you talked to him?"

"Not until today. He's driving to Budapest tonight. He wants to see me. He says he wants to talk before I leave Europe."

"What are you going to tell him?"

"I – I don't know. I'm scared. I'm still in love with him. I desperately want him, but what if he doesn't want me anymore? What if he's coming to tell me that? I've never loved anyone this much, Charlotte."

"Ahhh, Remy."

"This is why I made all those rules. I'm terrified that I'm going to be hurt – again. This time even worse than before."

"Once you've been badly hurt, it's hard to let your guard down."

"Charlotte, thank you for listening and not judging me." She sighed, "Frannie found out, and she wasn't nearly as kind."

"Frannie's young. I've learned not to judge anyone. No one's perfect. I'm so glad you told me – I knew that you needed to talk about something. You know, Fong told Tracey about what happened with Lee, but Tracey only told me that some woman came between them. I told him it's never one-sided. Then he clammed up. Even though I begged him, he wouldn't give me any other information. He said he was told in confidence, and it wasn't for him to share. You could hear the lawyer in him."

Remy laughed ruefully, "And now, we all know what we all know."

As they paid the bill, Charlotte looked at her watch, "I hope Tracey enjoyed the concert."

§

Tracey sat at the bar, sipping his cognac, flipping through the concert program, the final notes of the last piece echoing in his head. He held the last drops of his drink on his tongue, savoring them before pulling out his fountain pen, tapping it absently against his teeth as he contemplated the bill. "Forint to euros, and then how much is that in dollars?" he grumbled before signing the receipt to charge it to their room.

In the elevator, he hummed a few bars from the concert. He got off the elevator, still humming as he walked down the hall and stopped abruptly when he saw Fong, wearing his driving hat and heavy coat, standing across from their room, knocking at Remy's door. He watched. Remy, in a sweater and jeans, her feet bare, opened the door and pulled Fong into a warm embrace. She touched his face and then took his hand and drew him into the room.

Remy? Fong?

Early the next morning, Tracey got up quietly so he wouldn't disturb Charlotte. He looked down at her, listening to her deep breathing, and leaned over to kiss her on the forehead.

Dressed in jeans, a long-sleeved turtleneck and a pullover sweater, he threw on his coat and walked toward the door to go find a newspaper and coffee. He put his hand on the door handle and then dropped it when he heard voices in the hall. Leaning toward the door, he put his eye up to the peephole. Across the hall, Fong closed the door and walked swiftly toward the elevator.

He stayed the night. Interesting.

The Christmas Cruise

Onboard *The Lapis*

Over after-dinner drinks in the lounge the following evening, Remy said, "I had such a good time exploring Budapest, but I'm happy we're about to get underway. I keep remembering that first cruise when we all met one another. What a wonderful time we had, just floating along the river, enjoying the quiet evenings—"

"And the sound of the boat's motor?" asked Tracey as he gave her a quizzical look.

"But my love, we hear it because our suite is directly above the motor. Remy is down the hall. Maybe she doesn't hear it as loudly."

"On the last cruise, I was in almost the exact same stateroom as on this trip. For me, it's just a quiet vibration. Like white noise," Remy said.

Tracey looked at them, "The price of luxury, I suppose. Would either of you like another drink?"

Charlotte yawned as she stood, "Not for me. I've had enough cocoa and mineral water to last a lifetime. And I'm exhausted. I need my beauty sleep. Goodnight, Remy. I'll see you in the morning."

"Sleep well, Charlotte."

"No doubt I will," Charlotte grinned and carefully leaned over to kiss Remy on the cheek and whispered in her ear, "You haven't told me about Fong's visit."

Remy smiled happily and whispered back, "We definitely need to catch up in the morning."

Tracey and Charlotte held hands as they walked to their room. "What was all that whispering between you and Remy?"

"Oh, just girl stuff. I'm so sorry, my love. All the walking around Budapest over the past few days has exhausted me."

Tracey opened the door to their suite at the end of the hallway. She went in and quickly got undressed, dropping her clothes onto the small loveseat and pulling on her pajamas, stretching them over her midsection.

Tracey watched, "Brush your teeth now, and I'll tuck you in."

Charlotte gave him a little love-smack on the arm as she went by. "Brush my teeth. Like I'm a little kid or something. What a goof you are."

"I'm practicing to be a daddy. If you're good, I might read you a bedtime story." He heard Charlotte chortle as she closed the bathroom door.

Tracey hummed and listened to the water run as Charlotte got ready for bed. He folded the bedcover down, fluffed her pillows and arranged them just the way she liked them. She came out of the bathroom and crawled into bed. Tracey bent down and nuzzled her with sweet little pecks where her shoulder and neck met.

"Oof."

"What's wrong?"

"Baby Sarah is dancing up a storm."

He put his hand on her belly and shook his head, "How do you sleep with all that going on?"

"Babies are nocturnal creatures. Like our Little Phebe Cat. But tonight, I'm so tired, I'm sure I'll sleep through her party."

"And by the time you two wake up tomorrow morning, we'll be in Vienna."

Charlotte drew a long, sleepy breath, "You know, it was Remy. The woman Fong fell in love with," she murmured, half asleep, and her eyelids drooped closed. "Good night, my love. Enjoy your pipe." She drifted off.

Remy? Is that who he fell in love with? Is that who broke up their marriage? He spent the night in her room last night. Did they make love? Walking down the hall, troubled by what he'd just heard, Tracey pulled on his heavy jacket and, as he passed through the bar, he raised his hand with the pipe. Sasha nodded in response and poured him a large snifter of cognac before going back to preparing cocktails for guests seated throughout the bar.

Tracey took the stairs to the upper deck and then began his routine, filling and lighting his pipe. He took a deep, satisfying draw while leaning on the railing, pipe in one hand and snifter in the other. Looking across the river toward Fisherman's Bastion, he realized it was barely visible in the fog, and the lights from the hotel on the hillside, where they'd stayed the few nights before the cruise, had completely vanished.

The door to the wheelhouse was open, and he heard commands coming from the crew as they prepared the boat for departure. He puffed away, recalling that night of the first cruise they'd all taken together when he and Fong had sat on the upper deck, spinning tales about Henri. *Henri stood at the railing, satisfied that the painting was well hidden in his cabin. Soon—* "God, I miss you, Fong," he murmured to himself.

Fong, Lee, Remy. What good friends we all were. Remy, why did you have to sleep with Fong? Why did you do it? Didn't you think about how you would hurt Lee? Women do that to one another, they take what they want without any thought for who else gets hurt. Just like my mother with all her boyfriends. I wonder if she thought about their wives and families. I wonder if their families knew, if that hurt them. I wonder how many marriages were broken by her behavior and how many wives and kids were abandoned like Sarah and I were.

His thoughts continued to wander. *Good lord, Tracey, you're an adult now. You'd think you'd have gotten over that. But it hurt so badly when we stood in the parking lot that night, and my mother told me she had to go home to her family. Her family, she said, with no thought for me, her elder son. She just said, "Excuse me." It was clear I wasn't part of that family, of her family. I felt so bereft, so abandoned, so hurt. And angry. She made me so angry. And so I killed her. And I've kept on killing her through all those other women.*

He pressed his fingers to the area between his eyebrows and massaged it gently. *At some point, it became less about anger with my mother, when I started to do it because I like it. But I still kill women with red hair. Is part of me enjoying killing my mother over and over?*

He drew a harsh breath, appalled at his thoughts, and then they continued tumbling through his mind, feelings and memories all jumbled together. *I wonder if these urges to strangle women will ever stop. That young woman at the golf course — when she approached me. I just needed to leave, and she wanted to talk about all the things golfers leave behind. And then, when I told her I had to leave, she got snippy and tossed her head and made that same remark that young people do these days — "Well, ex-cuse me!" The skateboarder, she was such an engaging young woman. When I followed her — I wasn't sure why, but then, at the last moment, she just dismissed me, "Excuse me, would you give me some space?" It wasn't just the words. It was the tone. We'd had a nice conversation about her piercings and then—* He shook his head, continuing to be tormented by his thoughts. *There was something in her behavior that reminded me of how I felt when my mother dismissed me so easily from her life. Is it their tone? Their words? Their dismissal? Their looks? What makes me want to put my hands around these women's necks and squeeze the life out of them? And why does that give me such pleasure?*

He shivered. The fog had grown thicker. Even the palace just south of the Bastion had disappeared. He watched it hovering over the river and wondered how boats could possibly navigate in such pea soup. As he finished his pipe, he felt a jolt as the boat pulled away from the dock. He tapped his pipe on the side of the railing, watching the ashes blow away and vanish in the fog. *Remy,* he thought. *How could she do that?*

Remy stared out the window of the bar, thinking about the previous night, looking forward to seeing Fong again in Vienna. A smile crossed her lips. She noticed the fog growing heavier along the river and decided that she wanted to try to get some photographs capturing its eeriness. She stood up and almost ran into Sasha carrying a tray of drinks. "Are you calling it a night?"

"No, I want to get my camera and take photos of the buildings along the embankment in the fog as we depart."

"Don't forget your coat. It's cold and damp out there."

Remy came back through the bar, dressed in her winter coat, a scarf wrapped loosely around her neck and her camera in her hand. She glanced over, but Sasha was too busy with other passengers to notice her. She went forward toward the bow of the boat and through the doors onto the deck.

Tracey paused at the top of the stairs when he heard the lounge doors swoosh open. He watched Remy lift her camera and begin to take pictures of the parliament building, the moon and the spires peeking out above the fog. Then she lowered her camera and turned toward the Buda hills on the opposite side of the river.

She walked over to the railing and leaned against it for support as the boat rocked in the wake of a speed boat.

Tracey went down the stairs quietly and stopped behind her. "Are you getting some good shots, Remy?"

She jumped and swung around, bumping into him, "Oh, my gosh, you startled me. I didn't realize anyone else was out in this fog." She pushed a few wisps of hair out of her face.

The boat rocked again, and he put his hands on her shoulders to steady her.

"It's cold out here, I just want to finish taking these pictures before the fog shifts and get back inside. Excuse me, Tracey," she said as she turned her back to him.

Out of nowhere, anger coursed through him – at how she'd destroyed his friends' marriage, ruining the friendships that had developed between them all, at the way she had just dismissed him. Looking over his shoulder, he saw no one. With his right hand over her mouth and his left-hand tightening around her neck, he pressed her against the railing in the dark area beyond the stairs. Her camera fell into the river as she grabbed at his arm through his jacket, struggling against him. He felt the familiar tightening in his groin, and his breathing quickened.

Beneath his fingers, her screams were muffled, and she began to lose consciousness. He leaned close to her ear and whispered, "I'm sorry, Remy."

She moaned and went limp as the doors behind him swooshed open. Glancing over his shoulder, he didn't see anyone coming out into the cold fog. And he pushed her over the side of the boat into the river.

Leaning on the railing, trying to catch his breath, he heard the door open yet again, and he pulled his pipe out of his pocket and tapped it on the railing. A man's voice said, "Honey, it's really cold and damp out there. Are you sure you want to go out?"

Tracey glanced down at the river and only saw the fog.

He wandered casually through the bar. Sasha looked up briefly, still busy serving guests who were celebrating the beginning of their cruise and paused just long enough to raise his hand in quick acknowledgement before going back to mixing yet another cocktail for yet another guest.

At the end of the hall, Tracey stopped in front of his cabin, took several deep breaths and forced his thoughts back to his wife, asleep on the other side of the door. He waved his keycard in front of the lock and entered, closing the door quietly behind him so he wouldn't disturb Charlotte. After he'd hung his jacket in the closet, he went into the bathroom, looked in the mirror and touched the earring in his left ear. He pressed his fingers against his temples and reached into his shaving kit for his headache pills.

Then, with his toothbrush in his mouth, he leaned back against the counter, reliving how it had felt, his right hand over her mouth, the other tight around her throat, her struggles to breathe, to break away, the quiet splash as she vanished into the water – and into the fog. His heart pounded as he rinsed his mouth, and he decided against a shower, splashing water onto his face instead.

Hurriedly stripping off his clothes, he dropped them onto the loveseat where Charlotte had left hers earlier. He climbed into bed behind her and slipped his arm under her head, and she nestled back, squirming against him. With a sound of sleepy pleasure at his arousal, she pushed back over and over, feeling him harden in response. She arched her back, squirming against him. "Help me out of these PJs, my love."

With Charlotte naked in front of him, he held her steady with one hand on her hip, his excitement spiraling as he pressed himself against her bottom. His breath came in harsh gasps, faster and faster—

Charlotte reached back and rested a gentle hand on his leg. "Slow down, my love. Help me catch up with you."

Reluctantly, he slowed his movements. He reached his hand between her legs and began to caress her, knowing all the places she liked to be touched.

"Ahhh – yes – there – like that," she moaned. "And now – now – I need to feel you inside me – now!"

Tracey entered her in a hard thrust while his hand continued to tease her. His relentless movements, the touch of his fingers, drove Charlotte higher and higher. "Ah – ahh – ahhh—," she called out, and Tracey moved his hand from between her legs to cover her mouth, stifling her cry as she clenched around him one final time and yelled, "My – love!" He gave two more powerful thrusts and buried his face in her hair in a soundless shudder of release before he collapsed against her back.

A Body Washes Ashore

Vienna, Austria

The next morning, Charlotte and Tracey walked into the reception area as they prepared to depart for the day in Vienna. "My love, would you please get our badges?" Tracey went over to the container holding all the passenger badges and flipped through to find his and Charlotte's. "Remy must have gotten off very early because I didn't see her at breakfast. Would you check to see if her badge is there? If it is, I'll call her to see if she wants to join us."

Tracey walked back to Charlotte, slipping his hand from his jacket pocket. "Here's your badge. Remy's isn't there. She must have headed out already to take early morning photos."

After the damp fog of the previous night, the clear, cold morning was welcome. Coming out of the Spanish Riding School, Charlotte and Tracey continued their stroll through central Vienna, as they talked about where to have lunch and which museum they would visit that afternoon.

Tracey pulled his ringing phone from his pocket. "Hello, Fong."

"Tracey, have you and Charlotte seen Remy?"

"We had dinner with her last night. Why do you ask?"

"We were supposed to meet here in Vienna at the Palace Court Hotel for breakfast. I've been waiting in the restaurant for her. She hasn't shown up, and she's not answering her phone."

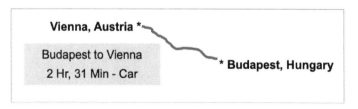

"Let me check with Charlotte." Tracey turned to Charlotte, "Are you sure Remy didn't say anything about her plans for this morning?"

Charlotte shook her head, "I never saw her. She said we'd catch up this morning."

"Fong, not even Charlotte knows where she is. And when we checked for her badge this morning, it was already gone. She must have gotten off here in Vienna before we did."

While he listened to Fong, Tracey took from his pocket a handful of receipts – Remy's badge concealed within them – and walked over to drop them into a nearby trash can.

"I'm worried about her. She's always called us when she couldn't make it or even if she was just going to be late. This isn't like her."

"Maybe she got distracted taking photographs. I'm sure she'll call. Would you like to have lunch with us?"

"I'm going to hang out here in case she shows up. You could join me at the hotel if you'd like."

They discussed how far Tracey and Charlotte were from the hotel and decided to try to get together for drinks later that afternoon instead.

After they'd hung up, Tracey took Charlotte's hand and continued walking along the street, "I saw Fong and Remy the other night outside her room." He wondered if Charlotte remembered what she'd told him as she was drifting off to sleep the night before.

"Really? She said he'd called, and he was coming to see her in Budapest."

"It seems they're supposed to meet here in Vienna as well."

After they had drinks with a distracted and increasingly agitated Fong, Charlotte and Tracey caught a taxi back to the boat. Tracey looked out the window, thinking about the previous evening as the car negotiated the beginnings of rush-hour traffic. Charlotte's hand on his arm startled him, "My love, Fong is quite worried about Remy. I am too."

"When we get to the boat, we'll check to see if her badge is there. Maybe her phone battery ran down."

As they entered the reception area, Tracey went over to put their badges back. Looking over his shoulder at Charlotte, he said, "It doesn't look like Remy is back yet. Her badge isn't here."

"Let me call her." With her phone to her ear, Charlotte said, "She's not answering, and her voicemail is full."

"She's very independent, Charlotte. And we don't depart for Krems until early in the morning. I'm sure she'll show up before then."

"This is so unlike her. I'm going to ask Sasha if she said anything to him."

§

Budapest, Hungary

Earlier that morning, on Csepel Island, after the fog had cleared, the young man shielded his eyes against the rising sun. "I found her at the very edge of the water."

The police officer glanced over at the ambulance attendants carefully lifting the woman, now covered in a blanket, onto the gurney, "What were you doing out before sunrise?"

"I'm a distance runner." He shivered and began hopping up and down and swinging his arms, trying to stay warm. "I try to get my run in before I go to work."

"Did you touch her?"

"I pulled her up from the water's edge, and then I just touched her on her neck. I slipped my fingers under the edge of her scarf to see if I could find a pulse. I also put my jacket over her because her clothes were still wet. It's a good thing it's above freezing. Otherwise, she probably wouldn't have survived."

"How do you know all of this?"

"I'm a nurse. Her pulse was very, very weak. I have no idea how she survived."

"Has she been conscious at all? Has she said anything?"

"No. Nothing."

An ambulance attendant handed the jacket to the police officer. "I don't know if you need this. We're all set." He turned around abruptly.

The police officer handed the runner his jacket, and he quickly pulled it on, grimacing at its dampness.

They watched the ambulance drive away, carrying the redheaded woman. "I think we have everything we need for now. Thank you for answering my questions. We have your contact information if we need anything else. You're free to go."

§

Onboard *The Lapis*

Late that afternoon, Sasha was polishing glasses at the empty bar when the captain approached him and showed him a piece of paper. "Isn't she one of our guests?"

Sasha looked at the fax with a grainy photograph of a woman, a Spectrum keycard and a chart with the name of a hospital. He looked at the photo carefully, "Yes, that's Remy – Rembrandt Martin. Oh my, what happened to her?"

"This woman was found on the riverbank on the outskirts of Budapest very early this morning, barely alive. She's in a coma at the hospital," the captain explained. "They found a Spectrum room key in her pocket and contacted headquarters, who sent her picture to all the boats in the area to see if anyone could identify her."

"She was on this cruise. A couple of other passengers, Tracey Lauch and Charlotte French, are her friends. They're traveling together. They've been worried because they haven't seen her all day. I told them that sometimes people get off the boat and come back on at a later port." Sasha set down the glass and towel. His face crinkled with concern as he said, "Is she going to be okay? She's a friend of mine as well."

"Spectrum headquarters didn't say, and I don't know if the police are releasing any other information."

Sasha said, thinking out loud, "I wonder if she fell overboard last night after we left Budapest. I saw her after dinner. She said she was going back to her room to get her camera and then out on the bow to take photographs. I didn't see her after that, but I was very busy."

"We might speculate among ourselves, but we're not volunteering that to the police or mentioning it to anyone else. That would be such a mess for the cruise line. We don't know what happened."

"What do we tell our guests?" Sasha asked, thinking about Tracey and Charlotte.

"Nothing yet. Now that you've confirmed that this is Ms. Martin, headquarters will give the police her emergency contact information. They should be contacted before anyone else is told."

But I have to let Fong know where she is. I can't leave him thinking she's avoiding him.

§

Milan, Italy

The next day, Gia walked into her room as Frannie was frantically packing her suitcase.

"Where are you going?" Gia asked. Frannie burst into tears and threw herself into Gia's arms. Gia held her away so Frannie could see her face, "What's wrong?"

"The last thing I told Remy was that I hated her, and I never wanted to see her again. And then she didn't put me down as her contact for this cruise. They had to call my parents all the way in California," Frannie hiccupped. "Then my mom and dad called me. They said the Hungarian police called them and said she's in a coma in a hospital in Budapest. I have to go to her."

"What happened?"

"Someone found her on the riverbank, she was unconscious and almost frozen to death. That's all I know."

"But she was going on a cruise out of Budapest."

"Mom said she asked the police a lot of questions, but they

wouldn't share any information until they could investigate what happened. And they are hoping to talk to Remy when she comes to." Frannie stuck her fingers into her hair and pulled at the roots, and she began to wail, "But what if she doesn't? What if—"

"Don't go there, Frannie. Just don't go there." Gia wrapped her arms around Frannie. After she'd calmed down a bit, Gia held Frannie away again, "I'm going to pack and come with you. I'll sit in the waiting room if I have to. I'll be there for you."

§

Budapest, Hungary

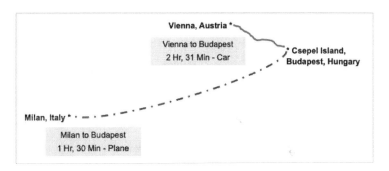

Fong sat in a hard, plastic, hospital chair next to Remy holding her hand in both of his. He looked at her pale face and reached over to run the backs of his fingers along her cheek. "What happened to you, Remy? How did you end up in the river?" Standing up, he leaned over and kissed her on the cheek and touched the abrasion on her neck, "That must hurt – a lot."

When the doctor entered, Fong turned around quickly, pushing the chair out of his way as he went over to talk to him.

Jó napot kívánok, said the doctor, holding out his hand in greeting.

"Hello, I'm Daniel Fong. I'm afraid I don't speak Hungarian."

The doctor switched to English, speaking in a perfect British accent, "How long have you two been married?"

"It seems like almost no time at all."

As the doctor walked around to the other side of the bed, he said, "The good news is that she is stable. When she arrived, we were uncertain if she would survive. She is fighting hard though."

Fong picked up her hand and held it to his cheek. Her fingers twitched under his. "Her fingers moved. Is she waking up?"

"Not necessarily. That sometimes happens involuntarily."

Fong continued to hold her hand in his. "Then what's the prognosis?"

"She has suffered severe hypothermia. When a person's body temperature drops, their heart, nervous system and other organs cannot work normally, but she didn't suffer cardiac arrest. We did extensive rewarming as soon as they brought her in. We watched her in intensive care for the first twenty-four hours. We decided to move her here to critical care to continue monitoring her. Her body is recovering. But I want to be honest with you, now, it is just a matter of waiting. With a coma, whether she will come out of it today or never, we do not know."

"What made the marks around her neck?"

"We do not know that either. She had a scarf on when she was found. So that could have made the mark. Possibly, it was pulled tight by the current, or it could have snagged on something."

"Except for the marks on her neck, she looks so peaceful."

"The nurse bathed her and brushed her hair before you arrived. When she wakes up, we want her to feel as normal as possible."

"When?"

"I like to remain optimistic."

Fong continued his one-sided conversation with Remy. He told her things that she knew and things that she didn't, about the vineyard, how peaceful he found it living there, about the harvest, how that year had been better than ever. And he told her he would be with her as long as she wanted him.

He heard voices in the hall, and when he looked up, he saw Frannie standing in the doorway with Gia behind her.

"How did you get in here?" demanded Frannie.

"I lied and said I'm her husband."

"But what about Lee?"

Tonelessly, he said, "It's over. She divorced me."

Gia took Frannie by the shoulders and gave her a slight shake before signing, "Come on, Frannie. This is about Remy."

Frannie signed back, "You're right. But why is he here?" She glared at Fong.

Gia put her hand on Frannie's arm and pulled her around, so she was facing away from Fong, "Enough already," she signed. "Just stop it."

Frannie nodded sullenly and went to stand beside Remy, opposite Fong. She lifted Remy's hand and placed it on top of hers and signed into her palm, "Remy, I'm here for you. I'm so sorry for what I said. I didn't mean it." She jumped when she felt Remy's fingers move over hers, "Oh, my gosh, she just moved her hand. She moved her hand!"

"I'm sure she heard what you just said to her," said Fong. He looked at Gia. "Why don't we get a cup of coffee and give Frannie some time with her cousin?" As they walked down the hall, he said to Gia, "I'm in love with her. I got here as soon as I could when Sasha told me what had happened. Fortunately, I was only in Vienna."

Once they'd left, Frannie leaned over and kissed Remy's hand. She held it to her cheek, "Mom and Dad send their love. They'll be here in a couple of days. They are just getting things in order in case they need to stay here a while." When she saw no reaction from Remy, she went on, "They've been talking to doctors in California, so they understand what you might be facing."

Remy moved her head slightly toward Frannie as though she was listening.

Frannie went on, "Mom and Dad had to put Bowser in the kennel. Apparently, he isn't happy about that." She laughed, "You always told me you thought that was a stupid name for a dog."

One corner of Remy's mouth moved like the beginning of a smile.

"Remy, remember when you arrived in Berkeley, and I just followed you around? I used to say 'cousin' over and over. I loved the sound of it, and I loved you from the very beginning."

A tear ran from the corner of Remy's eye. "You can hear me, Remy. I know you can." She looked around frantically and saw Gia and Fong, who'd come back with paper cups of coffee in their hands, standing in the doorway. "She tried to smile, and she cried when I said I love her. She's waking up. I know she is."

Fong whispered to Gia, "She hasn't responded until now. This is wonderful."

They walked in, and Gia went to stand beside Frannie while Fong stopped at the end of the bed. Remy's eyes slowly opened. She squinted against the light and saw all three of them standing there.

Frannie said, "You're in the hospital. And we're all here for you."

Remy looked around the room and then directly at Fong. She frowned and tried to speak, but all that came out was a hoarse croak. With her hand under Frannie's, she signed, "Do I know him?"

"He's a friend," Frannie signed back.

"I'll get the doctor." Gia turned quickly and hurried out of the room.

Remy signed, "Tell him he looks like someone I loved, who I still love." Frannie repeated it out loud for Fong.

Fong said quietly, "I'm sure he loves you too."

Epilogue

Early 2014, The Ashram

While Jane sat outside at a table under a tree, enjoying a post-yoga cup of tea, a slender woman with very short reddish hair approached her, "May I join you?"

She looked up and saw that it was Lee Fong, a woman who had been living at the ashram for several months and had just been in the same yoga class, "Of course."

As Lee sat down, she carefully placed her teacup in front of her and began to play with the leaves and twigs lying on the table, "What did you think of the class?"

"It was nice. I like that instructor best of all."

"Mmmm, me too." Lee flicked a broken leaf off the table. Before taking a sip of her tea, she took some more leaves and lay them in a row. Then she scooped them into a pile before rearranging them.

"It doesn't look as if you're as relaxed as I am after that class."

"Mmmm. I tried to watch your documentary."

"And?"

"I'm curious. Whatever made you pick cheating as the subject?"

"My sister's husband had an affair. She is quite a bit older than me, and I was in high school when it all happened."

Relieved the focus had moved away from her, Lee said, "May I ask, what happened?"

"Not very long after they got married, my brother-in-law started sleeping with our third cousin. We had all grown up together, and we were very close. Everyone knew it was going on, and we tried to tell her. She didn't believe us for the longest time. She was head-over-heels in love with him."

A painful look crossed Lee's face. *Head-over-heels in love – like I was with Daniel.* "I'm sure she didn't want to believe it either."

"Exactly."

"Are they still together?"

"No. She was out with girlfriends one night and saw them having a very intimate dinner. It was obvious they were more than just friends."

"Oh, dear, what a terrible way to find out."

"She was devastated, and she left before he got home that night. She moved back in with me and my parents. We were all broken-hearted by his lying and cheating. I was an impressionable teenager at the time, and to be honest, that experience is partly the reason for my degree in psychology. I wanted to understand people better, what makes them do things like that. What makes some people willing to cheat while others choose not to. What makes people tick emotionally."

"How did you get from psychology to film?"

"Film has always been my thing. Writing isn't. I've always liked movies and especially documentaries. So, as an undergraduate, I did a double major in film and psychology. I like to use film to tell people's stories."

"Your documentary was certainly powerful, showing the different points of view. I found it very hard to watch all the way to the end."

"Oh?"

Very softly, Lee said, "My husband cheated on me."

"I'm so sorry to hear that. I can see how my documentary would have triggered you. Although – sorry, but I can't help wishing I'd met you sooner and interviewed you."

"I wouldn't have agreed to do that. The details are something I keep between me and my counsellor."

"You don't have to continue, Lee," Jane said gently.

"'I've learned a lot about myself since I came here last summer. It's helped me to process what I went through." She gave Jane a half smile.

"Do you want to talk about it?"

"I haven't ever before, to anyone. But now, I think it might be good for me."

Jane waited for Lee to continue.

"My husband cheated on me for almost twenty years."

Jane reached out and put her hand over Lee's.

"It was when he went away on extended business trips. He said it meant nothing. It was just sex and a warm body in his bed for the night. He said he never slept with the same woman more than once. We talked about it in the beginning, but then it was something I knew would happen again, and finally, I didn't bring it up anymore. I was so in love with him – but it always hurt."

"How did you put up with it for so long?"

"I told myself it was just a physical thing, and then I put it in a little box in a corner of my heart where it couldn't hurt me quite so much."

"Doing this documentary, I learned that a lot of people compartmentalize things they can't or don't want to deal with in their relationships."

"That's what I did, until—" Lee swallowed hard and looked away.

Jane waited.

"Until he fell in love with one of my best friends."

"There was no room in the little box for that?"

"No. As long as he didn't *love* those other women, I could live with it – but there was no room there for my best friend and my husband. Not when they fell in love. Not for their betrayal."

"I don't want to sound clinical, but I saw that a lot in my interviews. People were able to suppress things for a long time, but then there came a tipping point where they couldn't do it anymore."

"I guess I'm not alone then." Lee began to cry softly, "It feels good to finally figure that out." Then she gave Jane a little grin, "But I still wouldn't have given you that interview."

We want to hear from you.

As Jane sets up so clearly at the beginning of *A Body Washes Ashore*, this book is about relationships, and in particular, those that cross the line and turn into affairs. Affairs are messy and complicated, there are always two sides to them. In the outsider's eyes, the mistress is frequently viewed as the evil homebreaker. We wanted to use this story to show how complex an affair can actually be. Often, the cheaters get to enjoy their secret liaisons, but their loved ones – spouses, children, family, friends – have to live with the pain of that betrayal. And other times, the cheaters are just as badly hurt in the end.

Despite all of her flaws, we really like Remy. She was an exciting character to develop. As we worked to add layers to her personality, it was important to figure out why she would need such an unusual set of rules to protect herself and her relationships with men as well as what would happen to her if she broke those rules.

You asked us to tell you more about Tracey, the man and his emotions. In this book, he becomes a central character filled with love, enriched by his new friendships and, in contrast, beginning to like his role as a serial killer. He is charming and funny – and vulnerable. We think you'll like him as much as we do. Oh, if only he didn't like strangling women so much!

After book one was released, you said you'd fallen in love with Gia, and you wanted to know what happened to her and Sal, so we brought them back here. What do you think? Should we keep them around for book four?

Thank you for reading this third book in the Spectrum series. Please share your thoughts by posting a review. What did you like? What else would you like to have seen? Here's the link for *A Body Washes Ashore* on Amazon – **https://amzn.to/3tRa0yx**

Robin & Jody

After the Killings

Available on Amazon, Fall 2023

In this final volume of the Spectrum Series, pieces slowly begin to fall into place in the case of the Parking Lot Strangler. Emily's new romantic interest, a former member of the Hungarian police, helps search for murders in Europe which are similar to the Raleigh ones. Suddenly, the net begins to tighten around Tracey.

Happily, immersed in his life with Charlotte as they move from their home in Sicily, Italy, to Raleigh, North Carolina, Tracey continues to struggle with his compulsion to strangle women who remind him of his mother.

While he found his mother in book one – and killed her, so far, there has been no sign of his sister. Even with Charlotte's help and encouragement, will he ever find her? Or will he need to be content with the foster home he named for her?

Tracey's murders have caused a chain reaction, and Jane dives deeply into the effect they have had on the victims' family and friends.

The Killings Begin

THE FIRST BOOK IN THE SERIES is very well written and well-paced. I like the way the characters are being introduced, I feel like I'm really getting to know them! I read it in two days, you know you have a good book when you can't wait to get back to it. My husband is reading it now and enjoying it very much. You always hate to see a good book end, but we have the whole series to look forward to. The suspense is building!

OBSESSED STRAIGHT AWAY! Such an easy read and couldn't put the book down. Found the story gripping and so excited for the second! Never wanted it to end, truly talented authors!

THIS IS A UNIQUE TALE and I enjoyed how strong of a character Gia Delgado was...I don't know that I've ever read another book with this sort of arrangement...

THE KILLINGS BEGIN IS A CAPTIVATING READ. I couldn't wait to get back to reading it. Now, I look so forward to reading the next book in the series. It couldn't come too soon.

I BOUGHT THE BOOK IMMEDIATELY, and once I received it, I was hooked. I give books the first chapter to hook me before abandoning [them]. This book hooked me before the first page was over... I bought the physical book so that [my husband] can read it to me out loud, but then I had to get the kindle edition to keep reading throughout my day no matter where I was.

MY WIFE BOUGHT THIS BOOK. Because of the lockdown, I decided to read it. I was skeptical because it is called a romance, but I really enjoyed the story. It is very well written, a quick and easy read. The romance is not too heavy or sappy and is more than offset by the suspense, making it a great read, even for someone who would not typically read a romance story. I also enjoyed the focus on the geography and culture of the various cities visited in the novel.

Death in a Dark Alley

THIS BOOK IS A TANTALIZING AND THRILLING TALE of a lifelong friendship, a deceptive romantic liaison, a daring criminal alliance, and the pretentious murderer who walks free among them.

WHAT A GREAT READ! I was lucky enough to be selected as an advance reviewer and I truly enjoyed reading *Death in a Dark Alley*. The book is a very quick, easy and relaxing read. It was full of intrigue and had its share of surprises including one especially unexpected development. The book is called a romance, but I would categorize it as a suspense novel, with an element of romance. The characters are quite engaging, making you want to continue reading on. And on. I read the book over the course of two otherwise busy days. I just couldn't put it down. I highly recommend *Death in a Dark Alley* and can't wait for the next installment in the series.

I FOUND *DEATH IN A DARK ALLEY* TO BE COMPELLING and hard to put down! The character development is well done, the settings & locations are beautifully described, and the style the authors used to weave the storyline together builds in intensity. Well done Bradley Pay...book three cannot come soon enough!!

THIS IS A WONDERFUL CONTINUATION of the Spectrum Series and I quickly saw that it can stand alone, as well! I enjoyed how the threads of characters and stories are woven and surprisingly intertwined when I was least prepared. Can't wait for the next book in the series!

THIS WAS A FANTASTIC SUMMER READ that will have you flipping pages in a flurry! Intriguing characters and lovely descriptions of places, food and relationships. Once you've flown through this one, makes sure to grab the first novel in the series, *The Killings Begin*!

Acknowledgements

When we embarked upon writing the Spectrum Series in 2016, we had no clue what we were getting ourselves into. Writing a book looks so easy from the outside, but in reality, it is an unbelievable challenge – developing the storyline, the characters, making it plausible but fun, giving each character a voice and a personality of their own and, of course, ensuring that each character has a purpose in the story. Yes, there have been a few that just didn't make the cut. Writing a series compounds that because you need to take all those things (and more) into account while looking ahead to the next book(s) and looking back to previous ones to make sure you don't set up situations you may not want later and that you don't contradict what you have said earlier. So, we're giving ourselves a giant pat on the back for accomplishing that – with a great deal of help from all the people below.

We are indebted to our beta readers: Dale Burke, Jennifer Cranston, Julia Darrah, Rae Ann Dilks, Monica Elertson, Jan Erkes, Pam Hays, Amanda King, Gavin Pay, Mallory Paxton and Patty Steinike. Their insights and suggestions provided new perspectives about our characters, locations and story. They told us when we needed better transitions because things didn't hang together. They told us when they were interested in something and wanted more information. And, of course, they caught early grammar, spelling and punctuation errors as well. Thank you for all your input – our story is far better because of you.

To our advance readers, your love of reading and sincere comments give other potential readers insights about the book that they wouldn't have otherwise. Once again, thanks to each of you for your contributions and your early reviews: Julia Barugel, Denise Beyer, Vickie Costello, Jennifer Cranston, Julia Darrah, Monica Elertson, Diane French, Mary Gilbert, Gina Manola, Jessica McCaleb, Sarah Pay, Joan Perry, Ken Pitz, and Melissa Watson.

Creating this series has taken a team. In addition to all those readers, there's been an entire editing, design and publicity/marketing team, some of whom don't know the others, working behind the scenes to help us deliver this book. First, our heartfelt thanks to Miranda Summers-Pritchard, our exceptional copy editor – in addition to your notes on comma usage (groan, will we ever get it?) and your recommendations for alternative wording, you have an absolutely uncanny ability to get inside our heads and take what we were saying one or even five steps further. Our books are so much better for all your suggestions. Our gratitude is unending. Karina Granda, you are a fabulous cover designer. The hands and heart logo you designed for our book covers and social media is your graphic interpretation of our series. Wow – we are thrilled at how well you captured both the psychological twists and the romance in our books with that seemingly small logo, a pair of hands encircling a heart. Thank you for your patience and creativity. You have been so easy to work with and have produced covers that excite us each time we see them. And now, to Novel Cause, our wonderful marketing and publicity crew – the promotional material and metadata guidance is precisely what we envisioned when we went looking for members for this part of our team. What you have provided is something we could never have done ourselves. Thank you for your hard work and your patience as we've gone back and forth to get it right.

The very talented Rachel Kaiser spent time with us describing how she takes an idea and transforms it into a street mural. Her experience is extensive, and while we didn't mirror the process she uses to create her masterpieces, we would be remiss if we didn't thank her for the time, background and inspiration she shared.

While writing this book, the war in Ukraine broke out. So we were happy when the opportunity arose to mention the Toilet History Museum in Kyiv on behalf of our friends, Mykola and Maryna Bogdanenko, the museum owners. We met this charming couple (virtually) while we were writing *The Killings Begin*. We continue to stay in touch and hope for their safety and the safety of their family, friends and staff.

The one euro housing program – what a brilliant idea – was

first proposed over a decade ago by Vittorio Sgarbi, a TV personality who was also the mayor of Salemi in southern Sicily, as a way to save the old, crumbling section of the city. The idea caught on and evolved as a way to repopulate dying villages in Italy. Houses, many of which have been abandoned by their owners, are tumbling down, some scarcely more than a pile of rubble. For a long while, we've thought that the purchase of a one euro house was an intriguing idea, and so we decided to rehabilitate a house in Sicily for one of our couples. Thank you, Vittorio Sgarbi, for the inspiration.

And finally, a roller coaster, lemons and lemonade, lovers and friends – that's life. We drew upon the ups and downs, the happiness, sadness, laughter, pain, joy and anger that we've caused and shared as we described how devastated Remy felt about her best friend's betrayal, how Lee reacted to Fong's many affairs throughout the years, how disappointed Frannie felt at her cousin's behavior and myriad other emotions experienced by our characters. We folded so many bits and pieces of ourselves and our emotions into their lives. Thank you, thank you, thank you to all our current and former friends and lovers for giving us so many rich experiences.

We are grateful to each and every member of our team, and to our families and friends. We are fortunate to have so many extraordinarily talented and caring people who have helped us make the Spectrum Series a reality!

About the Authors

Robin Bradley grew up in a home where they had no TV, and so everyone read voraciously and played with words. She is often known to say things like "Speaking is one-way; talking is two-way, a conversation," or "Passive voice? Really?" She loves a good story, whether it's reading, hearing or telling it. She inherited her love of writing from her family - her mother was an English teacher and published poet, and her uncle was a reporter for the San Jose Mercury. Robin also writes poetry, although she hasn't published any yet. Besides writing, Robin loves wine, cooking, and reading.

Jody Leber-Pay loves writing because she gets to be a collaborator, an inventor, a researcher, a storyteller, a problem solver, a writer, an editor, a marketer, and a techie. She finds the process of going from an idea to a published book fascinating, and that's what keeps her motivated. Before writing fiction, Jody authored technical documents for work and published a technical book. When she's not writing, Jody enjoys the great outdoors - walking, hiking and golfing.

Robin and Jody met in 2016 on a European riverboat cruise from Budapest to Nuremberg. As a way to pass the time while they traveled through the series of locks from the Danube to the Main River, Robin, Jody and a handful of friends sat around in the afternoon, drinking Chianti, laughing and making up silly romantic stories.

The development of those stories into the Spectrum Series began with an email from Jody to Robin: "By the way – You still interested in the Lock Series? … it will be fun."

And so began their unusual, long-distance friendship and their collaboration on the Spectrum Series.

Working as Bradley Pay, they found that their unique interests and skills were complementary, but it was their enjoyment that kept the process going. Creating the first book and outlining the remainder of the series was hard work but far more fun than they had imagined at the outset.

Some of the original characters remain, albeit much evolved, and many new characters have appeared. These stories are no longer the bosom-heaving romances of our river-cruise days. Instead, although the love interests remain, they are now haunted by an international serial killer who changes the course of the characters' lives.

Made in the USA
Columbia, SC
12 November 2022

70922594R00191